THE GREY LIST

RATHER

"THE THERAPIST"

GREY HUFFINGTON

LET'S GET SOCIAL

Instagram:

Grey Huffington
(Cover reveals, releases, etc)
Instagram.com/greyhuffington

HuffingtonHQ
(News, updates, etc —headed by Team Huffington)
Instagram.com/huffingtonhq

TikTok:

Grey Huffington
(Vlogs, updates, promotional images/videos, etc — headed by Team Huffington)
TikTok.com/@greyhuffington.com

Pinterest:

Grey Huffington
*(Inspiration, quotes, snippets, visuals, boards, lifestyle, etc —
headed by Team Huffington)*
https://pin.it/695pEOV9m

TRIGGER WARNING

PLEASE READ THIS SECTION!

Seeing this note means the book you are about to read could contain triggering situations or actions. This book is subject to one or more of the triggers listed below.

Please note that this a universal trigger warning page that is included in Grey Huffington books and is not specified for any particular set of characters, book, couple, etc.
This book does not contain all the warnings listed. It is simply a way to warn you that this particular book contains things/a thing that may be triggering for some.

This is my way of recognizing the reality and life experiences of my Romance friends and making sure I properly prepare you for what is to unfold within the pages of this book.

violence
sexual assault
drug addiction
suicide
homicide
miscarriage/child loss
child abuse
emotional abuse
mental illness
infidelity
infertility
cancer
criminal activity

NOTE.

Between the covers of this book is **my** art piece —
beautifully paired words structured for **my** creative
satisfaction and later consumed by others for enjoyment.

It's **leisure for you**, it's **life for me**.
This is just a book to most. **It's art for me**.
My art. I've had *my* time. Have **yours**.

happy reading

CONTENTS

GREY**HUFFINGTON**

PROLOGUE

Nice and easy, my boy.

Tension coiled the pit of my stomach. The fork dangled in the air with medium rare, pan-seared filet mignon at the tip. With patience, I waited for it to disappear into the small mouth just inches away from me at the dinner table.

I didn't blink. I didn't move. I didn't make a sound. The moment was pivotal. Any interruption could be the ending of a hopeful beginning. Each second pulled at my heartstrings.

Fuck.

The fork lowered, inch by inch, until it reached the glass plate.

Clink.

Another milestone was buried in the graveyard where hundreds more had gone to rest until being excavated. Some had only rested for days. Some for weeks. Others for months. Some we'd never see again, because they were simply too overwhelming for the small imbalance and big emotions to manage.

A faint sigh slipped through my slightly parted lips. Displays of exasperation were prohibited in fatherhood. In my case, essentially. It promoted discouragement and triggered stressors we fought hard to keep hidden behind my son's handsome face.

Princeton wasn't average. And, nothing about the way I'd chosen to parent him was either. He was special. I knew it. He knew it. And, everyone around us did, too.

In a single gaze, orbs could easily determine his level of difficulties functioning in a world built with children like him on the chopping block.

"Mm mm. Mm mm."

The same, repetitive sound erupted from his lips as his head lowered and the side of his index finger went into his mouth. Flared nostrils contradicted the splintering of my heart.

The lack of communication, the inability to speak, and all the other shit stopping Princeton from being the adventurous, independent child he was trying so desperately to be gutted me so often. I wondered just how much I had left to carve.

"Hey." I softened, weakening my resolve to meet him on the level he demanded. "Hey. Another day. There's always another day, son."

Though my words had a visible effect, the rocking had already commenced. The whipping of his head from one side to the other continued. The switch had been flipped and until his body and mind aligned, he wouldn't be able to control his movements.

My lids sealed briefly. When I reopened them, an unfamiliar set of eyes rested on Princeton's wiggly frame. My body began to overheat as boiling blood cruised through my veins. The pistol that was seated on my lap was now in my hand.

My finger was on the trigger, ready to apply the four pounds of pressure required to put a bullet right through the eyes of the busboy with a smile on his face and the deflated chest from sniggering quietly.

I'll deflate that motherfucker for good.

"Mm mm. Mm mm."

The only sound I'd ever heard come from my son's mouth put life back into perspective for me. I released the breath I'd been holding and stood, instead. Catching an unnecessary body with him by my side would stretch his mind beyond its current capacity. I wouldn't forgive myself.

My feet began the short journey despite my thoughts taking a second to catch up. Not willing to cause my son any more trouble, I clutched my piece as I stepped to the very rude, very uninformed employee. My tolerance was nonexistent when it came to Princeton, and I'd never had an issue making it clear for anyone.

"Say." Clearing my throat, I wiped the sides of my mouth with my thumb and index.

My presence was unwelcomed. That much was obvious. I didn't give a fuck. I hoped that was obvious as well.

"Do me a favor, homeboy."

With the back of my hand, I patted his chest. His body swayed each time I landed.

"Yo, man, wh–"

"You see that young boy you're so fucking amused by over there?"

I nodded toward Princeton.

"I– sor–"

"Take off his uniform and clock out for me. Don't expect this period's pay. He's taking that and spending it on some legos in the toy section as compensation for the turmoil stares from inconsiderate fuckers like you cause him. See, though he's not up to your standard, he's a superb boy. He designed this entire fucking layout with a dull pencil he sharpened on the concrete because pencil sharpeners are triggering.

"And, after he finished with that nub, he arranged legos until his fingers began peeling, desperately needing to see his vision come to life. A vision that is providing for you, whoever you're fucking and whoever you're feeding. Before you judge another book by its cover, think about how you almost lost your life bout this one. Instead, it's your job."

I tapped the name tag on his shirt. "Have a nice night, Jerod."

Fucking heathen. Imbecile. I scoffed, heading back to the table where Princeton's stimming had begun to slow to a creep.

"You ready, son?"

I'd vomited words, a habit I picked up after Princeton's diagnosis. It was hard, saying less while more thoughts rushed through others. Deading their ignorance with words to protect my son's peace was thorns in my side when I'd much rather deaden the beat of their hearts. I'd sleep peacefully at night with one less fool in the world.

Princeton was a genius in his own right. It wasn't debatable. Though he wasn't frolicking around, blabbering, and active like the average three and a half year old, the intricacies of his brain were far from average. His mind didn't function like theirs either. He was wise beyond his years.

His head lifted and fell rapidly. I tucked my piece in my waistline and stretched my hand for him to find. Dark ink on even darker skin peeped from underneath the black shirt and black suit, concealing its intensity. Small, cool fingers collapsed around mine, replenishing the parts of me that were gutted with each obstacle life deemed impossible for him.

Food sensitivity.

It was one of the earliest signs of autism in Princeton. Eating had always been such an easy task. I never imagined how difficult it was for some. Not until him.

With Princeton by my side, I strolled through the establishment his contributions had made possible. It was one of the few business opportunities he'd presented to me. It wasn't often he handed me a sketch from his book. He was sensitive about his artwork.

Countless hours went into his drawings. However, four of them had been ripped at the seams and placed in my hand. Without words, my young son had given me the foundation for my next investment. Our next investment.

Low lighting emphasized the city's backdrop. Clarke's skyline lit the space perfectly at night. Natural lighting opened it tremendously with the rising of the sun and just before its setting.

The bar swept from one side to the other. Chatter that usually sent Princeton spiraling was welcomed. This place was familiar to him. He knew every inch of the building. Not only was it his creation, but it was a reminder that he was loved, cared for, and listened to even if he never said a fucking word.

There was a tug from below, pulling my arm in the opposite direction. Furrowed eyebrows demonstrated my confusion.

Son.

His strength was impeccable. Though it wasn't enough to redirect me, it shifted my gears.

"Princet–"

A soft, disheartening voice disrupted every thought of mine, completely obliterating my sanity with little regard. Quickly followed by generous giggles that signaled contentment, happiness, and enjoyment, I was given very limited time for recovery. Confusion rearranged my facial structure.

And, that laugh.

I remembered it well. For two and a half years I'd heard it continuously. Every day. Several times a day. It was once the most beautiful sound to come from a human's lips.

My human.

That laughter made everything alright. Made everything well. So, inevitably, I longed for it. Craved it. Encouraged it. And, I listened with my heart more than my ears when it surfaced.

"Son, n–"

My words were incapable of rendering him motionless. They didn't stop his tiny feet from taking off, obliterating the distance from the subject and leaving me in the dust.

Fuck.

Swiftly, he climbed onto the leather, planted his body firmly against a growing belly, and laid his head against the chest of the woman who'd birthed him. Contorted features and the lack of reciprocation made it difficult for me to continue in stride.

My heart had broken a thousand times and nine hundred and ninety-nine of them were dedicated to my son. This one wasn't any different from the others, but it hurt a little more because I witnessed his longing for attention and love from a woman who wanted absolutely nothing to do with him.

As beautiful as Lola was, she was poisonous. Flawed. Inauthentic. Scandalous. Pathetic. A real fucking piece of shit.

I hadn't always considered her in those regards, but the birth of our son exposed her true character, forcing me to be more vigilant and considerate of who I involved myself with.

At one point, she was destined to be my wife. I was certain we'd wed. Our union would be the first of the family. I was the oldest of my siblings. It was fitting. But, Princeton changed it all.

His diagnosis didn't align with Lola's vision. Perfect life. Perfect home. Perfect husband. Perfect children. *Perfect–*

"Baby," her date voiced, clearing his throat in confusion. "Do you know this kid?"

Tension grew as I approached the table, carefully scooping Princeton into my arms. His resistance pierced the center of my chest, aiming straight for the heart he owned every inch of.

"Mm Mmm! Mmmmm!"

"I– I– uh," Lola stuttered.

She was as stunning as I remembered. But, those pretty layers were concealing so many ugly characteristics. Honey-colored eyes refused to hold my gaze. Shame filled her to the brim, splitting her nerve endings and making it difficult to sit still.

For six months I'd been trying to catch up with her. The round belly and incredibly offensive engagement ring on her finger helped me connect the dots and understand why I hadn't bumped into her. She was busy nailing the coffin of her next victim.

My eyes grew tired of trying to locate the beauty of the diamond on her finger. It was dull. It was embarrassingly small. It was, in fact, a carat or less. And, I could almost guarantee it was on a payment plan. Satisfaction lulled my aching heart. Lola had gotten exactly what she deserved. A fucking downgrade.

"She carried him for nine months and spent the first year of his life by his side. I'd assume she knows him."

"He's– he's yours?"

Disgust lined her frame. With her nose stuck in the air, she began to explain.

"Howard, I–"

"He was," I interrupted, not interested in the filth she was preparing to spew.

I unlocked my personal cell phone and accessed the files. I didn't have to scroll far, because there were only a handful of documents saved. They were all pertaining to Princeton. The final one, however, was the only one I was interested in at the moment.

It was a court-ordered document that had been stored after several attempts to have the papers signed in a legal setting where lawyers and a judge were both present. Lola's absence at the custody hearings made the completion of the paperwork impossible.

"The paperwork you requested," I reminded her, placing the phone on the table in front of her.

"I– Priest. Wait."

"Sign those for me, Lola."

I lowered Princeton onto the floor. He clung to my leg, hiding his face behind my pants. When I unlocked the second phone to document the signature process, which my lawyer had suggested as proof of authenticity, hazel orbs glared at me through the lens of the iPhone.

"Lola."

"Can we do this another time? I am having dinner with my fiancé," she sassed, rediscovering her power, suddenly.

As much as a cordial meeting and simple signing was my desire, I didn't mind matching the hell she was ready to indulge in. The difference between us was that she ran when the heat was increased. I planted my feet and waited patiently to be engulfed in flames. I didn't mind burning, especially for Princeton.

With my free hand, I removed my piece from my waist and aimed it in her fiancé's direction. My arm extended until his temple met the coolness of my Beretta.

"Hey. Hey. Man, wh–" he gasped, hands in the air as if they would stop his ending.

"When he's eating dirt, those papers will still need to be signed."

I nodded toward the phone. Her hesitation curled my lips upward.

"Suits me–"

My finger pressured the trigger, ready to witness her

squeal while begging for the same attention and love from a corpse as my son did whenever they crossed paths. She, too, was dead to me, so the score would be even in my opinion.

As if she was waving a magic wand, her finger began twirling across the screen.

"Here!"

Sliding the phone across the table, she released a shaky breath.

"My God."

Agitation was one of many emotions displayed through movements and expressions.

"He can't save you, either, Lola. Not from me."

"Prie–"

"Fortunately, you're no longer on my radar."

"Lola, what the fuck is going on?" Clueless, her fiancé breathed.

"I'll leave you two alone. Congratulations on the baby, Howard. Hopefully she gets around to telling you about the one she birthed and deemed unfit for her lifestyle yet is responsible for the architect of the very restaurant you're sitting in tonight."

I pulled Princeton into my arms and tucked my piece, simultaneously. With both cell phones in hand, I trekked toward the door. Though I was seething at the lack of interest Princeton's womb donor had for him, obtaining her signature, terminating her parental rights, soothed the aches and made for a perfect dinner night.

"Mr. Valentine."

"Mr. Valentine."

"Goodnight, Mr. Valentine."

"Good evening, Sir."

"Let me get the door for you."

It wasn't a secret I owned the establishment. Front-of-the-house staff were privy to the information. Not because I'd shared it but because they were the bread and butter of the company.

When Christmas bonuses were distributed, I handed them out personally. Those familiar faces that saw me every other week for my night out with Princeton at the only restaurant he didn't need his headphones for were flabbergasted as they accepted envelopes stuffed with hundreds of thank yous.

The evening air was free of humidity. A slight, steady breeze lowered my temperature and kissed my cheeks. Victory was mine. Princeton was mine, wholly. Mine alone.

A single tap of my fob unlocked the doors of the Ghost. The tip of its nose caved to reveal the jet-black Rolls Royce emblem. It rose to the occasion as my engine roared due to a remote-controlled start.

Sleek and black in color, it suited the name it had been given. Without the city lights of the night, one would have a hard time adjusting their vision to pinpoint the damn thing. Though it was massive in size, it camouflaged well. The simplistic design gave it that ability.

"Here."

Princeton's best friend tumbled to the ground as I opened the door. The reverse concept was ideal for mothers and fathers with children still in elevated seats for their safety and protection.

Together.

Separately.

I repeated the steps in my head, remembering to fasten

every snap so I didn't find Princeton on the floor, attempting to crawl underneath my seat, again. The mistake of ignoring the second step because we were running slightly behind for *The Gathering* one Sunday evening proved to be a mistake just minutes after taking off.

With Woody in his hands and his body secured in his car seat, I checked the child safety lock out of sheer habit before shutting the door and taking my seat behind the wheel. Out of the parking lot and into the Clarke streets, Princeton and I cruised. Every other Thursday evening, it was more of the same.

Routines.

They made our world revolve as seamlessly as it possibly could. On Thursdays, we ditched the dinner table for dinner at *Spectrum*.

The leather's warmth intensified under the pressure of my hand. Tightly, I gripped it as I angled the wheels toward the exit of the lot. A calm, steady flow of instruments filled the ride, keeping Princeton settled and in tune with reality.

Slowly, I bent every necessary corner and stopped at every traffic light glowing red. Nineteen minutes later and I killed the engine in the six-car garage. Eagerly, Princeton waited to be removed from his seat and placed on his feet. With his hand in mine, we entered our home through the back.

One by one, we removed our shoes, using our toes to slide them off the heels of our feet. We took the stairs to the second floor and straight to my son's bedroom. There, I kneeled before him, removing his tie and unbuttoning his shirt.

I pushed the tailored jacket down his arms and hung it

on the hanger dangling from the wardrobe rack where his dirty clothes were housed. Next was his shirt, and then finally, the Hermès belt and slacks. Stripped down to his boxers, he stood with Woody nestled against his chest.

I pulled back his sheets and patted the bed, wishing I could suggest a bath but he had associated the task with daylight and there wasn't any convincing him of anything else.

Routines. I reminded myself.

He lived by them. He functioned with them in place. It was part of the reason he was as bright as he was and as collected on a daily basis.

"Here, son."

Nodding, he skipped toward the bed with his eyes low and his head hung.

Please, my boy.

Before he leaped into bed, I stopped him in his tracks and took both of his hands into mine.

"Hey. Hey."

I lifted my head, becoming the example he needed. I'd lifted his head with my fingers far too many times before. He had the strength to do it himself. We were working on the confidence to keep it there and maintain eye contact.

"Up, up."

With a shake of the head, he pierced my heart.

"No?"

He shook his head again. His inability to maintain eye contact wasn't the case here. It was his unwillingness. He was exercising his right of expression in our home, though words weren't a part of his display.

"Talk to me, son. Is something bothering you?"

Silence.

"Something hurting?"

He nodded.

"What's hurting?"

He placed a hand on his chest. I swallowed the lump in my throat and pulled my legs around me to sit down. I closed the gap between us by scooting closer to Princeton. This time, I struggled with words.

"I– I apologize, son. For anything I've said or done to hur–"

He shook his head slowly, halting me.

"Then, what's the matter?"

Learning I wasn't the culprit saved me a year's worth of heartache.

He spread his fingers, reopening the wound in my chest. When he lifted his right hand, I tried closing my lids. My brain, however, didn't send the signal. By the time his thumb hit his chin, signaling the only verbal attempt he'd ever made since his first birthday.

Mom. He signed.

Mom.

Mom.

Mom.

Again, and, again, as his foot pounced on the ground as the anguish on his face stretched his features a little more each time. Until, eventually, tears blurred it all.

Mom.

Mom.

Mom.

Mom.

He wept.

It was all he knew. All he'd ever known. And, for the first year of her absence, it was all he ever signed. All day. Every day, until the space between his thumb and index finger grew raw. His chin still had a lighter tone where he placed his thumb religiously for thirteen months straight. It had only been a year since stimming had turned into a more settling, more controllable rock he could pull himself out of when his body and mind aligned.

"So— son," I coughed out, masking the cracking of my voice. I hardly recognized it as the word surfaced.

Mom.

Mom.

Mom.

Mom.

I pulled him into my arms, because there wasn't anything I could say or do to heal his broken heart. At three, he wasn't privy to the despicable traits his mother harbored. All he knew was at one point she loved him unconditionally and then she was gone.

While most children didn't remember much until the age of five, they never forgot people they loved and people who loved them well. Until his diagnosis, his mother had loved him well. He was having trouble forgetting that shit and the fact she wasn't willing to anymore.

"Hey. Hey. Hey. Princeton. You're okay," I promised, unable to maintain my composure.

When my son hurt, so did I.

"We're okay. We're going to be okay. Everything is going to be okay. Son, there's no need to cry. Not everyone deserves you. Not everyone deserves us. You have me. And- and I'll never- I'll never leave you. I will be by your side until my last breath. You'll always have me. You hear me?"

I separated our chests, needing to see those brown eyes as I spoke life into his lifeless heart.

"Princeton, your father will never leave you. Ever. You mean the world to me, son. Yo– you're better than my wildest dreams. You're so smart. So sharp. So talented. So gifted. You– you're okay, son. You're loved.

"Wholly. Widely. Largely. Unconditionally. Not just by me but by all your uncles. Your grandfather. Your grandmother. Both of them. Mommy isn't coming back, son. It's just you– you and me. You hear? And, we're going to be alright. Okay?"

Slowly, he nodded up and down. This time when he lifted his hand, it wasn't to his chin. It was to my face to wipe the tears I'd kept at bay for two years.

"Appreciate that, buddy," I scoffed, pissed I'd even allowed her to fuck up our night. "Appreciate that."

Tucked away in bed, I began a large circle on Princeton's back. It was the calming mechanism I'd learned nearly three years ago and it still soothed him when his emotions were larger than he could bear. Slowly, he drifted, sniffles continuing to riddle his little body.

T H E G R E Y L I S T

With the glass of brown liquor in my hand, I slouched in the large chair that accommodated my extensive limbs. Inward, my nostrils shrunk. And, then, outward, they expanded as I stared out into the dark of the night. Aside from the city lights, glowing blue water in the pool of my backyard, and the twinkle of the stars, nothing else was visible.

Fucking bitch.

My chest caved as the glass went flying. On the floor, it landed, clashing against the marble. Respect and women were hand-in-hand. My tongue was hardly sharp when in the presence of, speaking to, or speaking about such beautiful creatures. But, there was one who'd left a bitter taste in my mouth I hadn't been able to shake in two years.

"Urgh."

Because of her, I hadn't touched, noticed, or entertained a woman since she walked out of our son's life. Not because I didn't want to or because I didn't crave the very essence, the very scent of a woman, but because my focus hadn't departed from obtaining full custody of my son. Now that his womb donor had signed over her rights, I could rest.

Or at least, I imagined I'd be able to on this day. I imagined it would be one of the happiest of my life, but instead, I was nursing the same wounds my son had, praying my love for him was enough to set his little soul on fire.

"Mr. Valentine."

Nikola's soft voice failed to move me. To soothe me. To soothe my ache.

"Is everything okay?"

She tiptoed around the chair, noticing the shattered glass, immediately.

"Sit tight. I'll clean it."

"Thank you," I cleared my throat.

As my home's manager, she oversaw all things, including Princeton. He was the reason she was home as much as she was. She took good care of him on a daily basis. Thankful would be an understatement when trying to explain my appreciation for her.

"Don't thank me," she begged, "Please. Go ahead. You made plans tonight. Don't let whatever is bothering you keep you inside. Go. Go. Princeton will be fine and I can handle this."

"I–"

"Mr. Valentine," she warned with slits for eyes, "Go ahead. We'll be here when you return."

I had made plans tonight, but after Spectrum, there was nowhere I'd rather be than home with Princeton. I strolled toward the full bar with an entrance near the staircase while fastening the button of my suit jacket.

If I stuck around a second longer, I'd dismiss my plans, grab Princeton from underneath his sheets, and lay him under mine. He deserved a little more love and affection tonight. Shit, we both did.

Inside my cave, I grabbed a bottle of Hennessy and poured myself a healthy shot. Before I could close the cap, the glass was emptied. The invitation I'd scanned carefully for the twelfth time sat on the counter where I'd left it. Picking it up, I stared at the chocolate-colored textured paper.

The Mansion

Private Suite 102

Foiled coating on the letters made it shine, even in the dark, as it moved. The ten-thousand dollar tab was a hefty one to pay for entry to *The Mansion*. The six-thousand dollar bill for the designated suite felt like a stretch but curiosity had me sending the wire transfer after the fourth month of contemplation.

I'd suppressed the urge to commit for some time. Tonight being my first appearance made more sense than I'd considered when I made the appointment. The tension in my neck and chest matched the tension in my dick and balls. They were both begging to be relieved and it started with the card in my hand.

The Mansion was the organization. Private Suites were their specialty. Their business was designed with the wealthy in mind. Their establishment wasn't a club. It wasn't a sex operation. It wasn't a party. It was a place of residence for those who lacked time due to their business obligations, yet still recognized their body's natural yearning for sexual gratification.

The kind that didn't lead to more. The kind that was never mentioned in conversation with others. The kind that was a secret. The kind that was as plentiful as one needed.

And, clean.

Private.

Risk-free.

Available as needed.

There weren't women walking around who were looking to score a few bucks. Each woman who entered *The Mansion* paid just as much as the man they were in search of to be there. Her pockets were laced and her time was limited.

Identities were concealed behind masquerade masks. The color of your mask revealed exactly what you were interested in. There were only four to choose from.

Cream – Vanilla
Yellow – Gender Play
Red – Romance (Domestic Roles, including S/D)
Black – BDSM

I was torn between the first and third options. On one hand, I wanted the simplicity of sex to work in my favor, emptying my balls fast and viciously, so I could get back home. Simultaneously, I craved the adventure the red mask would lead me to.

Clicking my tongue against my teeth, I tapped the invitation on the counter before stepping away completely. I had time to finalize my decision. When I stepped into my suite, I was certain I'd know exactly what I wanted and exactly who I wanted.

The night was still young. The clock had barely struck ten. With any luck, lust would have me home by one. However, I wasn't quite certain what the night entailed or what experience I was truly embarking on. Blindly, I would be entering Private Suites. Knowledgeable, I would emerge.

The wheels of my Ghost glided across Clarke's cemented streets. Silence coated the air. No Hip Hop. No R&B. No Soul. No Jazz. Just thoughts. Obsessive thoughts. Intrusive thoughts. Relentless thoughts.

While Lola's pregnancy and engagement weren't the root of my issue, they only intensified my resentment for her existence. She was the donor of my son and a woman, nonetheless. Hadn't she been either, her brains would be on the pavement for the world to see.

She'd been spared and that was my issue. It was uncharacteristic of me–sparing any fucking body.

Princeton.

He was the exception. And, for him, the woman who'd birthed him was still breathing, against my better judgment. She'd written our son off, found another motherfucker to unleash one of her thirty personalities on, gotten impregnated, and engaged.

"Hmph."

Scoffing, I shook my head. Life spit you out, lubed you up, and then fucked you over and over. It was pathetic to even consider. She was bringing another life into the world while trying to forget the one she created and abandoned. One who lived in the same state. The same fucking city.

Pathetic.

Disgust consumed me. Confined me to my displeasure. Reminded me of my disdain. Summoned my distaste. There wasn't a motherfucker in the world I hated the way I hated that motherfucker. In fact, there wasn't a motherfucker in the world I hated at all besides her. The rest of them were dead.

Me and a motherfucker I despised couldn't both breathe on the same planet. They were better wherever one transitioned to. The afterlife, I imagine. And, if they knew any better, they wouldn't be there when I got there, either. History would only repeat itself, no matter when, where, or how many times.

A ping from my cell reeled me back in, removing me from the depths instantly. Keeping my eyes on the road, I managed to unlock my screen with a six digit code. My mother's face popped up on the screen, casting a calm over my spirit, over my body almost immediately.

A smile pierced my face before I had a chance to open the message. It didn't matter what her words said or what they meant, their timing was impeccable. Always was, just as she was.

Dear Lady. Her contact was one of the few that brightened everything around me.

In bed and you're heavy on my heart. You're a dream, son. Princeton and I are blessed to call you ours.

I don't belong to you two alone. I teased, imagining her scrunched features.

Gray bubbles appeared. Without a doubt, she was speed typing.

Well, that is true but you're ours the most. I just gave you a compliment. Should I take it back?

Goodnight Dear Lady.

Goodnight son.

My mother and father had profound respect for one another, however they weren't and never would be anything more than friends. I'd come to terms with the fact that my conception was accidental and a very pivotal point of both of their lives. Shit wasn't sweet then, but it is the sweetest now.

My father was with the woman he'd rest beside when their time on earth expired. And, my mother still maintained her singlehood since the love of her life was laid to rest. They were both utterly happy and settled into their roles as my parents and Princeton's grandparents. They were his glue. They kept him together even when he only felt like falling apart.

Turning my attention, that should've never been divided, back onto the road, I made the final turn. As I approached the gates with *The Mansion* scribed in iron, I readied the code sent hours prior as a result of confirming my attendance for the night.

"Good evening, Sir. Code, please."

Dressed in black with a white shirt peeking through his suit, security stood beside my car with his arms folded and his chin lowered.

"PS102. Angeles," I recited the words displayed on my screen.

"Mr. Valentine?"

He wasn't familiar with me, but he was familiar with the schedule. Seemingly, he studied it religiously so he was well-versed on the comings and goings of the guests. There were designated times for everyone on the list. They were firm and stood ten toes down when it came to their privacy policies and protecting the privacy of the people who trusted them with their fantasies, fetishes, kinks, and secrets.

I respected it. Privacy wasn't exactly my purpose for joining, though I'd maintain it. Convenience and suppression of my own sexual desires were. I needed my dick wet. It was simple. And, I didn't want a bird bitch to wet it. I wanted a woman of elegance.

A woman of virtue. A woman with just as much to lose as I did. A woman who could hold her own. A woman who needed nothing more from me than good memories, an occasionally sore frame, and mind-boggling orgasms. She had to be ready and willing to have her back blown to smithereens.

"Correct."

"This way, Sir. We have complimentary transportation to your suite if your privacy is–"

"There's no need."

"Good, then, Sir. This way," he said, pointing straight ahead. "Around the waterfall, across the bridge, and into the garage marked PS102."

"You'll have immediate access to your suite, but the door will not unlock until the garage is completely closed. This is for your safety and privacy as well as others."

"Noted."

The gravel cracked under the pressure of my tires. Leaving the window down, I caught the slight breeze with gratitude. My lungs needed the fresh air. My mind needed the escape nature provided.

The grounds were manicured perfectly. Sculptures sprouted occasionally. They were massive in size and strategically placed so their presence wasn't too daunting for guests, I assumed.

Garages, some doubled and other oversized singles lined the first floor of each building. There were four, fairly small and all with two stories.

PS102. It was already lifted, waiting on my arrival. I pulled in, deadened my engine, and climbed out of my car. Before I managed to grab the garage opener from its slot on the wall, the door closed behind me.

Once it lined with the concrete beneath it the light on

the steel door changed in color. Swiftly, the red circle glowed a bold green. A lone, feminine voice came over the loudspeaker right beside the door.

"Welcome, Mr. Valentine. I am Ursula, your personal consultant. I'd like to personally welcome you to *The Mansion's* Private Suites. There are a few rules I must reiterate though I'm sure you've familiarized yourself with our policies. Are you listening, Mr. Valentine?"

Moved by the gentleness of her tone, I chuckled. With a tilted skull, I placed a thumb against the right side of my chin, baffled by the enchantment. It had caught me by surprise, so had my virtual guest.

"I'm listening, Ursula, but I'd listen better if you were in my face and not o–"

"Mr. Valentine," she sniggered, losing her composure.

"I don't like being cut off, Ursula."

"I'm not in the ballroom. I'm not up for grabs."

"Anyone I feel is up for grabs is up for grabs. Don't insult my intelligence."

Breath hiked, she continued, "Will you make this difficult or will you just listen?"

"I can listen, but only because I want you to do your job. You seem to do it well."

"I'd like to think so."

"How far do these cameras see into the suite, Ursula?"

Stuffing my hands in my pocket, I measured the distance in my head.

"As long as the door is closed, we can't see into the suites."

"Disappointing," I tittered, kissing the skin of my teeth.

"How so? Privacy is–"

"Because, you should see what you're passing up on."

"Exhibitionism."

"Whatever the fuck you want to call it."

With a shrug, I removed my hands and smoothed the black shirt I wore beneath the black jacket.

Silence trailed my words. A heavy, quaking breath left her mouth before she began, again.

"I'm listening," I urged, removing the garage opener from the wall and rounding my car.

Hesitantly, she began again. This time the confidence she'd exude had diminished. Curiosity piqued with each word. With every dollar in my bank, I'd bet she was contemplating employment or enjoyment.

If her occupation permitted, and she wasn't afraid of what the night would hold, enjoyment was the latter. Otherwise, it was best she stayed behind the desk. I wasn't in search of forever. Just for now.

"Needless to say, names are prohibited. Under any circumstances. Never, remove your covering. Under any circumstances. Never request personal information. Never encourage encounters outside of Private Suites. Never move forward if refusal is apparent, mentioned, unclear, or the topic of conversation.

"We are compliant with the law and keep our guests' safety at the forefront of our operation. We do not take assault claims or cases lightly. We will help prosecute to the fullest extent. Lastly, it all ends in the suite."

"Nothing passes the threshold. Nothing. What happens inside, stays inside unless it conflicts with the interest or safety of our guests. Do you understand these terms and conditions along with the others in our handbook?"

"I do."

"Welcome to *The Mansion*, Mr. Valentine."

The clicking over the loudspeaker confirmed what I already knew would happen. Ursula rushed off before I had the chance to speak again.

Another day, Ursula. There's always another day.

On the console near the door was a pamphlet and a set of keys. Above it, a shelf held the four masks available to choose from.

Pick your poison.

The masquerade masks staring back at me made the choice easier than I'd imagined. I removed the red one, flipped it around, and placed it against my skin. The straps, I tucked behind my ears. The mirror next to the console was one of the four in the entire suite. I remembered their beauty from the tour. A quick glance and I was grabbing the keys from the console and headed through the door, satisfied with my choice.

Slowly, I entered the suite where I was met with cool, inviting air. The dark decor shifted the mood immediately. The suite was far more spacious than the virtual tour let on. Downstairs was the garage and plenty of space to personalize, along with a long hallway that led to a set of stairs encased in glass.

One by one, I climbed each step and reached the second floor fairly quickly. The loft area of the suite was one large room. A bed with new linen was in the center. Because I'd chosen a corner unit, there were two large windows in the suite. One facing the grounds and the other facing the second level of the ballroom, where connections were made.

Exhibitionism.

Instantly reminded of Ursula's words, I clicked my tongue against my teeth. That wasn't my jam, but some loved it. Where I stuck my dick and how deep I stuck that motherfucker was between me and the woman I was bathing in.

In addition to the bed, there was a cabinet with additional linen, a table that seated four, an upholstered couch, an ottoman that matched, and a television. Without a doubt, I knew many ditched their homes on a regular basis to live out their wildest dreams in their suite. It was, indeed, a home away from home for some.

Everything needed was on-site. Unfortunately, there was a fourteen-day stay maximum. In any given thirty days, you were only permitted fourteen full days.

336 hours. In total. They couldn't run consecutively.

I peeled the dinner menu from the wall where it rested in a small basket. There were two more. Breakfast and lunch. Though I'd dined already, not much was eaten. My attention was fixated and didn't part from my son. His discomfort and lack of ability to complete the new task of chewing steak shortened our visit. The comic relief of an employee and presence of his womb donor ended it.

Four options made the decision easy. I used the tablet provided to begin the request. The timer began almost immediately. I had exactly thirty minutes to return. Dinner would be served.

Twenty. I set a personal timer. That's all I'd need.

Instantly, I was catapulted into another universe. A

long figure clashed into me, pressing my right arm against my chest.

"Oh shit. Excuse me. I'm sorry."

I reserved my words as I took a second to scan the thin frame from head to toe. My response depended on my level of intrigue. I wasn't very impressed with what I examined. Slowly, I shrugged, wiping away any possible residue from my shoulder in a few swift motions.

She continued on wobbly legs. Either she was anxious to get fucked or had just gotten fucked into oblivion. I was unsure but I didn't give a damn either way. She was decent, but she wasn't the woman I was in search of.

I wasn't exactly sure who she was or exactly what qualities she actually possessed, but I was certain I'd recognize them when I encountered her. I was also certain she was amongst the crowd I scanned from the balcony, though I hadn't spotted her yet.

Men and women of the same or a higher caliber mingled in the underglow of the lounge below. Laughter was plentiful. Hands roamed. Cheeks swelled with pleasure. Hearts beat with passion. Bodies yearned for satisfaction. Eyes scurried from one mask to the next. Music played softly in the background. And, I descended the long staircase.

There were two routes. Both on opposing sides with an equal amount of steps. With a hand on my chest and the other near my side, I began taking in every aspect, jotting every detail, and etching what was visible of figures in my head.

Right hand, tattoo.

Buzz cut. Neck tattoo.

A mother.
Gold rings, both hands.
Horribly tanned.
Veneers.
Botched surgery.
Friendly.
Overcompensating. Easily impressed.
Roberto. Fine designer. I commended the man closest to the end of the stairs.

Very expensive, very funky ass cologne.
Not into women.
Presidential, hidden clasp.
Hair transplant. Recently.

One after the other, I recited details about the guests that would help me locate them in the event that anything went astray. Hiding their faces wasn't merely enough to keep me from uncovering their identity if circumstances required it.

The blueprints I'd acquired upon learning about *The Mansion* and Private Suites were beginning to make more sense. I combed over the floorplan in my head while scanning the building in real-time. Nothing seemed out of place.

6 exits – first floor.
4 restrooms – first floor.
3 generators – first floor.
2 fire escapes – second floor.
One main power source.
One control room.
One elevator.

This only included the wing I was housed in. There were more and I'd studied them all.

"Evening, Sir."

Draping the neatly folded towel over his arm, the butler greeted me. Half-full flutes of champagne I wasn't interested in sat on the silver tray, awaiting a dry mouth and willing participant.

"Champagne?"

I shook my head, stretching my palm in his direction.

"Perhaps something stronger?" he posed.

With a nod, I responded.

"Right this way, Sir."

He moved with precision, using the arm smothered underneath the white fabric to point me in the direction of the open bar as if it wasn't massive enough for me to see myself.

I took off, continuing my stride. I was headed there, anyway. I didn't need instructions on how to get there. But, the generosity was appreciated.

"Good day, now, Sir."

Women lined the bar, all built with precision and polished with paper. Whether it was their inheritance, husband's money, alimony, employment, or entrepreneurship that paid their monthly tab, I didn't give a fuck. They were here and had paid their dues.

Carefully, I examined the thread with hopeful eyes. Though beautiful in stature, none fit the mold I was continuing to form as I scoured. According to what was presented so far, I managed to bring myself clarity and construct the idea of the woman I was yearning for. She wasn't here. Not at the bar, at least.

I cleared my throat as I stepped up to the empty space at the bar. The bartender scurried toward me. Dressed in black from head to toe with black paint smeared on her eyes and nails to match, she blended perfectly.

"Hennessy, please."

"How would you like that, Sir?"

She dried the glass in her hand, eyes meeting mine as she waited for a response.

"Neat."

I flattened my left hand and pushed it outward for emphasis.

"Coming right up."

The plush velvet chair beside me slid out with ease. I sat atop, growing slightly more comfortable under its influence. With my shoulders squared and my spine straight, I grabbed the edge of the glass that had been slid in my direction.

"Suite?"

The tab would be covered at the end of the month along with the hefty suite expenses.

"PS102."

"Thank you."

"Of course."

The coolness of the Hennessy was followed by a sting. I lowered it onto the counter after a small sip. I wasn't in a rush to reduce my cognizance. I needed full control over my words, my thoughts, my actions, and my night's ending. A Hennessy-influenced night sounded far more forgiving than a drunken one. That wasn't exactly my style. It never had been.

I trained my eyes on the massive staircases. It was the

entryway of the ballroom. Because I'd scanned it almost in full, I knew there was no one inside for me. The only chance of ending my night on a good note depended on those fucking stairs.

THE GREYLIST

"You know, I was starting to lose hope."

As the voice grew closer, a lone hand landed on my shoulder.

"A French75, please."

"Sure thing," the bartender responded.

Gathering my thoughts and shoving the words on the tip of my tongue down my throat, I carefully removed the hand from my suit. I wasn't sure where they'd been, but I was certain they didn't belong there.

Beside me, a fair-skinned, masked woman stood with her perfectly contoured smile on display. She was wearing a cream mask with crystals that sparkled in the dark like the diamond ring on the finger reserved for marriage bands.

"Ariel," she introduced herself, extending a hand.

"No names, Ariel."

"It's a pseudonym. Relax," she chuckled.

"Do I look anything but?" I asked, feeling the crinkling of my forehead.

"Hmm. So serious."

"Life is no playground, Ariel. Are you suggesting I be something else?"

"The man to make my night."

"Your husband isn't fucking you right?" I wondered out loud.

"He's not, in fact."

"Neither will I."

I tilted my drink, sipping it quickly before resting the glass on the table again.

"I have a feeling you can."

"That wasn't founded upon my inability, but more of my unwillingness."

"Just this once?" She posed, combing over her teeth with her tongue.

"There are forty-seven niggas here, tonight, baby. I ain't the one."

The keyring holding the key to my room began buzzing in my pocket. The vibration was startling, straightening my spine and stretching my back an inch more. Upon removing it from my pocket, I discovered the small timer on the ring.

4:52.

Four minutes. Fifty-two seconds.

I took the final sip of my drink and stood on my feet. The wrinkles in my suit were minimal, but I swept them away anyhow.

4:41.

Four minutes. Forty-one seconds.

"Goodnight," Ariel called after me as I widened the distance between us.

It was a shame. Wealthy. Beautiful. Adventurous. Married. And, forced to find a suitor for her pussy's needs because she'd married either a nigga with a baby dick, one who didn't really like women, or one who simply didn't like her. Either way, she was fucked and needed to be fucked, simultaneously.

Selfishly, I wholeheartedly believed not every woman should have access to me. And, not every woman deserved it. Not my time, energy, or dick. Those were valuables I'd given and been burned in the process. The experience had left me with a precious gift, but it came with stipulations, trauma, and heartache.

I nodded my head, addressing her farewell, but never turning back to address her presence. It served no purpose. As my eyes returned to the staircase, time halted. Sound disappeared. Movement concluded. And, right on its axis, the earth stopped spinning.

Dark skin. Legs that went on forever. Hair that hung past shoulders. Perfectly sculpted, natural teeth. Eyes of mystique. Arms that ran the length of a mile. Breasts like small, unripe melons. Flawless curves.

Art. A masterpiece. One worth every dime I'd spent on this night alone came strolling down the stairs with a hand on the railing. My nostrils grew wider as my dick grew longer in my slacks.

Watching a motherfucker offer her assistance while whispering in her ear turned the temperature of the room up. *Hot*. I'd quickly, inevitably become. The shake of her head reduced the heat and made everything around me begin again.

But, the second those dark eyes found mine, everything ceased. Everything was terminated except her, for what felt like a lifetime, but in reality it was merely a few seconds. It was only until her feet touched the first floor. With her eyes still planted on me, she stalked it, seemingly headed in my direction. I waited, anxiously.

The red mask made her intentions and expectations clear. Mine were the same. More or less. Her strut reminded me of the models, the ones who were on runways for a living. She placed one foot in front of the other, moving so gracefully across the room.

All eyes were on her. Her eyes were on me, exactly where they needed to be and would remain throughout the night. I'd make sure of it.

Just short of our connection, she was pulled in the opposite direction. With a smile, she nodded at the nigga in her ear. Pouring alcohol on the open womb, she opened that pretty mouth of hers and began to release the most precious sound I'd ever heard.

Laughter. **Her** *laughter.*

I swallowed the nothingness in my throat and cleared it right after.

"Uhh mhm."

I dipped my index finger between my neck and the collar of my shirt, then ran it along the edge. Suddenly, it had grown tighter and the room had gotten smaller. That finger, my trigger finger, had begun itching and it was better I tuck it away than scratch it with the steel of my Beretta.

Her eyes, still on me, stirred something within me. The challenge she was posing wasn't one she wanted to see come to fruition. The switch she was toying with wasn't one she wanted to flip. But, the beckoning of her raised brows and daunting gaze led me to believe she wasn't bluffing and would be disappointed if she was able to call mine.

I waited, wondering just how far she'd take things, just

how far she was willing to push until she received the response I knew she craved. At the table of the man who was oblivious to her true interests and where her mind truly was, she sat.

Oh, I scoffed. *She has no idea she's barking up the wrong tree or she simply doesn't give a fuck.*

Though I would've loved to give her the benefit of doubt, I read her like a book in a few seconds. Her arousal was loud. Her choice was clear. Her stance was coherent.

If you want me, come and get me.

Blood filled my mouth as I came to the realization I'd bitten into my bottom lip. I freed it from between my top and bottom row of teeth. A tilt of my head in her direction said all that needed to be said.

Challenge accepted, my dear.

Her wish was my command.

The fact that she was a stranger and could command anything from me should've had me running the other way but it had me running toward her. Ready for whatever. Ready for whoever. Including her.

Vexed, I trudged forward, stopping for nothing and no one until I reached my destination for the night. Until I reached *her*.

"Come with me."

Short and straight to the point, I commanded of her as she'd been commanding me since she walked in the fucking room.

"Hello," she greeted me, unbothered and unmoving.

Stretching my body across the table, I drew closer to her ear.

"I don't know you and you don't know me, yet, but if

you'd like to find out about me quicker than I'd recommend, then keep sitting your fine ass next to a motherfucker that isn't me. You'll let everyone in this bitch know the firearm rule doesn't apply to me."

I pulled back and found her lips curved upward. She kissed the skin of her teeth as she maneuvered in her chair, still seated. A nod of approval from that perfectly shaped head with perfect features to match meant nothing.

"Movement," I explained, "That's all I want to see, dear."

Without haste, she slid the chair back slightly, making me regret being so far away. She deserved assistance. I didn't give a fuck if she didn't need it.

"Your audacity," she chuckled, "Enamoring. Comical. Alluring enough."

Though I didn't respond, I'd heard every word.

"Excuse me," the chump sitting next to her finally spoke.

Turning, I placed my eyes on him, hoping he understood what was at stake without a word spoken.

"I was talking to her, man. Sweetie, have a seat."

This time, it was his side I leaned into, "I don't like causing a scene but if you don't shut the fuck up, I will break your neck in front of everyone in this fine establishment, walk away, and still end up with my dick inside the woman you're yapping about before the night ends. Save another one. She's taken, homie."

Two pats on the back and I was upright, again. I extended an arm to take the woman of the night into my hand and lead her to my suite. Unfortunately, she'd vanished. Slightly frustrated with her ability to penetrate my thoughts so quickly, I began counting down from five. By the time I reached zero, my head whipped in three different directions. It was the final one where I found her. She was waiting at the staircase, clutch in hand and eyes on me.

I reached the stairs in an embarrassingly desperate amount of time, showcasing my internal and external desires for the woman in waiting.

Tighten up.

"Any slower and someone would've taken the opportunity you'd been given."

I decided against speaking my mind, again. Instead, I took her by the hand, noticing a unique detail. The birthmark between her thumb and index finger was shaped like a heart.

Birthmark.

Heart.

I scribbled the notes in my mental pad as the keyring began buzzing again.

Perfect timing.

The softness of her skin let me know she was a well-kept woman. She didn't know a single struggle. She wasn't a fan of hard work. And, hardly used her hands. Assistance was plentiful. I wasn't surprised. Not at all.

A woman of her essence made motherfuckers around her want to fight her battles, fold her clothes, hire help, and make her days so easy that lifting a finger was a choice. Not an obligation.

On her breath was traces of peppermint. On her skin were traces of bergamot, vanilla, caramel, amber, and neroli. The perfect balance, she'd managed.

"Your fragra–"

"Riot."

"Don't interrupt me," I grimaced.

"Or what?" She tutted, lowering the right side of her head and angling her chin toward me.

She was the calm and the storm. The conclusion quickly formed. While she settled something within me, she uprooted much more.

I smoothed the hair of my beard with my freehand as a chuckle fell from my lips. If stripping her of the expensive threads she wore and fucking her on the stairs for everyone to see wouldn't cause my privileges to be revoked, I'd give her all seven and a half inches of my dick to teach her the lesson she was begging for.

Quiet when I speak.

Never interrupt me.

Remain by my side unless otherwise instructed.

Act like you have some fucking sense in front of others.

I imagined she wasn't raised by wolves, so they should've all been understood without specifications. However, she was leading me to believe rules didn't apply to her either. Unfortunately, mine would even if the others didn't. With me, her unruliness ended.

"Has your father not taught you a fucking thing?" I questioned, baffled by her subversiveness.

"Bosses or nothing, baby. But, remember, you're nothing short of one yourself."

"Some lesson," I exclaimed with a shake of the head.

"If I'm too much for you, there's someone down there who I'm just enough for."

"It's sex, my dear. Nothing more. Just pray I'm not too much and it's not too late before you've discovered it."

One step at a time, I led her toward the second floor. Her long legs made it easy for her to keep my pace. Her hips swayed each time they moved. And, I was a bit more hypnotized each time they did.

Every few steps, my eyes landed on the chocolate goddess behind me. Her smile was radiating, unlocking parts of me I'd tossed the keys for. Her cheeks lifted each time my gaze struck her.

"You're going to walk or keep staring?"

"Both," I admitted, finally reaching the top where I led her to my door.

Before going inside, I gathered my bearings and brought her closer. I freed her from my grasp and allowed her to catch her footing and her breath. From the unsteady chest movement, I knew it was a struggle.

"You smell divine, by the way."

Hoping to soothe the nervous energy flowing through her body, I finished the compliment I'd started a minute or so ago.

"Thank you."

She nodded, clutching her purse with both hands.

"First time?"

"Here? No. But indulging, yes."

My head was spinning. She was swimming around my shit, no bathing suit and no reservations.

Fuck.

I turned and unlocked the door, ready to welcome her to the suite I'd yet to get acquainted with myself. The freshness of the food piled atop the plates covered with clear domes filled the air, coating the vanilla-scented fragrance I'd encountered earlier.

"Dinner?"

The rhetorical question didn't need a response, so I didn't give one.

As I watched her round the table, taking in the presentation, I removed my jacket and hung it on the designated rack. I busied my hands with soap and water, eyes hardly leaving her frame. Mentally, I was logging her in, making sure I didn't miss a detail.

She joined me near the sink, finally freeing her hands and sitting her bag on the counter. Red lipstick coated her lips. It was as fierce and bold as her. Against her dark skin it was timeless.

Her orbs stalked mine. Holding my gaze, she leaned against the counter and interlocked her hands in front of her. She waited. She wondered. She withered.

Her head fell. I lifted it, instantly. Naturally. The reaction shook me to the core. But, the defeat in her posture did the true damage.

"Heartbroken?"

My readiness to let my chopper sing was frightening. Whatever was happening with her heart had nothing to do with me. It wasn't my business, but somehow I wanted to make it mine.

"Not even in the slightest."

Relieved, I nodded. "Head up, my dear."

I yearned for distance. She was too much, too soon.

Just sex. I repeated in my head. *Just sex.*

Obliging, my feet drifted in the opposite direction, near the table where dinner was waiting.

"But you are," she said, barely above a whisper.

On the heel of my feet, I rotated. "What did you say?"

Standing tall, she squared her shoulders and straightened her posture. "You are."

My eyebrows caved inward as I tried comprehending her dissection. It was quick. It was lethal. And, it was accurate.

"Tonight won't fix it, but it'll help. For a little while, at least. And then, yo–"

"I didn't pay for a suite to get advice, therapy, tarot reading–"

"You're right," she admitted with a smile. "Neither did I."

"Mind your manners, dear."

She lifted two fingers and ran them across her mouth, "Zip."

As if she hadn't just exposed my insides, she started the water and began washing her hands. Low, harmonious sounds erupted from her, soothing the wound she'd just pulled the bandaid from.

Maybe red was a bad fucking choice.

Within the suites, it represented romance, normalcy, passion, and partnership. The long legs and beautiful voice in the wash area was leading me to believe I'd made a bad decision. Slowly, she started for the dining table. The humming transformed into words.

"I need a gangsta... to love me better than all the others doooo."

Loosening my tie, I scanned the room for the thermostat. According to the warmth surrounding us, it was up far too much. Or, maybe, just maybe it was her. She was the heat, slowly and strategically setting me ablaze.

"To always forgive me. Ride or die with me. That's just what gangstas doooo."

As she approached the chair I'd chosen for her, I removed it from beneath the table. She lowered onto it and waited for me to readjust it. Once she'd settled, I rounded the table and sat.

At that moment, just inches away, with gleaming jewels, soft skin, and the essence of a woman staring me right in my face, I remembered why I was so appreciative of the privilege. Having a woman in your world, the right woman, made it all better. Made it all right. Even when it was all wrong.

My addiction to the very existence, the aura of a woman, had been suppressed for two years. Femininity was the most sacred, unprotected aspect of a woman and I loved that shit dearly. It enhanced my masculinity. Made me wiser. Stronger. Better in every way possible.

And, though this wasn't my woman to have, she was mine for the night and I'd bask in her ambiance for the little time I was blessed with her. In my warped perception of self, I wholeheartedly believed I was not one who was supposed to live their days in singlehood. While others despised the idea of marriage, companionship, and lifelong commitments, I craved them and everything that came with them.

Stability was the foundation I'd bank on any day. The world was ever-changing. Having someone who continuously evolved but never truly changed by your side was, that shit was necessary in this game.

"A penny for your thoughts."

She pulled me from my head and back into the moment.

"Somehow I feel like you know exactly what I'm thinking."

"I wouldn't have asked."

Discomfort toyed with my words, my thoughts, and my response. I tugged at the mask on my head, ready to remove it completely.

"Don't," she warned, "Don't break the rules. It defeats the pu– the purpose of this all."

Quickly reminded that rules were involved, I nodded. Again, she was right. Rules and restrictions, I'd always found them to be inconveniences. But, the desire to sustain her comfort made them easier to abide by.

"Are you going to tell me what's on your mind?"

"I'm not."

I removed the lid from her plate and then from mine. Stuffed oysters, scallops, and grilled salmon fought for room on the plate beside seasoned rice and asparagus.

"Then, tell me what brings you here?"

"What brings you here?"

"I asked first," she sniggered.

She didn't cover her mouth when she laughed. She didn't shy away when she found something funny. Her confidence was oozing, making her even sexier than she was seconds before.

"That thing you mentioned earlier."

Nodding, she sucked in air before releasing it.

"Sorry."

"Sorry?"

"Broken hearts are no fun."

"They aren't."

"Fresh out of a relationship?"

"No," I replied, shaking my head.

"No?"

I continued shaking it from one side to the other, "Complicated."

"Hmmm."

"You?"

"Entertainment."

"That's it?"

"No. Not exactly."

"Then, what else?"

She stared at me, hesitating to answer.

"I asked a question."

"A freshly lasered pussy, a thudding in my center that won't go away, and the need to escape reality."

Impressed with her ability to express herself without sugarcoating anything, I sat back in my chair.

"Is reality that fucking bad?"

We both need to escape?

"Is that the only part you caught?"

There was that sniggering, again.

"Because I mentioned my freshly lasered pussy and that thudding us women get when–"

"I'll address that, my dear. That's why I'm here. In the meantime, your reality."

"It doesn't matter."

"How bad is it?"

"It's not bad. Not at all. But, sometimes... a girl just needs a break... some relief."

"Understood."

She bowed her head and stretched her arm across the table, grabbing ahold of mine. We joined hands. All the ruckus in my head quieted as she began to speak.

"Dear God, thank you for this life. Thank you for good health, good people, good family, and good food. Please continue to bless us in our daily lives. Continue to lift us and love us. Fix whatever has been broken in the man before me. Guide us. Protect us. Never leave us. In your darling son Jesus' name, Amen."

"Ame–"

Our eyes locked for the hundredth time. Her words began to loop in my head.

"Are you going to eat your food?" She probed, digging into her salmon.

She wasn't fooling me. Hunger had evaded her as it had me. The small bite of salmon was hardly enough to appease a woman with an appetite for food. She wanted her belly filled but not with what was on her plate.

"What I'll be eating isn't on ceramic. It's freshly lasered with an uncontrollable thud."

Nodding, she smiled, opening my chest cavity and freeing my heart of a portion of its strife.

"Good, then."

"I don't put my mouth anywhere, my dear. But, somehow, I can't fathom leaving this suite tonight without putting my mouth on you."

"I'm not anywhere. I'm not anyone."

"That, I've learned."

"Then, there's no need to explain."

"I wasn't explaining. I was prefacing."

"For–"

"I'm not interested in a new partner upon my return. In fact, I won't return if you can't promise you will."

"There are at least fifty beautiful wome–"

"And, I want you."

"Fair enough."

"Until we both get tired."

"What will I get out of this arrangement?"

"Exactly what you came for, my dear."

"I want more."

Whatever you want. I thought, never allowing the words to fall from my lips.

"What is it that you wa– What is it that you *need*?"

Hesitantly, she dropped the fork in her hand and grabbed the iced champagne. Up on my feet, instantly, I removed the bottle from her hand and poured the liquid into the fluted glass. I didn't stop until she held her palm in the air.

She swooped the champagne from the table and sat the rim against her lips. Slowly, she sipped. Her eyes rolled into the top of her head as she shook it from one side to the other. Whatever she was preparing to say almost felt silly to her. Almost felt beneath her. Almost felt shameful.

Yet, she was preparing to reveal it, anyway. She wanted her needs met and knew for a fact I'd meet them. Otherwise, she wouldn't be in my suite. She'd made it clear this wasn't her first time at The Mansion, but it was her first time indulging.

I waited, ready and willing to serve my purpose because she was serving hers well. She was stunning. She was exactly what I'd been missing every day and every night. She embodied womanhood so well. My attraction to it, at least.

The commanding presence. The dominating spirit while remaining ever so gentle. The ability to strip one of their logic and have them thinking of nothing, *seeing nothing* but her. The effortless influence to join whatever wavelength she was on.

"Authority."

"Authority?" I questioned, quite surprised by the simplicity of her request.

"Guidance."

"Leadership."

"That's what you want?"

"That's what I *need*."

The thirst she had wouldn't be quenched by the champagne she took another sip of.

"I have everything a girl could ever dream of. There's nothing I need from you– from a man at this point in my life but domination. And, not the freaky shit the rest of them consider when they hear that word. I mean mentally."

"Mentally?"

"Yes. In that reality I sometimes need a break from, I was born to lead. I'm expected to lead, and I am not given grace. That's not the way it works. So, here, I want to relinquish my power. I crave submission."

Eyebrows raised on my forehead, I leaned in to hear more. My attention was undivided.

"And no one here has been able to offer that?"

She shook her head, taking a third sip. "No. It's usually the other way around. The men are repulsive. They're either into something sickening or crave the same as me.

When I enter a room, they're willing to do anything to win me over. Willing to meet any of my demands when all I want is to be commanded. Controlled."

"Controlled?"

"In a sense. A healthy sense. There are leaders in my life, but it's all family. It's all business. I'm one of them. When the work day ends and the sun settles, I want to shed myself of those responsibilities. All responsibilities. Give them to someone else. Give myself to someone else."

"To me."

She nodded.

"I don't want to think for myself," she rushed out as if she'd been holding it inside for some time now.

The suppression had been obstructing her windpipe. Once it was released, she breathed easier. Lighter. Steadier.

"Don't look at me that way."

"What way?"

"Like I'm insane."

I shook my head, "I think you're stunning, my dear. And, I'm looking at you with adoration. Nothing less. I've never heard a woman address that natural instinct so beautifully."

"Natural instinct?"

"To submit. To be led. To be guided."

She allowed my words to penetrate.

"Can yo–"

"Don't insult me. If you didn't think I could, then you wouldn't be here. Would you?"

"No," she replied, swallowing a gulp of air. There was nothing else in her mouth.

"I can manage."

There was an immediate shift. Things were already taking place. Our positions were being established. Without shrinking, she began to recuse herself of her organically derived sense of leadership.

"One rule."

"Yes?"

"All in or nothing."

"I–I'm all in. There's just one last thing– one last thought I've had on my mind since I laid eyes on you in the ballroom. I won't live with myself if– if–"

Suddenly, her thoughts were jumbled. The way she was shedding the weight of her world and falling in line was so fucking persuasive. So fucking sexy. So fucking unforgettable. Without a doubt, I'd return. Again. And, again. And, again.

"Once it's come to fruition, that settles it. Consider your thoughts mine. Your movements mine. Your words mine. Your body—*mine*. So, what is it, dear?"

She stood almost six feet tall. I observed as she slid the chair back and peeled the straps of her dress from her shoulders. Her pace was agonizing but so fucking worthy of the wait.

She took her precious time sliding the black dress down her body, exposing round, perky breasts, a garter belt, and a matching thong. A black holster wrapped around her leg held a small .22. Mindblown, I sat up in my seat, rubbing my hands down my face to make sure I wasn't making this all up in my head.

The fuc– fucking rules don't apply to her either.

She twirled on her heels, offering me the full view. I appreciated that shit more than she knew. Her breath hiked in her chest as she stared at me. Her silence was loud. She was waiting for my approval, seeking my validation.

"You don't need me to tell you you're fine as fuck, dear. Me and nobody else. You know that shit."

I loosened my tie before pulling it from around my neck completely.

"Two rules," I began, "Never, and I mean never, get too far removed from reality that you don't remember you're a prize. You're the prize. And, I'm lucky to have you here. Your presence is a gift, my dear. One I will treasure in spite of everything else. Understood?"

She lifted her head and then let it fall.

"Words."

"Yes."

Still breathless, she backed up against the bed, only stopping when her legs pressed the sheets. Just as she was, she stayed for seconds, allowing me to have my fix. My dick was threatening to bust through the seams of my slacks. I stood, unbuttoning my shirt while still fixated on her.

She was a fucking dream. Whoever had come up with the theory that perfection didn't exist hadn't met her yet.

Her eyes lingered, landing on the bulge in my pants. Finally, she released the breath she'd been holding, but was quick to pull in another and hold it.

"Breathe."

She released it.

"Talk to me," I commanded.

"Com–"

She swallowed hard.

"Come here."

As if the words hurt to release, she scrunched her face.

It was at that moment I knew the thudding she mentioned had intensified.

"Is that all you were thinking of, dear? Something leads me to believe there's more."

"There is," she confessed.

"Then, show me."

The thong was removed. The holster was next. The gun landed on the side table, announcing its presence with a thud. She rounded the bed and lowered her body onto it. Her legs widened, exposing the prettiness between them. Her pussy glistened. She was heated.

I removed my slacks, giving my dick the room it needed to expand. My briefs followed. My shirt and tie were the last to go. Holding a matte black condom wrapper in my hand, I followed her scent. Between her legs, I stood, peering down at her.

"Is that all you thought of?"

She shook her head.

"What else is it?"

"Your head buried between them."

I tilted it toward her.

Say less, my dear.

I began to lower, but her voice halted my movement.

"With restraints."

She pointed toward the rope wrapped around the bars of the bed. Impressed with her private thoughts, I wondered if freeing her of them was a good idea. I made my way around the bed and pulled her closer to the top. With the rope, I restrained her by the wrists. When the knot was secure, I gave it enough slack to pull her down toward the edge, again.

"Is that all?"

I was anticipating more, but she had nothing more to offer.

"Yes."

"Fair enough."

Without warning, I plunged my index and middle fingers inside of her. It was necessary to check her temperature and make sure she was warm enough. I preferred my food hot when I consumed it.

"Oooooh fuuuuuck," she yelped out of sheer pleasure.

The lava flowed onto my fingers, assuring me her volcano was near eruption. With the right amount of pressure, it would explode. Hot molten would seep from her center and settle on my tastebuds.

The railing of the bed leaned forward, slightly as her body squirmed from the intensity of the moment. I twisted both fingers upward and began to stroke her clit, internally. This time, when I lowered my body to the ground, I didn't stop until my lips were on hers.

One.

Two.

Three.

Four kisses landed before I bowed my head and graced my meal.

"Dear God, thank you for the food I am about to receive," I whispered.

"Mmmmmmmmm!"

Her hips rolled as my tongue pressed against her center. Her pearl was slippery wet, a result of her loud and flamboyant arousal.

"Please," she begged from above.

Lifting slightly, I stared deep into those dark eyes of hers, still massaging her internals.

"Shhhhh."

Juices lubricating my beard, I instructed her to maintain her silence even if she was losing her composure.

"Shhhh, my dear."

I dived in, again, already missing the entree I'd pulled away from. I was still famished though my meal was right in front of me.

Her bitterness was balanced with her sweetness. She had a healthy diet. The potency of her cream said so. Her scent said so. The health of her fluids said so. The results of her routine tests for continued residency at *The Mansion* said so.

"Ahhhh. Ummmm. Yeeeees."

She squirmed under my influence, barely able to keep her ass on the sheets. I honed in on her clit, sucking it into my mouth and circling it with my tongue. The distance between her legs began to shorten. Soon enough, I was trapped between her thighs, exactly where I wanted to be. However, the tightening of the space made it difficult to move how I wanted to. How I intended to.

"Loosen up," I breathed, drenched in her gratification.

Not wasting even a second, I pulled her clit back in, assaulting it over and over again.

"I– Oh God. I can't."

"Yes," I paused and then got back to work before finishing my statement.

"You can."

"I caaaaaaan't."

She had reached the tippy top of her mountain. She was

in the homestretch, just before homerun. I pushed her legs further apart with the hand that wasn't lodged in her insides. With the same hand, I replaced my tongue, desperate to see her unfold. Desperate to see her bloom.

"Look at me."

Her eyes closed as she began to chase that feeling.

"Open your eyes."

"I can–"

"Open your fucking eyes and look at me," I growled.

Those orbs landed, socking me in my chest.

"There you go, dear."

"Ummmm."

"How you feeling?"

I asked, determined to distract her, prolonging her climax.

She shook her head from side to side, ready to close her eyes and be taken to that far away place.

"How you feeling?"

"Ahhhhhh. I'm going to cum."

"I'd like that a lot. Would you?"

She nodded with low lids.

"Eyes on me, baby. Eyes on me."

Completely and utterly engrossed in the moment, I observed with a dick harder than the bricks used to build the dwelling we were in. She was sex. She embodied the word so beautifully. Without sticking my dick in her, I was oozing. And, pre-cum wasn't a factor. My dick was spitting up on the floor as she unfolded.

Unraveled.

Untangled.

Unearthed.

Untied.
Became completely undone.
"Oh fuck!"
A gush of white, thick cream seeped from her center.
A gusher. My world was complete at once.
Fuck. She's a gusher. Fuck.

I left her on the bed, gasping for air as I stalked the floor, contemplating my departure. Somehow, I'd had enough of her to last a full month. Any more, and I couldn't promise my addiction wouldn't grow far more rapidly than I'd anticipated, than I'd planned. Finding a woman with some good pussy amongst the many in the ballroom would've suited me.

That's what I'd come for. But, one with the ability to maintain my attention, soothe parts of me that were restricted, and climb over the barriers I'd put in place two years ago was not what I was expecting.

Against my better judgment, I left the restraints around her wrist and slid the condom on my dick. It was so brittle it ached. I climbed atop the bed, unable to control my limbs. My neck stretched until my lips were against hers.

"Taste yourself."

Hungrily, she accepted me into her mouth, tonguing me down without reservation. My hand lifted the back of her head, pulling her deeper into me. She was in my space, in my hands, and in my mouth. Somehow, that still wasn't enough to satisfy my appetite.

I curved my body and spread her eagle style without disconnecting our lips. And, as her breath halted, so did mine. Simultaneously, I entered her.

"Goddamn, baby."

She contracted against me, attempting to extract more semen from my dick. Hadn't I already released a premature load, she would've succeeded. She was still riding her wave and wanted me to join her. My ride had ended. I was ready to board another with her at the wheel.

"Yesssss."

Slowly, I began to scribble on her walls. The snugness of her pouch had me fighting for residency, pulling me deeper and deeper. In utter disbelief of how fucking powerful her suction was, I lifted my upper body, needing to witness it with my own eyes.

Wrong move.

I recognized my mistake as soon as I'd made it. Seeing my dick covered in a thick, frothy concoction derived from her pussy had me delirious. I pressed a hand against the bed, right next to her head, and the other around her neck.

"Ummmmm."

Looking her dead in those hypnotizing ass eyes, I folded. Whatever spell her pussy and presence had me under, I doubt I'd come from under any time soon. I'd need more than a night to recover from this one. I'd need a few. Because if I didn't take it easy, I'd overdose on this shit. Overdose on her. She was intoxicating, barely giving a nigga room to breathe.

"You're a fucking problem. *Already*."

With my hand still wrapped around her throat, I cruised her ocean, familiarizing myself with the new, barely charted territory that was mine to have as long as we were in the confinement of my suite. She struggled to free her hands. There was no use. I wanted her just the way she was, unable to resist and unable to lessen the intensity of her next orgasm. It was coming. I could feel her pussy as it prepared to spit up, again.

I freed her neck and gripped her waist with both hands. Gently and very slowly, I began to apply pressure to her lower stomach. My strokes grew deeper as I guided them toward her g-spot, tapping against it each time I plunged into her.

"Wa— Uhhhhh. Wait."

"Nah. Give me that shit."

"Fuck. Fu– Ummmmm."

There she was. Like a flower, she began to open.

"Fuccccck. Oh God."

I removed myself and then the condom. With my right hand, I stroked my dick. With the left, I rubbed the swollen nub of her pussy. Her ejaculation preceded mine. Together, we made a mess of the sheets beneath us.

"Urgggggh. Shit."

My veins peeked through my skin as my fingers stiffened and my hands locked up. A tingling sensation curled my toes and sealed my lids. It was my turn to close my eyes.

"Again," I breathed, dick still hard in my hands.

"Again," she agreed, still catching her breath.

I regained feeling in my fingers and managed to untie the rope. Indentions pierced her skin. She was a beautiful burgundy beneath. As she massaged the pain away, I dug into my slacks and retrieved another condom and a warm cloth. The wash area was stocked with small towels. I turned the faucet on and put one underneath the water. It was warm upon contact, saving me time and energy.

I found the distressed damsel sitting up on the bed, polishing the sheets with more of her lubrication. She was still quite impressive. I enjoyed the disheveled version of her as much as I did the well-groomed one. Her messy hair. Her naked body. Her labored breathing. Her low lids. And, the lust that radiated from her frame.

My dear. I thought, sealing the distance between us.

With the damp towel, I pressed against her center.

"Ssss."

She winced, not from pain but from the overwhelming pleasure. Her sensitivity was the result of two orgasms, one right after the other. In an attempt to soothe her discomfort, I invited myself in for a forehead kiss. Then, one on the nose. Then, the lips where I lingered.

She was magnetic. She was the healthy sugar my body needed to function. The dosage for the night was high, but it would last for days to come. Possibly weeks.

"All fours, dear."

"Um hmm."

Nodding, she pulled away. The task was as hard for me to watch as it was for her to complete. That's why I'd given it to her.

She spread her arms out on the bed and lowered her top half onto the comforter. With her ass in the air, she loosened every bit of restraint I thought I had. The condom was out of the wrapper and on my dick.

"Urgh." Groaning, I parted her walls for my accommodation.

"Uhhhhhhh."

The arch in her back was offensive. Her knees nearly touched the bottom of her breast. A few more inches and they'd make contact.

Lethal.

She didn't fight fair. With all her beauty, that mouth-piece, her aura, her essence, her request, her pussy, her gushes, and her ability to fold in half while accepting every inch I had to give was sending me on a fucking trip.

"Throw that shit back," I insisted, slapping her right cheek with every intention to leave a mark for days to come.

She squeezed her muscles, involuntarily pulling me in deeper. I removed myself completely, knowing that if I stayed off in her shit, I'd be busting again. I leaned in, stuffing her with three fingers as I kissed her pearl.

"My God."

I licked her patiently, calmly as she fought against the sheets, trying to dig her way underneath the bed. Realizing she was attempting to flee, I dislodged my fingers. I held her tightly with both hands, my arms wrapped around her legs.

"Fuuuuuuuuck."

Just as she edged, I released her.

"Nooooo," she begged.

"You'll cum, my dear... *when I'm ready for you to.*"

I plunged into her, again, hitting rock bottom.

"Now, throw that shit back and don't stop."

Graciously, she balanced her body on her shoulders and began shoving her pussy into my pelvis. With her hands planted on the sheets, palms flat for stability, she drove me to the brinks of hell. I doubted, highly doubted, heaven would even allow this type of behavior. It was blasphemous.

Fuck. Fuck. Fuck.

"Ummm." Lowly, she groaned.

"Goddam– fuck." I grunted, trying to grab ahold of her so I could control her movement.

Irritation was apparent on her face when she turned to

look up at me, warning me with her pensive gaze. Still, I remained steadfast, needing her to cut me loose. My rocket was ready to launch.

She was unmanning me. Unearthing me. Uprooting me. Successfully eradicating me. With one hand, she swatted at my wrist, forcing me to loosen my grip on her.

Forcing me to take everything she was dishing and it was far too much for me to handle. My nut rose from my sack. The bulge traveled up my shaft and prepared to engage. Just as it mounted at the tip, she fell face first onto the bed, body quivering as her pussy began contracting.

It sucked the nut straight from my urethral meatus. Together, in pure harmony, we ruptured.

"Oh Goooooood. Oh God." She belted.

"Shit, baby. Shit."

My hips thrusted forward, digging into her as she gushed all over me.

"Ummmm."

She fell forward and I managed to get myself onto the bed. Against the headboard, I rested, attempting to get my shit together. I closed my eyes, counting down from ten, hoping it would stabilize my breathing and settle my thoughts. But, somewhere along four and three, I dozed.

A lingering shadow and the heat radiating from its source woke me from my slumber. Dark eyes penetrated my soul, unhousing feelings I'd buried in their eternal resting places. She didn't understand how much of a disturbance she was to the peace. *To me.*

"Hello."

Perfect teeth were exposed as her lips separated and stretched backward. The matte wrapper I remembered clearly as the last went into her mouth. She tore into it, and removed the contents. I followed each movement, watching as she picked up my hardening log and began rolling the rubber onto it.

I hadn't recalled the cleanliness I was witnessing. When I drifted, I was covered in her cum and mine. However, I was squeaky clean, now.

"How long have I been asleep?"

She paused, looking up at me with all her beauty in tow. "Thirty minutes."

I rocked, instantly. There was no denying her. I'd quickly come to that conclusion. And, in some sick way, her life outside of my suite influenced me to get him up one more fucking time.

If I fucked the life out of her pretty ass pussy, then another nigga couldn't. Because, every time she even considered it, she'd be reminded of the time we had and the things we did and the rounds we went.

"I have to go," she informed me.

"Where?"

"I wish I could tell you, but that's against the rules."

"You're so pretty," I complimented, saying exactly what had been on my mind all night.

Though I couldn't see beneath the mask, I knew she was. Inside out. Pretty than a motherfucker.

"Thank you."

"Lift up."

She obliged, lifting her butt. I slid down slightly before lowering her onto the head of my dick. She was soaking.

Is she always like this? Wet. Ready. Fuck.

Inch by inch, I glided into her. Our eyes engaged in a mental fuck that was far more intense than the act our bodies were engaged in. Her hands gripped my shoulder blades as I reached her pelvic floor.

"Uhhhhh."

Big, oversized lips brushed against my ear. Her sweetness lulled me to oblivion. Where she was taking me, I never wanted to come back from. Here, worries were few. Pleasure was plentiful.

"Ride this dick, my dear."

Like it's yours. Even if only for the night.

"Umm kay."

"Give me your eyes."

Another request surfaced after the first. Her eyes were on mine at once. Fingers digging into my clavicle, she lifted her body until she neared the tip and then slowly lowered it. Her head fell over to the side as her lids grew lazier.

Poetry.

She reminded me of poetry.

Intense. Sometimes brutal. Deep. Meaningful. Passionate. Painful. Prideful. Methodical. Idiosyncratic. Wavering. Heartening. Exclusive. Monumental. Experimental. Dazzling. Complicated. Desirable.

"Mmmm."

Her lips folded into her mouth.

Un-fucking-believable.

"Open them."

"Pleas–"

"Open them."

I ran my fingers through her hair, locating her scalp where I wadded a handful of her tresses and tugged.

"Open them."

Hastily, she widened her lids and gave me full access to her orbs. She never missed a beat. Her body still lifting and falling so beautifully. So graciously. So elegantly.

I cupped her right breast in my hand and stuffed my mouth. I rounded her nipple with my tongue before taking it between my teeth. Gently, I bit down.

"Ahhhhhhh."

She breathed out, grinding into me.

"Yessss."

I gripped the other, rotating it between my fingers while applying pressure.

"Ohhhh fuuuuuuck. Yesss."

Hungry for more of her chocolate-coated skin, I moved up her chest, leaving a trail of tender, lingering kisses. I reached her neck, unable to contain myself any longer. I sunk my teeth into her.

"Ahhhhh."

Her pussy tightened around me. Her pace increased, revealing her precise location. She was near her peak. I wasn't far behind her.

I sucked her skin into my mouth, still squeezing her nipple with one hand and holding the side of her neck with the other. Flawlessly, she still managed her balance until her legs began to buckle.

"Ohhhhh fuck. I– I'm— ummm–"

I set her free and pulled her ear closer to my lips. From below, I began to pump her full of dick. Faster and harder with each stroke.

"Cum on this dick, my dear," I whispered in her ear, allowing the blissfulness of the moment to consume me.

"Yes. Yes. Yeeeeessssss."

She leaned forward, clinging to me as if I'd vanish. Simultaneously, her pussy tightened around me. My semen spewed from my dick. I felt every drop as it filled the condom.

When her eyes returned to mine, I understood my logic and exactly why I didn't fuck women as much as I used to. Before my attempt at a family. Before my son.

I was far too invested in the act, the woman, and the ties we created. Without a doubt, I wanted the same warm body staring in my eyes as it deracinated my nut beside me when I closed my eyes and when I woke up. But, that wasn't my reality anymore. Her leaving and me going home to my son was.

She rested her chest against mine, placing her head on my shoulder. Her arms hung down my back. Slowly, she drew circles.

My mind struggled to adjust. Struggled to comprehend. Struggled to believe she knew what she was doing or what it was doing to me. Struggled to be anything but soothed by the gentle circles made by her fingertips.

"I– I've enjoyed this. Enjoyed you."

"Come back."

She waited for further instructions.

"In four days. Be here at ten. Go to your suite and then come directly to mine. No ballroom. None of the other common areas. Straight to my suite. Understood."

"Yes. I understand."

"Good."

I wrapped my arms around her, pressing her body against mine for a hug before ripping us apart. There was no easy way to remove the bandage we'd placed over our realities. Immediately, I was bombarded with feelings I was familiar with but hadn't addressed since stepping inside my suite.

At the same fucking time, fresh ones she'd birthed sat on my chest. The heaviness was as strange as it was inviting. I hated it and welcomed it at once.

I slid us both off the bed and placed her on her feet. By the chin, I brought her face up to mine and stuffed her mouth with my tongue. Quickly, before we were in too deep, I removed myself from her space and respected the distance we needed if either of us planned to leave.

I watched as she redressed. She had that fresh *–just got fucked–* face, hair, and wardrobe malfunctions going on. That shit looked good on her, especially knowing I was the one who provided it.

She finished up just as I was buttoning my shirt. My jacket and tie would not be part of my fit upon my exit. I imagined we both had that fresh *–just got fucked–* wardrobe.

She stood in front of me with all her grace and beauty. I brushed the back of her hair down with my palm. The bruise on her neck became a source of comical relief. Instead of warning her of its presence, I bid her farewell.

"Goodbye... *for now*." I kissed her forehead once and then again.

"Goodbye... *for now*."

· · ·

Four minutes later and I was in my car, pulling out of my garage. Rain had begun to fall, serving as the perfect backdrop for the night. I wasn't sure what *The Mansion* would have in store for me, but I didn't have a single complaint.

Suddenly, I didn't think they charged my account enough for the reward I'd received on the first night.

One night.

One encounter.

One room.

One request.

One woman.

And, multiple rounds had made everything okay. The weight of my burdens was no competition for the air under my wings she'd provided. I felt light. Everything was beneath me now and so fucking small from my current view.

T H E **G R E Y** L I S T

Four days later...

I toyed with the record player on the console table near the door. It was nine-fifty-two and in exactly eight minutes, the sweetest thing to grace planet Earth would be walking through my door. I'd expected the four days to take their precious time, but they'd come around far too soon.

On one hand, I was anxious for the night to begin. On the other, I wasn't prepared for the hangover I knew the night would result in. It had been four whole days and the haze was just beginning to clear. No liquor had ever lingered in my system like she had.

Willie Hutch's voice finally came through the speakers beneath the record player. Unfortunately, the pitch was enough to make me consider shutting the entire operation down. However, I twisted the knob near the edge to lower it.

"Perfect."

I turned the volume down, sure not to drown out our conversation or get any words lost in translation. Once I was satisfied with the outpouring of lyrics, I made my way toward the counter where my cup was sitting. I contemplated the first sip, knowing a whole bottle of Hennessy was on its way to my suite and before the night ended, I would have consumed it entirely.

Fuck it.

I needed something to take the edge off. It had been a hell of a day and seven minutes of waiting was too fucking long to sit with my thoughts. I sipped the brown liquid and waited for the slight burn.

"Argh."

As the glass hit the surface, there was a gentle knock on the door. I checked the face of my Rolex, quickly determining my guest was a bit earlier than expected.

Could she sense my misery? I questioned with a chuckle.

Between business and family, I wasn't sure which had contributed more. Nevertheless, I loved the life I lived and the people who surrounded me. I wouldn't trade either for a sunny day on the beach with no worries or responsibilities. This was the life I'd chosen and I did a damn good job maintaining it.

Because I already knew who was behind the door, I didn't bother asking. Instead, I unfastened the first button on my shirt and released the tension stemming from my day's work.

My feet were ahead of me, forming a mind of their own. My hands joined the cause, twisting the knob to reveal the luxury art behind the door's frame.

Red sheeted her body. The silk fabric clung to her curves. The red lipstick matched perfectly. Black shoes I'd provided were hidden underneath the expansive piece that cut across her breast with precision and pushed them toward her chin.

The vision that must've replayed in my head a hundred times or more was nothing in comparison to what I was seeing. I took a second to absorb her presence. And, when I was ready, I stepped aside to allow her entry.

I twisted the lock of the door behind her. Still completely in awe of every fucking aspect of the woman before me, I rounded her.

Once.

Twice.

And, the charmed one.

Silently, she waited with her breath lodged in her throat. Without instruction, she wouldn't move. Without instruction, she wouldn't speak. Her thoughts no longer belonged to her.

They were mine to have. So were her movements. Her words. Her voice. Her body.

Finally, I stood in front of her with my hands entangled

in front of me. It was the only way to keep me from putting them on her so soon. She was far too stunning to strip her just yet.

"Good evening."

I invited her to speak.

"Hello."

She paused as I took her all in.

"How'd you know the number of my suite?"

"Don't ask any questions, my dear."

Silence trailed.

"Over the last four days, I've found myself returning to thoughts of a woman who's name I don't even know."

"We have rules... rules we must follow for any of this to be as exhilarating as it is. When it gets personal, the thrill will dissipate."

"It doesn't have to," I expressed, "But, you're right. Rules are rules."

"Rules are rules."

I rounded her, unable to comprehend the method to God's madness. Whatever fucking point he was trying to prove making her, he'd proven.

"So, what should I call you?" I asked the rhetorical question, not waiting for or looking for a response.

"Whatever you want. What would you like? What do I remind you of?"

With a quick tilt of the head, I kissed the skin of my teeth. Dipped in red, there was one thing in particular she reminded me of.

"Rose."

A smile tugged at her lips. "Rose?"

"Delicate, beautiful, soft, influenced by her environment, silky, has gorgeous folds, withers gracefully —as she cums— and retains moisture... plenty of it," I rattled off, still circling the garden beauty.

"Then Rose it is."

The sultriness of her voice was inebriating. Dark eyes chased my frame with each full revolve until I came to a complete stop in front of her.

"On the bed, Rose."

I loosened a second button and the two on both wrists. One foot in front of the other, she strutted toward the bed. When her shins touched the sheets, she halted, waiting for the sound of my voice.

"Disrobe."

The dress I'd dreamt of on her fell to the floor at once. Underneath, she exposed the crimson-colored lingerie.

"Bend over."

Both hands rested against fresh sheets. Slowly, I closed my eyes, angling my head to the right to relieve the mounting pressure. The view was sickening. Heat consumed the room.

A few buttons weren't enough, anymore. I needed the entire shirt off my body, but it would reserve my attention for far too long. It belonged to Rose for now. I dared to depart.

The panties were missing an entire strip in the middle, exposing her center, all the way up her back. Saliva filled my mouth. My craving intensified as I watched the pinkness of her pussy peek through her plump, chocolate lips as she deepened her arch.

Sweat beads formed on my hairline. Rose was unreal. It

was the only way to describe her nature. Her depth. Her existence.

"O– on the bed."

I pulled a chair from the table and placed it three feet away from the bed. Rose's body was pressed against the sheets, ass piercing the air.

"On your back, my dear."

She abided. Her small, full breasts left me dazed. Those pretty nipples hardened, sticking straight up.

"Open up."

She spread her legs, allowing them to fall on both sides of her.

"Have you thought of me since our last encounter?"

"Yessss," she moaned.

"Show me exactly what you've done when alone with me on your mind."

She rushed to her vagina, dipping nearly her entire hand inside her canal and returning with well-lubricated, cream-coated fingers. Four of them, exactly. She'd rounded them, making a cylinder of sorts.

She smeared her residue across her clit. My dick began pressing against the zipper of my slacks.

Fucking ridiculous.

With an arched back, she inserted her middle and index finger, again. Her thumb, she brushed across her clit. Slowly. Gently.

"Ummmmmm."

From side to side, she swiped her clit while using two fingers to massage her g-spot.

"Mmmm–"

She couldn't keep still. Her hips grinded against her fingers. Her ass rubbed against the sheets.

"Uhhhhhmmmm."

I lifted, slightly, and shoved my pants down my legs. They landed on the floor next to me, along with my shoes. My briefs were lowered but clung to the bottom of my ass cheeks. My dick was no longer fighting for freedom. That motherfucker was in my hand.

The solution to the dryness was only a few feet away, but I was afraid the show would end if I interfered. Simply lubricating my dick would prove to be difficult.

Without a doubt, I'd slide right in that shit. It was too fucking good. Too fucking wet. Too fucking ready.

Still, I was unable to resist. I stood and stalked her scent until I reached her center. I hovered as she continued pleasuring herself.

"You are stunning, Rose."

"I– I'm gonna c–"

I swatted her hand away, dislodging it from her center.

"Not yet."

"Fuccccccck," she cried in agony.

She was close to her peak. So close tears were falling down the sides of her face. She was ready to release, but I wasn't ready for her to unfold.

I tapped against her center with my dick.

"Pleaaaase," Rose begged. She was wasting her breath.

Her body jerked each time my dick landed. Purposely, I made contact with her clit each time. Until, finally, I began rubbing up and down her slit, getting my dick nice and wet.

Slide in.

No.

Slide in.

No.

Slide–

I parted her sea with my girth.

"Ohhhh fuccccck."

Her body rose from the bed. Just as quickly as I'd entered her, I was ejected.

Wrong fucking move, Priest. I chastised, knowing exactly what those consequences were. Going in raw meant staying in raw and would result in the birth of a child with a woman I had no connections to, wasn't supposed to have connections to, and didn't know from a fucking can of paint.

No.

I pulled away from the bed, reeling from the momentary bliss. She was as warm and welcoming as I'd imagined, but so much better.

"Continue."

With her secretion covering my pole, I began to stroke it. My pace matched hers. Together, we found a rhythm that brought us both to the very edge of our seats.

"Ummm. Fu— Uhhhhh."

"Eyes."

Up on her elbows, immediately, Rose stared daggers into my chest. Her pretty face was distorted. Pleasure disrupted her features. Still, she was so fucking striking.

"Fuck," I grunted, feeling the rise that always came before the fall. "Fuck."

"Uhhhhh. Uhhhh. Ummmmmm. Oh my G— Uhhhh."

Semen sprouted from my dick as I continued to fist it,

unable to release it from my grasp. Simultaneously, Rose's center was covered in a cream, ultra thick glaze. Her speciality.

"Mmmmm." She froze in place, fingers dripping with evidence of her peak.

I managed to turn my shit loose. It was still rock hard, still ready to aim and shoot when I made it to the wash area. I grabbed a new towel, one for me and one for Rose. Once the water was at a decent temperature, I wet them both.

Mine was left in the sink as I used the second to carefully clean the mess she'd made. She was sensitive to touch. When I climbed on top of her, peering down at her, I noticed the laziness of her lids.

"How are you feeling?"

"Like the full day of rest I got to prepare for tonight wasn't enough."

"It wasn't," I proclaimed. "Under the covers, my dear."

I cleaned myself back at the sink and discarded both towels. There were more to choose from. New towels would be ready upon our return. Linen was not an issue. That had been made clear in the informative pamphlet.

With an entire box of condoms in tow, I strolled across the room. I emptied them into the stand next to the bed. Forty were inside the container. It would be a while before I needed more.

One didn't make the drawer. I rolled it down my dick and tossed the wrapper into the trash next to the stand.

She's tired. I thought, knowing exactly how to put her to sleep. Staying a night at *The Mansion* wasn't ideal, but I wouldn't regret waking up to Rose. Having her in my arms didn't feel like a bad decision even if it happened to be.

I peeled the covers back and joined Rose underneath them. Immediately weary of her distance, I pulled her closer and into my chest where she belonged. As I flexed my triceps, locking her in place, I used my left hand to navigate my dick through, now, familiar territory.

"Ssssssssss." She released as I entered her.

"You feel so fucking good," I groaned, face nestled in her hair.

From behind, I held her body close to mine as I stroked her with precision.

Satisfied grunts, groans, and mumbles escaped us both as we basked in contentment. For the moment. For each other. For the night.

Fuck.

In and out.

In and out.

She smelled divine. Her fragrance was being ingrained in my senses with each whiff. Her body fit against mine like a missing puzzle piece. The moans erupting from her mouth every few seconds were enough to send me into a state of ecstasy.

Rose's grip on my arm tightened. My appreciation for the euphoria on her face as she came led me to my knees. I pushed her legs backward until they reached the headboard, keeping them together to maximize the healthy friction between us.

"Yessss–"

Her pussy was so generous. So giving. So selfless, offering me every inch of it for my own consumption. I got lost in her ocean, desperately trying to find a raft to avoid drowning. There was hardly any use. It was inevitable. As she began to mount, my semen began its journey from my sack.

"I'm cu— Mmmmmm. Uhhhh. Plea– don't sto– Mmm."

"Eyes."

My limbs stiffened.

"Eyes."

Low and lusty, her eyes penetrated me, reaching depths that were roped off and deserted. I removed my dick just as the bulge reached the tip. Her legs fell flat onto the bed. I stood on wobbly legs.

"Come here."

Hurriedly, she twisted her body until her head was in my hands. I pulled the condom off and began stroking my tool.

"Open up."

With a hand full of hair, I tilted her head backward. I stuffed her mouth, refusing to stop until I reached the back of her throat. Rose sealed her lips around me while placing a hand on the base. Another cupped my balls. The trio unified with promises to strip me of every sperm cell my body was capable of producing.

Slurping, with hardly any shame in the amount of saliva she managed, Rose disarmed me. My ass cheeks grew tighter and closer together. My toes curled, nearly cutting slits into the sheets.

And, then, when I thought I'd reached the brink of insanity, she pulled back and spat on my shit as if it wasn't wet enough.

Fuck.

When her lips touched me again, all hell broke loose. I

gripped her tresses, gently removing myself from her vacuum of a fucking mouth.

"Tongue," I begged, desperate because I was losing my shit on the inside.

The second she revealed the vicious monster that was only part of the complete system, I let off. On her tongue and the roof of her mouth, my seeds found their home. Being a very good girl, she swallowed, erasing visible traces of them. However, I knew they'd linger.

"Good fucking girl, Rose."

I patted her cheek, ready to fall on my fucking face. By the time I lowered my body to the mattress, her head had already hit the pillow. I pulled her closer to me, burying myself in her neck for an endless supply of her scent as her heartbeat lulled me to sleep.

THE GREY LIST

The sun's viciousness shined through the slits of the blinds, but it wasn't what had awakened me. It was the feeling of those dark eyes and that pensive gaze of Rose's.

"Good morning," I rasped, still unsure how I'd managed a full night's rest.

"Good morning."

The sadness in her voice tugged at my lids, pulling them apart in spite of the brightness.

"How are you feeling?"

Those dark eyes were big and intrusive, saddened and regretful.

"Like I want you to wake up."

"Then, why'd you let me sleep?" I yawned.

I grabbed her leg and pulled her closer. She was sitting up, still naked, with her legs folded Indian-style.

"Because–" she paused.

Her request. I was quickly reminded. "Understood."

"Thank you."

"I'm awake now."

"Yes. Yes, you are. I've been bored without you."

"You haven't gotten out of bed?"

"You haven't told me to."

I hadn't.

"I have to piss."

I slid from underneath the cover, itching to take the fucking mask off. However, I was too committed to the thrill it produced to break the rules once contemplated abiding by. It was highly unlike me, but they were to my benefit so I settled with them. *For them. For Rose and I.*

"Breakfast?"

"I have business to tend to."

Though I hated to break the news, business came first. And, Princeton wouldn't touch his plate until he saw my face. It was best I got my shit together and got my ass home before his stomach was touching his back.

"Come," I instructed, extending my hand for her to grab.

"Okay."

Across the cold floor, she tiptoed behind me. The large shower was tempting, but I wasn't ready to clean her remnants from me. Instead, I emptied my bladder with her standing near the sink. She hadn't taken her eyes off my shit since I'd leaned over the toilet.

"Something on your mind?"

"Besides the fact I'd like to hold it next time and that it's very, very handsome... no."

"Next time," I promised her. "Handle your business so we can brush our teeth and get out of here."

"Yes, sir."

I flushed the toilet and maneuvered for her to get to the toilet. I located the towels in the bathroom while she did so. New tubes of toothpaste and packs of toothbrushes were in the cabinets as well. I began opening and discarding the paper. By the time she finished, her toothbrush was on the counter with paste across the bristles.

I made room for her at the sink I was using though it was Jack and Jill style. Together, we scrubbed our teeth of gunk and the sex that was still on our breaths. I warmed the water in the other sink and drenched the towels once it was a suitable temperature. Because I knew women loved burning their skin half off when cleansing, I burned my hands squeezing the excess water from her cloth.

"You first," I suggested, handing her the towel.

I slowly backed out of the bathroom so she could remove her mask and properly clean her face. Beside the door, I waited, wondering exactly what she looked like beneath. Her beauty was obstructed, but still radiant. I only had pieces, so I knew the full puzzle was ravishing.

Check on Princeton.

Morning meeting with Pops.

Forty-five minutes in the gym.

Lunch with my mother at Stadium.

Make my way to Spectrum to meet the new chef.

Wrap up the logistics for the upcoming shipment by five.

Dinner with a potential partner at House of Dragons. Eight, precisely.

I ran through the day's work until the door creaked. Rose appeared on the other side, handing me a towel.

"Your turn."

"Thank you."

I accepted it with a kiss to her lips. It was her turn to wait as I cleaned up. The mask left lines on my face. The mirror allowed me to map out the damage. It was nothing an hour or two couldn't cure, so stressing about it was pointless.

I hit every inch of my face and neck, then dabbled in both ears before tossing the towel in the trash can behind me. When I resurfaced, Rose was still next to the door.

"Get dressed, dear."

Reluctantly, she crossed the floor and retrieved her dress. She slipped it onto her body without the extra shit I'd provided. She wouldn't be needing them. She'd have more with time. I busied myself with my own garments. It wasn't long before I was fully dressed.

I found her right where I'd left her. Those saggy features said things her mouth hadn't and probably wouldn't. Her vulnerability was peaking.

I enjoyed it. Every bit of it. It was one of the traits I loved about women. Their ability to be completely and utterly open, transparent, and true. That shit was addictive.

"Hey. Hey."

I cleared my throat as I lifted her chin.

"Tomorrow. Here. Same time."

I removed the bills from my pants and stretched her palm.

"Maybe this will keep you busy until then."

She lifted the other one. With raised eyebrows, I scoffed. So quickly, I'd forgotten the caliber of woman made available in *The Mansion*.

I emptied my pockets, giving her every single hundred while wishing I had more. For once, I felt like a fucking bum. Six thousand wasn't shit for her. I was sure of it.

"Tomorrow is no good for me."

"Why not?"

"It's not. I have a family dinner."

"Then, the next day. At eight, since tomorrow is out of the question for you."

Two hours more wouldn't be enough time to repay me for her absence tomorrow, but it would be a start. I walked her toward the door. She stopped just a few steps shy of it.

"Here."

I turned her around, knowing exactly what she was waiting for and what she was in need of. I kissed her forehead and then her lips. There, I lingered, taking her all in as I explored her mouth with my tongue.

"Until next time, Rose."

I pulled away as my dick started to harden.

"Until next time."

THE GREY LIST

Big round circles were drawn with the tips of my fingers. One circle at a time, I nursed my son's mind back to health. It was a routine I'd created for his morning refresh. Each day he woke, he was able to start anew because I'd made sure he went to bed free of any stress.

He had yet to close his eyes, but his grip on Woody had gotten tighter. This could only mean sleep was near. Tonight, I'd managed to convince him to get in the bathtub before dinner.

It had taken a handful of Cheez-its and his favorite applesauce to keep his triggers at bay as he bathed. He lasted only ten minutes, but that was enough for me to cleanse his entire body one good time.

My vibrating phone claimed my attention. I removed it from my pocket to find a few names scrolling across the screen. As much as I wanted to ignore the others, there was one in particular I'd never let ring out.

"It's your aunt," I explained to Princeton. "I need to take this."

As the words left my mouth and I began to stand on my feet, his eyes finally grew tired. A yawn widened his mouth and he pulled Woody even closer to his body. His day was coming to an end and mine was about to begin.

"Kleigh," I answered as I exited my son's room, sure to close the door behind me.

Out in the hall, I waited for the rattling in the background to cease so I could hear my sister's voice. Though she wasn't on the line and there was so much ruckus, I knew she was home. Her ceiling tiles afforded me with comfort.

"One second, Priest. Sorry. I thought no one would answer."

"When have I not picked up your call?"

"Okay, the others!" She admitted, finally picking up the phone and letting me see that gorgeous face of hers.

Kleigh was next to the youngest, but we considered her the baby of the bunch. Kofi, we hated to even claim that nigga and still wondered why my stepmother and father decided to have the nigga.

Not only was he a liability to the family, the mother-fucker was downright ignorant. Sometimes, I questioned if we were truly raised and loved by the same people.

Strangely, he was Kleigh's pride and joy. He was only two years younger than her, so she felt like she'd raised him, in a sense. And, that was the possible explanation to the mystery we were all trying to solve.

Mom and Dad were exhausted by the time he came along. They'd poured their energy into raising three children before him. Though I wasn't Ashland's biologically, I was hers in every other sense of the word. She and my father left Kofi for us to raise it seemed. That hadn't turned out well. Not only was that nigga defiant, he was a fucking hell-raiser and he kept us all on our toes.

"Don't ever insult me in that manner, dear."

"You're right." She recanted. "I apologize."

"Is something the matter?"

Kleigh was notorious for her dramatics, but I loved her nonetheless. She was the only girl of four siblings. Her life was the epitome of theatrical according to us. We were men.

She was simply a woman evolving with each passing day. As the oldest of the herd, it was a blessing to watch her grow and become the person I'd seen in my dreams a million times or more.

She was the spitting image of our mother. The two of them, including my biological mother, were the ones to blame for my obsession with a woman's aura. Her role in a man's world. Her femininity. Her softness. Her gentleness. Her ability to calm raging storms or become the storm herself.

The way women's power lies dormant would forever be incredible to me. They had the power to rule nations, yet most chose to dilute their competency and reign over households, children, and immediate circles.

They were structured so beautifully. And, built with so much intention. Their talents were endless. Their instincts were mindblowing. Their presence was undeniable.

"No. No, not at all. I just found myself missing the men in my life and wanted to steal some of your time if I could."

Spoiled. Having three brothers and a father who catered to your every need had its privileges and Kleigh took advantage of those often.

She flaunted her independence and did so very well, yet, there were moments she remembered it wasn't necessary. Moments like these, when she was ready to relinquish her power and allow us to guide her.

Rose. I was reminded of the woman who'd be waiting at my door tonight, ready and willing to fulfill every command supplied. My throat thickened at the thought of her. My memory and senses joined one another in their efforts.

I could taste her on my tongue. Feel her grooves

extracting me of my manhood. I conformed as her thought-lessness increased my capacity.

"That's never a question. What do you have in mind?"

"I was thinking lunch with us all in attendance, but–"

"No Kofi."

"My God, leave him alone, Priest. He's getting better."

"In fact, just you and I. Lunch at *Pier*. One-thirty."

"Fine. I'll be there at one-thirty."

"And, Kleigh."

"Yes?"

"Bring that nigga you've been swapping spit with for the last month. I need to make sure he fits the mold."

"Pri–"

"If not, he can get the fuck out of your face."

I didn't wait for her to respond before ending the call. Though she would still be trying to pick her lip up from the counter seconds from now, the information I'd just shared shouldn't have been news to her. It was my job to know the dealings of every one of my siblings. I was the Captain of our ship and I kept my shit tight.

I returned to Princeton's room, prepared to continue luring him to sleep. However, his eyes were sealed shut and his grip on Woody had loosened, two signs his slumber was in progress. I kneeled down beside his bed and placed a kiss on his cheek, careful not to wake him.

"I love you son," I confessed, barely above a whisper, "So much."

I lowered the light beside his bed without shutting it down completely. In the event he woke during the night and his room was pitch black, he'd have a meltdown. I'd made that mistake three too many times and had learned my lesson now.

I freshened up and left Nikola to her nightly duties. On my ride, I sipped from a foam cup. Ice diluted the flavor of the liquor slightly, making it a bit smoother. Whatever was playing on the shuffled list made my stomach turn. There was simply too much yelling and too much hatred being spewed.

Rose's influence was substantial. Shamefully, I angled my wheels toward the curb and came to a complete stop. I placed my cup in the holder and grabbed my phone with my right hand. My left was curled around my Beretta, waiting for a nigga to get stupid and get riddled.

I unlocked my phone, heading for the music application. The words of the song Rose had sang the first night we'd gotten acquainted replayed in my head over and over again.

I need a gangsta
To love me better.

I recalled the cadence as I typed the words into the search bar. Immediately, I was prompted to click the image of a woman with fair skin and short hair. I tapped and the low, seductive voice surrounded me. Quickly I understood why Rose was singing the piece.

I was back on the road a few seconds later, cup in hand and mind traveling to that place only the girl in my suite could lead me to. By the time I was entering *The Mansion* gates, the track had looped at least six times. With it blasting through my speakers, I pulled into the garage and shut off my engine.

Got me so high I'm barely breathing. I whistled the tune. *So don't let me. Don't let me. Don't let me go.*

"Ursula," I called out.

Chuckling came through the intercom. "Yes. Mr. Valentine?"

She was waiting, knowing I'd be summoning her before slipping into my suite. I had plans for Rose and to make sure they went accordingly, the staff had to get their feet wet.

"All good?"

"Everything you requested."

"Good. Good."

"Goodnight, Mr. Valentine."

"Goodnight, Ursula."

9:56.

I stepped into my suite. The coolness caressed my skin. White foam was visible at the bottom of the cup in my hand, which became a problem.

I discarded it on my way upstairs. When I made it up, I located the bottle of Hennessy on the counter and poured a healthy shot into the glass next to it.

The vinyl player didn't appeal to me tonight. Instead, I unlocked my phone and began searching for the Bluetooth connection the suite provided for surround sound.

9:59.

My screen displayed the time big and bold, reminding me I had less than a minute before Rose showed up to my door. I restarted the song I'd played in the car several times.

The lyrics were beginning to grow on me. I even memorized a few. It was a fairly simple repetition of words with a few new ones in the verses. Still, it was easy to remember.

10:00.

I studied my phone until the digits changed. As they did so, I lowered the volume as I stalked the door with my eyes. Anxiously, I awaited the knock I'd only heard once but had somehow fallen victim to.

Knowing a lethal being who was cold-fucking-blooded on the other side was ready to suck me dry and bring me back to life by hydrating me with her built-in ocean did something for me. Did something *to me*.

My dick grew longer and harder, ready to bust out of my briefs as the seconds ticked away. I waited to feel her presence. Waited to be engulfed in her essence. Ready to inhale her fragrance. Ready to bask in her aura.

10:04.

My fingers tightened around the glass. Rose's absence made little sense. I wasn't sure if I should be concerned or combing the ballroom for her. Somehow, I knew going downstairs would be pointless. She wasn't there. She wasn't here. I couldn't feel her. I didn't sense her.

10:15.

From one end of the second floor to the other, I paced. The drink I'd only taken a sip from was still in my hand. Too anxious to put it down, too anxious to drink it, I allowed its presence.

10:30.

I began the grueling thought process. Decisions were always and had always been easy to come by. My decisiveness was one of the many reasons my father's retirement happened to be my promotion. With an iron fist, I led my family to greater heights, better profits, and more legal business opportunities.

Somehow, I struggled to determine if thirty minutes was far too long to wait for someone who didn't treasure my time. I considered tardiness a sign of disrespect.

It wasn't tolerated. It wasn't rewarded. It resulted in punishment of some kind. Yet, Rose's tardiness had my nostrils flared, my balls aching, and my heart heavy.

Where the fuck are you? I questioned.

And, why the fuck aren't you right here? Right now? With me?

10:45.

All hope was lost. The decision was easier to make, especially with the song I was beginning to hate still on rotation. It had been drowned out until I snapped back to reality.

The fuck am I doing?

I tossed the drink back, clearing the glass. Sitting around waiting for anyone, especially a woman, was unlike me. Princeton Valentine was the only human I'd wait on hand and foot. And, even he was respectful of my time, effort, and energy.

In a minute's time, I was out of the door, back in my whip, and pulling out of the garage. If Rose happened to come, she wouldn't find me in my suite.

With any luck, she'd see me another night. One when she was prompt and didn't keep me waiting.

11:21.

I dead my engine and made my way into the house. Against my better judgment, I poured a third drink. On my way into my bedroom, I began shedding my clothing one article at a time until I was down to my briefs.

In my closet, I flipped on the light and was immediately reminded of why I'd waited. Why I'd been unable to make the decision to leave sooner. Why I'd broken my own fucking protocol for a woman I didn't know the first fucking thing about.

The emptiness of the left side of the closet was hollowing. It twisted the dagger already in my heart.

Bare.

Hangers, empty shelves, and empty racks were accurate analogies for the emptiness I'd been experiencing for the last two years. On one hand, I was full to the brim. Life, business, and family filled one side to capacity. But, that other fucking side was bare bones.

Blood mixed with my saliva as I turned, completely disregarding what was staring me right in the fucking face. I grabbed a pair of pants from the sleepwear collection. I pulled them up over my briefs and shut off the light on the way out of the closet.

Dwelling wouldn't change my reality. Nothing would, because I wasn't willing to let it. That pain was too familiar to take a chance on experiencing it again.

By the time I made it to the bedroom sofa, my interest had shifted. The television was no longer in my plans. The darkness I was surrounded by suited me well.

I tipped the glass against my lips, sipping the harshness right from it. As I lowered it, the fact of the matter smacked me across my chest.

She didn't come.

10:23.

The following day, my wheels reversed from the garage at *The Mansion*. Foolishly, I'd revisited. Foolishly, I'd waited twenty minutes. Foolishly, I'd kept my eyes trained on the door that never received a knock.

With my tail tucked and some unfamiliar feelings attached to the resentment I was experiencing, I exited the gates.

Each passing minute she wasn't within my grasp, I craved her more. Any human with a decent dome would accept the neglect and push forward.

But, I was stuck. Invested. Immobile. Paralyzed. I didn't want Rose any less than I had last night when she didn't show. I wanted her more. A lot more.

10:18.

Day three, I walked out of my suite, knowing she wouldn't come knocking. The smile on my face as I slid into the driver's seat was contradicting. Misleading in the worst way.

I was festering. I was longing. I was yearning. I was aching. I was not happy, though the upward corners of my lips said otherwise.

Where the fuck are you, Rose.

And, who the fuck are you with?

The thought of her belonging to someone else was repulsive. My stomach flipped as I imagined her legs spread, her pussy wet, and her mouth waiting for another nigga.

Our rendezvous was supposed to remain in the suite and it would, but she was making it hard for a nigga not to come and find her ass. Before believing she was purposely avoiding the suite, I needed to hear that shit from her mouth.

Because, the sadness in those pretty, dark eyes told me she was counting down the seconds we'd meet again long before we even left one another's side.

10:32.

I combed the ballroom on day four. There were no signs of Rose. I didn't have to search to know she wasn't there. It was simply a way to pass time and get my thoughts in order.

A conversation with Ariel and a drink at the bar led me to the conclusion it was best I took off for the night before my dick ended up somewhere I didn't want it to be.

10:48.

On the seventh day, I waited the longest without a cup in my hand or even the jacket to my suit. The day had been long and my patience was thin.

However, I still waited. And, in waiting, I began to forget all that was troubling me.

The delayed shipment was pushed to the back of my mind. The accidental fire at the plant was right beside it.

The fact my youngest brother had wrecked his fourth car in sixteen months and would need three surgeries and a year's time to heal wasn't far behind them.

In my suite, as I did the unthinkable by continuously waiting, I collected myself. Right on the bed where my worries had gone to rest and where I'd laid her body down, I closed my eyes as the finality of my time at *The Mansion* toyed with me, mentally and physically.

Fuck it.

I summed up the losses I'd taken day after day, coming to wait in vain. I trashed them motherfuckers right along with the attachment to the suite and the woman who brought it to life. From the moment I saw Rose, I knew what type of woman she was. Yet, and still, I played with fire.

Slowly, my temperature lowered and the coolness of the room was acknowledged again. I pulled myself up by the bootstraps and took the stairs to the first floor.

When I entered the garage, I placed the mask on the shelf where it belonged. For a second, I lingered, thoughts in disarray, again.

"Ursula."

A pregnant pause paralyzed me. And, then, finally, there she was.

"Yes, Mr. Valentine."

Rose's neglect was too fresh of a wound to let go of at the moment. Maybe I would one day, but that day wasn't today.

Not because I was afraid of rejection, but because I didn't believe for once I was being rejected. Rose would be back. I just didn't have the audacity to keep waiting.

"Where is she?"

With a sigh, she responded," Who?"

Cameras were plentiful. They knew almost every move we made. Who we were fucking. And, how much we fucked them.

They didn't have eyes in the suite, but I'd be damned if they didn't know what was going on in them.

"I'm no fool, Ursula, and neither are you. Where is she?"

"We don't keep tabs on our guests outside of the establishment."

"Then, who is she? Tell me so I can keep tabs on her my motherfucking self."

"I'm afraid I can't."

She wasn't saying shit I wanted to hear. The privacy and safety of guests were their priorities. I got that shit, but I didn't give a fuck about the rules, the waivers, the clauses, and nothing else right now.

"How much?" I bribed.

"Mr. Valentine."

"How much?"

"I'm sorry. I– I wish I could, but I can't."

Blowing out a thick stream of air from my nose, I shook my head.

"You can't, or you won't, Ursula? Because, there's a big fucking difference, baby."

"Mr. Valentine, it's against our policies. I understand your frustrations, but our rules and regulations were clear. I even went over them before you stepped foot inside your suite. Again, I wish I could. I really do, but I can't."

She was doing her job. Denying me was what she was

paid to do and I couldn't blame her. But, I'd be damned if I ended the night the same way I'd started it.

I'd continue the wait, but it would be on my terms. And, when I finally caught up to Rose, she'd better hope her beauty made me forget her disobedience, because it was as maddening as she was.

"Well, what can you do?"

"Anything within these walls except give you her information."

"Put her suite on my tab. Leave it running for as long as it takes her to return. And, when she does, call me. Call every fucking number on the extensive ass file you have on me. If those don't work, start sending emails."

Frustrated with her absence, I snatched open the door of my car just as Ursula responded. The only thing keeping me from undoing everything my time alone in the suite had done tonight was the fact that Clarke was never too big to find anyone I was searching for.

And, the girl with the birthmark between her index finger and thumb was on my radar. Her. Her pussy. Her presence. Her passion. I needed that shit in my life. All of it, even if only through the night.

"As you wish."

GREY**HUFFINGTON**

ONE

Rather

Two years later...

With jumbled thoughts packed as tight as my suitcase, I fastened the gap with the weight of my body. I sat atop the hardshell case as my bottled feelings began to surface. This wasn't a waiting game anymore. This was happening.

In ninety days, I'd be draped in white with my hand stretched, waiting for my husband to slip the band he'd purchased on my finger. As a young girl, my sisters and I had gone over our wedding day a hundred times over, obsessing over every detail. Yet, neither of those details included the arrangement that had been made on my behalf.

While I wasn't opposed to the idea of it all or the shortcut to forever that I was lucky enough to have access to, it left me with so many questions. Marrying a man I had never met and having ninety days to learn everything there was to know about him while simultaneously falling in love felt dramatic.

For the most part, I knew if I wanted a life with a man on day one, so that wasn't the issue. It was the fact I would be isolated from the people who meant the entire world to me while trying to maintain my freedom, preparing for marriage, getting to know my future husband, and falling in love.

"Here," the deep baritone of my father soothed the anxiety creeping up in my chest.

I whipped around and toward the door is where I found Chem. He lessened the distance between us, stretching his long legs across the lengthy floor. With each passing day, he looked more like our father. Sounded more like our father.

Though I'd like to believe it was the reality, I understood the brain, how it worked, and how it coped. Chemistry was a splitting image of his brothers. One would believe his stepfather was his biological father. They all resembled Catherine. However, my father was scribed into his features somehow, someway.

His posture. His voice. His temperament. His vocabulary. His walk. His stance. It was all Richie.

So, maybe he was transforming and becoming the man

I missed so much it hurt. Or, maybe I missed him so much I filled the void he'd left with bits of Chem because he gave so much of himself to us. He always had.

And, in so many ways, he'd always been a father to us. My father's passing only magnified those qualities. It intensified those traits.

It highlighted his fatherly instincts. It aged his voice. It aged his skin. It quieted his resolve. It made him feel more like and look more like the man we'd buried in our family compound to keep him close to us at all times.

"Thank you, Teddy."

"Don't do that, baby."

He tapped my leg as he forbid my verbal acknowledgement of his greatness and my gratitude. Chemistry was the light of our lives. Mine. Rugger's. Roaman's. Royce's. Roulette's. Range's. And, Rome's entire universe.

He was the sun and the moon in her world. He was everything to her. Though he'd never admit it or claim favoritism, we all knew she was everything to him. She and Jru were on equal playing fields and she hadn't come from his nutsack. She'd come from Richie's.

"Lift up. I've got it, Rather."

My emotions made a fool of my limbs. Led by their intensity, I lunged forward and swooped Chem's body into my arms. His squared shoulders rounded as his spine flexed to accommodate me. His arms caressed my back as he squeezed me tightly, planting a kiss on my forehead.

"Is everything okay, baby?"

Anything for you, Teddy. Everything for you, Teddy.

Though the words didn't emerge, I knew he'd heard them. Felt them. And, understood them. He'd bend the world to rescue us. It was important he understood each of us would do the same without question or reservation.

"Y–yes," I choked, knowing I wasn't at all insane.

He sounded older. He sounded wiser. He sounded safer. He sounded *homely*.

"Is today the day you start lying to me? Because, I'll restart this motherfucker."

Still wrapped in his embrace, I felt his firmness soften. The invitation into his heart, into his head was met with slight resistance. I never wanted him to feel as though I was reluctant to make good on my sacrifice.

That wasn't the case. I'd stand ten toes down behind him, behind my family. It was that lone fact that had my heart in my throat.

"I miss him," I admitted.

His heart beat faster, harder against his chest. The vibration from his scoffing rattled my ear.

"I can't begin to tell you how m– how much I do."

His absence during our father's demise had taken a toll on him. It was vivid. It was telling. Richie was such a sore subject for Teddy.

"But, that's not it, baby."

He pulled away. A thumb on my cheek as he forged a smile was a warning I was all too familiar with. Chemistry was wise beyond measure.

Not only was he a literal genius, but he was a mastermind. In order to possess these qualities, he was required to do things others couldn't fathom and often dreamed of.

Read minds.

Yes, I read them for a living, but it had taken practice and lots of studying. I knew them because I was fascinated with the way the brains and the mental structures it created operated and adapted to life. That wasn't the case with Chem.

He was a reader. He sometimes knew what you were going to think before you thought it. Knew what you were going to do before you did it. Knew how you were going to react before you reacted. Knew how you'd move before you made the move.

It was frustrating how brilliant he was. Because, moments like this couldn't end without complete under-standing on both our ends. If we needed to, we'd sit right here until I was honest and until I felt better about what-ever was bothering me.

From where we sat, Teddy would stop the ocean from swaying, stop the earth from spinning, stop the sun from shining, or wage war if it would bring me peace. Because when our hearts were in turmoil, he didn't know peace.

"Say the word, Rather. Tell me you're not fucking with it and I will empty every account necessary to pay the debt."

"You don't have a debt."

"I'll make one if you don't wan–"

"No. No. Stop talking nonsense, Teddy. That won't be happening. I'm fine. I don't have any reservations with the marriage. I'm a little apprehensive because I don't know what to expect, but that comes with the territory.

"I'm hopeful, though. I don't think this is an awful thing. I don't. You're saving me the trouble of kissing a hundred frogs to meet my Prince," I chuckled.

"Baby, these men have extensive lists full of bodies. Probably one longer than mine."

"I doubt it," I interrupted.

He continued, knowing I was likely accurate.

"Nevertheless, the body count is not slacking. They sell dope by the boatloads. They are part of the underbelly. They make deals with the devil. They aren't strangers to trouble. They consider it a good time. They are on the opposite side of the law. They won't hesitate to kill. To shoot. To scuffle. To go to war. They have no limits."

He described our family. The thought brought joy to my heart. Knowing we weren't an anomaly and there were people in the world on the same page made me slightly more comfortable. In someone else's world, we were normal. Our lifestyle was normal.

"Does that sound like a Prince to you, baby?"

"Given the life we live sounding quite parallel to his—*Yes*, Chem. He actually does sound like a Prince to me. He sounds perfect."

"Then you girls are a bit more fucked up than I imagined. Pops and I could've done a bit better raising you."

"We surround ourselves with who we are, who we want to be, or who we think of ourselves as. Does it surprise you my interest is piqued knowing I'll be meeting a man who indulges in the lifestyle of you and Richie? And, please don't bullshit me with your response. I don't need to be pacified, Teddy."

Angling his head leftward, he took a second to respond. He calculated his words, mixed and matched them to suit his true feelings.

"I'm listening."

"I haven't started talking yet, Rather."

"What are you waiting for?"

He paused, staring back at me with the same dark eyes I'd stolen from Richie.

"It doesn't surprise me, but it doesn't keep me from being optimistic. Keep me from wanting you with a *normal* nigga."

"Is that not being optimistic? You say that as if being with a man of your stature is– is absurd. Damning. As if it's ludicrous. I beg the difference. It's not far-fetched and it is not nonsensical, either, Chemistry.

"I adore you. I adored our father. You have always been and still is the epitome of a man in my eyes. Richie was the blueprint. You were a better version of his design. Being with a man who isn't even close to what you are, who you are... that's what's illogical."

Offended, I stood, prepared to pace the room as I continued my explanation.

"Sit down, Rather."

Obliging, I sat beside him, resuming my position.

"I'm insulted."

"For me?" He chuckled.

"Yes. And, Dad."

I laced my arms and rested them beneath my bosom.

"You shouldn't be, Rather."

"Well, I am. Now, tell me, why would any of us seeing a man opposite of you be considered a better choice in your eyes?"

"I–"

"Because, honestly, Chem, what man other than one such as yourself would understand I've burned a man's balls to a crisp just so he could give me the combination to a safe that wasn't rightfully ours?"

"It became ours when he decided to cut my work."

"It was his work."

"It was stamped with my name. It was my formula. Don't fuck with my formula. That was one of the rules. He knew the consequences."

"Which, again, proves my point. What *normal* guy would understand the heights I'd go to for my family, our operation, and our–"

"Rather."

"No. No. Tell me. And, don't forget the man I refused his insulin until he gave up his boss. The guy walking around right now with one eye and missing fingers. He was only a witness. He wasn't the perpetrator."

"He acted like he couldn't see motherfuckers playing on my name, baby. That was his first mistake. He didn't try to stop them when the shit went down, either. That was his second one. Being caught on camera, simply watching it all was the third. His eyes and hands were pointless then, so there was no point of them afterward, right?"

"Oh, I'm with you on that. But, that doesn't answer my question. What *normal* guy, Chem?"

He watched me carefully, knowing I was far from finished.

"And the old man I fed viagra for a week straight."

Amused, he shook his head. He was so handsome. His pending smile made me smile.

"How you handle your business is none of my business, baby, as long as it gets handled."

"The guy with the permanent halo, now."

He tossed his hands in the air, "He should've used his head when he had the chance."

"His muscles are still deteriorating."

"His brain seemed to have done so first. Not my fault. Stupid shit gets you stupid results, every time."

"The question."

"I understand, baby."

"Well, then." I shrugged, "Don't do that, again. Optimism is hoping and praying I end up with a man who loves and cherishes me, one who reminds me of all the amazing things I love about my father and brother, the men who set the bar high in the sky."

"That's optimism, Teddy. Because, if you thought for a second I wanted a normal boy, then I'm afraid you don't know me as well as you think you do."

"I know you, Rather."

"Then, today is the day you started lying to me."

"I didn't. I'm aware of your preference. It has little to do with mine. That's not dishonesty. That's opposing views, desires."

"Hmph." I frowned, dropping my hands by my side.

He started for the door, stopping at the threshold to continue his antics.

"Fix your face, kid and come down when you're ready. We're waiting."

"Just make sure my niece never forgets me and how much I love her while I'm gone."

He turned with saddened eyes. His epiphany was in progress.

"That's it, huh?"

I nodded. "It's not my obligations that I'm struggling with. It's the separation. I don't want to leave you all. In my twenty-six years of life, I've never been alone. I've always had nine people by my side. One left me for good. I'm not ready to leave the others."

"You have four men waiting for you to touch down, Rather. They'll take good care of you. They'll make sure you're straight. They are me. I'm them. I trust them with my life and with yours."

"They're hours away, Chem."

"Minutes, baby. They're minutes away and should you ever need them it will feel like seconds."

"Malachi is in no shape to come running to my rescue."

"Malachi will shake himself off and come full speed ahead if you need him. Don't dirty his name or smear his character because he's hurting. He remains the same somewhere deep inside even if we can't see it right now. He's hurting but he's not useless."

"Sorry."

I dipped my head, remembering the beautiful life we'd all lost.

"Head up, Rather. Don't let me see it fall again."

I lifted my chin.

"Tell me something I want to hear," he deflected.

"I love you."

The words mounted my emotions. They threatened to spill from my eyes but I held it together.

"Like a *normal* kind of love or?" He smiled.

"Don't make me strap you to a chair and peel back your eyelids. Turn on the lawn mower and let the blades of grass kiss your orbs. The–"

"Rather, I'm not a client. I won't ever be. Before I sit down in your chair, I'd end your life and mine. I couldn't bear the thought of losing you and I wouldn't rest under the dirt knowing you'd lost me."

"You're sick," I sniggered, pulling the handle of my suitcase up.

"In this lifetime and next, baby."

"Come and find me?"

"Make sure you're waiting."

I laid a hand on my chest. My heart was raging. I'd love Chemistry in the next lifetime. It was written in stone.

I watched him turn to leave, somehow breaking my heart into pieces. I wasn't ready to leave them. Two years of preparation wasn't enough. I needed this lifetime. The whole thing. Unable to watch him go so soon, I summoned the words from my mind.

"Furthermore, a *normal* guy couldn't handle me if he tried. I'm not water. I'm not flowers. I'm not sunlight on a rainy day, Teddy. I'm wind. I'm fire."

"Don't I fucking know," he tittered, slapping his hand against the wall as he exited the room.

This time, I allowed him to leave because if I kept him here now I'd try to keep him forever and never board the private jet waiting for my arrival.

I gathered my things and began to make my way downstairs, sure Chemistry would return for the bags. Because our compound was massive, there was a pad for a chopper and a decently sized tarmac strip for pilots who were experienced flyers and could get the wheels up in the air quicker than others if necessary. It ran the length of the compound and was stationed on the back end.

"Hey, baby girl," I greeted Jru.

She was hanging out on the bottom step unloading and

reloading the extended magazine of the toy pistol Rugger had customized for her. Though we all hated to see her grab it, we knew it was her favorite and she was only getting her lesson early.

It was still a lesson she needed no matter what age Chem decided to give it to her. She toted it around like it was a Princess doll and chose it over any toy we tried persuading her to grab instead.

"Hi."

The rasp of her voice reminded me of Range and Rugger. If Chem wasn't careful, he'd be raising their triplet. He and Rugger were so parallel it was sickening to witness. Jru was following in those very footsteps.

Water and guns.

Water and guns.

And, though she had balance and was a genuinely sweet girl, she would be lethal. I knew it and so did everyone else around us.

"Want to ride with Tee Rather?"

"Yes."

Her pearly skin and tiny teeth made it hard not to stare. She was beautiful. Chemistry and Egypt had done well for themselves. Maybe it was a bit selfish of me, but I couldn't wait until they decided to have another one.

Jru was perfect. She needed a playmate. A brother, specifically, because it was who her father deserved. Having a son would ease those thick, crinkly brows and those worry lines on his forehead. Teddy was surrounded by women. It was time he met his match.

"Come on."

I bent down and pulled her into my arms. We traveled

through my home and into the living room where most of the family were waiting.

"Is it time, already?" Rome questioned, bolting to her feet.

The sadness in her tone had me fearful of her emotional well-being during my absence. She was Chemistry's heart, but she was the lungs of the family. She kept us strong, breathing, and motivated.

"Yes. Aden and Otis are waiting."

We'd need two vehicles to transport us the mile down the road. Of course, walking and motorized carts were an option, but they both felt like major inconveniences at the moment.

"Then let's go, girls," my mother suggested, ready to round everyone up if necessary.

She was the first out of the door. We all followed her lead. Roulette refused to pile up and decided to take her own car. Rugger rode in her passenger seat. Everyone else used the two available SUVs to get to the tarmac where the plane was waiting for departure.

Goodbyes were never easy, but as Rome's grip around my body loosened, peace consumed me. More than two whole years of my life had been spent on Chemistry's island with the people I loved most in the world. However, the idea of getting back to the States was somewhat enticing.

"I love you, baby. Keep Jru warm for me. You know she loves her cuddles and Tuesday nights at Tee Rather's house."

"It's Tee Rome's house, now."

"I couldn't be happier."

I pulled Jru closer. She wrapped her small arms around my neck and squeezed me tightly. I'd been preparing her for this moment, but it didn't stop those big eyes from tearing up as she tried regulating her emotions. At only two, she was mature beyond comprehension. It wasn't surprising to any of us. We were all the same.

Our advancement in life started at very young ages. At two, Jru knew every color, every alphabet, every number, every animal, every continent, every ocean, every fruit, every vegetable, and the list continued. Roaman was teaching her the intricacies of the brain, their functions, and surgical procedures that were designed to cure the diseases, disabilities, and dysfunctions they studied.

Rome had her on the tips of her toes the first day she learned to walk without assistance. She was stunning on the floor, just like her aunt. Range was increasing her comprehension skills and making her quick on her toes with quizzes about laws, rules, and regulations. Without a doubt she'd win an argument and make a solid case against any three year old although she hadn't reached that milestone just yet.

For starters, she spoke fluently and her vocabulary was expansive. They wouldn't stand a chance. Royce taught her simple life skills that would help improve her independence. Roulette's lessons were simple. *Fuck niggas, get money, but never spend your own.* Jru was the sheep being raised by wolves. But, by the time she reached adulthood, she'd be everything we dreamt.

"Baby, it's tim–" Chemistry began, rubbing the center of my back.

"Alright, Chemistry. I'm going."

I slipped from Jru's arms.

"I love you, Bubs."

"Evewry lie-time."

"Every lifetime, baby."

She was out for my heart. Her head landed on Rome's shoulder and those tears she was trying to fight came falling. To save me some pain, she turned her head so I wouldn't see her release her emotional discontent. I felt it. All of it.

My baby.

"Rather." Chemistry said barely above a whisper.

"Coming. I promise."

We were working with a very small window. Timing was critical. Hadn't it been, Chem would keep the pilot waiting until the plane ran out of fuel. However, he couldn't. We couldn't.

I climbed the steps alone as my family waited at the very bottom. Roaman's heart couldn't handle my departure. She had run off to her house after the quickest farewell I'd ever experienced. Her heart was pure, though, and I knew it was just as fragile.

I entered the cabin without taking a look over my shoulders. It was heartbreak waiting to happen. To spare us all, I strutted down the aisle of the aircraft and sat in the very back where the shades were stretched over the window and my view of the island was obstructed.

As I settled in and the door was sealed, I removed *The Self-Discovery Project,* a piece of work I'd been working on over the last eight months. The workbook doubled as an adult activity book with plenty of space for self-reflection and journaling.

Everything I valued and stood behind as a licensed therapist, woman, sister, friend, and human rested within the pages I carefully curated day in and day out. So many had bit the dust and not made the second round of evaluation, because they didn't suit the vision or truly embody the message I was trying to get across. It was fairly simple.

Women are doers.

Women are human.

Women are feelers.

Women are thinkers.

Women are more than objects.

Women deserve softness and support.

Women owe no explanation for our rightful nature.

Women should govern their own bodies, minds, and hearts.

Women deserve grace from everyone in their lives, including self.

Women are the most fragile beings on the planet and should be treated as such.

Women are the superior gender. Put a man in our shoes and his ankles will bleed.

Women's femininity is a direct reflection of the masculine energy that surrounds them.

Without women, life isn't possible. The quicker the world remembers that, the better the world will be.

Society's secret vendetta against the woman's body, heart, mind, femininity, fragility, sensitivity, and vulnerability has shaped the thoughts and expectations of women near and far.

It has most hating nearly everything about themselves simply because the world is quietly whispering just how much she should each time she unlocks her phone, sees a billboard, boards a plane, walks into an office, or tries to abort a child who is the result of an assault.

Women are hated by everyone, including each other. It angers me. The way women are torn apart, piece by piece, is disheartening. And, I've learned the work begins on the inside and that came from being surrounded by powerful women day in and day out.

Discovering yourself is the first step. Becoming sure of yourself is the second step. Loving yourself, unconditionally, is the final step.

Along with the draft I'd created, I removed the box of markers from my bag. My headphones were next. I covered my ears and put my favorite playlist on shuffle. As the marker struck the page, the Wifi connected and melodies finally filled my ears.

"I need a gangstaaaa."

At the sound of Kehlani's voice, my entire body stiffened. After the third line, I regained mobility in my limbs. Dramatically, I mashed my screen with my fingertip. Skipping the song that reminded me of a finer time led me to *On Read*, a Lucky Daye piece that was timeless.

Fuck.

Sifting through my thoughts, I found more pleasant ones that included the women who filled the pages of the draft I was preparing to color. The line art meant for the mental and emotional therapy for women everywhere happened to be images of the women in my world who helped me discover myself. They captured them so perfectly.

Quickly, I got lost filling in the lines that connected to

make Roaman's frame. Next came Roulette. And, then, there was Rugger. By the time I turned another page and found Rome's pretty face staring back at me, the wheels of the plane contacted the pavement carved for the private aircrafts.

With any luck, it would be the family I was marrying into on the tarmac and not the Federal agents tasked with my family's demise. I gathered my art supplies and stuffed them in the container they'd come in before stuffing it into my bag along with the first copy of my pending publication.

The Hermès Birkin fit them both, along with my head-phones and other necessities, perfectly. I stood on my feet as I began typing a simple text to the group full of my siblings and our mother.

I've arrived.

A slew of responses began pouring in. I dropped the phone into my purse, deciding to update them once I was settled and comfortable. I exited the plane with my chin in the air and my chest to centimeters further than its normal positions. My shoes collided with the plush rug beneath me before making my presence known as they sounded off on the concrete.

A handsome, older man removed his hat from his head and placed both hands in front of him as I neared. The woman beside him with the blinding rock on her finger was all smiles.

"Kalvin Valentine." The man spoke first.

"Ashland Valentine." The woman I'd swiftly learned was his wife followed his lead.

The in-laws. I surmised.

"My condolences for your loss. Richie was a fine gentleman and a good friend of–"

"Richie didn't have friends, Kalvin. Richie had associates. His friends lived in the same house as him, he raised them, and caught them all during birth with his bare hands."

A long pause left us all staring back at one another. And, finally, a smile peeled his lips back.

"Rather, is it?"

I angled my head as I tittered, blinking slowly. "We both know my name is not a mystery here."

"Richie Jr. That's what they should've named you."

"That would make it quite difficult to determine the names of the rest of his children and quite impossible to tell us apart."

"I like her, Ashland. She and Kofi will get along just fine," he chuckled.

"Or not at all," his wife joined him. "Welcome to the family, Rather. Your car is waiting. Dinner will be served in two hours. We're expecting you there. Tardiness is unacceptable."

"And an insult to character. I'll be there. On time."

"Good," she responded with a nod.

The Maybach waiting was black in color. I couldn't wait to see it glisten in the night.

"Good evening, Mrs. Valentine. My name is Quentin. I will be your driver for the night."

"Nice to meet you, Quentin."

Mrs. Valentine. It had a slight ring to it. Determined to remain composed, I didn't allow the skin of my teeth to show until I was seated and the door had closed behind me.

"Kofi Valentine," I whispered as it all began to sink in.

It wasn't until now that I knew the name of the man I'd be marrying. Chemistry was aware, yet he refused to divulge.

Kofi Valentine. Mrs. Kofi Valentine. Rather Valentine.

My cheeks flushed with curiosity. My fingers were anxious to begin searching the name, but I stopped myself before I was able to get carried away.

This is why he refused to divulge. He knew that piece of information would send me down a rabbit hole.

I silently thanked Chemistry for his logic and rested my head on the seat behind me. I wasn't sure how long of a drive we had or where my new home had been prepared. Chemistry had handled the details and made sure I was set up nicely during the ninety day period I was to remain unwed and in the event I needed shelter at any point during my time in the States.

Optimism.

The conversation I'd had with Teddy came rushing back to the forefront of my thoughts. I wouldn't need the home beyond the ninety days. If things moved according to plan, I wouldn't need it after the first thirty. There was no need to prolong the inevitable.

I was marrying Kofi. We were going to design a life we loved. And, we'd live happily. As long as we both understood and agreed, the foundation would be solid. Because I knew Chemistry nor our father wouldn't feed me to the wolves, I believed it was truly possible.

And, it will happen.

With those thoughts engrained, I rested my eyes as the wheels kept turning. It was another thirty minutes before the door swung open and I could tuck away my obsessive thoughts.

"We're here, Mrs. Valentine."

"Thank you, Quentin. For now, it's Ms. Childers."

He nodded his round head in understanding. "Got it."

Rather Childers-Valentine. Lengthy, but better.

Dropping my last name was never a desire of mine. I'd been Rather Childers my entire life. Rather Childers had worked hard. Rather Childers had made a name for herself in the therapy she specialized in. It was Rather Childers on all three degrees and the high school diploma.

Rather Childers was the name written on the awards and noted in the accolades. I'd remain Rather Childers even long after my death. Acquiring a man's last name was an ancient practice that didn't necessarily carry the same benefits and principles, now.

Then, it was a medal of honor, a way to let others know you were someone else's property. To let them know you belonged to someone. To a man. I didn't belong to any man but God. The days when marriage was a woman's greatest accomplishment in life were long gone.

So, although I was in love with the sound of Rather Valentine, Rather Childers-Valentine sounded better.

"Thank you."

He busied himself with the bags as I made the journey toward the door. I unlocked it using the key Chemistry had given me just before my departure. The smell of fresh roses filled the entryway. I followed the faint, yet distinctive smell through the foyer where I found a large box of roses waiting for me.

"Ms. Childers," Quentin called out to me.

Turning to find him with the luggage I'd brought along, I nodded toward the stairs.

"Up the stairs will be fine."

Though I didn't know what was up there or where the master suite was located, I knew I wouldn't be hauling suitcases up. Bringing them down if necessary was less daunting.

"Sure thing. And, then, I'll be out of your hair."

"Good day, now, Quentin."

"Have a good day, ma'am."

I removed the fully-loaded, full-sized Px4 Storm from my purse. With one toggle of the black notch, the SD Type F transformed from dormant weight in the bottom of my Birkin to a deadly piece of machinery.

Patiently, I glossed my lips as I waited to hear the door close behind Quentin. When I was certain he'd gotten to his car safely, the barrel of my gun pierced the air. The gift from Teddy was a soft brown, nearly golden tone and a beast in the field. Without a doubt, it would get the job handled.

The clicking of my heels announced my presence as I stalked each room on the first level. After clearing the backend, I moved toward the kitchen where the smudges on the freshly polished floors caught my attention.

Proven. I'm not insane.

The imperfections were proof of presence in the home other than my own. The flowers were the first piece of evidence. Chemistry made it clear he'd chosen my location, my home, furnished it, and sealed it so entry was forbidden until I arrived. The red roses upon arrival were red fucking flags.

Through the kitchen, around the pantry, and into the

laundry room, I followed the trail of faint marks. Because the laundry room was down a small set of steps, it was completely separate from the rest of the house. Still, it was completely finished and useful.

The smell of fresh paint traced the air. Inside, I searched for the continuation of the smudges but came to a dead end. Instantly, the door tightened behind me. Though I'd completely fallen apart inside, I collected myself and moved forward.

From behind the mud rack, darkness arose.

Black top.

Black bottom.

Black shoes.

Black hole.

My life wouldn't end today, but theirs surely would. I'd always been taught to shoot first and ask for specifics later. And, not from the person on the ground. Because, if they could answer any questions you hadn't done your job.

Fow!

I fired a shot toward the figure, quickly regretting the discharging of my gun as soon as it sounded. The long frame disappeared as quickly as it had appeared. Fear gripped my chest, tightening my throat past the point of discomfort.

As my stomach began to turn and my emotions began to spill from my mouth, I was blessed once more with the fleeting presence.

"Chemi–"

"Good evening, baby."

"How– How'd you– You were just in–"

"And, now I'm here. If you thought I was sending you

off without making sure you were well, then you had it all fucked up, Rather."

"I didn't think much, Teddy."

"Understood. This is a huge step."

"But, I'm prepared. I'm ready. And, somewhat excited."

"Good. Good to hear."

"How'd you get here before me?"

"You took the scenic route. I flew straight here. You didn't notice the extra forty-five minutes?"

"I was lost in my crafts."

"Don't get lost again, Rather. Pay close attention."

"You're right," I admitted, "Why the flowers?"

"Wanted to make sure you weren't slipping and had your antennas up."

"Sorry for shooting at you."

"Be sorry you missed, baby. That's the only thing that's pissing me off. You know better."

"If I hadn–"

"But you did."

Snap. Snap.

Once. Twice.

It was the universal code for business in our family.

"I'm listening."

I straightened my spine and pushed the small button on the side of my handle. Chemistry was all the safety I needed. Unlike me, he didn't miss. Even with his eyes closed and his back turned, he'd hit his mark. His precision was undeniable. I'd witnessed it too many times.

"This way."

I followed him around the corner he'd rounded and then disappeared behind as I pulled the trigger. To my surprise, it wasn't a corner at all. It was a very discreet pathway.

"What is it?"

"Your path to freedom if you're ever in a jam."

He was beyond his time and beyond any human I'd ever encountered, even Richie. Chemistry wasn't a step ahead. He was miles ahead. While others were waiting at the start line for the race to begin, he was crossing the finish line. It never failed and he never ceased to amaze me.

Quietly, we walked down the long stretch. With each passing second, I waited for it's ending. It seemed as though we'd never make it there.

"Teddy–"

We were getting deeper and deeper. I eventually came to the realization it continued for miles.

"Don't give me that look, baby."

"You did all this for me? I'm promised protection, right?"

"I know what they said and I appreciate the gesture, but you're my responsibility. And, you will be until I'm in the ground. Fuck their protection."

With a nod, I continued.

"The heat sensors aren't able to pick up a signal down here. If, for any reason, you feel compromised, simply stand in front of the door we came through. Your entire body will go through a one second scan.

"It will detect your rapid heart rate and elevated vitals. It'll know if you're distressed and open that door. Not sure if you remember Lawe, but his people installed it for me."

Of course I remembered him. The few weekends in summer we had the privilege to visit Berkeley while he was at Pops couldn't end fast enough. He was a train wreck and wasn't sorry about it. Paired with Makai and every place they visited became a shit show.

"Follow this exact path. There are three others, simply for confusing anyone who steps foot down here. Use this path and take the fifth exit.

"There you will find Benny waiting to take you to a secure location. There you'll wait for further instructions. If they don't come from me, from my voice, they are not your instructions. Alright?"

"Yes."

"No one knows about this but you and I. Benny will only know when he needs to know. The family you're marrying into isn't to know a fucking thing, baby. You hear me?"

"Yes."

"Not even Kofi."

My heart swelled in my chest hearing his name roll off Chemistry's tongue. It was the first time but I was certain it wouldn't be the last. He and I were destined to spend the rest of our lives together.

"Chemistry."

"Yes, baby?"

"What's he like?" I sighed, desperate to know something, anything about the man I was set to marry in ninety days.

"He's a man," Teddy explained, "He's a fucking man, Rather."

"What's that supposed to mean?"

"It means guard your heart, maintain your sanity, and don't let that motherfucker get to your head. Remember who you are and don't ever forget it. You're a Childers, Rather, and we don't move foolishly. Most of all, maintain your individuality.

"Don't let that nigga speak for you, think for you, or move for you. Make your own moves. Do your own thinking. And, speak your mind. Don't, not even for a second, let any of them play with you or think they can play with you. Because the truth of the matter is they can't. Understood?"

"Understood."

"Then why are you looking at me that way?"

"One more question."

"One more."

"Is he that bad?"

"He's not bad at all, Rather, or you wouldn't be here. He's a liability. We don't like liabilities, baby. We like assets. That's the sacrifice. That's how we repay the Valentines.

"That's your job. Turn him into an asset. Not just for his family, but for all three of the families. If you don't, the government will... but surely you know it'll be for themselves."

"He'd become a rat?"

"No. He'd become bait."

Needing him near, I closed the gap between us and wrapped my arms around him. He kissed the top of my head before stepping back.

"I have to get going. Now that you're here, our communication will be limited. But, I have a line dedicated to your calls. Whenever you need me, call me. There's a phone in the nightstand next to the bed in the master suite."

"Okay."

"Rugger left a gift for you in the kitchen. Turn all the knobs right until they click. Behind the stove you'll find it."

I didn't stop him when he turned and headed in the opposite direction. Over his shoulder, he tossed a peace sign. It was all he had and all I could accept at the moment.

Because, truthfully, I wanted him to stay as bad as he wanted to stay. To make things easier for us both, we settled for the mediocre gesture.

I scurried back into the house where I stood in front of the stove minutes later. My Beretta rested on the counter behind me as I stared at the precious chunk of material. Some amazing dishes would be made in the near future.

Click.

Click.

Click.

Click.

Click.

Click.

The backsplash lifted, exposing a small artillery. And, though small wasn't an accurate description, it was in comparison to Rugger's ideal of a decent collection. Sure that Chem had given her limitations and made her settle for much less than she cared to settle for, I was left with a smile.

Well, shall we get dressed?

Massive.

Manicured.

Enchanting.

Festive.

Not only could my thoughts describe the home I'd stepped into, but they could also describe my family's home. I missed it as much as I did my father. Entering the Valentine's family home reminded me of the countless dinners we had and the bonds we thickened around the table that nearly stretched the length of the entire room.

"Right this way."

A staff member directed me toward the dining hall where the same man and woman I'd met hours ago were standing. Slowly, I continued down the long hallway, reaching them only when my thoughts were clear and my head was on the straight and narrow. Chem's words stuck with me.

It means guard your heart, maintain your sanity, and don't let that motherfucker get to your head. Remember who you are and don't ever forget it. You're a Childers, Rather, and we don't move foolishly. Most of all, maintain your individuality.

Don't let that nigga speak for you, think for you, or move for you. Make your own moves. Do your own thinking. And, speak your mind. Don't, not even for a second, let any of them play with you or think they can play with you. Because the truth of the matter is they can't. Understood?

"Understood," I whispered as I approached.

"So, we meet again," Ashland spoke.

"We do."

"Into the dining area, shall we?" Kalvin said, tugging on the door behind his wife.

"We'll introduce you to the family. Starting with Kofi, you'll make your way around the table and greet each person you come into contact with. Not everyone is as friendly as–" she explained.

"There's only one person you must overlook, Rather. Our eldest. Don't take his brashness personal."

"In other words, he's a bit of a grump. The others are fine. You'll be fine. I *hope*."

"Do you not understand who your son is marrying?" I tittered. "There's no doubt in my mind that I'll be fine. As for the people I encounter–"

I shrugged.

"Worry about them. Please don't worry about me."

"Oh, I'm not," Kalvin chuckled, "Not even one bit."

The doors swung open and I was confronted with chatter that was plentiful and faces that were beyond beautiful. Chiseled cheekbones, perfectly lined fades, suits, ballroom dresses, white teeth that varied in perfection, gaps, gold, diamonds that sparkled, and laughter that was infectious. I couldn't understand why my lips lifted into a smile but they had.

Family.

I imagined that was the cause. And, this family was gorgeous. Wealth was abundant. And, structure was apparent.

My family.

Not only was this my new family, but it reminded me of the times I'd had with mine prior to our relocation and our father's death. They reeked of excellence. *So did we.* Their riches were loud and bold even though it wasn't their intention. *So was ours.*

"Settle down, everyone. Settle down. We have a very special guest tonight, so I need everyone to behave themselves. Especially you, Kofi," Kalvin warned with his eyes trained on the darkest of the bunch.

His eyes were low, hooded almost, but it wasn't due to genetics. Marijuana was cruising through his system. He was on a high and that bold smile with all his teeth visible validated my revelation. Red eyes confirmed it.

"I haven't done a thing, old man."

"Not yet," a deep baritone barked. "But, it won't be long."

"You have no faith in my offspring. It's insulting," a woman who resembled Ashland sighed, loudly.

"Kofi, Rather. Rather, Kofi."

He pushed the chair back and stood on his feet. His extensive limbs ambled in my direction. When he was near, his arms widened and encased me.

He's hugging me.

It was swift, but his scent lingered.

"Kofi," he introduced himself as if his father hadn't already.

With flared nostrils and a throbbing center, I managed my manners.

"Rather. Rather Childers."

"Not for long," he reminded me as he took his seat.

"Ninety days to be exact," Kalvin added.

"That voice you just heard belongs to Killian, next to the oldest. My daughter's name is Kleigh. You've met Kofi. And, the one at the very end of the table... that's Priest."

"Hi," Kleigh greeted me with kindness and delicacy.

"Hello."

The contentment on everyone's face surrounding me was pleasurable. However, the man she'd just named didn't seem to share the same sentiments as his siblings and parents. Intimidation was a foreign feeling and one that didn't visit me often or ever.

I made a mental note to meet the grump with the same energy he delivered so he was never confused about where I stood with him. I would begin and continue standing wherever he stood with me. And that went for everyone. My father hadn't raised a fool and I wouldn't begin acting like one in his absence.

I began my round, first stopping by to shake Kleigh's hand. She was the most welcoming. Kofi and I had already exchanged bodily bacteria that lived on the surface of our skin. It was time to pass the germs I'd collected since my bath on to someone else.

"You're so pretty," Kleigh complimented me, standing on her feet.

She was uninterested in a handshake and opted for a hug. I embraced her, knowing instantly she'd be an ally. The rest of the siblings were still up for evaluation. Feminine energy radiated through us both as we kissed one another's cheeks.

"What are you wearing?"

"Riot. From a small fragrance company my sister loves. It was a gift from her."

"Tell her I need a gift, too. You smell so yummy."

"Thank you. I'll be sure you get some."

I continued down the side of the table where Killian was next up. He stood, taking my hand into his. Though firm, I immediately assumed he was the more tolerable of the three men at the table other than his father. A charmer.

"Nice to meet you, Rather. I've heard great things." He lifted my hand to kiss.

"He's lying. We've heard literally nothing about you," Kleigh admitted.

"This nigga, man," Kofi scoffed, slouching in his seat.

I moved right along, rounding the table to reach the end where the dark presence was brooding. A nod of his head corrected Kofi's behavior. Words weren't exchanged, but Kofi clearly understood his posture had become an issue. He sucked his teeth while straightening himself up and stiffening his spine.

Don.

Boss.

Head.

Leader.

Capo Mandamento.

I realized.

Chemistry. My brother's position made it easy to understand his and it didn't take a few minutes. Milliseconds was all I needed to fully comprehend.

"Rather." I extended my hand to shake his.

He stood tall and he stood long, buttoning the jacket of his suit in the process. Not until he was ready did he take a good look at me, studying me like an open book, and take my hand into his. Words never evaded him. His eyes fell from mine, onto my hand where my grip was firm and full of confidence.

Yet, somehow, the sight of it seemed to have grown more repulsive by the second. He released me forcefully, abruptly ending our introduction. Unfazed by his disdain for my presence, I stood unmovingly, peering into his dark eyes. Maybe he was head of the people around him, but there was only one head of the Childers and his name was Chemistry.

With a roll of my eyes and a frustrated stream of air from my nose, I decided to end the stare down. Though I didn't want to give up, I'd seen his kind and knew they didn't give up easily, either. I made it clear, however, he wasn't establishing his dominance over me. It didn't exist. He'd be better off saving that energy for the people he shared blood with.

I gathered my bearings and sat in the chair designated for me. Because I could feel his eyes piercing my flesh, I went against my logic and took a look across the table where he sat. Finally, he set his sight on something else. On someone else.

Asshole!

TWO

Priest

I needed air in my lungs.

Rose.

I needed a pacemaker to monitor my heart.

Rose.

I needed to peel my eyes out of my skull.

Rose.

I needed to erase the memories from my head.

Rose.

The heart-shaped birthmark between her index finger
and thumb was taxing my thoughts, jogging my memory,

stealing my breath, and trying to dislodge my heart from my chest.

Two years.

Two whole years.

Two fucking years.

And, after two years, she re-enters my world with vengeance, preparing to flip that motherfucker upside down.

Two fucking years, I'd waited and so easily she falls into the hands of a kid I nearly raised with marriage as their fate. To make matters worse, marriage within a ninety-day timespan.

Kofi wasn't ready and we all knew he wasn't. However, his last incident nearly ended his life and brought ours to a screeching halt. Putting it very fucking lightly, he'd scared us all. While death didn't faze me, it wasn't a fate I wanted for my siblings. Not while I was still walking the earth, at least.

"Aye."

I heard Killian, but I couldn't hear Killian.

The beat of my heart was too loud. The beauty of her laughter was too unnerving. The memories of our time together were coming in too fast.

"Priest," he whispered. "Aye."

It was the most daunting task I'd ever encountered. Realigning my vision and freeing her of my orbs cost me a heartbeat or two, but I managed. I cut my eyes toward Killian, needing to know what the fuck he wanted and why the fuck he was beckoning for my attention.

"Are you alright?"

His concern etched away at my sanity.

The woman who tattooed her pussy on my face and stitched the scent of her pussy in my brain is marrying my little brother in ninety days. No, nigga. I'm not okay. I'm losing my shit.

"Um hm," I lied, cutting my eyes toward my mother and father who were all smiles.

This was a good thing for Kofi. This was a great thing for our family. And, I'd been on board with the idea for two whole years. But, finding out those two years were directly connected to the two years I waited for that damn woman had me conflicted. Because, they could've chosen anyone... *anyone but her.*

"You think this nigga has it in him to go through with this shit?"

I hope the fuck not. I thought, selfishly.

"It's Kofi. One will never know until the day comes."

"This isn't one of those things, P. He'll be dead wrong for breaking that damn girl's heart. And, she's not like the rest of his flock. She might end his life," Killian chuckled, "We're worried about the streets killing that motherfucker. It might just be the sheets. I heard them women get down."

We'd all heard it. We all knew it. Unlike Kleigh, the Childers sisters were immersed in their family's operation. They weren't the clueless girls most syndicates raised. They had been primed and prepped since they were young children. They were the oil that kept the fucking machine of an operation fully functioning.

Chemistry kept them hidden in plain sight. I hadn't had the pleasure of meeting any of them, or so I'd thought, but I knew they were lethal. He was lethal. And, if they were as cold-hearted and wise as the man they praised, then

Kofi needed to get his shit together sooner than later. Otherwise, we'd be searching the city for parts of him that were scattered in a very strategic, thoughtful manner.

"In the worst way," I agreed.

The world is as small as it is round. I couldn't speak for the others, but the one I'd fixated my orbs on got down, *down*. Not only in the room with clients but in the bedroom as well.

The Therapist.

She'd fucked me.

Fucked my mind.

Fucked my soul.

Fucked my heart.

Though it was a quickie, she'd left a lasting fucking impression.

"Seeing her makes me wonder where the fuck them sisters hiding. I could use a Childers in my corner."

"They're not your type of woman, Killian. Besides, it'll be a cold day in hell before The Chemist allows it. He's kept them hidden from us all these years for a fucking reason. He's only given us access to this one because of our arrangement."

"Business. Business. Always about business."

"What the fuck else is there for shit to be about?" I asked, genuinely curious.

"Shit, life."

"That is life."

Nodding, he agreed, "I know. I really thought I was going somewhere with that one, but I guess not."

"I guess not."

Killian, second born of my father, was possibly the most

logical of the three boys. The most tolerable. And, that was mainly because he was most relatable. However, he was far from average. There was a switch in that head of his, one that led me to believe he suffered from multiple personality disorder.

Once it was flipped, he became something so fucking beastly that not even our mother could get through to him. Keeping Killian on the other side of the fence where he was social and sane instead of straddling it was our safest bet. Killian was a fucking nutcase. With the same smile still on his face after having the time of his life, he'd gut the mother-fucker who'd provided the experience.

You'd always see Kofi coming. He made it obvious. He never wanted you to be surprised by his presence. When it was your turn to receive the hell he was ready to give, he'd make sure you got the message. He sent a warning before destruction.

Killian was baffling. He left so much to be determined. Everything was always up in the air with him. You didn't know when, where, why, if, or how he was coming. He was the mystery that solved itself.

Silent and artful. I left little to the imagination. Victims were certain of my presence and certain I'd meet them in hell to relive their final moments when my time finally came.

"She's pretty."

She's wondrous.

"Yeah."

Rose.

"This nigga better not fuck this up and ruin my chance of meeting those sisters."

"It's not happening. Drop it."

"I can take on The Chemist. Drop that nigga where he stands."

"But, you won't. Besides, that motherfucker is too smart. He's probably already found a hundred ways to kill each of us if he needs to. We are in possession of one of his. If there's nothing else I've learned about him, it's that he doesn't fuck around when it comes to those girls."

"Or at all. Cause, who the fuck crosses an ocean for a woman who took you down an–"

"A man in love, Killian."

"Women can't even get their niggas to take out the trash and this nigga was out there swimming with the fucking sharks to get back to his."

"For a woman he loves, even a woman he likes enough, a man will not have to be asked, told twice, urged, or reminded... He just will. Anything. Any day. Any time. Any place. Nothing will ever be too much to ask of or expect from him. So, crossing an ocean for a woman you love isn't surprising to me. It's inspiring."

"Inspiring?" He sniggered. "Do you even like women anymore, brother?"

With my lips twisting into a smirk, I nodded. *No, Killian. I don't like women. I like **that** woman.*

"The first course is being served. Pay attention."

The vibration of my cell during dinner hours could only mean one thing. As the appetizers were placed on the table, I excused myself.

"Excuse me."

On my feet, I made strides toward the door. Simultaneously, I slid my finger across the screen. When I reached the hallway, my ear was glued to the device, waiting to hear what Nikola had to say. Princeton wasn't in the best of moods when it came time for dinner. The adamant shaking of his head led me to believe he wasn't interested in the family affair.

Because I respected his decision, I refused to bring him along and have him feeling the weight of my decision when he'd clearly made his own. He was in bed with his knees to his chest and his pajamas on when I left. Whatever was happening in that little head of his had him down a bit. Unfortunately, he wasn't capable of telling me what was on his mind so I could help. I was still hopeful we'd get past the communication barrier one year, but year five probably wouldn't be it.

"How is he?"

"He's fine. He just seems a little... down."

"Yeah. I felt that, too."

"He's usually sleep by now, but he's not. He's awake. Quiet and calm, but still awake."

I cleared my throat and loosened the tie that had began choking me at the sound of her words. Something was bothering my son and I had no way of easing his mind. That shit pained me in the worst way.

"If anything changes, call me."

"I– okay."

"You what, Nikola? What else is there?"

"I just left his bedroom and– I don't know if I'm just– nevermind."

"It's never nevermind when it comes to my son. Tell me what you saw when you left his bedroom."

"I turned as I was closing his door. I'd just tucked him in, again. And, he was signing. Not to me. Just– discreetly."

Though he knew many, there was only one he chose to utilize and it had been over a year since I'd witnessed its use. The idea of his discontentment stemming from the neglect his mother's absence taunted him with left me stomped.

"Goodnight, Nikola."

I wasn't interested in prolonging the conversation. Instead, I ended the call and returned to the table. The churning of my stomach wasn't from the lack of content. My appetite wasn't as demanding as it had been before I stepped out. It was a result of my son's heartache.

Every inch of me grew uneasy. I leaned forward with my elbows on the table. The clearing of a throat reminded me of the lack of etiquette on full display. Slowly, I removed them and opted for the arms of the chair. A single wink and Kleigh's attention shot across the table.

My eyes followed hers, landing on the incredible creature that sat next to Kofi and my mother. Upon settling on her beauty, my heart rate slowed. The aching eased. My nerve endings gathered. And the void I'd been plagued with didn't feel so fucking insatiable.

"Was that Nikola?" Our mother questioned, forking the stuffed ravioli.

"Yes."

I observed furrowed brows as the muscles in her face flexed. The perplexity of Rather was quite intriguing. Something within her was stirred at the sound of my voice. Or, maybe it was my imagination. Either way, I sensed her displeasure.

"Is everything alright?" My father followed up. "With Princeton?"

"Yes."

"Good. Good. We missed him tonight," Ashland spoke for everyone at the table.

"So much," Kleigh groaned.

Because I didn't have anything to add, I remained silent. Dinner salads were the next course. They were all pre-dressed with a healthy amount of house dressing our mother created at the top of each month.

Rather was pleasantly surprised by the new flavor. Her eyes lit up. Her posture straightened. And her cheeks peeked as the first bite touched her taste buds. I was quickly reminded of the way her cheeks fattened the first time I touched her taste buds.

Fuck.

I blinked away the vision of her cleaning herself from my shaft. This wasn't the place. Neither was this the time. I'd spoil my appetite.

Entrees were served. Dessert was the final course. I had very little interest in either. I was craving something a bit more savory. The second the plates were cleared from the table, I was up on my feet, prepared to bolt out the front door. Kleigh grabbed a hold of me before I could dismiss myself.

"You barely touched your food, big guy."

"A lot on my mind."

"Anything I can help with? Anything you care to talk about?"

"No."

"If you won't talk to me then maybe you can talk to

Kofi's new fiancée. She's a therapist and a damn good one from what I hear."

"That's good for her... and him. He needs a fucking therapist."

"I won't disagree with that, but so do you."

I won't disagree with that. I thought.

"I'm leaving, Kleigh. Can you let me go?"

Her arms were wrapped around me as she looked up at me. She didn't understand boundaries or personal space. Having a sister was a gift and a curse. Kleigh didn't give a fuck. Physical touch was her love language and because she loved her brothers dearly, we were always in her underneath her palms, in her arms, under her lips, and against the side of her face.

"Say please."

I placed a hand on her shoulders and pushed, slightly. Like a rag doll, she slid backward.

"Goodnight."

"Rude!" She yelled behind me, "And, goodnight to you, too."

Unbothered by her theatrics, I continued out of the door. I wouldn't hear the end of our parents' mouths tomorrow for departing without letting them know, but that was another obstacle for another day. Today, though, I had somewhere to be.

THE GREY LIST

I shuffled around in the glove compartment of my latest addition to my fleet. Within the last two years, I'd upgraded my whip twice. My latest purchase and most frequent set of wheels housed the small garage opener. It transferred cars each time I did. I never left it behind in the event I received the call I'd been waiting two years for.

At the very last minute, I scheduled a visit to *The Mansion*. As I pulled into the gates, I noticed just how much had changed since my last visit. A new set of suites had been built on the property. The landscape layout had been changed. Though manicured, the lawn was much different.

The garage lifted at the push of a button. Once inside, I shut off my engine and lowered the door behind me.

9:55.

The time on the dash seemed bigger, bolder tonight. With five minutes to spare, I reclined my seat slightly and brushed a hand over my face. Everything was beginning to make sense. The odds of it being two years since I'd last saw Rose and it being two years since The Chemist had succumb to the consequences of falling for a Fed weren't coincidental.

9:58.

I exited the car. Though I was expecting dust to clutter the shelf holding the masks, it was squeaky clean. For seconds, I contemplated, staring at the options presented. There were two additional masks, making six in total. Things had certainly changed. I made a mental note to check the updates I'd been sent through email.

Red.

My drug of choice. I slid the strap over my head and

pulled it down my face. Simultaneously, a familiar voice came over the loudspeaker.

"Good to see you, Mr. Valentine."

"Good evening, Ursula."

"Is there anything we can do for you tonight? We weren't expecting you."

"Unless you can bring her to my suite within the next thirty minutes, no... There's nothing you can do for me."

"Goodnight then, Mr. Valentine."

Goodnight. I thought, turning the knob of my suite door.

10:00.

I cracked open the door of my suite for the first time in two years. While everything was exactly the same, nothing truly was. Everything was different. I'd stepped onto foreign territory or so it seemed.

10:06.

I settled in with a glass of ice topped with Hennessy from a fresh bottle. The staff were quick on their feet. I'd notified them of my pending arrival less than an hour ago and my liquor was waiting along with snacks and a welcome package as if I was a new resident.

10:08.

I stood near the door, leaning on the counter with my irises fixed on the center. I waited, anxiously, to feel the prominence of Rose's presence. I waited to hear the gentleness of her knock. I waited for the potency of her aura.

Waited for her to move when I said so.

Waited for her to speak when I said so.

Waited for her to think when I said so.

10:25.

I stood in the same spot, finishing my drink with a smirk stretching my lips. A shake of my head led me to push off the counter and straighten the slight curve of my spine.

"Pull your shit together, nigga."

I tossed my glass back and began chumping on the small cube of ice left. It melted almost instantly.

"Pull it the fuck together."

I removed the mask from my face as I descended the steps. Shortly after, I was out of the door, inside of my car, and pulling out of the garage. I pushed the pedal, ready to get home to my son where I should've been all along.

11:04.

I silenced my engine and made my way inside. I shed my clothing piece by piece until I was completely naked and standing in front of the shower. The low light inside the glass was the only source of illumination. I twisted the knob and adjusted the temperature.

My phone glowed on the counter. Its vibration was muted by the water flowing from the showerhead. I picked it up to find my youngest brother's name on the screen.

"Speak."

"Come outside, nigga. We're celebrating."

"Celebrating what, exactly?"

I ran my hand down my goatee, smoothing it down.

"Me being forced to give up my fucking freedom to be tied down playing husband and shit."

"Kofi."

"In ninety fucking days to be frank."

"Kofi."

"Yes, I had a long fucking time to prepare but who the fuck can prepare for some shit they didn't want, my nigga?"

"Kofi– are you intoxicated?"

"Did you not hear anything I just said? Whether I'm drunk or not is no–"

"Where is Killian?"

I didn't give a damn about his saltiness. His safety was my only concern.

"I don't need a babysitter."

"You've proven you do."

"I assume that's why you and Pops worked out this little deal? A babysitter. Is that what she is?"

"If we wanted a motherfucker to babysit you, we would've hired one. She's a fucking person, Kofi. Someone to keep you occupied so you're not risking your life every day of the week with your definition of a good time."

"Whatever man. You coming out or what?"

"I'm not. I'm at home with my son where I am staying."

I ended the call and immediately dialed Killian's cell.

This fucking nigga, man. Fuck. Kofi was the most careless fucker I knew. He had Honor, from the Baptiste family, beat. But as the years passed us by, he was becoming more of a nuisance than the joke we took him for in his earlier days.

Killian picked up on the second ring.

"Yeah."

"Where are you?"

"With this nigga. Kleigh and I."

"Good. Where's Ro– Ro– Where's his fiancée?"

"She's home sleep, I suppose."

Good. She didn't need to witness his bullshit on her first night home.

"Alright. Eyes open. Keep Kleigh safe and that fool from killing himself."

"That's why I'm here."

I ended the call with one person in mind.

She's home sleep, I suppose. Killian's words looped in my head.

She has six sisters. I reasoned. *She's not the one, Priest.*

"She's not," I groaned, "Unless God has fucking jokes or some shit."

I stepped into the shower and allowed the water to cascade down my chest and back.

But, the smell of her perfume.

It was special. Unique. And, smelled so fucking good.

"Riot. From a small fragrance company my sister loves. It was a gift from her."

"Tell her I need a gift, too. You smell so yummy."

I recalled the words exchanged between her and Kleigh.

"Her sister. There are six more of them," I whispered to myself, "She's not the one."

The birthmark.

I couldn't explain that one, but I prayed her sisters shared the same one to make sense of this all.

She's not the one.

THREE

Rather

Dressed in a pair of barrel jeans, a white wrap top, and vintage Dior slingbacks, I sipped from the prettiest textured glass filled with coffee. Without a doubt, I knew it had been sourced from a vintage shop or a generous estate sale.

Genre, the corner coffee shop, was notorious for their glassware and trinket dishes for serving their guests. It was almost impossible to find a match or set that wasn't at least sixty years old. Pat, the owner, had a very unique vision that I was happy to see come to life.

The coffee was incredible. The scenery was perfect. The crowd was diverse. The fact that there was a library full of books by Black writers that guests could read freely the duration of their sitting made the visits even sweeter.

Currently, my eyes were nestled between the pages of a very cute, very short story about strangers becoming lovers. Ironically, their union had been arranged as well. I'd smiled a hundred times since I split the book's pages to read the prologue.

So lost in the story of Kema and Dillan, I struggled to recall the purpose of my visit. The time on my phone's screen revealed another hour was on the horizon. Eleven was approaching and I'd been seated since ten, precisely.

Kofi.

My brows crinkled in search of the center of my forehead. The genuine disgust that quickly began mounting led me to my feet. Irritation was heavy on my heels as I marched toward the counter. Giving up Kema and Dillan after reading the first five chapters of their story felt too much like torture.

Through the lens of my black shades, I set my sight on the register, fully prepared to request the price of the publication so I could checkout, gather my things, and head out. The solid chest that met my shades, pushing them further onto my face, had appeared from thin air. My entire body shifted backward.

Swiftly, I placed the book in my left hand and slid my right hand into the back of my jeans where my weapon was partially concealed. The palm against my elbow, pulling my arm in the other direction was seconds away from being blown to shreds.

I retrieved my weapon, ready to shoot first and ask the nagging questions later. However, the debilitating baritone

I'd heard many hours prior at the first family dinner left me paralyzed.

"Don't blow your cover."

Taking the request into consideration, I shoved my Beretta back into my jeans and fixed my shades. I took a healthy step back, separating us while simultaneously trying to gather oxygen the man before me had stolen from my lungs.

"You're late."

"I know," Kofi groaned, removing the shades from his face while rubbing his forehead.

"And, hungover," I sighed, heading in the opposite direction.

He followed behind me, taking a seat at the table I stopped in front of. I placed the book I was reading face down, sure not to lose my current page.

"Unacceptable."

"Good morning to you, too."

"Tardiness is a sign of disrespect, Kofi. I'm certain I don't have to tell you this. You're a mess."

"I'm not." He shook his head.

"You haven't recovered from what I assume was a good night. You're late. And, though you seemed to have bathed, liquor is coming from your pores. If this is any indication of how much you value the connection we've been tasked with developing, then you have a ways to go before I happily walk down the aisle. This behavior will not be tolerated."

Without saying a word, he stared directly at me with a smile on his face.

"What is it that's on your mind?"

"My father wasn't lying," he sniggered with a shake of the head.

"What does that mean exactly?"

"You girls are special."

"If that was meant to be a compliment, thanks."

"It was, which is why I don't want you to take much of what's said at this table personal."

"Thanks for the warning, but I can't promise you anything."

"Fair enough."

"Would you like coffee?"

"Nah. I'm in no mood to be shitting all day. That's all coffee does for me."

Taken aback by his remark, my face contorted. The smirk I was trying to keep at bay fought for relevancy.

"You're going to be on the toilet in an hour tops, so we need to hurry this shit up, anyway."

"Is that right?" I chuckled, amused by his honesty.

"Yeah. Though I apologize for my tardiness, make no mistakes. I respect your time. I value this shit we're being forced into, but who the fuck wants to meet for coffee at ten in the morning on a Monday?"

"Me," I reminded him.

"Obviously."

"This doesn't have to be difficult, Kofi. This arrangement– it'll be whatever we make of it. And, for me, I want to make the best of it. That starts now. I just need to know you're on board, because I will not exert all my energy while you hardly give any. There needs to be an equal amount of effort to balance this all out. I'm willing to give it everything if you're willing to do the same."

With an angled head, he brushed his beard. My heart fell to the pit of my stomach as I waited for whatever was in his head to come from his mouth. I knew it was only a matter of seconds. Kofi had made it clear last night that he had a difficult time holding onto his thoughts.

"That's where the bitterness to this otherwise sweet opportunity comes into play. This was not my idea, love. And, that's not to discourage you or devalue you in any way. That's just me being frank. My people consider me a walking train wreck. Because of my history, they have every right to."

"However, forcing me into a relationship I didn't ask for nor want at this point in my life in an attempt to save me from self-destruction is so over the fucking top. I almost lost my life two years ago. It took me eighteen fucking months to recover. Eighteen."

"And, that wasn't a full recovery. Until four months ago, I was still fighting to get back to myself after breaking almost every bone in my body, including injuring my spine. I'm not supposed to be sitting here talking to you today, but I am. And, in my opinion, jumping into a relationship after that shit is— it's not what I want to do."

"They're scared. I scare them. The idea of my death scares them. And, you happen to be a casualty of that fear. When I say I am not ready, Rather, please believe me. Don't let me show you. That shit will be painful and the last thing I want to do is hurt you. But, I'm not ready."

"This isn't up for debate, Kofi. I have been sacrificed. Do you understand this?"

"I do. Fully. But, as you said, this will be exactly what we make of it."

"So, what are you proposing?"

"The full ninety days."

"For what, exactly?"

"For preparation. I'm not ready, but I can get ready if you just give me that time. I lik– I love pussy, Rather. All kinds. All sizes. All depths. And, I will not stop sliding in them just because my fucking father thinks I'll die soon if I don't settle down and have a fucking family."

"I'm only a few months into full mobility. It wasn't until the last two months that I started feeling like myself again. I'm not ready to sit down and I won't. Not yet. So, for the next eighty-something days, I'll continue to explore. Continue to do whatever my single ass pleases."

"But, the day I am obligated to our commitment is the day it all stops. Everything. And, I devote myself completely and wholly to you."

"And, during that time, I just hang around hoping you'll actually be ready?"

"No, we still get to know each other. We date. We court. We learn each other's fears and favorite colors and shit. Whatever they do in relationships."

"You've never been in one?"

"I haven't and wasn't planning on it either."

"Yet, here I am."

"Here you are," he said, nodding.

Taking a look at his handsome face, I softened. His honesty was appreciated though it wasn't something I'd expected to ruffle my feathers. This wasn't the ideal meeting, but it was progressive, nonetheless. I knew where he stood, what he wanted, and how he was feeling. He knew where I stood, what I'd accept, and how I was feeling as well.

"Fine."

I sipped from the cup of coffee.

"Fine. I'll give you the full ninety days, because whether you're ready or not the wedding is happening and before I allow you to make a fool of me in marriage, I will make you regret surviving that accident."

"Wh– wait. Wha–"

"I let you talk. Now it's my turn. You've laid down your ground rules, so here are mine."

"I'm listening."

He straightened his posture and leaned in.

"You have until the night before our wedding to wrap it up. In the meantime, while you're sliding your dick in others you will not be sliding it in me. If you're not ready, then neither is my pussy. It's a sacred place. No man who is planting seeds in other gardens can enter mine. It's not happening."

"Damn, I can't even sample the pussy before we walk down the aisle?"

"The walk down the aisle is happening whether we like it or not. So, deal with that on your own time. You've had two years to come to terms with it and so have I."

"True. True."

He nodded.

"When I call, answer."

"Doable."

"Don't make me feel alone. Don't make me feel like a burden. Don't make me feel like I'm begging for your attention, because I won't. Not now and not ever."

"Noted."

"Dates. Dinners. Outings. We will still indulge. You will actively court me, no matter what happens when you bring me home. That's not my business. Not until we commit."

"Understood."

"Maintain your health. Wrap it up, Kofi. No babies and no diseases or infections."

"Of course."

I sipped my coffee.

"Anything else?" He smiled, making my center throb.

"Keep your hands to yourself, because if ever you fall into my garden your escape won't be as easy as you assume."

"Hands to myself," he promised, holding both hands in the air.

"Good, then."

He leaned over and took the glass from my fingers. I observed as he tipped the glass up against his lips and finished the warm beverage. Satisfied with my suitor, my lips curved up into a smile.

Does that sound like a Prince to you, baby? Chemistry's words rang out in my head.

Maneuvering to suppress the yearning his beauty had begun to bribe, I thought, *Yes. Yes, it does.*

Eighty-eight days getting to know a man who was still interested in his freedom while I rejoined society and explored my own sounded like a plan. Though his selfishness was ingrained in the deal, it would produce so many rewards for me.

My protection.
My freedom.
My peace.

And, the lack of overwhelm was only a few.

"Pack your shit up, love. I'm not feeling this spot. I have somewhere better in mind."

Suddenly, my story became more interesting than Kema and Dillan's. I'd revisit them if I landed in *Genre* again. For the moment, I was more interested in Mr. Valentine and what he had in mind.

"Give me a second. I have to turn this book in."

"You feeling it?" He asked, standing on his feet.

"I am, actually. It's about an arrangement something like ou–"

The book was snatched from between my fingers and slipped underneath Kofi's arm. He extended the other, ready to take my hand.

"We can't j–"

"Quiet, Rather, and bring your pretty ass on, girl."

"But you have the–"

"No one will know if you don't tell them."

A kleptomaniac. I concluded, taking his hand and slipping out of the coffee shop with second-hand embarrassment flushing my cheeks a deep maroon. We rounded the corner where I spotted a red Ferrari parked illegally with flashers blinking.

Bingo.

I didn't need the three degrees I'd acquired younger than most to know I was staring at Kofi's car. If the obnoxious color hadn't told me so, the illegal parking might've. And, if that wasn't the case, surely the music that was loud and lewd was the giveaway.

"Where are we headed?"

"You'll find out when we get there. I need you to learn

to trust your fiancé," he joked.

"Is that what you are? Because, I don't see a ring yet. And, didn't you just tell me you'll be sticking your thing in things dur–"

"Aye. Aye. Stop bringing up the past," he laughed, showing those pearly teeth and that perfect smile.

"That was only a few minutes ago."

"Still, the past. And, if it's a ring you want then a ring I'll get you. Say no more, love."

With a roll of my eyes, I sunk into the passenger seat and allowed the buttery soft leather to embrace me. I watched as he dashed around the car and joined me on the driver's side. With one hand on the steering wheel and the other planted on my thigh, Kofi pulled into traffic.

THE **GREY** LIST

My back slammed against the seat the second the light changed in color. The missing roof allowed the wind to pour inside of the car. It pushed my hair backward and rearranged the light makeup on my face.

Kofi shifted gears, racing down the street as if flashing lights were behind him. I searched my handbag for the wallet I'd stuffed inside as I was leaving home. Surely we'd be on the side of the road with an officer at the passenger door before we got to our destination. The falsified documentation would be necessary if they requested my identity.

As I located the black leather YSL wallet, the tires came to a screeching halt. I looked up to find us in front of Adren-

aline. Though I'd never visited the arcade, I recalled the week of its grand opening. The city was excited and happy to present their largest adult activity facility.

"Put that up," Kofi suggested, jumping out of the car without opening the door or allowing valet to do so. "If they get behind us, I'm not stopping, baby."

His declaration was music to my ears. It was lubrication for my center. The throbbing intensified as I watched him adjust his jeans on his waste and the shades on his face. The fact I wouldn't have the opportunity to indulge was a shame. But, as long as he was craving other women, my appetite for him would be suppressed.

The Mansion.

It had been two years since I'd entered those gates, but the idea of returning to the residence soothed the itch I was developing. I unlocked my phone, prepared to send a message to the concierge. With any luck, my urgency wouldn't pose a problem for staff. In the event it did, they'd be compensated well for their troubles.

My door swung open as a hand extended for me to grab. The attendant welcomed me with a smile and pretty, white teeth.

"Welcome to Adrenaline."

"Thank you."

"When I come back, there better not be a scratch on my shit."

"Yes Sir," the attendant chuckled.

"Don't go joy riding, either. You can't handle what's under that hood, nigga."

"I won't."

Kofi linked our fingers and ushered me to the door. The

breeze wrapped my body in small, fine bumps. I leaned against the six foot frame beside me, hoping to capture his warmth.

Dark carpet covered the floors. Dim lights traveled the length and width of the building. Games sat inches apart from one another, waiting for human interaction. Through the main floor, we continued until we stopped in front of an elevator.

"Cold?"

Attention to detail.

Thrill-seeker.

Promiscuous.

Short attention span.

I parted the notebook that held nearly every thought I'd ever had and began making mental notes. Kofi was in a separate section. A special section. The section I'd revisit more often than not for the success of a marriage that I was beginning to look forward to.

He's a fun guy.

In so many ways, I could use one in the world. Everything was always business. Always work. Always calculated. Always planned. Always a step in the right direction. Always the best decision.

The last two years of exile taught me so much about myself and how much of my identity was wrapped into my family's operation. Without cases in front of me or assignments from Chemistry, I was lost for the first full year. It wasn't until year two that I began discovering Rather. Who she is. What she likes. Where she is mentally and emotionally.

The balance between work and life will come easy,

because he'll make sure we're living as much as we're working. Surely.

"I am."

As we waited for the elevator doors to close, his hands slid up and down my arms.

"They're going to have to turn this shit up."

"The heat?" I questioned, a bit confused by what he was referring to.

"Yeah."

"I'm sure I'll feel better when I start moving."

He bear-hugged me, pressing his chest against my face and covering as much of me as he could. Inhaling his fragrance, I closed my eyes and disappeared somewhere in our pending future when the sheets possessed his scent.

And, no matter how many times I washed them I couldn't remove it because he was ingrained in the threads. They remembered him. So did I. So did my body. So did my mind. So did my heart.

"We're not going to wait to figure it out."

We reached a secluded area seconds after exiting the elevator. Immediately, Kofi encountered a staff member.

"Welcome t–"

"She's cold. I need the temperature a bit more suitable up here. Handle that and then we can talk."

"Sure thing, Sir. I'll get right on it."

"That's what I like to hear–" Kofi paused to read the nametag of the employer while tapping his cheek with his palm in a steady motion. "Joel."

Joel scurried in the other direction as we continued in stride. It wasn't long before I realized we were the only two people on the third floor.

"Ready to get your ass whooped?"

Near the netted machine that dispensed basketballs and counted the number of baskets each player made was where Kofi stilled. With his head angled toward the basket and his brows attempting to fuse with his hairline, he waited for my response.

"I'm afraid I don't lose, Kofi."

"How much you trying to bet, baby? And don't bullshit me. My money long and yours isn't skimpy, either."

I took a look at my empty wrist, still upset about a few things I'd left behind in St. Catana.

"I could use a new Rolex," I sighed, sucking the skin of my teeth.

"Say no more."

"What about you? What if you win?"

"You've gambled enough by agreeing to give me your heart, Rather. Asking for anything else would be too much. I've already won."

My hand rested against my chest as my eyes closed. I swayed my body from one side to the other, humming the words to *Comfortable.*

"I don't think she's listening, Royce."

"Rather!" Royce called out, ignoring Rome.

"Hm?"

"Why are you smiling so hard?"

I lifted my wrist so that my new presidential piece was eye-level. The 36mm Rolex with the hidden clasp and diamond dial was such a beauty.

"Him." I admitted, lowering my arm.

I placed the pencil at my lips and began tracing my natural line until I met the dark brown shade from the other side.

"Well, I'm happy to hear you at least feel an attraction to him. Admittedly, I was worried," Roaman explained. "But that smile on your face tells me everything I need to know."

"He wants the entire ninety days to empty his nutsack," I informed the group.

Everyone was on the call and in their respective homes.

"Men," Egypt scoffed, "You hardly find one who thinks with his big head."

"Unless they're old and it hardly works anymore," Roulette chimed in, stuffing a chip in her mouth, "That's why I won't be thinking with mine until my coochie is loose and releases a little pee when I sneeze or laugh. Until then, it's fuck niggas. Get money."

"But you literally have a man," I reminded her.

"It's not and never will be that type of party over here and you know it."

She was right. She'd been dibbling and dabbling for years now. I doubted that she would change.

"So why are you smiling?" Rugger wanted to know.

"Richie raised many things, but a fool wasn't in his repertoire."

"Good to know your head is on straight," she replied. "Now, tell me more, like how you came across that new timepiece."

"He bought it. I beat him in basketball at the arcade and this was my prize."

"I can't be mad at that," Roulette chuckled, "I taught you well."

"If that makes you feel better, then I assume."

"Let her finish, Roulette," Rome complained.

"It's the potential I'm most excited by, and not his alone. I know better than to fall for who I believe a man can be when who he truly is, is staring me right in the face and calling me a bold-faced liar. It's the potential of a union I wasn't sure what to expect of that has me smiling."

"When I learned of the sacrifice and stepped forward so Rome didn't have to walk into a life of uncertainty, it was because I didn't want a man breathing down her neck and demanding anything of her she wasn't willing to partake in on her own."

"I didn't want that life for her, but I knew I could handle myself. You know. Not saying you couldn't, babe, but I'd much rather it be me. So, I stepped off that plane clueless with my guard up and my guns drawn –mentally of course."

"Why not physically? That's what I'd p–"

"We know, Rugger," Roaman concurred.

"You know me, sister. They were ready just in case. But, as I was saying–" I sighed, finally glossing my lips, "I was expecting the unexpected. What I wasn't expecting was to walk into a room full of people who reminded me of the people I love most."

"I wasn't expecting the handsome man I'd be marrying to be so enjoyable. So attentive. So honest. Men lie. That is a proven fact. So, I'd much rather him tell me not to hold my breath waiting for him over the next ninety days than him let me run out of oxygen while doing so."

"He lifted a weight off my shoulders when he expressed his desires, because I have a few of my own."

"Aw shit, now. Talk to me, sister," Roulette effused.

"Quiet," Range demanded.

"Desires?" Rome questioned.

"Yes. I was getting overwhelmed thinking about moving back to the states, maintaining my freedom, missing my family, getting to know a stranger, falling in love with him, planning a wedding, finding a dress, and getting down the aisle in ninety days."

"When it's all said and done, I'll be marrying that man in less than ninety days. It doesn't matter if we're in love or if we are meeting for the first time. The deed is not up for discussion. Learning he's tolerable and actually has plans to commit fully to our marriage when the time comes lifts the burden. But, until he's obligated, his only commitment is to himself."

"He's fresh out of recovery. I am not opposed to his idea. So, I've tasked myself with enjoying each and every day leading up to the wedding as well."

"Starting with–" Roulette asked, waiting for what she knew was to come.

For six months, after our departure and Chem's arrest, I fed Roulette breadcrumbs about my experience at *The Mansion*. Not only because I wanted her to expand her business and create a similar experience, but because there was one detail about the experience I simply couldn't get out of my head.

PS102.

"A quiet place where I can forget the rest of the world exists."

"Which is where you're headed now? At nine o'clock at night?" Rugger searched for answers.

"It is. Hopefully, I'm there by ten. And, the only way that'll happen is if I get you girls off the phone."

"Oh, she's rushing us off the phone?" Rome sounded partly surprised.

"Dick will do that." Roulette sniggered as she hung up.

"We all know not to mind her. She's a special case," I reminded everyone, "But, I need to finish getting dressed and head out. I'll talk to you girls tomorrow. I love you. All of you."

Rugger responded by ending her call. Rome, Royce, Roaman, and Range all said their goodbyes before leaving the call. With my line free, I continued humming to the background tunes, prepping for a night out.

I stood in the closet that only held a handful of tops, bottoms, accessories, and dresses, trying to decide what to wear. Chem had insisted he recreate my wardrobe, but I denied him the opportunity. So much had changed in the last two years and most of the clothes I'd collected prior didn't correlate with the woman I was becoming.

Ding. Dong.

The bell sounded around the house, slightly startling me. Not because I was afraid, but because I wasn't expecting anyone and my phone was still on my bathroom counter. There was no way for me to see who was trying to gain access to my home... *access to me.*

My limbs stretched beyond their average capacity, helping me retrieve my phone quicker than usual. I located the application on my phone that showed all angles of my home. The front door was the view I was most interested in until I tapped it and realized there was no one there.

While strolling through my home, headed for the kitchen, I tapped the view of the driveway. A black Mercedes appeared, but there was no sign of human activity.

I twisted every knob on the stove and stepped aside as my small arsenal was revealed. I removed the prettiest and sassiest of them all, the *Tiger Striped PMXs*. It fit between my fingers like a glove. I grabbed a smaller, more compact pistol and shoved it in the pocket of my robe. It dangled, stretching the fabric due to its heaviness.

Still, I pushed forward and made my way toward the door, no longer worried about the cameras. When I opened the door, I'd see everything I needed to see. I trusted my own vision more than technology, anyway.

Ding. Dong.

I drew closer and closer to my door as the bell sounded again. With the PMXs ready to go and trained on the frosted glass that I couldn't see out of and no one could see inside, I unlocked it and pulled the handle. As I began to press the trigger, ready to squeeze and end the life on the other side of the door, I noticed the sienna-colored skin and curly barrels of hair.

"Oh God. Please don't end my life tonight. I just got a new manicure and haven't taken the photos like I promised Tina. She'll hate me all the way in heaven," Kleigh begged.

"Don't ever come unannounced," I warned, pulling her into the house and locking the door behind her.

"Sorry, but I didn't have your number. I stole your

address from the family's database. There wasn't a number for you, though."

"Your brother has my number."

"Well, I tried reaching him but wherever he is, the music is too loud and his attention span is too short."

"Figures."

I lowered my weapon and straightened my spine as we stood in the foyer. I was waiting for her to state her order of business so I could get on with my evening.

"Aren't you going to put that away?" She wondered out loud.

"I'm not. I'd like you to tell me your reason for being here."

"God, so intense. Are the rest of the girls like this or is there at least one that's less serious and into gir–"

"State your busin–"

"Okay. I see I've started off on the wrong foot by popping up, but please disregard my lack of etiquette. My parents taught me better. I apologize."

"Accepted."

"I've grown up around boys my entire life and always wanted a sister or a girlfriend I'm really close to but– Well, neither of those ever happened. I mean, Lola, for a few years but she turned out to be someone other th–"

"Lola?"

"Princeton's mother."

"Princeton?"

"My nephew. Priest's son."

Asshole has a child. Asshole Jr. I noted. *Hopefully he didn't take after his father.*

"At dinner I felt like maybe our conversation was the

start of a healthy relationship between you and I. You're here alone and I've been alone since I discovered Kofi was another boy and not the sister I'd dreamed of. So, I brought snacks and pajamas, hair rollers, my laptop, a few credit cards, wine, and a movie."

Because she was empty-handed, nothing she was saying made much sense.

"Did you now?"

"Bad idea?" She cringed, squinting her features.

No. The Mansion just happens to be a better one.

With a raised brow, I remained silent, knowing she had more to say. She was the cutest thing, brimming with excitement she was trying to contain. Letting her down would break my heart. I could settle for a deflated pearl between my legs.

What I couldn't settle for was the look of disappointment on her face and the chance to indulge in what I loved most about the human existence. *Womanhood. Sisterhood.*

"Not at all."

"Whew," she sighed, loudly.

"Where are all the things you've spoken of? You're practically empty-handed."

"I know. I ran back out to the car thinking I could carry everything in myself, but I can't. I'm going to need your help."

"My hands are a bit occupied, but I can help get a few things."

Putting away my weapons while stepping outside in the dark of the night in the company of another woman in a brand new neighborhood was absurd and simply wasn't happening. For her safety and mine, they would accompany us outside and back however many times the load required.

"Good. Come on. Everything is in the backseat. I was thinking we could do a little shopping, yeah?"

She opened the door and headed toward the car. I followed, keeping my eyes and ears on guard.

"The way my closet looks, I'm thinking we could do the same."

"Fair enough."

Priest

Tardiness wasn't tolerated, but absence was unacceptable. Princeton's was the only excusable absence, which was why it didn't bother me much that he'd be home for the second week in a row. What was chipping away at my sanity was the lack of information or a decent explanation as to why.

Princeton was accustomed to routines. He learned them. He loved them. But, as of lately, he loathed them. His naps were more frequent and his fuse was shorter. At the drop of a dime, literally, the stimming began and outbursts beyond his control took over his small body.

A trip to his physician revealed nothing out of the ordinary, but I knew something was wrong with my son. And, autism wasn't the case. He'd had that all his life. Something deeper, something more unsettling was the matter and I needed to get to the bottom of it. I just didn't understand how or how much time it would require.

I met our home affairs manager at the door. Because I knew everyone was inside seated already, there was hardly any reason for me to move any swifter. I was late. The damage had already been done.

"Good evening, Sir."

"Good evening," I responded, pushing past the tray with champagne flutes atop.

My bladder was already urging me to visit the closest toilet. I cut a quick left off the main hallway in pursuit of the bathroom reserved for family. We weren't allowed in the guest bathrooms which were just down the main hallway on both ends.

I loosened the button on my suit in preparation. The realization that my button had gotten caught by a thread led me to investigate. As my head lowered and my eyes followed, the sound of heels clapping against the floor reserved my attention.

Creased eyebrows and a wrinkled forehead contorted the rest of my features. Chocolate-coated stilts led me to impressive curves and eventually a face that would surely go down in history as one of the greatest. Hair flowed effortlessly down a chiseled back and arms.

Down boy. I warned.

My attempt to suppress my yearning was useless. I swelled in my pants as I watched carefully as Rather placed one foot in front of the other, headed in my direction. Her head was high and her heels were higher. Her chest protruded, piercing the air with her pebbled nipples.

That fucking perfume. I groaned, internally, as she passed me by.

Our eyes locked briefly. Without a word, she continued to pound the marbled flooring. My heart sped although time seemed to stand still. Her progress was slow. Methodic. Alluring. Agonizing.

Gradually, my head turned to meet her backside. A reel of our time in *Private Suite 102* played as the distance between us began to increase.

Her legs wrapped around my body.

Her lips against my ear.

Her request.

Her creamy center.

Her volcano.

Her climax.

Her warmth.

Her lava.

Her in that fucking red.

Her boldness.

Her face just before our departure.

Her sadness.

It stuck with me. It haunted me. It worried me. Encountering her two years later and understanding her absence wasn't intentional validated my concerns. Involuntarily, she'd kept me waiting. I didn't want to wait anymore.

"Rose."

Those long legs stiffened instantly. Without seeing that pretty face of hers, I envisioned its distortion. The same horrifying thoughts going through her head, I understood because they'd gone through mine over the last week. Since coming to the realization I'd handed the woman I'd been waiting for to my brother on a silver fucking platter, I'd been suffering from the same torment.

Slowly, she twirled on the tips of her shoes until our eyes met. Enlightenment scrunched her beauty, but it was still viable. Still alive. And, still recognizable.

There was a shift, one I felt the second her dark eyes found me. She suddenly shrunk in size. Her ego didn't seem as massive. Her pride had been minimized. The ferocious being I knew as *The Therapist*, as Rather, quickly retreated.

The walls of my family's home transformed. Darkness surrounded us. We were no longer standing in the hallway. Mentally, we'd teleported.

Those thoughts she once owned were no longer hers. Words no longer belonged to her. Movement was no longer determined by her. She yielded to my presence, immediately conforming to the structure we'd built in a single night's time two years prior.

Good girl.

Her cheeks were flushed. Heat radiated from her body. I could smell her arousal as it began to seep from her deepest fold.

Her gaze was pinned against me. She was still processing. She was still trying to consider the odds. She was still gathering herself.

Unable to maintain the distance, I depleted it with two long, urgent steps. Instantly, I was surrounded by her greatness. Engulfed in her aura. Bathing in her vulnerability. Encouraging her softness. Rebirthing her femininity. Praising her presence.

With me, she didn't have to be the person everyone wanted her to be or knew her to be. She could be nothing while simultaneously being everything. Because, at the moment, that's exactly what she was to me.

The fact she didn't belong to me or my inhibitions didn't resonate. Neither did it matter. She was whatever the fuck I said she was. She was whoever the fuck I said she was.

"I waited."

I rounded her, admiring the subtle weight gain. She was being fed well, but I had a better meal plan in mind for her. *For me. For us.*

Nervously, she shifted her weight from one side to the other. She was ready to free words from her mouth. I stepped back, allowing her room to breathe. Room to release the tension she was feeling, *tension I wanted to resolve.*

"Speak, Rose."

"We can't. We can't do th–"

"You kept me waiting."

"I would– I would've come back every night if I could've bu–"

"There you are," my father exclaimed as his hands fell by his side. "Thought you got lost."

Rose remained silent. She was waiting for instruction. Frozen in place, she kept her eyes trained on me despite my father's presence.

Good girl.

"Priest. You're late."

"Princeton was having a rough evening."

I tipped my head in the opposite direction, silently

commanding movement from Rose. She was free to leave and rejoin the rest of the family.

"I'm sending for him tomorrow. Maybe a day or two in nature will help. Get him out of his environment."

"Maybe."

With my father in my ear and Rose inching away from me, I forgot I needed to take a leak. Together, he and I began down the hallway.

His hand rested on my back as he turned to me and asked, "What do you think of her? She's a gem, aye? Good for the family?"

"She's a perfect fit for the family."

Perfect.

"You know son, she's a therapist. A really good one."

"Trust me, Pops. I know."

"You should consider letting her work with Princeton. Talk to him and see where his head is. I'm worried about him."

We entered the dining hall. The chatter freed me of the obligation to speak. Everyone in attendance stood to their feet. I leaned in and kissed my mother's cheek. Beside her was Kleigh. I pecked her cheeks and forehead as well.

Killian greeted me with a hand. Our palms slapped against one another. He pulled me in, patting my back as if we were church members who often had a dinner plate together on Sunday evening after the Lord's word settled in our souls.

"Stop patting my fucking back," I insisted.

"Would you prefer I rubbed your ass?"

"If you want to see your mother cry tonight then try it."

"Boys–" Kleigh cautioned. "Please."

Because Killian had made it clear he was fishing for a reaction from me, I continued around the table. Kofi's embrace was as theatrical as his choice of attire. While we all were draped in black with hints of color, Kofi was fully clothed in red.

Our embrace provided a better view of the woman who was trying her hardest to disappear in plain sight. Although she was losing it inside, one wouldn't be able to guess it. From first glance, one would believe she was a well-put-together, unbothered ball of fire.

But, the tapping of her fingers on the table and her lack of ability to acknowledge my presence suddenly revealed just how much she was falling apart. She was losing it inside. But, she wasn't the only one. The difference between us was I knew how to remain collected and unchanging. Rather, not so much.

I rounded the table, again, stopping at the very end where I sat directly opposite of my father. Because he was the owner of our family home, he sat on one end. Because I was the head of the family, I sat at the other.

Simultaneously, we all sat. Naturally, my eyes gravitated to the most interesting being at the table. She was clothed in a black dress that stopped inches away from her knees and hugged her body like a glove.

"So, Rather and I had a little girl time this week," Kleigh revealed. "I really enjoyed myself."

"Was it because you're still holding onto that dream of having a sister or is it because you actually had a good time." My mother asked.

"Both, actually."

"Rather." My mother turned to our guest. "What about you?"

"I've spent the bulk of my life with six girls. Last night didn't feel any different."

"Awwww," Kleigh dragged, "That feels like a compliment."

"Probably because it is."

Rather nodded, seeming genuinely appreciative of the time they'd spent together. The appetizer dishes were removed from the table. The second course was served shortly after.

THE GREY LIST

My mother's cheeks were stained with tears from the laughter that had her doubled over as Kofi recalled his encounter with a loose pit bull in a neighborhood he wasn't supposed to visit alone. While she was amused by this strange interaction, I was counting the amount of regulations he'd disregarded before, during, and after it.

Easily, he could've found himself in a situation we'd have to extract him from. An encounter with a pitbull was the least of my worries and there wasn't a thing I found funny about it. I added to the list of topics to address at our next meeting, but allowed the story to continue.

"I am going to get going. I have an early start tomorrow and I need to be getting to bed. Kofi, have that wound checked out. You never know what diseases that dog carried."

"I've already been," he assured her, "All is well and he's somewhere in Doggy Heaven– or hell."

"My God. I didn't expect that ending."

"May he rest in peace," Kofi scoffed.

My mother stood, drawing us all from our seats.

"Sit. Sit. Sit," she told us, waving her hand. "Goodnight everyone."

"Goodnight," we replied in unison.

My father followed close behind her. Though he wasn't ending his night so soon, he would surely see her off to bed.

"The old people are off to bed, but they left one of the crew members," Kofi snickered, taking a peek in my direction.

"I'm not sure why they left their toddler who is going through his terrible two stage behind but I hope they notice soon."

"Fuck you." All of his teeth showed.

Laughter rounded the table.

"The feeling is mutual."

"Don't act like you're not about to cut out of here and go home like the other old folks who are in bed by nine."

"I'm not. Cut out of here, yes. Going home, not yet."

"See, I told you he still liked pussy," Killian burst out, pointing at Kofi.

"I do. One in particular, actually."

My eyes found Rose.

"Hm. Sounds fun. When will we get to meet her?" Kleigh questioned with wide, curious eyes.

You have already.

"You think you have to meet every piece of pussy we slide in?" Kofi asked our sister. "The man didn't say he had a woman. He said he has a little something, something."

"Where'd you meet?" Kleigh couldn't help herself.

"At *The Mansion*."

"*The Mansion*?"

"Oh shit, that place you told us about a while back?"

"Yes. That place."

The clearing of Rather's throat quieted us all. Our eyes were trained on her chocolate skin and pretty, forged smile.

"Kofi," she said lowly, almost inaudible.

Her nerves were controlling every movement of her features and her frame. I could feel the energy across the table. Kofi turned, lending his attention to her. He matched her volume, but we could still hear every word spoken.

"What's up, Rather?"

"I'm not feeling my best."

"What's the matter?"

He scooted closer, hoping his presence would bring her peace. She was in an uproar, internally. She didn't know peace. Wouldn't know peace. Not now, anyway.

"I think I'm going to call it a night. Feeling a bit queasy."

"I'll walk you to the ca–"

"No. No. That won't be necessary. Stay here. It's right out front. I can manage."

I waited, hoping Kofi would contest her stance and still make sure she got to her car. She was on our property. It was heavily secured, so of course she was safe. However, our level of security was beside the point. Manners and etiquette were the only stars at the moment.

"Call me when you make it home."

My nostrils flared as I watched Rather stand on her feet. We all stood and waited for her exit. It took so much of me not to chase her down and see her to her car. But, I rested my ass in the seat along with everyone else as she rounded the corner and disappeared.

"Why aren't you going after her?" Kleigh was the first to speak.

"She said she doesn't feel good," Kofi explained.

"Which is exactly why you should've driven her home or made sure she was taken home."

She's not going home, I argued in my head.

"I have plans, Kleigh. And, they don't include being in the house before the ten o'clock hour. I understand you two have bonded a bit and gotten to know each other better, but that's my business. Not yours."

Taken aback, Kleigh rested her body against her chair. "As a woman, another woman will forever be my business so get used to it, shitface."

I didn't interfere, because Kofi had that one coming.

"She's right, brother," Killian added, "Going home early is ideal when there will be an open buffet waiting."

"I have something else lined up," Kofi explained.

"Something else?" Killian shrieked. "Nigga, you're getting married in less than three months and Pops footing the bill. Fuck you mean you have something else lined up?"

"His idea, Killian. He should foot the fucking bill. Had it been my choice, my decision, then I would've gladly paid for my own wedding."

"But you didn't and you're fucking right it was his decision. It's a desperate attempt to try and save his baby boy from destruction," I reminded Kofi.

"Who could blame him?" Kleigh sighed.

"When it's time to walk down that aisle, my shit will be intact. For now, all you motherfuckers worry about your wack ass love lives and stay out of mine."

Red blood stained his suit from a fist to the face. He was forever in violation and my duty as the leader of the family was to reprimand him each and every time. Since his accident, I'd been sparing him, but tonight I wanted to make him remember his place so he could stay in that motherfucker.

Not tonight.

For my sake, I didn't fall through on the satisfying visual that left my hand itching. The urge to re-break his jaw after it had healed so beautifully was almost impossible to resist.

"Let this be the last night you talk to anyone at this table like you've lost your marbles. You've made a full recovery now. What I tolerated during your healing won't be tolerated any longer. You're a disrespectful, selfish piece of shit and that's fine."

"But, in our presence, you will respect every single one of us. Both Killian and Kleigh are right. For once, get your shit together. A woman's heart is at stake. Treat her right, Kofi."

Or I will.

I stood and headed for the door, leaving the three of them to converse amongst themselves. I had somewhere to be and the clock couldn't strike ten before I got there.

• • •

On my way to my car, I dialed the number I knew best of them all.

"How is he?"

"He's asleep," Nikola informed me.

"How long?"

"About twenty minutes. He's all tired out. Tonight might be the night he gets his rest. I'm hopeful, Mr. Valentine."

"So am I. He needs it."

"He does."

"Alright."

"Goodnight, Mr. Valentine."

I stopped just short of changing gears.

"Goodnight? What makes you believe I'm not coming home?"

"Because you would've been here instead of calling."

"Goodbye, Nikola."

I ended the call, knowing she had a point, but I wasn't sure if it was accurate. In fact, her point of view stuck with me on the entire ride to *The Mansion*. When my wheels came to a halt at the booth before gaining entry, my plans quickly shifted.

As the gates opened, I reversed my car, high-tailing out of the lot. I maneuvered the gear into Drive and unlocked my cell simultaneously. My nights of waiting had ended.

"Ursula," I called out the moment she answered.

"Mr. Valentine."

"Has a reservation been made for the night under her name?"

There was a moment of silence before she responded, "Not for this week."

Her words threw me for a loop. "This week?"

"Yes. There was a reservation made for nine-thirty last week. Monday, it seems."

"And, I wasn't notified."

"Because that's not what you asked of me. You didn't say to inform you if she reserves. You said to inform you if she returns. She hasn't. She didn't make it Monday night."

Yet and still, she wanted to.

The lone fact led me to my rolodex where all things Rose was stored. The comments Kleigh had made about popping up at her house Monday night replayed. She was the reason Rose hadn't made it. But, the smile on Kleigh's face as she told us about their night together was far more precious than a night at *The Mansion*, no matter how long I'd been waiting.

Nine-thirty. I chuckled at the thought. Surely she was trying to make the ten-o'clock deadline.

"Thank you, Ursula."

"You're welcome, Mr. Valentine."

"Before you go—"

"Yes?"

"Reservations. Contact. Presence. It all matters."

"Noted."

Rather's possible condition concerned me. Now, Kofi's lack of decorum had truly begun to grind my gears.

Fucking heathen. His actions were unacceptable.

She's unwell. I imagined. My destination changed instantly upon reaching the highway.

Multi-tasking while driving wasn't exactly a choice I'd usually make but there was nothing usual about the current circumstances. I searched my family's private database to locate the home address of our newest member.

Though Rather wasn't officially a Valentine, she was under our protection as a promise to her family. Because of that, her details were readily available. All but her cell because hers would be changing more often than not.

96239 Pinnacle Way

Clarke, Huffington

Though I'd never visited the address, I knew exactly where she was resting her head at night. She was in good company. All the beautiful women with more than enough to lose lived in Browning alongside the wealthy men who were afraid to be in their company or provided a life of luxury for them. Chem had her put up well. I didn't expect anything less.

Browning was the highest point of Clarke, near the mountain's core. Hilltops made the roads wind upward for miles and miles. Browning included three neighborhoods, all varying in size and all growing in financial responsibility as you climbed.

Mount Clarke, where Princeton and I lived, sat atop The Summit and Meridian. Rather wasn't very far from us. Comfortably, she was nestled between Mount Clarke and Meridian. I reached her neighborhood in twenty minutes. Her home, in particular, I reached in twenty-three.

The two-story, Victorian-style home with the subtle modern upgrades to the original design was fitting. Almost every light in the home was on. I pulled three houses down, where the street curved into a half-circle and there was room for parking.

Out of the car and on foot, I walked the distance to

reach Rather's home. Across the street, preparing to make my way to the other side, I watched as she moved about her home. Her shadow defined the new curves that had come with aging and Father Time.

A queen in her castle.

As I stepped into the street, ready to alert her of my presence, a familiar set of wheels turned down the dimly lit street with R&B blasting from the speakers.

Of course.

I stepped back, blending with the dark of the night and finding a pole to rest my arm against. The black Mercedes pulled around the driveway and Kleigh hopped out without a care in the world. She never checked her surroundings. She never closed her door.

She has to do better.

Not involving her in the family's affairs was a choice we'd made in an attempt to lighten her burdens. Life was complicated enough. We wanted her to remain soft and gentle in every aspect of her world.

However, seeing how carefree she was had me second guessing our choice. Even if she wasn't involved, she needed to understand the way the world truly worked. It wasn't daisies and roses. It was sometimes mud and shit. And, if she wasn't careful, she'd walk right into it.

She stood at the door, patiently waiting for Rather to appear. It wasn't long before she did. Dressed in a beige silk number, she greeted Kleigh. Because there was so much distance between us, her facial expression couldn't be determined, so I resorted to body movement to see if she was, in fact, unwell.

Kleigh's arms wrapped around her after a short

exchange. As quickly as she'd come, she was leaving. Baby girl was a Valentine through and through. Her heart was large and she understood the value of relationship-building. Kofi wasn't willing to come by and make sure Rather was alright, so she did. So did I.

Her black coupe sped down the residential street, bending the corner with far too much speed. Nevertheless, it was still intact when she pushed the gas on the next street.

Kleigh's departure should've been my queue to leave, but my legs wouldn't move. My eyes wouldn't move. My arms, they just wouldn't move.

I watched from afar as Rather turned off one light at a time throughout her home. When she made it upstairs and the darkness began to consume her dwelling, my time began to wind down. Resentment filled my bones. And, it took every bit of strength to refrain from moving my limbs and heading in her direction.

Finally, her bedroom light shut off, signaling an end to her day. I gathered my bearings, straightened my spine, and began in the opposite direction. Before getting too far, I took a final look over my shoulder, hoping the night brought her the peace she needed because once she woke, her world would be turned upside down. Mentally. Physically. Intimately. Sexually.

Sleep well, Rose.

[illegible]

FIVE

Rather

"Tuesday, you've been good to me," I yawned.

It had taken two full days for my body to regulate and rebuild its nervous system. Anxiety kept me up later than I'd like for the past two nights. Even as I closed my eyes in the dead of the dark in my bedroom, sleep evaded me. For hours and hours, I rested my head on the pillow with my eyes peering into the abyss my obsessive thoughts were digging.

His brother? It was the question I'd asked a hundred times or more.

My God, Rather. The fact my center still throbbed at

the thought of him was even more damning. The two nights I'd spent with him at *The Mansion* had left a lasting impression on me. Hadn't I gone to St. Catana with my family and things gone horribly wrong with Chem, one would need pliers to pry me out of the room and off him.

That's how good he was. That's how passionate he was. That's how impressive his performance was. That's how quickly our connection had formed.

For six months after my departure, I still parted my legs at night with him behind my lids. Licking me. Kissing me. Fucking me. So beautifully.

Without haste. Without hesitation. Without fault. He was perfect. He was ideal. But, his new position in my life wasn't.

Forget about him. I'd been telling myself for the last two days. And, today was the first day I believed it could happen. Kofi was to be my husband soon. The quicker I established that in my head and heart, the better I'd be.

But, my pussy. My, was she giving me a hard time.

The mid-day nap left me with an appetite. I flipped the covers and slipped into my fuzzy slippers, heading down-stairs. A large Cesar salad with extra crouton crumbles was heavy on my mind. My stomach growled at the thought of my oversized salad bowl filled to the brim with leafy greens.

The sun had begun to settle, casting the most enchanting purplish glow across the sky. Its beauty was such a delight to witness. I rounded the counter and opened the fridge, prepared to take advantage of the sun room or built-in breakfast nook. Both had immaculate views of the sun.

"Alexa, shuffle my playlist."

"Shuffling Rather's playlist," Alexa responded.

Immediately, Toni Braxton's voice dressed the beat. The song of choice sent a sharp pain through my chest, causing me to halt all motion. The third line forced my eyes close as those visions I was desperately trying to suppress began playing.

"I love me some you," she sang. "Another man will never do."

Ding Dong.

The sound of the doorbell rescued me from the depths of hell. I pulled my robe tighter around my body and retrieved the closest firearm without disturbing my small arsenal. The coat closet was my first stop. Opening the door, mid-day, dressed in a robe and an extra long hair roller was unacceptable. I'd never hear the end of my mother's mouth in my head.

I removed the roller and traded my gown for a long, flowy dress that I was tasked with keeping near the door since I'd gotten my first home. According to my mother, my comfort was top priority but decorum was second place. Greeting houseguests morning, noon, and evenings required proper attire. After nightfall, they were subject to my nightly threads and I shouldn't be sorry for it.

Because, unless it was an emergency, they shouldn't be at my doorstep. All else could wait for sunrise. My sisters and I had lived by those words since we were gifted homes of our own. This was my second and nothing had changed.

I tucked the robe and gown away, promising to revisit as soon as I was alone again. One foot in front of the other, I moseyed my way toward the door. I opened it to find a gentleman on the other side with a parcel in his hands, extending it for me to take.

"Good day, Ma'am."

"Thank y– you?" I questioned, genuinely confused by the box in my hand.

Kleigh and I had done a number online, shopping without limits and charging everything to a card that belonged to her family. She'd remembered the number by heart. The shipping had been expedited for every delivery and they'd all been made. I'd spent the last two days sulking and organizing the closet. Everything was accounted for.

Without another word, he was off to his car. I stepped away from the door after locking up. As if it was contaminated, I held the box a few inches away from my body and led it straight to the mailroom. It was small and just off the study, but the perfect place to sort through mail and packages so they weren't sitting in the foyer collecting dust before I actually decided to deal with them.

I split the lone strip of tape holding the package together. Easily, the top lifted, revealing a vaguely familiar lingerie set with an envelope settled in on top of the threads. Out of pure curiosity, I removed the envelope and pulled the slip of thick paper from it. The message was short but it packed a punch. Long after they'd been read and reviewed a hundred times, they'd still haunt me.

Rose,

PS102.

9pm.

Tonight.

I swallowed the saliva that pooled in my mouth, nearly

ending my life. I began a coughing spell that made my face burn and my throat tight. I patted my chest with my hand. My palm slapped my skin each time it collided with my chest.

"Shit."

My ears began ringing. My face grew warmer. I struggled to breathe. And, for what felt like forever, I tried correcting the mistake I'd made. A full minute later when my recovery began, I read the letter again, still wondering where they were selling the audacity Priest had purchased. I'd only dealt with two entitled men my entire lifetime. One had birthed me with his bare hands. The other thought he'd birthed me.

Bumping into Kofi and his oldest brother was appalling. They both possessed that character flaw. Because it had been instilled in me from a child, I was hardly upset. But, revolted, nonetheless.

Rose,

PS102.

9pm.

Tonight.

His demands were simple, yet so complex. In hindsight, I had two months and two weeks before my commitment was established. My body belonged to no one until then. But, somehow, I felt like it might not be the case. Not to him, at least.

Rose,

PS102.

9pm.

Tonight.

"Ugh."

Nine? Why nine? I questioned.

"It doesn't matter. I'm not going. So, no. It doesn't matter," I finalized, shoving the box and note to the side and heading back into the kitchen.

As quickly as I'd gone in, I bolted out. Once more, I had to read the contents of the note.

Rose,

PS102.

9pm.

Tonight.

"I ca– I can't. Ugh."

I exited again, this time with the note still in my hand.

"Roulette, please pick up," I begged of my sister before I'd even dialed her number.

I needed her in the worst way. The time difference would toss a wrench in, but it didn't hurt to try. Maybe when she heard what was happening in my world she'd wake right on up and give me the best sisterly advice she could muster. Because, putting it very lightly, I was in over my head.

By the third ring, I'd lost hope. However, the grogginess in her voice a second later brought me comfort beyond explanation.

"Is everything okay, Rather?" She groaned.

"Yes and no!"

"Are you safe? Are you hurt?"

"I'm safe, Roulette. Wake up. Please."

Silence coated the line. I was losing her. I could feel it.

Exhaustion was riding her tail. There was nothing either of us could do about it.

"Roulette."

"I'm tired, babe. Sorry, but pretty bitches need sleep. We have such heavy loads on a daily basis."

"Load? Roulette, you're currently jobless and on an island," I reminded her. All of our loads were light. Chemistry made sure of it.

"And, sleep. You didn't add that."

She yawned, assuring me she couldn't be of service.

"I'm sorry, babe. The time difference. The morning, okay? I promise."

"Okay. Goodnight."

"Goodnight, I love you."

"In this lifetime and all the others, babe," sadly, I replied before ending the call and letting Roulette get the beauty rest she was adamant about.

My rumbling stomach reminded me I was due for that Caesar salad. As I removed the dressings, croutons, parmesan cheese, pre-boiled egg, and leafy greens, I grew uneasy. With everything on the counter, I began putting together the salad, simultaneously keeping an eye on the clock.

7:51.

I crushed the croutons, pounding them against the wooden mortar with the wooden pestle that matched.

9pm.

Tonight.

I combined the ingredients in the salad bowl and dressed them well with Caesar and then sprinkled parmesan cheese on top. The tidying began immediately after. Once everything was put away, I left a trail of dread behind as I headed for the nook. I'd stored my latest read on the ledge with promises to return.

I opened the book with the intention of occupying my thoughts. The novel was a tale of two friends becoming lovers without either of them truly knowing until that love was tested. I'd never had the pleasure of befriending a male, but wasn't opposed to the idea. Having Chemistry was the closest I'd ever had to a male best friend. While I knew I could decipher feelings and keep from falling for a friend, I understood Kaylin's dilemma.

Ugh. Frustration widened my nose and thickened the air around me. Though my eyes were on the words and I was reciting them in my head, nothing was sticking. The salad I desperately wanted minutes prior sat in the bowl, untouched and undesired.

8:08.

I closed my eyes, trying my hardest to replace thoughts of the pending meet up. Priest was expecting me, but I wouldn't be there. It didn't matter that Roulette wasn't awake long enough to listen and tell me it wasn't a good idea. I knew it wasn't and I knew I couldn't fall through with it.

8:10.

The warmth of the sun's setting welcomed me as I exposed my orbs, again. Anxiousness grew heavier in my spirit, blocking everything else with little effort. I became numb with paralyzed limbs. My thumb hurt something awful from separating the pages of the book for as long as I had. However, I couldn't close it. I couldn't move.

8:15.

I slammed the book shut and released a shaky breath.

I have to go. I have to tell him this is unacceptable. We can– we can't do this. He should know.

Mentally, I calculated the distance from my home to *The Mansion*. Because I knew I'd need to put on something more presentable, I wouldn't get out of the house for another ten minutes at the very least. Fifteen gave me a bit more of a cushion to lean on.

It would take almost a full thirty minutes to get to the gates and another five to park and get my balance settled before making my way to his suite. I'd surely keep him waiting a while before I delivered the news.

Not if you leave now. I protested.

I bolted from my seat at the sound of my voice in my head. And, within seven minutes, my teeth were brushed, new clothes were pressed against my skin, and I had the parcel in my hand on my way out of the door. I slid into the Panamera, a gift from Teddy that was waiting upon my arrival in the States.

It had taken me three days to take note of the car sitting in the garage. Nevertheless, I was in love with the sleek, black model. The motor purred as I tapped the gas, speeding down the winding path leading to the expressway.

Lucky Daye made my stomach turn with his addictive voice singing so pleasantly about hearing his woman making the fucking sound.

Ugh.

I smashed the large display screen with the tip of my index finger, immediately ready to hear the next song. To my dismay, Chris Brown claimed to not give a fuck about the man his lover had, promising to pull her hair and beat it right now.

Ugggh!

Sexual frustration threatened my sanity as I pushed the screen again for the next song. *Comfortable* was next on the list, putting my mind and body at ease with only the first line. I fought to maintain control of the visions in my head. Kofi's handsome face brought a smile to mine.

Though he was rough around the edges and lived life on the ledge, I wasn't opposed to the idea of us. Not because I wanted things to work, but because they had to or I'd live a life of misery and that wasn't happening on my watch. I'd been in worse situations and made the best of them. This one wouldn't be much different.

My survival skills went far beyond that of the average woman, because I was far from average. No one I entertained or kept company with was average. Even the thought of anything regular was repulsive.

Comfortable was followed by *Long Nights*, an unofficial classic by 6lack. For the rest of the ride, more pleasantries served as background music as I floored the gas in pursuit of *The Mansion.*

THE GREYLIST

With one foot in front of the other, I marched up the stairs with a martini in hand. Confronting Priest didn't require liquid courage. Avoiding his advances did. In the last ten minutes, I'd learned my year-long residency balance had been settled and restarted the following year. For the entire two years I was away, he'd kept my tab paid and my suite in pristine condition.

I waited.

His words in the hall began to resonate more. And, the box in my hand felt pointless. However, there was a life outside of these walls we were both involved in and whatever had happened prior to that discovery simply couldn't happen again.

No matter how much it melted my heart to learn he'd, in fact, waited for me. No matter how much I missed his girth plunging into my canal. No matter how good he made me feel. No matter how much pressure he relieved. No matter how ideal his arms were after a busy day. No matter how much I wanted to get back to him after going away.

The truth was, I wasn't his to have anymore. At any capacity. I was taken. Reserved. In-waiting. I was promised to another man. That man happened to be his brother. And, he'd played a huge part in our arrangement. In my opinion, this was all his fault. He was the reason whatever we had we couldn't have anymore.

Standing in front of his door, I tipped the glass and finished the drink. As a tray full of champagne passed me by, I sat it on top of it. Sighing deeply, I stared at the numbers I remembered better than any I'd ever been tasked with logging into my memory. We'd spent two short nights tangled in each other's limbs, but they felt like half a lifetime.

My knuckles rested against the door, softly. At the very last second, I decided against knocking. Instead, I twisted the knob, somehow figuring it wasn't locked and I was free to enter.

The door swung open. As the path illuminated with the light from his suite, I stepped in with my chest expanded and my head high. My breath hiked in my chest.

Unlike the two times before when I'd entered his suite, there wasn't a mask covering his features. Priest stood on all ten toes with his arms folded across his chest and one hand pulling at the hair on his chin. He was in deep thought and not even my presence had interrupted him.

I'd bet any amount of money those thoughts surrounded me, just like his presence surrounded me. Consumed me. I chastised myself for the thoughts beginning to circulate. As quickly as they came, I pushed them aside and remembered the task at hand.

I shoved the parcel in his direction, shutting the door behind me simultaneously. Instead of taking it, he turned and retrieved his drink.

Once.

Twice.

Three times.

And then a fourth.

His steps were calculated. *Concise.* He neared me, the smell of his cologne overpowering my arousal. I was thankful for the aroma, because mine was aggressive, seeking satisfaction.

In one swift motion, he removed the red mask from my face, revealing features he'd gotten acquainted with over two family dinners and a brief moment of privacy in the hall. Priest didn't stop in stride. He continued in the other direction, leaving me breathless. As he walked deeper into the suite, he pulled at my heartstrings, demanding I follow him without a single word spoken.

"Why aren't you dressed, *Rose*?" He tossed over his shoulder.

Though he hadn't truly shown it, I sensed his aggravation. I'd ruined whatever fantasy in that big head of his.

Good.

"Because, I'm not here to soften your dick, Priest. I'm here as a courtesy. Here to let you know that whatever this was between us, whatever we've been waiting for, whatever we've been yearning for... it ends tonight. Right here. Right now. Things have changed. The stakes are high. And, I have a duty to uphold. My brother has never asked anything of us. Nothing."

"This is my chance to prove to him that all he's ever done for us wasn't in vain. This is my chance to prove we have his back just like he has ours. I can't fuck this up. I won't fuck this up. It doesn't matter how drawn to you I once felt. I'm marrying your brother. That's it. That's final. That's my reality. Get it through your thick skull. Get i–"

"Oh, Rose," Priest grunted, sitting his glass on the dining table.

"My have you forgotten," he hissed, "but I'm here to remind you. When you cross that threshold, you're in my world, baby girl. You don't think without my permission. You don't speak without my permission. You don't move without my permission. You don't do a motherfucking thing without my permission. You move when I say move. You open when I say open. You fuck when I say fuck. You suck when I say suck. You cum– *when I say cum*."

Priest gazed at me as he removed the jacket of his suit.

He laid it on the chair to preserve its perfection and avoid wrinkles.

"When you enter that motherfucking door, I own your thoughts. Your words. And, your body. Maybe I'm not the smartest man on the planet and my education isn't as extensive as you and your siblings, but I don't need a fucking degree to know that if you didn't want to be here you wouldn't be."

He removed the cuff links and unbuttoned the sleeves of his shirt.

"Your absence would've told me everything I needed to know. But, your presence... it has told me a whole fucking lot, Rose. Not only do you miss this dick, but you miss the experience this suite gives."

Sarcastically, he chuckled with a shake of his head.

"I don't blame you one bit, baby, because it's addictive. Two hits and I'd become its slave. As headstrong as a girl you are, you fell victim too and that's alright. Remember something, Rose. I had that shit before that deal existed. The sacrifice doesn't change things between us. It simply ups the ante."

He unbuttoned the last button on his shirt and pushed it from his shoulders. His body was agonizingly impressive. Fit. Sculpted. Defined.

"Understand that I have more than two months before I have to give you up and I intend to take my precious time doing so. You might be my brothers after the day we've set for you, but right now– *you're mine*. So take off them fucking clothes and put your hands on that fucking bed. We have unfinished business."

"We– Pries–"

"Fine."

He was tilting his head one second. Next, he was in front of me. His breath on my nose. His hands cupping my ass. His rod against my center. His lips on mine. His tongue down my throat.

Just like the rose he claimed me to be, I opened for him. The passion he infused in the kiss was reciprocated. I mimicked his energy. I inherited his thirst.

He took his precious time carrying me to the bed where he peeled the linen dress from my body with disgust. Underneath was a black seamless thong, a thigh holster, and my Beretta. He inched toward my gun, ready to remove it and the holster, but was sadly mistaken.

"Don't."

He continued, not caring much for my demand. Once my gun was on the ottoman beside the bed, Priest hovered over me with his head low and his eyes trained on me.

"You don't run shit in here, Rose."

My nipples had hardened to the point of pain. His large hand over the right one felt criminal. With an open palm, he rotated it in the center. Though the movement was subtle, the effects were unbearable.

"Understood?"

At once, his index finger and thumb tried fusing themselves to my left nipple. Priest squeezed. I squirmed below him, wanting to beg for his consideration but refusing to. The defiance he was met with struck a chord within him.

Instead of tender circles around my right breast, he trapped my nipple between his fingers to double the pain and suffering that made me slippery below. My heart raced in my chest, galloping at one-hundred beats per minute.

Please! I begged, internally. I'd heard it a million times or more from clients in my chair. Never had I ever been at the mercy of another man. Never had I been on the receiving end of the torture. Never did I think I'd resort to the same feelings, same thoughts as my clients.

Yet, here I was, waiting for Priest's form of therapy. The kind that had me cumming non-stop two years ago. The kind that had me rubbing my clit every night for six months at the thought of it.

The kind I had every intention of seeking when Kofi established the rules of our arrangement. The kind that had me springing from my chair to meet him here though I promised it was only to tell him we couldn't be involved.

Sexual therapy.

Emotional therapy.

Physical therapy.

Mental therapy.

"Answer my fucking question, Rose, or we'll be right here until you do."

The idea of not having him inside of me lifted my head up and then down. Up and then down.

"Words. Use your words."

"Yes."

He loosened his grip and stood straight up against the bed. Where the sleek black wrapper in his hand had come from, I wasn't sure of, but I was delighted by its presence. Within seconds, it was on his tool and my thong was pushed to the side.

Anticipation clogged my lungs and put an end to my breathing. I was stuck. Mesmerized by Priest's features, his readiness, his desire, and his skill. We'd been here before, so I knew his capabilities were beyond my comprehension.

His thick, meaty dick pounced on my clit, causing me to shudder with each blow. My stomach imploded as I began to breathe again. I inhaled deeply and pushed out fresh, shaky breaths.

And, without warning, Priest parted me. He drove himself into me. He split me right down the center. Naturally, my hands roamed in search of something to have, something to hold.

"Oh my G—"

He sealed our reunion with a kiss. The guilt slowly crept from my frame, transferring itself to Priest. The energy was unwelcomed.

The first stroke recaptured my breath, but replaced it by the second one. The third stroke reminded me why I was here and not home eating the salad that was now in my trash bin.

"Ummmm."

We were no longer attached at the lips. I closed my eyes, desperately trying to savor the moment but my climax was approaching rapidly. Too much time had elapsed. Too much was at stake.

His strokes deepened. My center sounded in the privacy of his suite, feeling the air with pleasantries we both understood were a result of my gratitude. The creaminess assisted his intrusion, leaving us both in a state of delirium, desperation, and delusion.

I could feel Priest peering at me as his right hand roamed my body, eventually ending around my neck. Gently, he squeezed.

He was majestic. A fib. Fiction. Unreal. Majestic in every sense of the word.

"Eyes," he requested.

"Pr—"

He removed himself from my gaping hole.

"Eyes, Rose."

I reopened them, hopeful that my obedience would lead to his reinsertion. I was wrong. My eyes glossed with tears. I needed him inside of me as bad as I needed my heart to continue beating, however fast or slow that suited the moment.

Priest stood at the edge of the bed with a hand on both hips, never taking his eyes off me. He was collected. He was calm. I was losing every bit of control inside.

He sensed it. He saw it. He acknowledged it.

"Speak."

"Please—" I whimpered, watching as he removed the condom from his shaft.

Saliva production made the bottom of my mouth tingle. My sublingual glands were hard at work, moisturizing my mouth to keep my throat wet. Preparation was key and if Priest decided to stuff my mouth with his tool, I needed to be ready.

"Please? Please what, Rose?"

He massaged his dick. It was beautiful, just as he was. The girth was consistent along his phallus. His scrotum was in pristine condition. It didn't hang very low, but his testis had ample room for movement.

His cockiness surpassed his other characteristics and demanded attention. Priest was no fool. He knew just how potent his presence was. He knew just how possessive one became during and after an encounter.

He knew just how fucking irresistible his pole was. He knew his pace was perfection. Everything and nothing in particular about his bedroom skills justified his arrogance and I couldn't be upset about it.

"Put it back."

"Back where?"

He touched himself, blowing my mind with every stroke of his hand.

"Inside of me."

"How, Rose? How do you want me inside of you?"

"Just like thaaaat," lowly, I beseeched.

He lessened the space between us. His skin met mine, catapulting me into the land of doom. We were both playing a very dangerous game, but the risk was worth the reward. Without a barrier, Priest slid his thickness against my slit, lubricating it with my secretion.

"Like this?"

"Yessssss. Yes. Like that. Just like thaaaa–"

Priest entered me. Skin to hymen. With one hand beside my head and the other around my waist, he stirred the ingredients inside my pot. His eyes lowered. He was unable to continue the gazing. He was losing the uphill battle. He was weakening.

Without warning Priest, I prepared for the inevitable. With each stroke, I climbed higher and higher, in anticipation of my peak.

"Eyes," I pled with Priest. "Eyes."

I was speaking out of turn but my rebellion would lead

to my revolution. He had to understand. Those irises were the end of me and I was desperate for my demise.

"Eyes."

There they were. In all their true glory. My center caved and grew more slippery. More vocal. Deeper. Warmer.

"Ummmmmmm–"

I slammed my eyes shut for only a moment. I reopened them as my orgasm crowded my central systems, increasing my sensitivity. My head lifted from the bed, slightly, to see just how much of my womanhood was releasing onto Priest's manhood. He was covered.

The view intensified my elation and I began to truly unfold. To blossom. To bloom. Like a garden in the spring, I came to life.

Abruptly, Priest dislodged. He rested his pole against my clit as it pulsated, hungrily attempting to extract him of his goods.

"Urrrrrrgh."

His grunt signified the nearing of his ending. The sperm waiting in his vas deferens was anticipating his eruption, ready to exit through his shaft and fill me with responsibilities I wasn't ready for.

"Fuck."

Back and forward, Priest began to rock, massaging himself in the folds of my vagina. His limbs grew stiffer. His features stretched, putting his thoughts on full display. His breathing was no longer steady.

"Shit. Shit." He rounded his spine as he repeated, lowly.

Suddenly, his sprout released his load. Semen pierced the air before falling onto the skin of my bald pussy and down his erection.

THE GREYLIST

The warm water cascaded down my head, neck, and back. The fuss of it all, reluctantly happening right in my head, caused me to grow weary. I snuggled the oversized sponge against my chin and mouth wondering what consequences would become of my actions and how disappointed Chemistry would be if he knew where I was, what I'd just done, and who I was with.

It wasn't the man my family had promised me to. It was the man my family had promised. And for the life of me, I couldn't understand why he felt so good when he was so wrong.

"Speak," Priest coaxed, softening his tone. "Freely."

For the life of me, I couldn't find his eyes. Shame consumed me. Dread filled me. Anxiety tried drowning me.

I was in the depths of despair as the water's height grew taller around me. I wasn't sure if I'd be pulled to shore or swept away with the tides. The only thing I knew was the journey had just begun.

"I have nothing to say," I admitted with a hump of my shoulders.

For the first time in my life, I was leading with the one thing my family despised as a whole. *Feelings*. They were the beginning of every end. It was proven.

"But you do."

"It doesn't matter. None of it matters, Priest."

I sighed, releasing the sponge from my clutch and

placing it where it belonged before attempting to leave the shower. It was impossible. My shoulder collided with his chest.

"I need to get home."

"I never said you were going home, Rose."

It wasn't a desire of mine. I just needed words to fill the space. Though I knew it would be best to leave, I was stuck here. Mentally, emotionally and now physically. There was no escaping Priest. Not tonight, at least.

He cupped my chin and turned it toward him. He was so well-constructed. Dark skin. A fade with waves like oceans swirling his hair. A muscular frame. Peculiar eyes. Chiseled cheeks. A strong jawline. A nose that could smell roses miles away. Lips that were full and so fucking kissable.

"I'm not opposed to that idea."

"It didn't matter if you were," he assured me with a half-smile.

With a shake of my head, I tried exiting the shower again. Priest stopped me, again, but this time with his hand around my neck.

"Whoever told you your feelings were invalid, that they didn't matter– they lied."

"No o–"

"Yes, Rose. Yes they did. Even if it wasn't out of their mouths. Indirectly, someone has led you to believe your feelings don't matter. Shouldn't matter. But, they do. In this suite and any time I am around, understand your feelings are paramount. Your comfort is priority. Your desires... your needs... you– *Rose*. You will hold ranking."

"And, when it's all over in December?"

Kofi and I were scheduled to wed in winter.

"Stop worrying yourself, Rose. Tomorrow has yet to come."

Sighing, I stepped back and looked up at his handsome face.

"It should've been you."

"It will be me—*until it's not.*"

The last three words were daggers in my heart, but Priest didn't allow me to sulk for long. He twisted the knob to stop the flow of the water. He was the first to get out of the shower. Before grabbing a towel for himself, he wrapped me in one and led me out onto the plush mat. He slid the disposable slippers across the floor for me to slide into. I watched as he repeated the same steps, but for himself.

We re-entered the cool air. Priest had increased the temperature on the thermostat but with only twenty minutes elapsing, there wasn't a significant change throughout the suite.

"Downstairs, there's a small wardrobe for you. It's still in the box. I'll make sure it's ready soon so you're not digging through those bags for long."

I hadn't noticed the bags along the wall until his mentioning of them. He walked over to the smaller one and removed a red, silk crimson robe. A silk dress accompanied it.

"Your skin is covered in fine bumps, Rose."

He offered the 2-piece and immediately retrieved red slippers from the same bag. Even with all their fluff, they did very little to enhance the elegant pieces in my hand. The disappointment on my face brought a smile to his.

"Speak," he urged.

"I'm underwhelmed."

"Figured."

He took two steps and began digging into another bag. This time, he retrieved a square box. He removed the lid and feathers fell over the cardboard. My eyes glistened and my heart's pounding began another 800 meter dash. It raced, covering as much ground as possible as I anticipated the reveal of the box's contents.

Priest held up the red platform with a single, thick strap across the top. Feathers covered the entirety of the strap, but didn't exceed its stitches. The rest of the shoe was as plain as it was pretty.

I nodded, approving the second option. There was a twenty-year-old woman inside of me screaming uncontrollably because this was exactly how she'd imagined her life. Minus the fact it was my future husband's brother I was having sexual relations with. And, minus the fact that the marriage I'd dreamt of as a kid was arranged.

"More of your speed, Rose?"

I nodded, unable to redirect the curving of my lips.

"Speak."

"Only I'd imagined this outfit in black, though red is winning me over."

"Hmmm." He nodded, taking my suggestion into consideration. "And?"

"My heels pounding the floors of a penthouse or the top level of the home of my lover."

"That can be arranged," he chuckled, "As long as you understand you have a lot of fucking footage to cover on that top level, love."

I shook my head, "Let's not blur the lines. What we have stays here. Can you at least promise me that?"

"I can."

"Thank you."

"Don't ever wonder, Rose. Your comfortability is my responsibility."

"What about you?"

"What about me?" He asked.

"What will make you comfortable?"

"A spot between your legs with your pussy parted and these heels in the air."

Like butter, I melted. The lack of emotion as the words fell from his lips revealed the viciousness of his thoughts.

"Take them."

Because I loved a good challenge, I opened a hand, waiting for him to hand over the new beauties.

I exchanged them for the pieces of fabric in my hand. Priest wandered across the room in search of a place to hang the threads. He settled with the closet after a few seconds. Meanwhile, I searched through the pink bag with the large *M* in the center. I'd shopped at *Miss Lewd* enough times to remember the logo. Inside, I found a plethora of interesting products, but it was one I was looking for in particular.

"There." Barely above a whisper, I rejoiced.

The edible oil glided on the body so effortlessly. Though I hadn't had the pleasure of it being licked from my skin, I'd worn it a number of times. It was their best-seller and for good reasoning.

I removed the towel I'd been given and began oiling my body from head to toe. The *Pre-Heat* body oil didn't sit on top of your skin. It seeped into your pores while still giving you a healthy shine and a sleekness that could be seen long before it was felt.

It wasn't until he cleared his throat that I noticed Priest had joined me. I slathered the oil on my ankles, sure not to touch the bottom of my feet. I'd ruin the shoes. The cap twisted back onto the bottle with ease. I placed it on the nightstand just in case the seal couldn't contain its contents.

Seconds later, I slid into the red heels. Something within me was activated. Slowly, I began to transform. Slowly, I began to recharge and the power Priest stripped me of each time I walked through the door began its journey back to me.

"Uh hm."

He depleted me. Stripped me of the power, immediately.

"On that fucking bed."

I strutted across the floor without haste. Carefully, Priest observed every move I made. And, when I was finally on the bed, he joined me. Up on my elbows, I anticipated the feeling of his tongue against my flesh.

"Open."

I parted, just as he'd imagined. He angled his head at a mere thirty degrees. His eyes bounced from mine to my pussy.

"She's pretty."

Slow blinks ensued. With each word Priest spoke, consciousness became harder to manage. He was intoxicating.

"So fucking fat."

He lowered his head, planting it between my legs.

Comfortable? I shuddered as contact was initiated.

"Tell me something good, Rose."

He circled my clit with his tongue. My spine curved, lifting my back from the bed.

"I– I m– ohhhhhh."

"And don't stop talking or I will."

He spoke to my pussy, never taking his lips off me.

"I missed thiiiiiisss."

"You missed this or you missed me?"

"Bothhhhhh."

SIX

"Mmmm."

My son's voice pulled me from the trenches. It had been exactly nine days since I'd been between the thighs underneath the white tennis skirt and I was struggling to understand why. Four of those days, I'd been away on business, but the other five couldn't be justified. No matter what Rose's excuse was.

I nodded toward Kleigh, who was returning with the water Princeton had requested by tapping his finger against the empty cup repeatedly.

"Here it comes. Your aunt has it, dude."

Nodding up and down, rapidly with his finger lodged between his teeth, he turned and found Kleigh standing a few feet away, beckoning for him. He took off running in her direction, happily obliging her request.

The country club my family visited, in unison, once a quarter was equipped with a number of activities for us to indulge. Golf, tennis, swimming, pickleball, soccer, and volleyball were the few we were most interested in during visits.

Today, because the weather was too cool for swimming, the wind was too high for golf, no one was interested in volleyball, and the pickleball court was being painted, tennis was our sport of choice.

"Fuck!" Killian huffed, plopping down on the chair next to me.

He leaned forward, wiping his face with the end of his shirt. Sweat was pouring from his skin. With a shake of the head, he looked over his shoulder at the woman we were all awe of.

She was impressive. In general. Literally. Physically. And, on the court.

"She hasn't broken a fucking sweat!" He complained, "The fuck type of training that nigga have them in. She's a beast."

With a nod, I concurred.

Indeed, she is.

The words I was preparing to speak became lodged in my throat as she approached. As if she hadn't just kicked Killian's ass for nearly an hour and a half straight, she planted her hand on her hip without a trace of exhaustion in sight. I watched as her chest rose and fell calmly.

She surveyed the area, purposely avoiding my gaze. A small chuckle freed itself from my lips. Her theatrics were cute. They were tempting, too.

Because, though I'd promised to keep things between us at *The Mansion*, I didn't mind breaking her ass off in the worst way in the women's restroom with the door locked and her face so close to the sink she could smell the H2O from its pipes.

Kleigh and Killian both twisted their necks in my direction. Their curiosity wasn't allowed much time to pique. Rather condensed their abilities, making it impossible to see or hear anything other than her.

"Kofi."

She tilted her head, balancing her weight on the other leg. Her breast pressed against the fabric of her cropped shirt. Her eyes darted in my direction.

Just as they locked, her nipples pebbled. She shifted her weight a second time and cut her eyes toward Kofi, again.

"Your turn. Come join me on the court."

I waited for the response everyone knew was coming *but* Rather. Kleigh rolled her eyes before words surfaced. Kofi was ruining her chances at forming the unbreakable bond she was trying so hard to build with Rather.

Though he was her heart, she was growing tired of his bullshit, especially when it came to the woman she was beginning to harbor platonic feelings for. He was embarrassing her. That's where she drew the line, I assumed.

"Take a look around, baby," he told Rather, "I'm not dressed for the occasion. I can't keep my Glock on my hip jumping up and down the court."

Without a word, Rather lifted her skirt, exposing the

shorts beneath it. And, underneath them was the print of a baby pistol I was sure was holstered with a strap around her thigh that wasn't exactly visible.

My dick rose to the occasion. She was hell and it was only one of the hundreds of reasons I couldn't get her off my brain.

Lethal.

Rather was nothing short of greatness and it was an honor to observe her existence. Because, frankly, that was stunning enough. Even if she never spoke, I'd overdose on movement and silent power alone. She was a force and we were all victims of her all-encompassing nature.

"Any more excuses?"

Kofi's smile split his face in two almost.

"Convincing," he admitted, "But, I'm not that nigga, Rather."

"Good, then, because I had something better than the Rolex in mind this time."

She took off toward the court, not waiting for him to deny her, again. Instead, she stepped inside of the court and faced the fence in front of her, preparing to play alone with the fence propelling the ball in her direction each time she hit it.

"Nigga," Killian blurted, "Ninety days my ass. You'd better get your shit together or that fucking girl is going to grill you and eat you for dinner."

"She can taste my meat without killing me. All she has to do is get rid of that bullshit ass rule sh—"

"Rule?" Killian asked.

Though I was tuned into the conversation, my eyes were in a far, far away place. They were on her, watching as she made due with the shit my brother was spoon feeding her.

"I made it clear I wasn't stopping my extracurricular activities as we waited to walk down the aisle. She made it clear I wasn't sliding in that pussy as long as I continued with them."

"Oh shit–" Killian chuckled, "She's not a bird brain."

"Did you expect her to be?" My thoughts rang out, unintentionally.

Fuck.

"Not exactly, but you never know. The smartest women turn out to be the dumbest motherfuckers when it comes to a nigga. The shit you wouldn't expect or assume she should know better than tends to take the backseat when a man is involved. I've witnessed it too many times before," he explained. "But, how quickly I keep forgetting this isn't the average woman. Nothing about that damn woman is predictable."

Absolutely nothing.

Satisfied with his response, I stood and stretched my limbs. "Since her nigga is scared to kick her ass, I will."

"Hope you've set aside some bills. She doesn't lose and her requests are not average, either. Hence the Rollie on her wrist."

I don't lose either. And, a dick in her gut is all I have to gift her. We'll both leave victorious.

My presence on the court hardly fazed Rather. She continued pounding the ball, waiting patiently as it bounced off the fence. I grabbed a racket and stood on the same fence she was abusing with the ball.

Intensely, I watched her feet bounce in the white sneakers with double Cs on them. They'd cost her a pretty penny, but I was sure she didn't bat an eye when checking out. Now, she was using them to play tennis, bending them and scuffing them without a care in the world. I made a mental note to double up and send her a second pair.

As the thought crossed my mind, the ball suddenly headed in my direction. Unsure if it was intentional or simply a mistake, I stopped it just before it busted my shit. It would've been a nasty sight had it landed between my nose and mouth, busting them both. Unmoved, Rather stood with her hands folded and her breast pushed up on her chest.

The fact she'd attempted to leave me leaking with blood staining my clothes and the concrete beneath me meant almost nothing. Her beauty forced me to look past it all and focus on those pursed lips and annoyance in her stance.

"You're in my way," she fumed.

"You needed someone on the court with you. Here I am."

"*Wanted*," she corrected, "I didn't need anyone, Priest. I still don't."

The way my name rolled off her tongue, even in frustration, did things to me. Good things to me.

"You're frustrated," I revealed, wanting and needing to step closer to her.

So I didn't raise any red flags or go back on my promise to maintain her comfort, I stayed put.

"*Sexually*."

Her breath hiked in her throat, swelling her chest.

"Pri–" she tried, but was unable to finish because she was interrupted.

"It's written all over that pretty face of yours."

She looked off, peeking back at our people. They weren't interested in our conversation. They were occupied with Killian's humor.

"They're not worried about us, Rather, but I am."

"There's no us, Priest. Not here. Not right now."

"Then tell me why you're flustered? Tell me why you're short of breath? Tell me why your heart is racing? And, tell me why, without a doubt, I know that if I invited you to that restroom right down there, you'd come?"

"Because I would," she admitted with a sigh.

Now that we'd established that, I moved forward. There was no need to dwell.

"Where have you been? I've missed you."

"But, not enough to make it clear? Not enough to let me know?"

"Is that what you want, Rather? For me to put effort into–"

"It's been far too easy. I've been too easy. Effort, yes. That's what I'm requesting."

"My command," I told her, heading toward the center of the court on the side where I'd be playing.

Separation was eating me to shreds, but it was necessary. I wanted nothing more than to lift Rather into my arms, slide her shorts aside, and dip my dick in her filling.

"I don't play for free."

Her warning was enticing. We neared each other and

brought our rackets together. They collided just before we began to step backward, slowly.

"My dick is hard, Rather. I don't plan to play for free, either."

"I expect an investment when I win. Twenty-two thousand dollars."

"I expect to see you in my suite, pussy parted with my dick tapping against your walls when I kick your ass."

"Not happening," she challenged.

"It will. So will the twenty-two thousand. It'll be in your account tomorrow."

"That's not how this works. I'll win, fair and square."

"It works however I say it does, Rather. Now, shut up and play."

She closed her eyes, frustrated with our lack of intimacy and her lack of self-control. When her eyes opened, so did her mouth.

"My period," she explained.

"What?"

"You asked why you hadn't seen me. I've been on my period."

With a nod, I accepted the new bit of information she was giving.

"Hear me well when I say don't ever let that stop you again. I'm not a law abiding citizen, Rose. I run red lights."

This time, the separation lasted until she was bent over, hugging her knees with her palms while trying to catch her breath. I neared the center of the court, watching her struggle as the sun glared down on us both.

"You could put yourself out of your misery by quitting now."

We were on our third set. I'd won one and so had she. However, she was now down by two points. Another point and I would win the game.

Unlike before, when my family was hardly paying us any mind, everyone was tuned in. Kleigh, my mother, and Nikola were all cheering for Rather. Killian and Kofi roared every time I gained another point.

My father remained neutral externally, but I was almost certain he was daring me to lose to Rather. My success meant more to him than a simple game of tennis.

"It's not over yet, Priest."

"It can be."

"I'm ready," she panted, standing tall and clutching her racket.

Her fight was commendable but the games she'd played before had weakened her. If I was the first person she'd played, I wouldn't doubt she would've beat my ass. But, that wasn't the case. She was burnt out and I was just warming up.

I tossed the ball in the air and hit it with the racket. It nearly landed on the ground in the far corner of her barrier. However, she recovered it. Quickly, I hit the ball in the other corner, certain she was in no shape to make it to the other side of the court so quickly. I was wrong. She managed.

"UGH."

With urgency, she smacked the ball in my direction and ran toward the other side, expecting me to make the same decision twice. She was wrong and that's where she'd fucked up. The ball landed on the side she'd just recovered it from. This time, the greenery caught it.

"Fuck!"

My features were unchanging as I hung the racket on the hook where it belonged. Eventually, Rather did the same. She said nothing as she bent over, grabbing the tumbler filled with water.

"Just like that," I expressed, "I want you just like that tonight. Eight. And, don't make me wait or you'll find out just how much effort I'm willing to put into you."

I left her standing where she was and rejoined the rest of the family under the shade.

"That's what the fuck I'm talking about! Beat her ass," Killian yelled-whispered, slapping my back.

Our parents were near. It was imperative he remained respectful.

"Barely," Kofi chuckled.

"Had she not played this knucklehead and your mother, you wouldn't stand a chance, son. You suck." My father didn't sugarcoat things. He said them with his entire chest.

He was right. I couldn't deny it. Nonetheless, I had won and not for the reasons any of them wanted me to. It was simply because I wanted those legs parted so I could take a swim.

I didn't bother responding. Instead, I grabbed the bottle of water from the table and loosened the cap. It was one of many Kleigh had brought out in addition to Princeton's water.

I quenched my thirst while watching every move Rather made. She approached with darkened cheeks and her ponytail much looser than it had been before. My hands wrapped around it as I dug her out from behind was the only vision roaming my thoughts in anticipation of being brought to fruition.

She lowered into one of the oversized, comfy chairs underneath the private cabana our family owned at the country club. I was fixated on her, but her eyes were elsewhere. On the little body I'd played a part in birthing. On my whole heart.

When her hands expanded and she sat up in her chair, my brain refused to advise my lungs to keep working in my best interest.

Rejection, on her behalf and from anyone, was becoming my least favorite experience. Introducing Princeton to people who were accustomed to encountering neurotypical children was at the top of my list. Combined and I wasn't able to maintain my composure.

"Hi!" She greeted him, trying to entice him with that silky voice of hers. It wouldn't work.

"I can see you want to come. There's plenty of room for us both. It's okay. Can I see your friend there?"

She asked questions with expectations that were simply out of Princeton's reach. It pained me to hear another one emerge.

"Hmm? Can I?"

"He's nonverbal," I explained.

"We're talking," Rather said, immediately moving her fingers as she spoke.

Mindblown, I sat up straighter. I planted my arms on my knees and watched as the familiar signs continued.

"In his language and that's fine with me."

As her statement concluded, her arms stretched again. This time, Princeton's legs began moving. Six steps and he was in her space. Her personal space. A place he didn't visit when it came to strangers. This was his first time meeting Rather. His comfort was baffling.

"Is this your friend?" She asked Princeton, simultaneously signing.

He nodded, drawing gasps from everyone around.

"Oh, he's handsome. Does he have a name?"

Another nod nearly sent me to an early grave. My father tapped my arm, trying to acquire my attention, but I was unable to divide it. My thoughts were jumbled. My gaze was firm.

"What is it?"

This time, Rather didn't sign with her hands. Instead, she used one to place it on her ear and angled it in Princeton's direction.

She was making her expectations known. She was exerting her confidence onto him. She was making him well aware of the response he was capable of. She was encouraging him without trying to force anything out of him.

Princeton's head dipped slightly, slowly breaking my heart. But, just as quickly, he'd sealed the cracks with the verbalization no one but Rather was expecting. We couldn't hear him, but we were certain something had come from those lips.

"Hmm? There's just so much noise around us, I could hardly hear you. What's his name, again? I'd hate to call your friend the wrong thing. Tell me, again."

She began leaning in his direction, but before she was able to get too close, the word burst from his small frame.

"Woody!"

It sucked the life out of me. One word. One name. Two syllables.

His excitement was dazzling. His smile, the pride he felt in that moment, was endearing. While we all clenched our chests, the ruckus began.

However, I was lost for words. Kleigh, Killian, Kofi, our father, and our mother all joined in conversation stemming from the shock. Rather, on the other hand, pretended as if Princeton's verbalization was a normal part of his day. It wasn't. He hadn't spoken a single word since he'd been born.

"Woody? Oh yes. Now, I remember. He's the little guy in Toy Story, right?"

Princeton nodded.

"Yes. Yes. I've watched it a few times. Is that your favorite movie?"

Another nod led her to ask a more complex question that would likely get another response from Princeton. The fact she was able to hold his attention for as long as she had was baffling. Yet, I kept my eyes on them both, admiring every movement they made.

"Who's your favorite character?"

"Woody."

The same word surfaced again.

"What's his friend's name? I can't remember. The one that wears the helmet. Gosh, I can't remember," she lied, trying to coax another word from Princeton.

He didn't give in as easily. Instead, he shook his head from side to side. Toy Story was no longer on his radar.

The necklace around Rather's neck was. He laid his

head against her chest and tucked his feet beneath him. With the tips of his fingers, he began drawing circles on the dainty chain. Afraid he would become too much for Rather too soon, I beckoned for his attention.

"Princeton," I called.

His head never lifted. His body never rose. He remained pressed against Rather. She met my gaze, looking me square in the eyes as she shook her head, advising me not to uproot my son.

He's comfortable, she signed.

He's safe. She followed up with.

He is only nonverbal for now. Princeton has chosen not to speak and until he's ready he won't. But, he is capable of expressing himself. The word he just spoke might be the only one he speaks for a while, but have patience. One day, he'll have a full vocabulary. It won't make sense when he begins his journey, but eventually it all will. How old is he?

Five, I responded with my hand.

Time. He just needs time. There's likely a lot going on in that little head of his. He just needs time. But, remember, even slow progress is still progress. She told me.

Progress in itself is all I need. It doesn't matter the pace.

Then, he's on the right track.

Thank you.

So fucking impressive. She could have two-hundred-twenty-two-thousand dollars if she wanted it. All she had to do was say the word. What she'd just done for me, I could never repay her for. What she'd just given us, we could never thank her enough for.

Kofi had to get it right with this one, because she would be his to have in the end. Our time wouldn't last.

But, when it was over, she deserved to be treated well. Very well.

You're welcome. She signed.

"How do I get my grandson on your schedule, Rather?"

My father wasted no time creating a plan for Princeton.

"Unfortunately, I'm not practicing right now, so my time is plentiful."

"That'll all work itself out. I'm sure your brother is working hard to make that possible for you. In the meantime, your new patient is sitting right next to you."

It wasn't a good idea to be around Rather alone, even in Princeton's presence. He napped more often than not. We'd have too much time on our hands and the lines she was trying not to blur, I'd scribble all over.

"How does Thursdays sound?"

"Sounds doable."

"Thursdays are no good for Princeton," I interjected.

"Tuesdays?"

"As long as you agree to take him and get him back home," I demanded, speaking to my father.

For my sake and the sake of our family, sending me to Rather's house weekly would be catastrophic. I wouldn't be able to keep my dick out of her.

"Without hesitation."

"Then, Tuesdays?" She asked.

"Yes. Does two work for you?" My father questioned.

"It does."

"Then, see you Tuesday at two."

Her hand rested on Princeton's head. Her eyes rested on me. My heart, it opened for her. She left it with no choice.

SEVEN

Rather

Large hands pulled me backward and into his pelvis. My pleasure was visible on his dick, making his strokes flawless and nearly effortless. My climax had slammed my body against the bed and I was still trying to recover as his neared.

He felt like a slice of heaven. If losing to Priest resulted in mind-boggling strokes and back to back orgasms, I'd meet him on the court every fucking day. He was addictive. I was dreading the day I had to end this thing we had begun two years ago.

"Wh— where you want it?"

His muscles tightened as he grew harder inside of me. I

deepened my arch and assisted his elevation by pushing back into him, driving him mad.

"Fuck."

I slid up and down his dick so effortlessly. I was soaking. He'd unstopped my well and allowed my juices to flow freely.

"Wher— shit. Where yo- you wan-"

"Right there."

Admitting one of my deepest desires was difficult but necessary. I wanted him to fill me to capacity with his minions, though the consequences weren't of interest.

"Rose-" he grunted.

"Right there," I repeated, hoping he wouldn't fight with himself or his logic.

All logic was out of the window. The emergency contraceptive tablets I'd emptied into the drawer right beneath the condoms should've made my intentions clear, but he'd ignored them just like he was attempting to ignore my request.

I rounded my ass in search of the hole that wasn't occupied. Upon locating it, I submerged my index finger.

"Uhhhhhh."

"You not playing fair, dear."

"Right there," I reminded him, massaging my asshole with my finger.

"Right whe- where?" he inquired, exposing his hand. He couldn't resist. He wouldn't deny me.

"Deep insiiiiiide—uh of me."

"Deep inside of you?"

"Yeesssssss."

His explosion was massive. As he released, he pounded me from behind. His strokes were perfectly paced and packed *enough power to curl my spine and force both of my hands on the bed.*

"Fuck!"

Whack!

He smacked my right cheek before falling onto the bed beside me. I clenched my pussy from the pain and joined him on the pillow right beside the one he was laying on. He stretched his long limbs and opened the second drawer of the nightstand.

He grabbed a bottle of water from the top after securing one of the packages inside. He fought with the wrapper for at least a minute before removing the cap from the water.

"Open up," Priest instructed.

I obeyed his order, allowing him to place the pill in my mouth.

"Drink."

The water made the pill go down my throat easily. Once it disappeared, so did the water. Priest pulled me closer and wrapped those long arms around me.

The same circles his son drew on my skin, he managed to complete one after the other. My skin was dewy from the second round of intoxication he was wholly responsible for. The air conditioner did little to cool me off. It was no match for the furnace between my legs or the man beside me.

"Speak, Rose. I can feel your thoughts. They're heavy."

"What happened to his mother?"

"She's not dead if that's why your heart is heavy."

"Then, where is she?"

"Living her life. She's not my concern and yours either. She signed over her rights. Princeton belongs to me and only me."

"He's a beautiful boy."

"And, bright. His mind is a complex, very impressive place."

"I can only imagine."

"He is the mastermind behind the designs of several investments of mine."

"A budding entrepreneur."

"He is."

"He'll be fine, Priest. I know he will be."

Somehow, I felt like he needed those words. Needed that assurance. I would give it to him every and any chance I was able.

"Me, too."

Silence hovered over us as we stared into the blankness.

"Come back, Rose. In two days. Ten o'clock."

We were back on track, back to the original time set for our meetings.

"I have so many thoughts about our time here."

"If they're not pleasant, you do not have my permission to express them. Only good things must come from your lips in reference to us, this suite, and the things we get into. That's all I can stand, Rose."

That's all I had to give. It was my second visit since discovering our connection outside the suite. I'd made my bed and with him I'd lie in it every chance I got. Only happy thoughts surrounded me at the moment. Only good things.

"I feel so at peace here," I sighed, "So quickly I forget everything happening outside of these walls."

"That's how you're supposed to feel."

"And, you?" I wondered aloud. "How do you feel?"

"Blessed, Rose. I feel blessed when I'm between these walls, between these sheets, between your ears, and between your legs."

"It's not only in the suite when you're between my ears. I think of you often. All the time, in fact."

"You're not alone."

I quieted, allowing my thoughts to consume me. Priest wasn't having it. He wanted to extract them from my brain. It was against the rules for me to even have any of my own. But, he made that hard to manage.

"I'm listening," he breathed, deepening our embrace by tightening his arms around me.

"Why wire me the money? I lost."

"Because I want you to have it."

"Aren't you going to ask why I need it?"

"I'm no fool, Rose. You don't need the money. You just don't care to spend your own. You have it. We both know you do."

"I do."

"It doesn't matter. Now you have more."

"It's for the launch of a book I've been working on," I blurted, desperately wanting to fill him in on things happening in my world. "The marketing. The promotion. The first large print run. The small store I plan to open, filled to the brim with them. And, the horse trailer I plan to convert into a mobile bookstore for festivals and markets during the spring, summer, and fall. Once this all blows over, I'll already have it all worked out and ready for business."

"A book?"

"Not filled with words, but more like therapy bottled up in activities and affirmations and- it's hard to explain. You'd have to see it to understand."

"I'd love to see it. When can I?"

"When my final draft feels completed. I'm not there yet, but I'm almost there. I can see the finish line."

"How long have you been working on it?"

"Two years."

"The two years I waited?"

I paused, swallowing the lump in my throat. He wasn't ready to let it go and neither was I. Those two years changed our trajectory and I didn't think I'd ever recover from them. Without a doubt in my mind, things between us would've progressed rapidly and soon enough it wouldn't be The Mansion I was headed to at ten some nights. It would be his home. Possibly **our** home by now. We'd never know because this was our reality and we couldn't turn back the hands of time.

"I waited, too," I confessed. "There wasn't a day you didn't cross my mind. I wondered if I'd ever see you again. If I'd ever run into you in the wild since I'd been promised to another man. If I'd recognize your voice or your walk or your stance. Anything.

"And, if I did, how I'd react. I didn't know the first thing about you when I was put on that plane and shipped across the world for my protection. However, I told my sister about you– for six months straight until she claimed her ears were starting to bleed. It was around the time I'd run out of things to say because I thought surely you'd forgotten me by then.

"Surely you'd found someone else to pleasure you the way you needed. Surely you'd pushed me to the back of your brain."

"You were wrong, Rose. I waited. In vain."

"It wasn't my fault, Priest."

"I know. It was mine. And, I'll never forgive myself for not searching for you. If I'd just tried, I would've found you in a flash. You were so close, yet so far away."

"I was right there, all along."

"All along."

The blaring of my phone pulled me from my thoughts. Memories of my time with Priest were the most precious thing to me. Having them interrupted was frustrating, but the face on my screen made the interruption worthy of my praise.

Roulette and I had been playing phone tag for nearly two weeks. Our schedules simply weren't aligned. Whenever we did speak, we weren't the only ones on the line. What I wanted to talk to her about wasn't for other ears to hear. It was only for ours.

"Hello," I greeted her as soon as the line connected.

"Princess Rather," she exclaimed, "How's the castle?"

Her humor was infectious. "Roulette, please."

"Talk about a fairytale. You're living it."

"I wish it were that simple," I sighed, closing the book in front of me.

I was nose deep in the book full of therapeutic practices for pediatric patients with autism. The book was insightful. I'd began building the plan of action for Princeton's therapy before I finished the first page. It was full of gems that had my gears turning and my hopes high.

Priest was ready to tear down the communication barriers between him and his son. I was desperate to help. Not only because I wanted them torn down, too, but because I was wholeheartedly invested in the progression of the small human I'd only met once and fallen for.

The incredible amount of time I had on my hands and the patience I was forced to practice until I was able to see clients again had a lot to do with how invested I was as well.

"When it comes to men, it's hardly ever *that* simple. But, still, we move, love."

"You move," I chuckled, knowing how she truly got down.

"True. True. Now, what was it that you called me for that night? I called you when I woke up that morning but you didn't answer."

"I was kind of tied up."

I buried my head in the pillow as thoughts of Priest returned.

"Oh, answer this FaceTime!"

I looked at the screen to find she was in fact calling me on FaceTime. Without hesitation, I slid the bar across the screen.

"Now, I'm listening."

"When I needed you to help me make the executive decision, you needed sleep. The deed is done now. The mess has been made now. I'm in deep shit and I have no idea how I'm going to get myself out of it when the time comes."

"You're talking in circles, Rather. Tell me what's going on."

"PS102."

"You went back?"

I nodded.

"To *The Mansion*."

I nodded.

"And, he was there?"

I nodded.

"After two whole years? Goddamn, Rather. Your pussy got superpowers, too?"

Because I knew she was referring to the powers she claimed her pussy had all these years, I couldn't contain myself. I laughed, nodding in response to her question.

"He kept my tab clean. For two years."

"Shit. You have a beast between those thighs, babe. Congratulations," she chanted.

When she realized I was no longer laughing, she paused.

"So, what's with the sadness?"

"I'm getting married in two months, Roulette."

"To a man that's still getting his dick wet. If anyone is going to get played in the relationship, never let it be you, baby. Have I not taught you anything?"

She sipped from the cup that appeared from thin air.

"To his brother!"

She spat out the liquid she'd just poured into her mouth.

"T– to who? Wait. What? Back up. Hold up! Who's brother?"

"His name is Priest. PS102, his name is Priest."

"Priest, Priest?" She asked, knowing exactly who he was.

He was the man who'd made Chem's escape possible. We'd never forget him. Though we'd assumed we had never crossed paths with him, we were aware of who he was and the role he'd played in our brother's freedom.

"Priest, Priest."

"Goddamn, this world is a small place."

"It is."

"But, still, the question remains. What's with the sadness?"

"I'm fucking the man who's brother I'm set to marry in two months."

"And?"

"And?"

"It's an arrangement, Rather. You're acting like you were in love with the man prior and you're breaking some code of conduct. You were sliding down Priest's dick before you knew Kofi existed. The damage was already done. Finding out they were brothers wouldn't undo what had already been done."

"I know, bu–"

"But nothing. I've told you many times before, Rather. When a man shows you who he is, believe him. Kofi told you out of his own mouth. Right now, if he had the chance to stick his dick in one of your six sisters, he would and would continue until that ninety day mark. He'd have no issue kissing his bride with the secretion of ours smeared across his top lip.

"Some dogs you can't tame, love, so don't tire yourself out trying to or feeling guilty about joining them. It's your best move. Trust me when I say he'd have Rhea bent over, ass up if she gave him the opportunity. Don't spare him, Rather, or no man for the matter. Not one that doesn't have your best interest at heart."

Roulette was heartless. She believed that ninety percent of men on the earth's core were meant to be played and playing them was her favorite game.

"When the hell did we start moving with uncertainty?

That's not a Childers trait. When we move, we move. The guilt or whatever the fuck you're feeling right now is irrelevant. That man is likely climbing out of pussy right now. You better get it together. Chin up. Chest out, babe. You had the same ninety days he had. That's what he failed to realize. I'm starting to believe you failed to realize it too."

"I haven't," I assured her.

"Then make me a believer. Shit. Straighten up that pretty face."

My lips curved into a smile.

"If you're going to fuck that man's brother, don't feel bad about it, Rather. Seriously. I saw the look in your eyes each time you mentioned him. I saw the longing. The yearning. This was inevitable. It was going to happen whether you wanted it to or not. Whether it was his brother or not."

She was right. Even if Kofi hadn't burst my bubble at that coffee shop, before things between us got serious, I would've tried my damndest to get back to the suite. Back to Priest, at least once.

"I know."

"Keep your head high and your standards higher, Rather. What's done is done. At least you're fucking with two men that will make sure you're straight regardless, so you're in a situation you can't lose —that's my type of party."

"Yes, I know!" I nodded, because it was indeed her type of party.

"So, tell me about PS102."

"He's a dream, Roulette."

I buried my head in the pillow, again. But, not for long.

I needed to get everything off my chest and there was no one I wanted to talk to more about all the things I'd been thinking, feeling, and experiencing since I'd been back in the States.

"How'd you find out who he was?"

"I didn't. He noticed me by my birthmark. He waited a full week, trying to convince himself it wasn't me he'd been waiting for. Until one night when we were alone in the hallway, he called out to me."

"Called out to you?"

"Yes. He called me Rose."

"Shut up!"

"Roulette, I wanted to disappear. I wanted to melt. I wanted to drop to my knees and suck his dick right in that hallway. I wanted to teleport to the suite. Mentally, I did. His father came into the hallway and I couldn't move. I didn't move. Not until–"

"He gave you permission."

"Yes! Not until he told me I could."

"Oh, you're down bad, Miss Girl."

"I knoooooow! And, now, two months seems unfair. Where has a month gone already?"

"It hasn't gone, *completely*."

"Might as well. Only a few days away."

"Tell me more. Tell me about the last month."

"Nine days of it were spent away from him. It was a very hard, very grueling nine days. Seven of which I was bleeding. The other two consisted of recovery."

"Ugh, God handed women His ass to kiss. Menstrual. Babies. Boobs. Asses. Pussies. Ovaries. Like, what the fuck was happening? Why'd we need all of that?"

"Please let me know when you find out."

"Back to PS102," she urged.

"He wired thirty thousand dollars to my account."

"That's it?" Her shriek was incredibly humorous. "That's allowance, Rather. Chemistry sends that to our accounts monthly for simply existing. Are you losing your mind?"

"I only asked for twenty-two."

"My God, you're losing it. Truly," she chuckled.

"Well, I didn't really ask. I played him in tennis."

"And won."

"Actually, I lost, but he still put the money in my account."

"So, free money? I can't be mad at that. But, fifty or better, baby. Don't let him play in your face, again."

Sniggering, I responded, "Noted."

Roulette waited for more details and I had plenty to give.

"He has a son. His name is Princeton and he's the most handsome boy I know. I've taken him on as a client."

"You're not into pediatrics, babe."

"I know, but I'm making an exception. I miss my office. My clients. My life, Roulette. Pediatrics will have to work for now. I just want an ounce of normalcy. Since everything happened, nothing has felt ordinary to me. Not even now that I'm back in the States. I feel like things are ever changing and I'm just trying to find grounding. That's where I will find it. I truly believe that."

"I understand. I promise. We're all forever adjusting. But, honestly, our comfort needed a disturbance. We were so accustomed to thriving in our element. This is just another lesson for us all. Another chance to strengthen our core, tighten our bond, and learn to survive."

"You're right. As much as I wanted to hate Egypt at a point in my life, I love her for what she's done for us all. What she's given Teddy, I can never begin to repay her."

"She wouldn't accept it if you tried. Despite her obligation, she's shown us time and time again she's for us. Was always for us, even when she was supposed to be against us. I love my girl. And she doesn't mind letting that chopper *siiiiiinnnng*. I couldn't ask for a better sister-in-love."

Egypt was a beast in the field. She and Rugger were the most competitive during our exercises. They were both skilled and both able to handle a firearm better than us all. Everyone *except* Chemistry.

"How is Jru?"

"Spoiled and too smart for her own good."

"Of course. When I saw Princeton, she was the first person I thought of. I miss my baby."

"Why does he need therapy?"

"He doesn't. He's autistic and the family wants to see if therapy will support the progression they're in pursuit of. For now, he doesn't speak. We're looking to turn that around soon."

"*We're*– look at you, already speaking for the family. I don't know if I'm jealous or happy for you, sis. Let's not mention the good dick you're getting. Meanwhile, I'm playing with my pussy every night."

"Roulette, please!"

"It's true. I know my clit is tired of me. Hate to see my fingers coming. Like, pick somebody else, tonight!"

Laughter was good for the heart and whenever Roulette was involved, there would be plenty.

"Chem is working to get us cleared and back together again. It won't be long, babe. Just takes time."

"Yeah. I know. I'm not complaining. I like it over here. It's euphoric. It's a slice of paradise. Everything feels so much better from this side of the world. No worries."

"No worries," I agreed. "That type of peace is priceless."

"I need to get my other line, Rather. Call me. I have to go."

"Okay. I'll talk to you lat–"

The line went dead. With her advice on heavy rotation, I rested my head against the pillow as thoughts of Priest joined the line up. In under two hours, I'd be seeing his son. Right now, I wanted nothing more than to see him.

Kofi.

His handsome face fought for relevancy. I wondered where he was, what he was doing, and if a call would steer my thoughts in a different direction. I decided to test the theory immediately instead of waiting.

His number was one of few in my contacts. I tapped his name and placed the call on speakerphone. My heart raced at the sound of the first ring. Then, there was a second. By the third, I grew worried. It wasn't until the fifth ring that I decided to end the call, knowing he wouldn't pick up.

Maybe he'll call back.

Sighing, I opened the photo gallery of the fairly new device. I'd only had it for a month and the pictures were few. Jru made up most of them. Images the family had collectively sent filled the gallery. Then, there was a thread of new, hidden photos that required my FaceID for visibility.

Dark skin, thick arms, and tattooed skin appeared on the screen. Warmth caressed my body. Fine hairs stood on my arms, back, neck, and fingers. A tingling sensation shot up my spine.

Priest.

I needed something to remember him by. Still images as he rested peacefully beside me were keepsakes that not even he knew about. My growing obsession for his presence painted a picture of misery that helped me see well into my future.

Kofi would be alright in the end, but he'd never be Priest. And, for the life of me, I couldn't shake my thoughts of that piece of knowledge.

Priest was a man. A caretaker. A provider. A lover. He appreciated my presence. It wasn't a burden to him. I wasn't a burden for him. My job wasn't to create something of him that he'd been unsuccessful at creating himself. It was simply to exist. That made all the difference. That made all the commotion in my head and at my center.

Though personal satisfaction wasn't necessary anymore, the throbbing between my legs was intensifying by the second and I needed relief. I pushed my panties down until I was able to slip my leg through one side. Spread wide, I parted my lower lips.

"Sssss."

The tips of my fingers were cold to the touch, sending a chill through me. I pressed four fingers against my clit, desperate to warm them. My sensitivity made the task more difficult than it should've been. But once the fire pit had grilled my skin long enough, I removed two fingers and began rounding my clit with the other two.

Priest's image was enough influence to send me spiraling, but I'd try my hardest to maintain my composure. My sanity depended on it. Because, whether he knew it or not, he was driving me wild.

THE GREY LIST

I strutted toward the front door dressed in a gown that swayed effortlessly. The Hermès sandals allowed it to sweep across the thoroughly clean surface beneath me, making each movement theatrical. Poised and pretty were only a few words to describe how the L'AGENCE Bias piece made me feel.

My vibrating phone piqued my curiosity. A smile drew the corners of my mouth upward at the sight of Kofi's name across my screen. It had been nearly two hours since I'd made a call to him. He was finally calling me back.

"Hello," I answered, stopping to take his call.

"What's up, baby? I was tied up, handling business."

I leaned against the wall next to the staircase and folded my arms underneath my breast.

"Nothing. I was calling because I had nothing else to do and was wondering what you were up to."

"Handling business. Nothing much. You ate? My stomach touching my back."

"I haven't."

"Where you at? I can swing through and pick you u–"

"I have therapy with Princeton in a few minutes. I think your father just pulled up."

"Shit, it is Tuesday."

"Yes. It is."

"How long will therapy last?"

"No longer than an hour, but if he's comfortable then it could last longer."

"Hit me up when it's over. If I haven't eaten, we can go grab something."

"Well–" I hesitated. "I kind of promised Kleigh I would let her take me to the dress shop to try on a few dresses we chose online."

"Busy day, huh?"

"Sort of. When I called, I had two hours to spare."

"It's all good. I'll catch you another day this week."

"Okay."

"Alright."

Neither of us ended the call. Instead, we waited on the line for the other to disconnect it. After a few seconds, laughter from both of our ends ensued.

"You–" I pushed.

"No, you!" Kofi chuckled.

His laugh was heart-stopping. With a shake of the head, I combed my hand down my face.

"Hang up."

"Nah, you hang up," he toyed.

"Ugh. Fine."

It was me who finally ended the call. Just as I made it to the door, a text stopped me in my tracks, again. It was from Kofi.

I like you.

His words brought a smile to my face. I could feel my cheeks flush another shade of brown.

Good, because I don't think you have much of a choice.

I opened the front door to find Princeton and Kalvin headed up the walkway. Tiny arms wrapped around my legs the second they crossed the threshold. Taken aback by his display of affection, I lowered until we were eye level.

"Hello, Princeton," I greeted him with words while using ASL simultaneously.

Though he didn't respond, the smile he gave me sufficed.

"Well, that's new," Kalvin claimed, "Should I stay?"

"If you think it will make him more comfortable. The plan for today is simple."

"Yeah? What's that?"

"Start Toy Story."

Princeton's eyes brightened at the sound of his favorite movie. That was the reaction I was anticipating. Building trust was the most crucial portion of foundation when it came to pediatric therapy. A child needed to understand and be fully aware of their ability and privilege to trust you before you could move forward.

So, we were going to begin building our foundation with a movie he was familiar with. Together, on the same sofa, we'd have ourselves a blast watching Woody and friends come to life.

"Then, I'll leave you two. Kleigh will be here in about an hour, she says. I'll be sure to grab him before she comes or else he won't go with me."

"Sounds good to me."

"See you in a minute, son. Rather is going to take good care of you, alright?"

Princeton hid his face in my dress instead of responding. Kalvin gave him a good pat on the head before heading back to the vehicle his driver was standing beside.

"Okay, buddy. It's just you and me. Let's get settled in."

We walked in the theater room where I watched Princeton's eyes sparkle with joy. Where he stood, near the door, he bounced up and down with excitement. I'd managed to transform my theater room into a Toy Story monument in an hour's time.

The large order I'd placed Sunday night had a fairly swift delivery. Everything I needed was waiting in the mailroom by Monday. Just before showering and getting dressed, I opened them one by one and made the best of the contents in the package.

That simple, it reminded me of the man my heart had begun yearning for day in and day out. Princeton was a carbon copy of his father. Though children weren't in my near future, I couldn't help but wonder if my child would resemble their father.

"Popcorn?"

Princeton responded with a nod of the head.

I took him by the hand, leading him to the extra comfortable sofa in the theater room. I removed his shoes and let him climb up. I tucked him in the Woody blanket and sat his Woody toy right beside him. I grabbed the freshly popped corn and the tray full of healthy snacks that fit right over his legs. I made myself comfortable beside him, underneath the Jessie blanket with my snacks and popcorn.

"Ready?"

Excitedly, Princeton nodded. I pressed play on the remote and began the film. The glistening of his eyes and the captivation of his attention let me know we were off to a great start. I didn't think we'd get through the entire film in the first session, but we'd push for the full hour. It was just enough without overstimulating him.

By the four minute mark, Princeton had inched closer to me. He tapped the tray, requesting its removal. I sat it on the floor next to the couch for easy access if he needed it.

He snuggled up next to me and began rocking his body back and forth. He was content. Though it might've seemed otherwise, he was comfortable. He felt safe.

Good. Very Good.

We were headed in the right direction.

With Princeton's feet pressed against my leg, I angled my body so I could get a better picture than the first three I'd taken. He was so precious and hadn't lasted forty-five minutes before he was out cold. Just like his father, he slept with one hand behind his head.

There.

The perfect image filled my screen from one edge to the other. The sound of my doorbell alerted me of Kalvin's presence. In exactly one hour, he'd pulled into the driveway. For the last few minutes, he stood outside on a call that seemed important from my camera's view.

Instead of waking Princeton, I headed for the door to let Kalvin in. The coolness of the silk fabric felt good against my skin.

"Don't tell me you don't ever, ever– ever ever think about me," I sang Teyana Taylor's song lowly.

The lyrics were a bit more relatable, now. They were a bit more real. And, just like her, I knew all good things must come to an end.

"Mr. Valentine."

When I opened the door, I wasn't surprised to find Kleigh standing beside her father.

"Kleigh."

"You ready, babe?"

"I am. But, I have a sleeping Woody in my theater room. I have to send him off before I can join you."

"I'll be in the car waiting. If he sees me, it won't be easy for either of us to get away."

"So your father has told me."

"Where is he?" Kalvin asked, turning in every direction in search of a sign of Princeton.

"Right this way–"

I led him down the hallway and into the theater room.

"How did he do?"

He scooped Princeton up and took his shoes from my hand.

"Wonderful. He's a sleepyhead, so we'll have to finish it next week."

"Did he say anything? Did he talk at all?"

"He didn't. But, he will. This session was more about gaining his trust. We'll work on the more complicated stuff when we nail this."

"Right. Right. I had my accountant wire a nice amount to your account. That should cover him for at least a full year."

With a smile and a tilted head, I asked, "How much did you wire, Mr. Valentine?"

"Six figures."

With a nod, I waved my hand toward the door. "Right this way."

"Hopefully that's enough."

"It'll work."

Six figures was enough to cover fifty-two sessions. In fact, it was more than enough. However, I wouldn't open my mouth to tell him that. I opted for staying quiet and walking him out of the door. I rushed back inside to grab my belongings and met Kleigh at her car where she'd been waiting.

"Are you excited? Wedding dresses. My God, I've dreamt of my wedding preparations for years. I can't wait until my time comes."

"Whoever he is will be a lucky man."

Kleigh reminded me so much of Range. Wholesome. Bubbly, depending on her surroundings. Sociable. Kind-hearted. Optimistic.

"You think so?" She pursed her lips as she sped off.

"Wholeheartedly."

EIGHT

Priest

I scrolled, checking the sizes of each item in the cart to make sure they were accurate before entering my debit card information at checkout. The Chanel sneakers Rather had scuffed was one of twelve items in the cart I'd filled.

After the confirmation screen appeared, I sat back in the chair at my office desk. The void I felt when I'd entered the sacred space remained. Spending a little bread on her did little to cure the longing in my head and heart.

11:56.

Visions of thick sheets, an oversized comforter, and long, brown legs that were freshly shaved and moisturized invaded my thoughts. I closed my eyes, knowing exactly where I wanted to be and who I wanted to share the rest of my night with.

Not at *The Mansion*, but at mine. Or hers.

Fuck.

My buzzing cell freed me of my transgressions. Silk's name on the screen could only mean one of two things. Neither were good. I answered with haste.

"Yeah."

Up on my feet, I began to pace the room before words even escaped him. I'd gotten a call from him two years ago that nearly shattered my world. Seeing his name was triggering.

Kofi.

"Aye, yo, Boss man."

"I'm listening, Silk."

"Them niggas from the East that Kofi bumped heads with are in the building."

"And–"

"So is Kofi. He was toasted before he stumbled through the door. I'm watching that nigga and making sure he's straight, but I can already tell what type of time these niggas on and they didn't come alone."

"How many?"

"Six."

Six dead men, I thought, headed for my closet. *Dead on my arrival*.

"Stay put."

"You already know I am. We're at *Orchid*."

I ended the call. There was no time to linger on the line. Kofi was a sitting duck. Though I knew he could handle his own, the influence of alcohol and whatever drugs were in his system would delay his reaction, have his aim off, and diminish his ability to move as he should.

Being next to niggas you owed bullets to the dome was enough to tell me he wasn't in his right mind. It was law—*shoot first and ask questions never*. He'd broken that one and a few others.

Black tank.

Black hoodie.

Black skully.

Black sweats.

Black socks.

Black shoes.

Black Glock.

I stepped out of the closet with vengeance on my mind. If Kofi wasn't going to get his, then I was. I'd rather put them niggas in the dirt before they had my entire family dressed in their Sunday's best crying over Kofi's casket.

Instead of the Phantom, I opted for the Kia underneath the tarp in my garage with license plates belonging to absolutely no one. It was a dramatic downgrade from what I was accustomed to, but the second I slid into the driver seat, I could smell the blood that would be shed tonight. It was more of the same each time I started the engine and silence followed.

No music.

No phone.

It was just me, my thoughts, and the Glock I would be ditching before the night's end. It wasn't my preferred weapon but I couldn't deny its ability to bark or the bite it packed when I needed a job done with haste. It was easy to handle, compact enough for concealment, and would leave no stone unturned.

As long as my aim was good, then it would leave no witnesses. And, for me, good was an insult. My aim was impeccable. Flawless. Every time I fired, bullets were lodged in something, in someone. It was inevitable.

Orchid was thirty-five minutes away from my home in Mt. Clarke. For twenty-six of them I didn't make a peep. The descent required silence. I was headed to my depths where I exchanged my sanity for savagery. It was necessary for the task at hand.

Killing a man was as easy for me as snapping a finger, but it demanded a very specific mindset. In order for me to sleep peacefully when I returned home, its presence wasn't up for discussion. I dug deep, awakening the nigga required for the job.

He was thoughtless. Ruthless. Heartless. Careless. Fearless. And, lacked limits. Lacked logic. Lacked self-control. Lacked a reservation for life. He ended things. People. Empires. Operations.

"Priest," Ice picked up on the second ring.

"Silk holler at you?"

"Yeah. He called."

"Kill their feed in eight. I'll be there in nine, in the door in eleven."

"I'm on it."

"Ice."

"What's up, Boss?"

"Every camera. I need them blind."

"Say less."

Silk was my next point of contact.

"You here?" He asked as soon as he answered.

"In eight minutes I will be. In ten, kill the lights."

"I'm headed toward the powerbox now."

When the call on the untraceable line ended, I flipped it and tossed it in the cup holder. Though peeved with Kofi's inability to straighten the fuck up and put us all out of our misery, his protection would forever be my responsibility. Because, I knew if the roles were reversed, he wouldn't hesitate to shoot or catch a bullet for me. He was an asshole, but he was a beast when it came to the people he broke bread and shared the same blood with.

In eight minutes I was in the parking lot of Orchid with the strings of my hoodie tightened underneath my neck. The confusion written over the security's face when the power went out was my sign to exit the car. Right in front of the club, I left it running. Their state of bewilderment made it easy to slip past them and inside.

I pulled the goggles down over my eyes. Instantly, the darkness transformed into an array of greens. I could see everything, including the clubbers who weren't interested in exiting due to promises being shouted by club management.

"Ohhhh ohhhh. Don't go nowhere. Having issues with the power. The generators will kick on in a few seconds. Don't go nowhere."

Kofi.

I spotted my brother in the booth near the corner. He'd removed his pistols from his waist. They sat on his lap, clutched tightly in his hands.

Smart boy.

Against the wall. Fingers on the triggers. Ready for war.

Don't worry, brother. I got this.

My thoughts raced as I tried not to draw any attention my way by bumping the people standing around waiting for power.

"In fact," the loud voice continued yelling, "Let's count this shit down. Starting from thirty. I bet this shit be back in business. I hope you motherfuckers can count! You ready? I'ma start this shit off."

Thirty seconds. Thirty seconds, Priest.

The countdown began as my search continued.

Twenty-nine.

Twenty-eight.

I counted along with the crowd.

Twenty-seven.

Twenty-six.

Fuck. Where these niggas at?

Twenty-five.

Twenty-four.

I turned in the opposite direction, knowing that wherever they were it was likely they had a clear view of my brother.

Bingo!

Spotted were six niggas with curious eyes and too much movement for my liking.

Twenty-two.

Twenty-one.

The hunger in my belly intensified as I observed, making my way through the crowd to gain leverage and deplete the distance. Though I could end every one of their lives from where I stood, too many innocent lives hung in the balance.

Eighteen.

Seventeen.

I reached my destination. The gap near their section made things a bit sweeter. I planted my feet firmly on the floor and aimed my weapon. The silencer would make their deaths swift and quiet, just like I wanted them.

Fifteen.

The first bullet split the skull of one of the six men.

Fourteen.

The second one hit the chest of another.

Thirteen.

The third was a neck shot, ending the life of the third soldier.

Twelve.

A fourth succumbed to his injuries immediately.

Eleven.

Between the eyes of an unsuspecting victim, I lodged the fifth bullet.

Ten.

The last member of the crew received an honorary bullet to his chest in addition to the one in the center of his face.

Nine.

I pushed through the crowd, slowly making strides so I didn't become the center of attention.

Eight.

Seven.

Six.

Five.

I made it to the other side, following the line of people

who weren't crazy enough to stick around during the outage.

Four.

Three.

Two.

One.

I sat in the Kia and before the door closed fully, I tapped the gas. The power was restored as I pulled off the lot. Unfortunately, the cameras wouldn't be. Not until Kofi was home and safe.

I opted for the scenic route. Without fault, I abided by every traffic law known to man until I reached the overpass between The Tops *(Mount Clarke)* and the rest of Clarke. In the emergency lane, I shifted the gear into park and stepped out.

Lake Foster kissed the piece I was saying goodbye to. It smacked the water and began to sink instantly. With it now a thing of the past, I got back into the car and was headed for my next destination. Though it wasn't home, it felt like it.

Twelve minutes into my trip and I was back on foot, putting distance between me and the Kia that would be repainted with a new plate by the week's end. The quiet street was lined with homes that were all grand in stature but were all incredibly different. The personality of their owners were showcased by their structure, manicured lawns, vehicles of choice, lighting, and decor.

The lights along the lawn glowed as I treaded up the driveway and onto the walkway. I was aware that my presence was prohibited. I was aware that I was crossing lines clearly drawn. I was aware that I was breaking a promise I'd made. I was aware that I was disrupting the comfort I promised to keep.

But, I wasn't in control of my thoughts, my body, or the insatiable appetite I was developing. My lack of containment led to my fist pounding against the frosted glass, demanding the presence that would put me at peace. I was still in the depths of hell, having an outer body experience and I needed to be pulled to shore. I needed to rejoin society and be hit with a dose of reality. *A dose of her.*

The door swung open seconds later. The tiger-stripped Baretta pointed at my chest made my dick stand. I knew for a fact the woman behind it wouldn't hesitate to shoot.

"Priest," Rather sighed, lowering her weapon.

The short dress she wore clung to her. Jealousy sprouted and blossomed simultaneously. I'd never envied fabric more than I did at the moment. I'd never wanted to be a piece of it more than I wanted to be tonight.

"What are you doing here?"

"Where are you headed, Rather?"

"To mee– I'm supposed to be meeting Kofi at– Orchid. Priest. What are you do–"

I pushed forward, taking her body with me. My hands fit perfectly around her small waist.

"What are you doing he– I have to g–"

"You're not going any fucking where."

I removed her piece and placed it on the console table near the door. Rather was gorgeous in all black. Her beauty was unfathomable. Those heels were high, just like I liked them. And, I would take her in them. Still attached to those pretty toes and those legs I needed in the air or bent over the massive staircase that reminded me of one of the three in my home.

Shit, Rose.

Her breath hiked, lifting her chest as I obliterated the distance between us. She was near yet she was too far.

"Priest–" she begged, "You're breaking you– your promise."

"Because you made me," I admitted, "Getting you out of my head is easier said than done. Tonight, I don't have the strength."

I lifted her up against the wall, looking into those brown eyes that were reeling me from the pit I'd fallen into.

"You weaken me."

The confession left me vulnerable. Open. Exposed.

Her forehead leaned into mine. Her lips caressed mine as I pushed her dress up and her thong aside.

"You weaken me," she professed against my lips, "To the core."

I entered her mouth with my tongue. Our time at *The Mansion* would never suffice. I wanted her more. Needed her more. Not just her body, but her mind and that pure heart of hers. At my side. In my bed. In my kitchen. In my shower. In my world, not only in the one we'd created between those few walls in *PS102*.

Fuck.

"It's pathetic," she whined.

"It's beautiful, Rose."

I entered her.

No glove.

No regrets.

"He's waitinggggggg," she moaned in my ear.

"He's going to keep waiting," I confirmed, deepening our connection by pushing further into her.

She established a grip around me and tightened it as I began to dig into her. The moans erupting from her body were the sweetest sounds I'd ever heard. They could loop in my head all day and night and I'd never get tired of their cadence, of their melody.

"You're so good–"

We shared sentiments. She was better than good. She was the best. I'd never be able to accurately describe exactly what she was. It was impossible.

Her words were therapeutic. Her presence was analeptic. Her pussy was medicinal.

Damn, this shit is heavenly.

Like a magnet, I was drawn to her. Mentally. Physically. Emotionally. Spiritually. Denial wasn't enough to deter me anymore. She was quickly becoming the center of my world. Her absence only intensified the feelings that were birthing instead of burying them.

Ninety days was hardly enough. A lifetime felt more justifiable. But, that wasn't in the hand we were dealt. So, for the time being, enjoyment was the only feeling I needed to honor.

"Yesssss. Ye— Ummmm."

I could feel her raining down on my tool. With each stroke, she became more slippery. The sounds of her box and our thighs as they met made me delirious.

Smack.

Smack.

Smack.

Smack.

Each time our skin collided, we were notified.

"Yes. Yesss. God. Yes."

"Urgh. Fuck."

Smack.

Smack.

I could feel my ending near, but I wasn't ready to conclude my time in her wetland. Abruptly, I dislodged, refusing us both the climaxes we were chasing.

"Priest!" Rather protested.

Her stickiness strung between us as I lowered her to the floor. It wasn't until her heels touched the tiles that we completely disconnected.

"Please."

Cupping her chin, I pulled her closer and buried my tongue in her mouth. When I came up for air, I peered down at her.

"You don't have to beg for what's rightfully and undoubtedly yours, Rose."

I rested my forehead against her cheek, completely gutted by the idea of giving myself to someone else some-day. It didn't sit well with me. Not the thought. Not the reality. *Nothing.*

"You don't have to beg."

She nodded, understanding the words coming from my mouth but not the disruption they caused in my chest.

"Bend over, my dear," barely above a whisper, I instructed. "Palms on the stairs. Ass in the air."

She got into position, exposing her nectar. Though I wanted to bury dick in her again, I couldn't avoid the tingling of my tastebuds. On my knees, I parted her pussy with my tongue.

"Uhhhhhh–"

Her spine curled. I used a hand to arch it, again.

"Ass in the air, Rather."

Calling her anything other than Rose made this all feel real. It made it all feel right. But, depending on who you asked or what commandments were in mind, it was all wrong. All fucking wrong.

However, my dick, my dome, my heart, and soul wasn't hearing it. Couldn't see it. Didn't acknowledge anything but the gratification our connection provided. For now, it was enough for me. *For us*.

I sucked her clit into my mouth. She collapsed forward. Her inability to handle what I was dishing frustrated me and fascinated me simultaneously. I placed a hand under her stomach to lift her up. With the other, I stuffed her insides with two fingers, curved downward to initiate direct contact with her internal clitoris.

With my thumb, I rubbed the outer portion. And, my tongue circled her glossy asshole. It was beckoning for me. Demanding my attention.

"Priesssss–"

Slowly, I worked her over, pulling out more of her filling with each stroke of my finger. When her frame grew rigid and she became paralyzed, I understood her climax was approaching.

"Oh fu– oh fuck!"

Her gusher exploded. Lava flowed from her volcano onto my fingers and down my hand.

"Fuck!"

Her body jerked. She lacked control of her movements. I lacked control entirely.

Desperate to feel her contracting walls, I slid back into her. Like quicksand, her pussy buried my bone.

"Shit," I groaned, feeling her pussy signal for my semen.

Smack.

Smack.

Smack.

Smack.

I drove into her, connecting our bodies with each stroke. The bulge of my dick crept toward the tip. In her pussy wasn't where I wanted to leave my seeds. It was risky business and when able to avoid it, I would.

"Ummmm. Mmmmm."

"Knees, Rather."

Though the command was given, I couldn't seem to climb out of her. She felt too fucking good.

"Yess. Ye— Uhhhhh."

"Fuck."

I forced myself out of her. Hurriedly, she got on her knees and turned until she was facing me. Without hesitation, I stuffed her mouth with that motherfucker. It wasn't her pussy I was stroking anymore, but the slow strokes continued.

Like a fucking champ, she accepted as much of me as she could. Tears fell from her eyes. Her throat threatened regurgitation. It was enticing. But, before I could accept the challenge, those brown eyes that stared up at me extracted my nut.

"Shiiit–"

Rather sipped my seeds straight from my dick. She swallowed every last drop, leaving me with clenched ass cheeks and a hand full of her hair as she continued sucking.

"Rather."

She ignored my pleas. With each stroke of her neck, I accepted my fate. She wasn't finished. Neither was I.

"Fuck," I groaned, feeling my softened meat harden again.

Round two.

I pulled her up from her knees by her hair. I stretched her neck until her eyes met mine. Deeply, passionately, I kissed her. Her scent lingered. When I released her lips, she breathed out sharp and short air. I was in a daze. Under her spell. I didn't want out. Wherever she wanted me, wherever she needed me was exactly where I wanted to be.

"The bedroom." I nodded toward the stairs before lifting her into my arms.

We didn't make it to the next step before I plunged into her again.

"Ohhh fuckkkk," she moaned.

I shoved her dress down her arm, releasing her small, round breasts. The left fit perfectly in my mouth. I swiped my tongue across her hardened nipple. It was begging to be sucked. But, I could hardly help myself. I sunk my teeth into her skin.

"Ahhhh— Mm."

She curled on my dick as we reached the top of the stairs. I had no idea where I was headed or which room we'd end up in, but I chased the feeling in my gut. With each step, I stroked her pussy long and deep.

When we made it into the second room on the second floor, I was elated to know we'd reached our destination. Her scent lingered on the sheets. Her aura painted the walls. Her belongings confirmed our location.

"Pri– Oooh— Yes."

I laid her body down on the bed. Without removing my dick from her well, I climbed in with her. Her legs maneuvered with ease. I pushed them forward until they tapped the headboard.

She was such a beautiful sight. Her dress was gathered around her belly. Her nipples were aimed at the ceiling. And, her pussy was pulling me deeper.

Missionary.

Bad fucking idea.

Perfection stared back at me, making it nearly impossible not to let loose.

"Ro– Rose."

I released her legs and leaned in, using my elbows to hold the weight of my upper body. As if it was the last time I'd visit her garden, I dug into her. Slowly, I penetrated her with my gaze, trying to understand how a human could possibly possess so much beauty. So much charm. So much charisma. So much power.

From below, she rounded her hips. Each time I pulled back, so did she. Each time I pushed forward, so did she. We were making a mess between her legs. Though I couldn't see it, I could feel it. I could hear it. I could smell it.

So fucking good.

"Where you want it?"

Against my better judgment, I asked.

"Where you want it?"

She cupped both breasts, signaling exactly where she wanted my nut. I nodded, knowing exactly where I'd put it.

THE GREYLIST

A full hour had passed since I'd cleaned my cum from Rather's breast and eaten her pussy until she gushed in my mouth. Still, I was no closer to leaving than I was when I'd come. Reluctantly, I would but if the choice was completely mine then I'd stay until sunrise.

However it wasn't in either of our best interest. I knew it and so did Rather. That's why her head hung as she rested on the side of the bed. That's why the energy in the room was unbearable.

"Rath–"

"Don't," she rushed out. "Don't say it, Priest. It only makes it real. It'll feel better if I just pretend like you were never here, so you never had to leave."

Fair enough.

"Come 'er."

I pulled her back down onto the bed and wrapped her in my arms. I kissed those puckered lips and then met those eyes that were shooting daggers in my direction.

"Fix your face."

"Nothing's wrong with my face."

"You're pouting."

She released a sigh, still not managing to convince me of the mental shift. That face... those sad eyes. They reminded me of the last time I saw her two years ago. And just like that night, involuntarily, we'd be parting, again.

"I missed you."

The curve of her lips soothed my spirit. I pecked her lips and pulled back.

"Did you?"

"That's why I came. I couldn't fathom my night without you. I needed to see you, even if only for a little while."

"You ruined my plans."

"They weren't good plans, Rather. I don't have to go into details. Just trust me."

"I do– I do," she whispered, closing her eyes for a second. "I missed you. I *miss* you. All the time."

Come home with me.

The words were at the tip of my tongue, but instead, I went with the latter.

"I should be going."

Quietly, she nodded. Despair glossed her orbs. She was breaking my heart in half. I wondered if she knew just how hard our goodbyes were getting. Each took a toll on me.

Silently, we both gathered our bearings and made the trip downstairs. Hand-in-hand, we stood at the bottom of the stairs where a few of our belongings remained. She continued, opening the door so I could exit.

Before doing so, I lowered my lips onto her forehead.

Then her lips.

Then her chin.

And, then, again onto her lips.

Fuck.

I squeezed both sides of her cheeks, hating the heaviness of my heart. Hating the weight our reality plagued me with. I was burdened by the anchor budding feelings were carrying around. Yet, nothing felt better than moments with her.

They were worth the commandments I was breaking. They were worth the pain the loss of her would cause in two months. They were worth the lifetime of regret I'd be forced to live with. And, my brother's life would be worth the sacrifice we all made to see their union come to fruition.

Tonight was confirmation the correct decision was being made. Kofi was going to cause me pain, regardless. I'd rather it be from the loss of the woman I longed for than the loss of his life.

"My days almost feel pointless when you're not part of them."

Unable to look at her any longer without falling on my fucking face, I turned away and didn't stop until I was inside the car with my hands gripping the steering wheel. I inhaled and then released a shaky stream of air. The grip dissolved as my frustration peaked.

Once.

Twice.

And, a third time, I banged my fist against the wheel.

Feelings. Fucking feelings! They didn't outweigh the structure of our family's syndicate. Neither did they surmount the influence of the commandments. It was inevitable. I had to tuck them away so I wouldn't get in the way of Kofi and Rather's destiny.

As head of the family, it was imperative I kept my shit in order and led by example. This wasn't an example I wanted to set. This wasn't the standard. This was hell and I'd be here for the rest of my days on earth, as long as the woman I wanted was forbidden.

NINE

Rather

"Nah." Kofi grimaced. "Hell nah."

Instead of finishing the cake sample, he spat it into the napkin in his hand.

"What the fuck is that supposed to be?"

Chuckling, I pointed to the picture that displayed the samples, their flavors, and the ingredients.

"Carrot cake? Who the fuck orders a carrot cake for their wedding?"

"Some couples, apparently." I was doubling over in laughter.

I'd only been with Kofi for two hours and my jaws were already sore.

"Not us. We're not– Ugh. The fuck, man. People really eat that shit? It's like chewing a fucking sponge."

"I guess it's a no for the carrot cake," Marg, the owner of the bakery asked as she returned to the table with another sample.

"It's a hell no for me so it's a hell no for her, too. Matter of fact, don't waste anymore of your cake, ma'am. We're good with the white cake. That whipped icing or whatever that shit was you let us taste the second time. And, at least one layer of red velvet. The design, we're going with the big one. There will be a shitload of people. The details you can follow up with her on."

With a shake of my head, I agreed, "I can handle the rest. I think he's a bit overstimulated. We both want those flavors, though. Will that be doable?"

I was trying to hold in my laughter, but the faces Kofi was making beside me made it difficult.

"Yes, of course. I'll give you a call tomorrow if you're about over it for the day. We've been here for quite some time, so I completely understand."

"That would be great. Call me tomorrow and we can solidify the details and note the specifics."

"Alright. Sounds good."

"It was nice meeting you two. Congratulations on your pending nuptials."

"Thank you," I responded, taking the duplicate order form she'd been filling out since we took our seats.

Kofi was the first to stand. Before I was able to push my chair back up to the table, he was already at the door waiting for me with it ajar. The coolness of the October weather was inviting. It wasn't hot and neither was it cold.

The linen pants I wore paired perfectly with the beige button down and Louboutin sandals. We'd nearly eaten a week's worth of cake, so my appetite had diminished. However, I was interested in the drink that Kofi had promised today.

"You hate carrot cake. Marking that in my mental notebook of all things Kofi."

"And you love whipped icing."

"I do. It makes me so happy."

"Happy wife, happy sex life. Isn't that how the saying goes."

Completely taken by his charming personality and ability to bring a smile out of anyone, I shook my head.

"No. Happy wife, happy life."

"Same thing."

"If you say so," I tittered. "So, still on for the drink you offered or has duty begun calling?"

His phone had gone off quite a few times during cake tasting. He'd silenced every call.

"It's a spot right down the way. We can walk but if your dogs are barking then I can grab the whip from the valet."

"My dogs?" I shrieked.

"Yeah. Especially the one with that chip in it. You might need to put that motherfucker on ice when you get home. Does it hurt?"

I'd hit my toe on the console on the way out of the door. The white polish had chipped, pissing me off just before I climbed into Kofi's passenger seat. The fact he'd noticed was both comical and maddening.

"It is fine, just injured. I bumped against the console before leaving the house. It'll be fine and the polish will be fixed tomorrow."

"Here," he urged, peeling a hundred from the stack of money he'd pulled from his pocket. It was too thick to fold, so he slid it right back down the side of his jeans until it was no longer visible.

"That should help."

A hundred dollars was more than enough for a polished toe. However, I was considering the rest a small gift.

"So– down this way?" I tipped my head in the direction we were heading.

"Nah. That way." He tilted his head in the opposite direction with a snigger, "Fuck you think, love."

It wasn't until his response that I realized how unnecessary the question was. Of course we were headed in the right direction.

A sense of humor.

Lives life–fully.

Not uptight.

Kofi had good qualities. Though we'd only managed to see one another a few times, the budding friendship hadn't gone unnoticed. My body didn't warm to his touch. My center no longer throbbed when he spoke. My heart didn't leap at the sight of him. However, I knew being with him meant countless smiles, unlimited laughter, and a good time.

"It was a simple question."

"That your long head ass already knew the answer to."

With one arm, he pulled me closer by looping it around my neck.

"You thinking red and white?"

"Red and white?"

"For the wedding colors."

"Haven't your mother told you? The colors were already decided before my plane landed."

"No one has told me anything, honestly."

"Possibly because they know you don't care." I shrugged.

"That's not entirely true. I know girls fantasize about their special day from a jit. I don't give a fuck what we do as long as it makes you happy."

"A heart. I wasn't sure you had one," I expressed, looking up at him.

"My heart has nothing to do with what I just said, Rather. Decency does. I know this shit isn't easy for you, so the least I can do is make sure you get exactly what you want."

"I want a renewal."

"Damn, we haven't even gotten down the aisle yet."

"This isn't our wedding, Kofi. It's your family's wedding. When both of our hearts are in it, we can wed–*for us*. This one, it's for them."

"I'm fucking with that."

"So, it doesn't matter much... what I want doesn't matter much this time. Ask me next time. I'll have a heap of requests. I've been gathering them since I was six."

"Let me start putting up some paper for that shit now."

"Please, because it's going to cost a pretty penny."

We strolled down the boulevard, conquering two blocks before we reached our destination. The upscale bar was hidden in plain view.

Cassius. The name was written in a neat, curvy script. My eyes adjusted to the low lights. It was a swift, dramatic change from the brightness of the sun.

Kofi wasted little time securing two chairs at the bar. Though I preferred a more private setting, I remained open to the idea of being amongst others in the social setting. For a weekday evening, the bar was near capacity. Almost every chair was taken.

The bubbly bartender with the bone-straight blunt cut that stopped right at her shoulders bounced over to our end of the bar. She placed small napkins in front of us and followed up with glasses of iced water before finally halting.

"What can I get for you two?"

It wasn't until her gaze lingered on Kofi that I realized she wasn't fond of his company. A roll of the eyes was enough to let me know the two had history.

"Well," she retracted, "For you. I'm almost certain I know what he wants."

Her audacity was appalling.

"This evening, he's going to tell you again," I assured her. "I'd hate for you to get too caught up in the past and serve the wrong drink."

"Unless his preference has changed from three nights ago, I think I'll be fine, babe."

I refused to break a sweat or show signs of intimidation. Because, frankly, I was anything but intimidated. Kofi was a free agent and so was I. What and who he did in his free time was none of my concern, but respect was the principle here. Not territory.

"It hasn't," I confirmed, though I wasn't sure what his preferred drink was myself.

"Hailey–" Kofi scoffed, "We're not doing that, baby girl. Respect. You feel me?"

"Whatever, Kofi."

Though she was interested in every word that came from his lips, disdain covered her pretty face.

"Fix the fucking drink and your face."

With a roll of her neck, she turned and headed for the rows of neatly stacked liquor.

"I'll take a martini. A *dirty* one."

She tossed a hand over her shoulder to let me know she'd heard me loud and clear. I watched closely as she began gathering the ingredients. I didn't want to be the victim of a scorned lover, especially not for a man who I barely knew and cared almost nothing about.

"Is this what I have to look forward to when with you during these ninety days?"

I could hear him suck the skin of his teeth. My eyes never left Hailey.

"That's nothing, Rather."

"Does she know that?"

"I don't give a fuck what she knows or what she thinks. I'm telling you it's nothing."

"I don't need convincing, Kofi. You've made it clear that you're n–"

"It's nothing. If you saw the nigga that was deep in your guts three nights ago out with a woman, you might just be feeling a way, too. Yet and still, it's nothing."

"Nothing another night can't fix, huh?"

Finally, I peeped in his direction. He shrugged, but the smile on his face made his intentions clear. Hailey was on his radar tonight. With slightly ruffled feathers, I returned to continue observing every move Kofi's current fixation was making.

He doesn't belong to you, Rather. Not yet, at least.

I repeated the words in my head once more before letting the discontent roll off my shoulders. When Hailey approached the second time, she had both drinks in-hand.

"Thank you."

A tilt of Kofi's head along with raised brows forced a handful of words from her mouth.

"You're absolutely welcomed."

"Welcome," I corrected.

"Excuse me?"

"You added an unnecessary D to the word. It's *welcome.*"

Chuckling, she tossed her head back in embarrassment. "Seriously?"

"You're a very pretty girl, Hailey."

I sipped from the drink she'd given me. It was divine. She made a damn good martini.

"This is a nice establishment. One day, one day you might come across a man that's worth fussing about. Though, *in my opinion*, no man is worth fussing about. One day, you'll run into him. Right here. That's if you can manage to keep your feelings in your pocket and your employment status."

I shrugged, taking the olive from the rim and biting into it. Before speaking again, I swallowed it.

"And, when you do, you'll know the difference. You'll feel the difference. You'll understand the difference very quickly between a man that belongs to you and one that doesn't. Because this one, he'll belong to me in a few short months and the *D* he's been giving you will stop."

"You'll, then, discover it was a waste of time. He was a waste of time. Waste of emotions. Waste of risks—like losing your job for being downright nasty to a very important, very influential customer. Which would be a shame, because you make a hell of a martini."

I looked her square in the eyes and exposed at least twenty of my thirty-two teeth.

"So, instead of going low with someone who has seen the depths of hell and had a damn good time, let's get along. Kofi will be yours for the night. I promise. But, for right now, he's mine. Deal with it, babe. Fix your pretty face like he advised and keep making me pretty drinks."

"I tip well and it's not dick that I'll be paying you with. I *hope* you've managed to acquire more than that from him, too. If not, then we have more to talk about, girlfriend."

A wink and a swipe of the tongue across my lips and I was over the antics. If all went well, I'd finish a second martini before my departure. However, if Hailey couldn't comprehend what I'd just explained, I'd leave after finishing off the glass in my hand. By morning, she wouldn't have a job.

When her precious features began to relax, I got an inkling we were going to be just fine.

"You're hell, man. Goddamn."

"And, you're a heartbreaker. Why would you suggest a bar you know—"

"In my defense, I didn't know until we walked in. Her mouth is always full. She never told me where she worked."

The same smile that peeled my lips backward pushed his up with a curve.

"She knew what you wanted to drink. Sucking your little dick wasn't all she does when you're together."

"You're right. She fuc–"

"Kofi!"

"I'm just saying."

"Don't."

"Okay. But, on some real shit. I didn't know she worked here. I wouldn't have come. There are three other places we could've gone on this strip."

"It's fine, Kofi."

"I'll get the check if you're ready to roll."

"You'll do no such thing. I'm fine. I'm going to finish my drink and then have another one. It's been a long day."

Kofi got comfortable in his seat. He'd been at the edge, unsure if we were staying or not. When I assured him I was alright and could hold my own, he planted himself firmly in the seat. It wasn't long before he began doing what he did best, bringing tears to my eyes and making my cheeks ache.

THE GREYLIST

There was something about a reclined roof in the autumn breeze underneath the sun's subtle glow that dissolved my transgressions. Nothing matters at the moment. Not even the destruction of the loose curls I was proud of accomplishing before heading out the door. Not even the broken

Dior lipstick I'd dropped on the floor in an attempt to reapply it before leaving the bar. *Nothing*.

Exhaustion stalked me, but I was fighting to stay away. The day was still young. And, for the first time in a few days, I felt invincible. Sleep wasn't on my radar. Neither was a night with Kofi, so it was likely my only option.

Hailey would be waiting and I'd hate to disappoint baby girl. She was too good behind the bar and I had every intention to return to *Cassius* for her service. She'd refused the money Kofi tried handing her, and responded by telling us it was her treat. After she got her feelings in check, she was a joy to be around. She kept us entertained and didn't skimp us on the liquor.

"Uhhhhhhh."

I'd yawned five times in the twenty-three minutes we'd been driving. The drive to Windridge seemed much shorter than the journey back home. Maybe it was the two martinis I'd consumed or maybe it was the day's activities that had drained me.

Kofi's hand snaked across my shoulder and around my neck. Briefly, he took his eyes off the road to look at me. When our shades aligned, he squeezed gently. The amount of pressure was perfect, relieving the tension instantly.

I closed my eyes and leaned my head backward. The wind kissed my lips and forehead. Kofi's generosity continued as he knead away the kinks of my neck. If I hadn't been enough already, I was missing St. Catana even more now. Bi-weekly spa appointments with full-body massages, facials, lymphatic massages, and wood therapy had spoiled me.

As the wheels of his car stopped rolling, so did his

fingers. The music lowered and the familiar sound of steel forced my eyes open. Instinctively, I clutched my purse where my piece of protection was sleeping peacefully. At the click of a button, it would transform from a hibernating bear to a raging beast.

"Fuck is this nigga?" Kofi questioned, hurrying out of the car.

I wasn't far behind him. The casually dressed man placed a third and final box next to the door. At the sight of Kofi and I, his eyes grew twice their size. Before he was able to do so himself, Kofi snatched the headphones off his ear and trained his gun on his side.

"What's in the boxes my nigga?"

The better question is who sent you?

In any other instance, I wouldn't approve of the gun Kofi had jammed into the side of a stranger, but this wasn't any other instance. My freedom was on the line and I'd been promised protection. Everyone had to be vetted. *Everyone. Anyone.*

From the mailman to the delivery man, I needed to know who you were, who you worked for, and why you were at my home. And, if you didn't come empty-handed, I needed to know what you'd brought to my doorstep and why.

"I'm not sure. I– I'm just the delivery guy. My number is on the side of the truck. If you want, you can call the corporate office or– or my bos– or my girl. My momz can even confirm w– where I work. Man, I have a daughter on the way. I'm ju– I'm just doing my job."

"Name on the package?"

"I– I– Rose."

My heart fell from my chest onto the pavement.

"Sender's name on the package?"

"Let him go. He's not a threat."

Kofi looked over at me, wondering if I was sure. With a nod, I doubled down.

"He's just doing his job. Let him get home to his pregnant girlfriend. Please."

He loosened his grip on the shirt and stuffed his gun where it belonged. Roughly, he straightened the shirt he'd wrinkled.

"My bad, my guy. Can never be too careful."

With a nod, the frightened delivery driver nodded. "Yeah. Yeah. I feel ya, man, damn. Thought I was about to lose my life today."

Kofi shrugged. "There's always tomorrow."

"Kofi!"

Chuckling, he patted the guy on the shoulder and sent him about his day. I left him in the driveway, while he observed the delivery truck until it was no longer in plain view. Meanwhile, I shoved the large boxes inside as quickly and as quietly as possible.

Though it was a struggle, I managed. I pressed my palm against the wall near the front door to catch my breath.

"Rather?"

"In here."

Gathering my bearings was a bit harder than I thought. My heart was racing. My head was spinning.

"Where the packages?"

Kofi entered my home, confused. When he laid eyes on the package, his movement halted.

"You took that shit in by yourself?"

"It was nothing," I lied, heading into the kitchen and hoping he'd followed.

I hadn't read the names on the packages, but the last thing I wanted was for him to have the chance. Instead of following me into the kitchen, he dipped into the guest bathroom underneath the staircase.

I grabbed a bottled water from the fridge and quenched my thirst. By the time I'd gotten half down, taking small sips one after the other, Kofi appeared in the hallway.

"I'm going to head out. Duty calls."

Chuckling, I rolled my eyes with a smile. "Duty my ass. Hailey called."

"She didn't, actually. But, I have some shit to handle. You good? You need anything?"

"I don't," I admitted, "But you can give me the rest of what's in your pocket if you're feeling generous."

With a shake of his head, he dug into his pocket and stretched a hand filled with cash. He placed it on the counter closest to him and farthest from me.

"Thank you."

"Happy wife, happy life, right?"

"You're catching on rather fast. You'll be just fine," I sniggered, taking another swig of my drink.

"Can a nigga get a hug or something? You just broke me."

"Baby, if that's all you had, then I wouldn't be here and there wouldn't be an aisle to walk down in December. If there's nothing more I hate in the world, it's a man with a negative account balance."

"Then, you don't have to worry about hating me."

I rounded the counter and sat the water bottle down as

I neared Kofi. He leaned against the island and widened his arms, inviting me into his personal space.

"Mm hm. We'll see."

"Come 'er with your feisty ass."

"Feisty?"

"A fucking pitbull in a skirt. I'm going to have to warn these ditzy ass broads to pipe down or–"

"Go casket shopping with their besties."

I embraced his warmth, standing between his legs with my arms on his shoulders.

"A fucking grenade, waiting to detonate."

"Goodnight, Kofi."

His hands closed in around me.

"I enjoyed you today. I look forward to the next time."

"You're a busy man."

"I am. But when I have another free day, yours will be the first number I dial."

"I won't hold my breath."

"Don't, because it might be a while."

"I'm sure."

"Goodnight, Rather."

He released me, but not before pressing his lips against my forehead. Because the heat was slowly rising in the kitchen, I tried freeing us both from temptation. Though my views of Kofi were changing with each hour of the day, the attraction hadn't been abolished completely. It was intact.

He was quicker on his feet. His hand cupped my chin, pulling my face closer to him, closer to his lips. And, sooner than I could protest, his was on mine. They'd gone as quickly as they'd come. I placed a hand over my mouth, trying to determine if it was illegal to enjoy the feel of Kofi or if it was alright.

"Until next time."

Stunned into silence, I nodded, watching him walk out of the kitchen and down the hall. Seconds later, the front door closed and I was left alone with my thoughts. Thoughts of betrayal. Guilt plagued me.

Priest.

My chest caved. My heart plummeted. My mouth hung. My nostrils flared.

How the right thing could feel so wrong and the wrong thing feel so fucking right was beyond me. Kofi was the man I was set to marry. Kissing him shouldn't have felt criminal but somehow, someway it had. Because, despite him becoming my husband soon, my body didn't belong to him. Not now. *Later.*

Priest.

It was him. I was his.

Thoughts of him led me into the doorway where boxes were waiting for me. Locking the front door was my first order of business. Next was unboxing. I dipped a hand in the tray on the console table and retrieved the mail opener.

The tape split with ease. I cut them all before digging into the first box. It was filled with a few more. I removed the one on top.

My cheeks burned and my mouth filled with saliva as I stared at the Chanel box. Without removing the top, I already knew what was inside because I had one just like it upstairs in my bedroom. Priest had kicked my ass in tennis, doing damage to my Chanel sneakers.

"My God, he's *everything*," I sighed, pressing the box against my chest and closing my eyes.

Two skirts.

Four shirts.

A denim bucket bag.

Sunglasses.

A gold bracelet.

Gold earrings.

And, a pair of slippers.

I stacked the items from the box full of Chanel on the stairs with intentions of taking them upstairs when everything was unboxed. The next box was the heaviest. There wasn't much left to the imagination. The large LV box inside of it could only mean one thing. An extra large LV luggage slid out with ease.

The last package had me stomped. I wasn't sure of its components and the brand was unfamiliar. Nevertheless, I tore through the box to find two smaller ones stacked on top of each other.

The first one housed three red dresses, all beautiful as the next. The second one was full of the same dresses, but all in black. At the bottom of the large box was a note attached to the receipt. For a brand I didn't recognize, I thought the total of the purchase was pure insanity, but I was grateful Priest understood the caliber of woman he was dealing with.

I imagine your voice is like silk on the line. Make me a believer, Rose.

555-230-9917.

. . .

It wasn't until I read his words that I realized I'd never conversed with Priest in his absence. I heard his voice behind my sleeping mask when I laid down at night. I heard his voice in my dreams while I slept. I heard his voice in my ear when I drifted off into the world we'd created while wide awake. But, never had I heard his baritone on my line.

Diffidence pushed my cheeks toward the sky. I pulled my lip between my teeth and bit down until the pain I was causing registered with me. Roulette was the first on my mind, but the foolishness that would follow my genuine concern for things transpiring between Priest and I played in my head.

I quickly decided against calling her. It wasn't her chastising I needed. It was something else.

Wine.

Château Lafite-Rothschild.

It was a guilty pleasure. The dryness was perfection. Chemistry had introduced us all to the red beauty and I'd never forgive him.

A bottle was the cost of the average rent in the States. Every time I opened a bottle, I donated to a local charity. However, I was in no position to do so, now. Traceable payments were prohibited.

I rushed into the kitchen and kneeled in front of the wine fridge. I removed the lone bottle and sat it atop the counter. It wasn't long before the inside of the bottle kissed the air.

The smell of merlot and sauvignon tickled my nostrils.

Eagerly, I grabbed a glass from the rack above the small fridge and filled it less than a quarter of the way.

Swirl.

Sniff.

Sip.

"Ummmm."

The first sip was celestial. I had a second. Then, a third. It wasn't long before I was pouring another glass.

"I'll slow down this time," I promised.

Priest's request was heavily influencing my actions. I could consume the entire bottle and doubted I'd be ready to fulfill it.

A new form of communication had me doubting my ability to control my impulses. A new form of communication had me considering how much faster and how much deeper I'd fall for the man coated in dark skin and undeniable beauty.

I tiptoed across the floor, feet bare and tapping against the coolness. It wasn't until I rested my body on the sofa in the living room that I regretted not grabbing a pair of socks from the full-sized coat closet.

Call him. The voice in my head demanded.

I hugged my cell in one hand and the stem of the wine glass in the other. I didn't need to see the paper again. I remembered the number at first glance.

555-230-9917.

The first ring pushed me deeper into the couch. I gnawed my bottom lip, preparing to end the call if I didn't have an answer by the third ring. It was the second one that had my breath caught in my chest.

Anxiously, I waited for the familiar tenor to disrupt my

entire nervous system. Instead, I was lulled by rhythmic breathing. I drew blanks. One after the other.

His presence was so commanding. So paralyzing. It stripped me of my power. It stripped me of the education I'd spent my entire life acquiring.

I want to kiss you deeply.

See your handsome face.

Touch your dark, flawless skin.

Tell you things I've been doing... been thinking.

Listen to your heart as it beats against my ear.

Hug away your worries and patch your wounds.

The silence was loud and it was obnoxious. Though I wanted it to end, all the things I wanted to say, *all the things I could say*, I knew I shouldn't. So, instead, I breathed into the phone, matching each breath he pulled in and released.

"Rather." Finally, Priest spoke into the phone.

"Yesss?" Hungrily. Desperately. Shamefully, I responded.

"I don't like missing you."

"I– Me either. Where are you?"

"Have you eaten?"

I sighed, remembering I hadn't. "No."

"Then, get dressed and meet me at the location I'm sending you now."

"Pri–"

"I don't want to hear shit, Rather. I don't want to hear nothing if it isn't those few words that'll let me know I won't end up at this address alone. So, what is it?"

I had no intention of protesting. I knew exactly what he wanted to hear and before I asked anything else, I'd validate his feelings. I'd acknowledge his hunger. I'd quench his thirst.

"I'm on my way."

"Good. That's all a nigga needs to hear."

"That's not all."

"What else, my dear?"

"What do you want me in?"

"A red dress. Leave your piece. I'm all the protection you'll need tonight."

The call ended without notice. I fell back onto the cushion of the couch, unable to contain the explosion in my chest. My heart raced wildly, galloping like a horse at the Kentucky Derby.

THE GREYLIST

Most women experienced the negative influence of a man's presence. The kind that declined their health, sanity, and ability to navigate the world with a whole, fully-functioning heart. With a man beside them, they became the diminished version of themselves. And, when they passed a mirror, they hardly recognized the suppressed form of their beauty.

Not Priest.

One foot led the other toward the door where he stood. Not only was he magnetic, but he was slowly birthing something within me that not even I had the power to. I'd been a strong, confident Black woman since I'd reached the tender age of twelve. Though society hadn't deemed me age appropriate, maturity had. My mind aged much faster than my frame and face.

Even in all my confidence and strength, there was much room for elevation. Each time I saw his handsome features, was blessed with his infectious smile, heard his deep rasp, looked into his dark orbs, held his hand, or slid down his thick, lengthy dick, I accessed another level. The heights his presence revealed weren't ones my wealth, status, or connections could guarantee entrance to. They belonged to a man. A *good* man. *This* man.

"Hello, Priest."

I stood before him, fully clothed but simultaneously bare. I wore nothing. He stripped me of everything each time he laid eyes on me.

Silence etched away at the gloom of the night. The sun had settled and the drizzling had began. Lights blurred, just like the boundaries we'd clearly set. Life outside Priest's suite was forbidden, but here I stood.

The hands I was beginning to crave in the wee hours of the night touched both sides of my face, easing down ever so gently. Priest brought me closer. I could feel his breath on my skin. I could taste the mint on his tongue simply from inhaling.

"Hello, my dear," he sighed, visibly relieved to see me.

Knowledge of his yearning was a source of happiness for me. It made it clear I wasn't alone. It made it clear I wasn't imagining the connection between us. It was real. We were real.

"Unfathomable. *Empyrean*," his whispers made the hair on the back of my neck stand.

His voice grew slightly louder as he continued. "Don't

ever change, Rose. Remain delicate, remain graceful. Those parts, they're the best parts of you."

"And the jagged ones."

"They're most addictive."

I searched his eyes for signs of dishonesty. I found none. A smile stretched my lips backward.

"Where are we?"

"Exactly where we need to be, Rose." He paused to bring his lips to mine.

His kiss stirred my center.

"I couldn't stand another night between the walls of the suite. Though I've broken my promise, your comfort will remain intact."

"I–"

"This thing between you and I–" He explained, still holding me close and staring right into my eyes, "It's bigger than those walls. There's not enough room there to contain our bond. It's too big. Too wide. Too tall. Too plentiful."

I nodded, understanding exactly what was being revealed to me.

"Too encompassing. Too much. It's too much."

Too good. Like the fairytale stories I read in my down-time. Like the love I root for in the books I can't pull my eyes from. Like the movies that make my heart slow it's beat but increase in intensity.

"How are you feeling?"

The concern etched in his voice wiped the smile from my face and deflated my cheeks.

"I'm okay. I feel– I feel good."

Invincible. Unstoppable. Superior. On top of the fucking world.

"Good."

He turned and took me by the hand. We entered the building through the door that quickly shut behind us. Darkness coated every corner of the large room. Candles covered nearly every inch of the floor. And, wherever there was space, there were roses. Ivory roses. Scattered on the floor.

A small path had been carved. We followed along until we reached the lone table in the middle. It was set for two. At the table, Priest slid my chair back. The nod of his head served as nonverbal instruction to take my seat. Happily, I lowered my butt into the cushioned chair.

Priest rounded the table and did the same. And, for what felt like an entire lifetime, we said nothing. Yet, our eyes never left one another. So much was said while nothing at all was spoken. And, when he was ready, Priest finally broke the silence.

"Thank you."

"Thank me?" I asked, pointing at my chest.

I was unsure of why he wanted to thank me or what I'd done for him to show his appreciation.

"There's no one else at the table, Rose."

"I don't understand."

"Princeton has been in your care for only a little while. The improvements ar– they're incredible, Rose. I'm not sure what those days consist of or what you two have done in the two sessions you've had, but he's better."

"His temperament. His attention span. His eye contact. His sleep patterns. His behavior. He feels like a new boy. I almost don't recognize him. I mean– I do. But, he's different. I've always thought he was perfect, but damn. I'm not sure what to classify this new kid as."

"We've done very little in sessions, but we've made tremendous progress. With children just like Princeton, it's imperative we build trust first. That's been the goal for me."

"We spent the first day on the sofa. The second, we finished Toy Story and conversed about our favorite parts while he finished a colors-by-the-number illustration of Woody. He didn't need assistance."

"I framed the finished product."

"It was frame-worthy."

"Time. Affection. Attention."

"Hm?"

"That's your angle with Princeton?"

"No. Not exactly. It just happens he's part of a family I'm marrying into, so those things come along with the plan I've put in place. They're added benefits of *family* therapy."

"They're making all the difference. He only knows us, blood relatives. Nikola has been by his side since birth, so he considers her one of us, too."

"He's been longing for a relationship with someone outside of his immediate circle."

"He's been longing for a mother," Priest revealed, eyes penetrating parts of me that should've been reserved for my future spouse.

I swallowed the ball of nothingness in my throat. The room grew warmer. I took a quick look around, wondering if something had caught fire from the open flames. It didn't take long for me to realize it was me. But, the candles weren't the cause. Priest was the culprit.

"Figure," he finished with a tilt of the head.

"I know someone just like him." Teddy crossed my mind. "Five to be exact."

My mother was the figure in Chem's life that Princeton was searching for.

"Thank you."

"For what?" He sat back in his chair, loosening his limbs in the process.

"The gifts."

He scratched the side of his face though I was certain it wasn't itching.

"That was hardly enough, Rose. You deserve more."

"I won't protest."

"I won't let you."

I could feel the sides of my lips split as all of my teeth were put on full display. Coyly, I shook my head.

"You're like–" I paused, taking a second to catch my breath. "Warm tea on a winter's night. Like honey glaze on homemade butter biscuits. Like the stillness after the storm that lets everyone affected know things are okay now that you're here."

"Like ointment one slathers over their burned, bruised, or bitten skin. Like a love song. The kind they recorded in the eighties and nineties. Like a fresh face after a day in the brutal sun. Like lavender buds in cold water. Like light. Like warmth. Like comfort."

Caught in my feelings, I quieted myself and placed a hand on my heart.

Still now.

"Like you," he added, pointing his head in my direction.

"Like us," I breathed.

TEN

Priest

Clarke's beauty was something I'd never be able to accurately describe. It was one of those things you'd have to see to truly believe. Stepping off the plane and being met with it was better than stumbling into the living room with sleepy eyes as a kid on Christmas and finding boxes stacked under the tree.

It had been seven days since I'd kissed the city's air. Negotiations had lasted three days longer than expected. Implementation had been a breeze once the numbers were right. Yet and still, it was a four-day process.

"This way, son."

I ushered Princeton toward the car. As much as I'd wanted him home over the last week, I wanted him near. He and Nikola were packed and ready to board their flight the second negotiations were over and his therapy session for the week had ended. My presence was pivotal in Princeton's world.

A day or two without me and he'd be fine. Anything more and he'd begin shedding pounds from the lack of hydration and nutrients. Dinner wouldn't interest him. Neither would his usual activities. To keep his routine intact, they traveled along with him and Nikola.

"This way, son."

Stopping in my tracks, I lowered my body to the pavement. His eyes had wandered off, but his words were sitting right on top of my chest.

"This way, son. This way, son. This way, son."

He chuckled.

"This way, son. This way, son."

A hand covered his mouth as he continued to find humor in his repetitiveness.

"This way, son. This way, son."

I couldn't help but laugh myself as I tried to understand if he was mimicking me and my constant demand to have him by my side or if he simply couldn't stop himself from repeating the phrase over and over, again.

"This way, son. This way, son."

Woody. Mmm. That's all. That's all I'd ever heard come from those little lips of his. The fact that had changed in a matter of seconds had me struggling to find balance. My head was foggy. My heart was pounding.

My thoughts were running rampant. My limbs, they

felt pointless almost because I couldn't gather the strength to pull my son in my arms. I could only stare at him.

"This way, son. This way, son. This way, son."

He's talking. He's talking to me. His voice. His—

"This way, son. This way, son."

"Are you making fun of your father?" Nikola tittered, taking Princeton by the hand.

Her question snapped me out of whatever state Princeton's progress had tossed me in. A nod from my son confirmed our suspicions. I found my strength and managed to palm his head while standing on my feet, again.

"I'm going to remember that next time you're wandering around the house in a panic because you can't find me."

"This way, son. This way, son. This way, son," he repeated.

It didn't matter how many times he said it. It felt like the first time every time. My heart was happy.

"That's exactly what I'm not going to call out to you and say."

It had been seven days since I'd seen Rather. Since I'd touched her. Since I'd kissed her. Since I'd heard her voice. Today, however, I'd make up for all the days I'd missed.

We settled in the car with Nikola in the backseat with Princeton. The stereo was shut off completely. It wasn't music I wanted to hear. It was my son.

I took out my phone and opened the camera. As I pressed the button to record, I sparked his interest by revisiting the words he'd said over and over again.

"This way, son."

He lifted his head with a smile on his face. Immediately, the words began flowing again.

"This way, son. This way, son. This way, son."

"This way, son." I joined him before turning the video off.

My father was the first call I made. I wanted him to know there was no need for him to come by my home to get Princeton for therapy. But, most importantly, it was crucial that he heard the voice of his only grandchild. We'd waited close to six years for him to say his first words. Most parents only waited a few months.

"Priest," he answered.

"Listen."

There wasn't a response. Instead, he quieted and complied.

"This way, son. This way, son."

Elation filled me. Princeton rocked back and forward, tapping his index finger against his chin.

"This way, son. This way, son. This way, son."

"Priest. Is that my gran– Is that my grandson?"

Bewilderment was intertwined in my father's words. There was doubt. There was excitement. There was pride. There was joy.

"It is," confidently, I confirmed.

I could hear the broken pieces of his heart as they began finding their way back together. If Princeton never said a single word, we'd love him all the same. However, we understood his frustrations and desires to do more, say more, and progress more. Most times, it was as if the words were at the tip of his tongue, but he simply couldn't get them out.

"Goddamn, man," he spoke into the phone. The

cracking of his voice raised fine bumps on my skin. "I knew he could. I always knew my boy could. I always knew."

"Me, too, Pops."

"That woman is a Godsend. Kofi had better get his shit together quick. If nothing else, Princeton needs her. She's exactly what the fucking doctor failed to prescribe."

She's our antidote.

"I was just about to head that way to pick him up. Is he about ready?"

"Not quite. We just landed. You don't have to worry about getting him to therapy this week. I'll make sure he's there on time. We're already in the car."

"Alright. Sounds good, son."

In the background, Princeton continued repeating himself.

"I'll hit you back later, old man."

"Listen to him go. When you get tired of hearing him say that shit over and over, send him to us. We'll listen until our ears bleed."

"Then send him to my mom," I tittered, knowing she'd gladly join the round up.

"She'll kill us all if we don't. Does she know?"

"Nah. You were the first person I called."

"Good. Let me tell her."

"Okay, I have a video in case she doesn't believe you. I'm sending it over now."

"Alright. Talk to you later, son."

"Later."

I ended the call and sent the video I'd taken. I was sure my mother would be calling me after talking to my father, but I'd let him do the honors. Even at thirty-six, they remain co-parents.

Their healthy relationship was a goal for so many parents who didn't have romantic ties. It had trickled down to the care of Princeton which created the perfect balance. He was blessed with three grandparents who loved him dearly.

Lola didn't know who her father was and her mother had been strung out since she was three. She'd bounced around from foster care to foster care. I, later, understood the absence of her mother made her detachment from Princeton fairly simple.

She didn't know what a mother looked like, felt like, or acted like. She'd tried her hardest to be the best version of what she thought a mother was the first year of Princeton's life. But, when his diagnosis was revealed, she folded. All the things she was becoming, *the mother she was becoming*, vanished so easily.

As for me, all I knew was healthy, wholesome parenting. I'd been my father's pride and joy since I was born, despite the circumstances surrounding my conception and birth. Not only did I have a phenomenal mother, but I was gifted with a second one. God had been generous. My support system was solid, which is why I didn't bat an eye when Lola skated.

The body of the Phantom was massive. It claimed a sizable amount of the pavement that carved Rather's driveway. When the wheels stopped in front of her door, a part of me found peace. Since I'd seen her descending the stairs at *The Mansion* two years ago, this was exactly where I wanted to be.

Nikola was safely inside my home, preparing to change linen and reacclimate Princeton with his at-home routine. For the weekend, she'd be visiting family five-hundred miles away. I was looking forward to her taking the much needed break from our home.

It wasn't until I opened his door that I noticed Princeton had fallen asleep. He'd worn himself out mimicking me and my helicopter parenting. His sense of humor was the aspect of this all that I was looking forward to.

Laughing with my son was a dream I wasn't afraid to admit I had often. It was the purest form of gratitude a child could display. I was patiently waiting for the day Princeton brought me to tears and made my stomach ache from laughter.

"Come on, son."

Barely above a whisper, I encouraged his consciousness. A few nudges got his eyes open. At the realization of where we were, he found the strength to smile. He bounced up and down, trying to assist me with the task at hand. He tapped the red button as if I didn't know it was the key to his freedom.

"Woah. Let me get your belt undone."

Eagerly, he jumped down from the car onto the concrete after I'd loosened his seatbelt. I wasn't sure what sounds were coming from his mouth as he ran around the car and up to the door, but they were very new and very peculiar.

By the time I made it to the door, Rather was turning the locks. Routines. She lived by them all her life. It wasn't until two years ago that changed for her. But, Princeton's presence was a reminder of the life she once had. *The routines.*

Two o'clock.

Tuesdays.

Every week.

Upon opening the door, Rather dropped to her knees. She pulled Princeton in for a hug and wrapped her hands around his body. As they embraced, she stared up at me with crinkled eyebrows and concern written all over her pretty face. My presence was baffling. So there was no more confusion on her behalf, I made shit crystal clear.

I miss you. I mouthed, simultaneously using my hands to confess.

Her spine curled. Her eyes closed. And, a sigh escaped her lips. The tension in her spine dissolved before my very eyes.

Shortly after, she loosened her grip on my son and held him at a distance.

"Hi, Princeton. Are you ready for our session?"

He lifted his head and it fell almost immediately after.

"Hmm?" She asked, placing a hand on her ear and angling it toward him.

"Y—yes," he responded, barely audible.

Self-control proved to be difficult at that moment. From then, I knew I'd struggled with my impulsiveness throughout the evening. It was never an issue. Had never been an issue. I hardly moved without consideration and careful calculation, but when it came to her hardly anything was the same about me. I was different. *Mentally. Physically.*

"That's what I like to hear. Let's go."

I stepped inside, trying to piece together my memories. I'd been in the very spot I was standing in weeks prior, but hardly remembered anything about the space. All I remembered was the woman hand-in-hand with my son. I was in a completely different realm when I entered Rather's home that night. I was on a completely different wavelength.

"How about you go into our room and have a seat? I'll be right there. Let me see your father out. Okay?"

Princeton didn't respond. Instead, he hopped down the hall at full speed, turning the first corner he reached. She turned, taking me all in as I did the same. She was a breath of fresh air and stunning in the loose-fitted cropped top and long skirt combination. They were beige in color. The material of choice was linen.

She was timeless. Her beauty. Her class. Her elegance. So well put together. So manicured. So polished. Clean. Simple. Her aesthetic was quintessential. As was she.

Folded arms told me she wasn't exactly happy. They made it clear I'd disturbed her comfort. It was something I never intended to do, but she made that promise almost impossible to keep. I wanted her around. Near. Always. In all ways.

"I'm not leaving, Rather."

"Pries–"

"Have you missed me?" I interrupted, hardly interested in her protests.

"I– Priest."

"Answer my question."

Slowly, she nodded. Those big, all-consuming eyes glossed over. Her resolve softened. Her limbs loosened. Right before me, she modified her stance. She rediscovered her comfort. That's all I wanted. That's all I ever wanted with Rather.

"Too much."

Her response was low, but I heard every word.

As gentle as I cared to be in my head, my hands had a mind of their own. I pushed her up toward the wall behind her with my fingers wrapped around her neck. My feet were moving fast. Hers moved even faster, keeping up with my speed until she smashed into the wall.

My lips landed on hers. My tongue separated her teeth.

Fuck, I've missed you.

So swiftly, I so easily got lost in her. She was easy to navigate, but I purposely lost my sense of geography. My knowledge of worlds, the way they worked, and how they were operated was useless.

When my lungs could no longer support life and had dried to a crisp, I unleashed her.

Breathe.

She disrupted my oxygen supply. My body struggled to adjust. Labored breathing followed our disconnection.

"Where's your father? Is he well?"

"He is."

"Then, why are you here?" She angled her chin and widened her eyes.

Chuckling, I kissed the skin of my teeth, "I don't need

permission to see you, Rather. I do that as I damn well please."

"Those weren't the rules," she reminded me.

I leaned in and whispered in her ear, "Fuck the rules."

Taken by my response, she released a deep breath.

"Priest."

"I'm listening."

Instead of responding, she rolled those eyes of hers, bringing joy to my world. She didn't have shit to say.

"I could probably never repay you for what you've restored in here," I told her, pointing at my chest. "But, I'll keep trying until I figure it out."

"You owe me nothing."

With her forehead pressed against my chest, she shared.

"I owe you everything, Rather. Princeton's improvement– maybe it seems small but it's a big fucking deal. You did that. No one did that but you."

"It's not, Priest. But, it's my job. He repays me in full every time he opens his mouth. Your father never has to wire me another dime and nothing between us will change. Tuesdays. Two o'clock. One hour. A world of possibilities."

"Thank you."

She paused, looking up at me.

"I have a client waiting. Make yourself comfortable since you insist on staying. But, please don't interfere or get in our way. This isn't our time. It belongs to Princeton."

With her palms expanded, Rather pushed me backward. The softness she'd succumbed to was quickly hardening. She was asserting her dominance. She was regaining her power. She was becoming the woman her brother had kept hidden in plain sight this whole fucking time.

"Fine," I agreed with both hands in the air.

The last thing I wanted was to be kicked out on my ass.

"Hard boundary, Priest. *Hard*."

She made herself clear.

"Understood."

She turned, heading toward the direction Princeton had run off in. Before she was out of arm's reach, I smacked her largest curve.

Whack! It sounded in the openness of her foyer.

When her eyes met mine and her hand went for her thigh, I wrapped my arm around her neck and pulled her back into me. I grabbed her right hand, stopping all movement.

Laughing, I asked, "You were going to shoot me?"

"No, but the bullet would've grazed you," she assured me.

"You're that good, huh?"

"Let me go so you can find out."

"No. Not until you calm down."

She didn't respond. Instead, she inhaled and exhaled dramatically. Five times she repeated the exercise. Her body relaxed against mine.

"Better now?"

She nodded.

I didn't trust her. Not one bit. I walked her down the hallway with gapped legs and both of her hands under my control.

"Seriously?"

"Yeah. I'm not trying to get shot, Rather."

"If I wanted to shoot you, you'd be shot. I mean that... *from the bottom of my heart*."

It wasn't until we reached the room where Princeton was waiting that I let her go. She was amused and so was I. Before she made her way into the classroom, she stopped at the door's threshold.

Smitten by the woman before me, I blew a kiss in her direction. Again, those big eyes rolled as she shook her head. Her cheeks fluffed and her teeth peered from behind her lips.

I made a mental note to cancel my father's future pick-ups. I was now responsible for therapy on Tuesdays at two o'clock. Everything I was trying to avoid by giving him the task was transpiring. It wasn't shit I could do about it. It wasn't shit I was trying to do about it either.

T H E G R E Y L I S T

Fuck I'm supposed to do with myself? I asked for the fourth time in twenty minutes.

I hadn't quite thought my plan through. I neglected to acknowledge the fact I would be useless for a full hour while Princeton was in therapy. Now, as I sat on the living room couch, I couldn't keep still.

Doors. The doors.

I nodded, springing from my seat and heading for the first door in sight that led to the outside. It only took a few seconds for me to get a good look at the screw and determine it was one of the smaller ones that wouldn't stand a chance against a raid or someone's heavy foot. I was certain if this lock was held in place by the small screw, the others were, too.

The kitchen was my next stop. I searched every drawer to find where she kept screws of any kind, screwdrivers, or anything remotely close. I didn't find anything. The garage beckoned for me. I followed my intuition and quickly stumbled upon an unopened toolkit. I brought the sorted screws and screwdrivers of all sizes inside. I only needed one, but the kit wasn't opened so I had to bring them all in.

The first lock was changed in a matter of two minutes. The second was her patio door. It didn't give me any trouble either. I made my way down the hall toward the bedroom that led to the pool on the other side of the house. It was a second master suite, I assumed. Possibly an in-law suite.

I passed the room where Princeton and Rather were seated in the large comfortable loveseat. An oversized book was in her hands and she was reading each word with theatrics that matched. Briefly, I paused, taking in the view.

Exactly what she was giving him was all Princeton wanted. It was all he needed. Someone to nourish his mind and tap into his emotions... *and not just anyone*. It had to be someone he viewed in a specific regard. Someone he saw in the same light as he did Lola. Someone he associated with the person he was missing. A woman. *A mother*.

Sensing my presence, Rather peeped her head over the large publication. I was reminded of hers. She'd do well. I was convinced. And, however I could, I would assist her.

No words were exchanged. I continued down the hallway to finish the job I'd started. One by one, I changed the screws of every lock in her home. By the time I finished the final one on her front door, she was rounding the corner. I checked the time on my watch. Princeton still had ten minutes of therapy left.

"Is everything okay?"

"He's asleep."

"He was tired on the way over. I'm not surprised."

I'd broken a sweat and was out of my button down. Rather's lingering eyes jogged my memory. I had forgotten my shirt was on the back of her couch. We stood face to face, unmoving and silent.

Rather was a complete mind fuck. I found it hard to believe she didn't know it. She was a therapist. *The Therapist*. She was well aware of it.

"Why didn't you call?" Her words gutted me.

The vulnerability leaped out, snatching my soul and heart in its quest for relevancy.

"Rather, I–"

"I don't like missing you," she grumbled, "That's what you told me."

"Because it's true."

"Then, you sucked at showing me this week."

She lodged a fist in my heart. I searched for words. They'd gone missing.

The only thing I could conjure was, "I'm sorry."

"I don't want an apology, Priest. I want you to understand how I feel. I want you to understand what's happening here."

She pointed between us.

"Do you understand what's happening? Because, for the life of me, I can't stop it. I don't know that I want to either. We've blurred the lines. We've fucked up, royally. I don't know about you, but for me—for me it's not just sex anymore."

She shook her head from side to side. I heard every word. I felt every word. So that she could hear me clearly, I conquered the space between us. When I was close enough, I adapted to her eye level. Not only did I want her to hear me, I wanted her to see, feel, and understand me.

"It was never just sex," I confessed, "Not for me. It was always more. You were always more. Don't insult this thing we have. No matter how complex it is. Don't do that, Rather."

"I crave you," she admitted, closing her eyes and placing a hand on her chest, "Every waking hour of the day."

"Even when I sleep," I added, letting her know she wasn't alone.

"I've been trying to consume you in small doses, so afraid I'll overdose."

Her truth was valid. It was mine as well.

"It's not that easy, Rather."

"I know."

Her rounded shoulders and burdened gaze was tearing me apart inside.

"Join us at the lake house this weekend. Friday morning, be there."

"Pri–"

"I don't care. Whatever is about to come from those lips that doesn't align with what I've just said or the way you're feeling, then I don't care. It's not real. This is."

I tapped my index finger on her chest.

She massaged her temple, trying to make sense of something that would never make sense. Not to me. Not to her.

Not to anyone. But, we were beyond that point. It didn't matter. Nothing mattered but us.

"I jus– I need to see it through. I have to see it through. He'd give his life for me, one hundred times over. Just this one thi– thing. I can't screw this up."

"You won't."

"We've blurred the lines. Our secrets have spilled out of the suite and into our personal lives."

"The lines no longer exist. I've told you once, but I'll say it again–the suite can't contain us."

She agreed silently.

"Friday, by noon. 11206 Lakeshore Drive."

"Okay." She sealed her lids as the response escaped her. Slowly, her chin lowered to her chest where it stayed until my voice brought her back to me.

"How are you feeling, Rose?"

At the sound of her given name, her eyes were on me again. She opened her mouth to speak but when nothing emerged, she closed it, again. Her lips pressed together.

The internal conflict she faced was written all over her face and her unsteady fingers. She drew small, repeated circles on her thigh. I stepped forward, taking her hand into mine.

"How are you feeling, Rose?"

She lifted her shoulders and then dropped them. "Parch."

I'd known it with or without her confirmation. Her longing hadn't gone unnoticed. It wasn't water that would quench her thirst.

I pressed my palm against her cheek. She was open. She

was ready. But, the roles had yet to be assumed. Rather had yet to conform.

"Then, we should see about getting that worked out."

"I'm not her, Priest."

Blankly, emotionlessly she stared at me. Unmoving. Unconvinced. Unable to be anything other than her true self.

"This isn't the suite. And, my name isn't Rose. It's Rather. Rather Childers. *The Therapist*. And, unless you're not afraid to sit in my chair and serve as my client, then I suggest you pack your son up and head out of the door you came in."

I almost forgot to breathe. I almost forgot to blink. I almost forgot to respond. Dazed, I stilled and watched as the woman before me honed her power and stripped mine simultaneously.

She rounded me.

Once.

Twice.

And a third time before stopping in front of me.

"Mr. Valentine."

I was so far removed from our reality that I didn't know my chin had dipped and my head was hanging. I straightened my posture and matched Rather's stare.

"What will it be?"

I palmed my mouth, considering my options. I'd heard the stories. I knew just how brutal she was. I knew how well she did her job. I knew how bad things could get. Yet and still, I was intrigued by the thought.

Not many who sat in her chair survived to tell the story. Those who did likely couldn't tell their story because their injuries wouldn't allow. Those injuries weren't always phys-ical. They possessed mental scars as well.

"Mr. Valentine."

"I've never been a hoe, Dr. Childers. How shall we proceed?"

Her hands gathered near her chest.

Clap.

Clap.

Clap.

Slowly and quietly, she gathered her hands.

"Well, then–"

She brushed the invisible wrinkles from her skirt. The sternness of her stance and words made me wonder if I'd made a mistake. However, I refused to recant.

"This way, shall we?"

ELEVEN

Rather

"Rath– Fuck."

His bulge had reached the tip of his dick. His end was near, but I wouldn't allow him the pleasure of releasing. He didn't deserve it. Not yet. I removed my hands and watched his eyes close as his head fell backward.

Priest's hands were battling the restraints. His efforts were pointless. I'd bet every dollar in my bank account that he wouldn't free himself, just like I wouldn't free his semen until I was ready.

"What the fuck are you doi–"

"Shhhhhh."

I lifted my leg and brought his head forward. I fed him the pussy he was desperate to feel. As if he'd missed his last six meals, he opened his mouth to receive my meatiness.

"Tongue."

When it was visible, I lifted slightly and placed it right at my opening. Back and forward, I rocked my body.

"Ummmm."

With each stroke of his tongue, I shuddered. When the feeling became too intense, I lowered my body and pressed my clit against his tongue. Simultaneously, I leaned over and extended my arm to pull his dick into my hand.

"Rather," he whined.

Disregarding his pleas, I stroked his length.

"Shhhhhh." I commanded silence.

His bulge reappeared near the center of his shaft. It was such a beautiful sight. Hunger pains knotted my stomach. I aborted my mission to ride his face until I peaked. Instead, I fell flat on my knees with his dick in my mouth and his balls in my hand.

Ssspuh! I spat the saliva that had pooled in my mouth as I marveled as the beauty of his girth.

"Fu– ckkk."

"Mmmmm."

Each time he reached the back of my throat, I hummed. The tip of his dick met the vibrations over and over, sending Priest spiraling. Just when his ass tightened and his legs stiffened, I popped him out of my mouth and sat back on my legs.

"Fuck is you trying to do to me?" He groaned, frustrated with the edging.

"Hm?" I forged my innocence, pretending I wasn't aware of what he was complaining about.

As I did so, I climbed up and straddled him in the chair.

"You gone make me cum in that pussy, Rather. You gone make a nigga cum in that sh—"

I stood up, allowing his dick to fall right out of me and onto his thighs. A mess was made. My stickiness streaked his meat and the rest of his center.

"Uhhhhh!" My time had come, too. I was on the brink, but I wanted us to share the bliss.

"Fuck. Come back here. Get back on this motherfucker," Priest pled with me. "Rather."

"Shhhhh."

I covered his lips with mine. My pussy was aching for its release. I'd been teasing him, but I'd been teasing myself, too. For an hour straight, I refused to let Priest cum. I was ready, now, but I needed him to say the magic word.

"Say please," I whispered, kissing him deeply.

He pulled back from me, staring at me with regretful eyes. He wasn't sure what he was getting himself into an hour ago, but he'd surely found out. In the future, I hoped he made wiser choices. This was nothing in comparison to what I was capable of.

"Please!"

I reached behind me and fisted his hammer. I drove it inside of me and propped both feet up on the left and right stretchers for balance.

Up.

Down.

Up.

"Oh God!"

Down.

Up.

Down.

Priest didn't announce his pending arrival because he was too afraid I would remove myself. He didn't have to. I felt him stiffen inside me and all around me. Just as his semen filled me, I rained down on him. **Heavily. Heavenly.**

Shit. I tapped the steering wheel as the flashback caused a flood in my undies. Undoubtedly, they were ruined.

"Your destination is on the left. 11206 Lakeshore Drive."

Priest had rose to the top of my list of clients and he was not number two. For an hour, I had my way with him, driving us both mad. Things between us had spiraled into something neither of us could control. But, I wasn't sure I wanted to.

I turned into the long driveway that started at the top of the road and ended at the front of the incredibly beautiful home. Priest stood near the garage, waving me over. From my understanding, I'd be parking my car inside. Though we would be alone for the weekend, one could never be too careful.

"Shhhh."

I dipped the warm towel in the bowl of hot water as he protested.

"Untie me."

He was putty. He was tapped out. He was vulnerable. He was bare. He was powerless.

The subtle requests were quieter as each rolled off his

tongue. His submission hadn't come easy, but it was magnifying. He'd cared for me on many occasions. It was my turn to take good care of him.

"When I'm ready," I told him for the twelfth time.

He was struggling. His masculinity had taken a blow, but it was a beautiful one. Convincing him that he could surrender to me started with him trusting me. His history with women wasn't one he was proud of, so he was careful. He was calculated.

But, with me, he didn't have to be that person. I wanted the raw version. The one that hadn't been altered by the pain of his past.

"You can let it down, Priest."

He quieted, closing his eyes as my words penetrated him.

"I'm not here to cause you any pain."

I ran the warm cloth down his chest.

"It'll never be the case."

Gently, I cleaned my nature from his thighs.

"Eyes," I demanded.

He lifted his head, staring down at me with the weight of his world on his shoulder.

Let me have it.

I wanted his burdens. His pain. His worries. His stress. His hardships.

"Do you understand, Mr. Valentine?"

His limp shaft was crusted with a thin white layer of gratitude. My pussy was beyond grateful for his contributions.

"Answer me."

Weakly, he nodded. Slacked facial features and rounded shoulders displayed his defeat in high definition.

"In less than six weeks I'll be marrying the man that has been arranged for me. I'll mourn you each day. Since your identity was revealed, I've mourned the idea of happiness I foolishly boarded the plane back to America with."

"Because in no world and in no way will I ever have peace or utter happiness knowing you exist. The day I accept your brother as my husband will be the only time I will knowingly, and reluctantly, cause you pain. But, you won't suffer alone."

"I have the rest of my life to live with that pain. Until then, you can let down your guard. Allow me to experience you fully."

I stopped cleaning his body to look into those eyes that saw right through me.

"Please." The cracking of my voice was as frightening as it was revealing.

"I wouldn't have it any other way, Rose."

With my eyes closed, I counted down from ten. By the time I reached three, the door of my car swung open and Priest was guiding me out. Before both feet were settled on the concrete beneath me, his arms were around me.

"Good morning," he greeted me.

His lips pressed against mine.

Once.

Twice.

"Good morning."

"It's six. What are you doing up?"

"I– I couldn't sleep."

Chuckling, he rubbed his hand down his head.

"Me neither," he admitted, "Been wanting you here since we arrived last night."

"I almost came. Last night," I sighed, happy to finally have made it.

The call letting me know he'd made it came around eleven. I was in bed, under the covers, and headed toward my dreams. It took a great deal of control to stay put and find sleep.

Because he was getting settled, the call was swift. Had we stayed on the line, I wouldn't have been able to resist. He sounded exhausted, lonely, and like he could use some company.

"You should've."

Priest had left dinner with Princeton the previous night and come straight to the lake house. I couldn't stand the idea of being home waiting for the ten o'clock hour to head out. My internal alarm woke me up at four. Within thirty minutes, I was on the road and on my way to Priest.

"Come inside. It's chilly out."

On wobbly legs, I followed him into the house where the smell of marshmallows and caramel welcomed me.

"Coffee?"

He nodded.

"You seem like the type of woman that starts her day off with a cup. I started some when you notified me that you were headed this way."

It wasn't until I was halfway here that I called Priest. I was too afraid to wake him and too afraid he'd tell me to ditch my plans and stay home until sunrise.

"Coffee would be nice. I don't have it every morning, but it brings me joy the rare mornings I do."

"That, too, huh?"

He nodded toward the breakfast nook in the spacious, ranch-style kitchen. A stack of books piled high and topped with a large red bow stole my attention. I froze, momentarily, blinking rapidly to make sure my eyes weren't deceiving me. I rotated on my heels to find Priest with a smirk on his face.

"You didn't."

Shrugging, he responded, "I did. And, though I'm not a coffee lover, I thought we could take a moment to appreciate the sun's glow while you narrate whatever the hell is between those pages. Heated blankets are in the closet near the gazebo."

"Pinch me," I demanded, moving closer. "Pinch me."

"I won't do such a thing, Rather. Because after the stinging subsides, the books will still be right there and I'll still be waiting with a cup of coffee and a heated blanket to join you out back."

I rushed to unravel the bow and take a good look at the books stacked on top of one another. To my surprise, the final book in the stack wasn't filled with words. It was patiently awaiting mine. The *Ivy Dawn* journal was one that had been on my wishlist for some time now.

Every time I considered the purchase, I talked myself out of it. The line of stationary was far too beautiful for me to destroy with a single journal entry before quitting altogether. I didn't have much to write about then.

"Write about me," Priest challenged.

"Are you reading my thoughts?"

"No. Sharing mine."

"I heard everything you said the other day. I haven't

stopped thinking about it. It would pain me more to know you aren't living the happiest life you could because that's exactly what you deserve. Utter happiness. You tell me that you'll mourn my absence. I'll mourn the blissful life you could've had, had I never entered your world."

"Not for a second do I regret meeting you or the magic we've made since encountering one another. But, I regret the turmoil I've burdened you with. I'll never forgive myself for your fate or for your future. You deserve better than the pain you'll feel."

"I deserve you."

With a nod, he agreed. Pursed lips and a low chuckle were followed by the shake of Priest's head. "But I'm not who you'll have."

"I know."

"Come outside with me, Rather. We don't have long before Princeton is awake."

He extended his arm and waited for me to grab ahold of his hand. I snatched the first book from the stack, hoping it was intriguing enough to capture both of our attention. It wasn't until I made it out onto the extended porch that I realized I'd forgotten the cup of coffee I was eager to have. I let go of Priest's hand and started for the door.

"Is everything alright?" He called behind me.

"How do you like your coffee?"

"Black."

While he prepared the blankets and chairs, I busied myself in the kitchen with cups of fresh coffee. As I stood waiting for the mug I'd chosen to fill, everything around me stilled. The moment felt so surreal. Comfort quilted me better than any blanket man could create. The words of a song I loved more than the law should allow came to mind and out of my mouth.

"I feel so comfortable with you. You make me comfortable with you."

At some point of *The Start of Everything*, it was Priest who began to turn page by page, reading to me. And, at some point during his reading, I fell asleep on his shoulder. The electric fire pit he'd started a few feet away kept the chilly water winds from altering my body's temperature.

Sleep had overcome me. Many hours later and I was awakened by giggles and the sound of a raging dinosaur. Darkness surrounded me. As much as I wanted to blame the blackout curtains in the unfamiliar bedroom, I had a gut feeling I'd slept the day away. The sun set after the six o'clock hour. Though it was relatively early, it was too late for me to have slept in.

I slid into the fluffy slippers waiting for me in front of the bed. It was then I felt the silk fabric against my skin. I was no longer in the loungewear I'd come in. Priest had gotten me out of my clothes and into something more suitable for sleep.

Gosh, I couldn't have been that tired.

Sleepless nights were few and far apart, but late nights and early mornings were plentiful. My head and heart were both still adjusting to solitude. I hated every waking minute of it. I missed my family dearly.

My mother's voice wasn't enough anymore. I needed her by my side. And, the girls, I yearned for their presence. The FaceTime group calls weren't enough. Teddy was a completely different story. The void his absence left was hard to even think about. We didn't talk as often as I wanted or needed.

He wasn't much of a talker. Our calls would be filled with silence. But, even that would be better than the bits and pieces of him I had at the moment.

Maybe I was tired. Mentally, if nothing else.

Though I heard him loud and clear, it was taking me forever to get to Priest. The home was far from modest. The land was never ending. Acres on acres on acres of beautiful things and beautiful creatures occupied the territory.

According to Priest, there was a stable full of horses he owned two miles down the dirt road carved in the center of the property. An equestrian at heart, I couldn't wait to have a look. If the horses were mild-mannered, a ride or two before the weekend would be divine.

"Sleeping beauty has awaken."

Finally, I saw his handsome face. I released a breath I hadn't realized I was holding. Princeton's feet shuffled toward me, stopping only when he'd reached me and his hands were wrapped around my legs.

"Hi, buddy."

I rubbed his back in an attempt to settle his nerves. The sight of me was riveting, sending him spiraling. He took off in the other direction after a few seconds. Up and down, he jumped around, clapping his hands and stomping his feet. His excitement was heartening.

This must be how my mother felt waking up to Chemistry and Richie.

"How did you sleep?"

He was doing it again. Unintentionally stirring my feelings. Discovering the asshole I'd met at the dinner table was everything but the asshole I'd made him out to be was not on my bingo card. Finding out he was the complete opposite of the man his family painted him as had me on a high I never wanted to come down from. Naturally, he cared. The constant questions proved it.

How are you feeling?

What are you feeling?

How are you doing?

Are you okay?

How did you sleep?

The questions weren't always simple and could come with loaded, very heavy responses. But, no matter the response, it became part of his study guide. Each answer was stored somewhere in that complex brain of his until he found use for it.

The thoughtfulness of books on the table this morning had come from the place he stored my responses. The lakehouse visit. The mention of the stable. The slippers. Everything. Priest listened well.

"Seeing that the sun has settled leads me to believe I slept well. *Like a baby.*"

"Sometimes our bodies begs us for rest and we refuse until it stops begging."

"And, you wake up after ten hours."

"Eleven," he corrected me. "It's seven, my dear."

"Eleven?" My eyes widened in shock.

"Yes."

"I've wasted the entire first day out here. I'm so–"

"You better not do that, Rather," he warned, getting up from the floor and standing on his feet. "Never apologize for giving your body exactly what it needs."

I followed his long stature with my eyes until he made it to the kitchen. Princeton was finally settling. He grabbed him by the hand and brought him closer to the counter where he grabbed the white stack of laminated sheets that were held together by a single metal ring.

I knew what every page entailed because I'd made the booklet. Each week, the idea was to add two sheets to the ring to expand Princeton's palette.

His favorite foods were amongst the items pictured in the booklet to help him better communicate his desires and eliminate unnecessary triggers for him as it related to decision making. Princeton was capable. He just didn't know how to communicate his preferences in most cases.

"We're having dinner soon. What would you like?"

I watched carefully as Princeton went into deep thought. Priest's patience was appreciated as he made the tough decision. Only when he was sure, Princeton began pointing.

A grin turned my eyes to slits. Princeton was a joy to have around. He was becoming my saving grace. He offered normalcy in my world. Everything felt foreign to me except sessions with him–*and time with his father*.

"Good job, son."

Priest lowered him onto the floor and patted him on his head.

"I guess we're having grilled chicken, corn, and jello."

Shrugging, I joined forces with the decision-making five-year-old who was off to find Woody.

"That sounds delicious."

Priest and I both failed to conceal our laughter. Nevertheless, he began preparing for our hearty meal. I wasted little time stepping into the kitchen and running my soapy hands underneath warm water.

"I'll open the cans of corn and get them started."

"I'll get started on the chicken."

We worked our way around the kitchen, ultimately deciding that a salad was suitable for the questionable meal we were having. Within an hour, everything was plated and in front of us on the table.

"Dear God, thank you for the meal we're preparing to receive. Thank you for life. Thank you for health. Thank you for the breath in our lungs and the beat of our heart. May the food we're waiting to receive is nourishing to our minds, bodies, and souls. In your darling son Jesus' name, Amen."

"Amen," Priest added.

"Princeton?" I called out, "Amen. Right?"

He tilted his chin upward, bringing smiles to our faces.

"Good enough," I concluded.

Laughter and light quickly spread around the table as we stuffed our faces. Though it was rather quiet, no words were needed. Everything Priest was feeling rested in his eyes, posture, and every movement he made. I only hoped the feeling was visible in mine.

Princeton piled corn on his spoon a final time. He'd

eaten it all and only a few bites of chicken. But, when the metal hit his plate, he made it clear he was finished.

"All done?" I asked in two different languages.

"Umm hmm." Clearly, Princeton responded.

Priest's eyes cut in his direction. I shook my head, daring him to make a fuss about it. Normalizing Princeton's newfound ability was the quickest way to bring him comfort and encourage him to continue. Princeton didn't need a pat on the back for speaking. He needed reassurance so the words would keep flowing.

It wasn't his fault they were lodged in his throat when he tried getting them out. But, he was fully responsible for breaking down those barriers his little brain and body had agreed upon. If Priest began rewarding him for every new word he spoke, it would be never ending.

"What is it that you'd like to do next?"

I was aware of Princeton's routines and so was he. His body set internal alarms to let him know when the next task was required. Because he had the ability to determine what was next without being told, I knew he had the strength to tell me exactly where we were in his daily routine.

He pointed down the hallway. I wasn't sure what was down there, but according to the time it must've been his bedroom.

"What's down there?"

He pointed again.

"A pool?" I asked.

He shook his head.

"A gym?"

He shook his head.

"A lake?"

He shook his head again.

"B–bed."

"Oh, your bed? Is that it?"

He nodded. "Umm hmm."

"Oh dear, are you sleepy?"

"Umm hmm."

"Then, let's get you to bed, yeah?"

"Umm hmmm."

His little rasp was the most precious sound. Priest slid his chair from the table and met Princeton on the other side.

"I'm going to get him down. I won't be long."

"Of course."

I pulled Princeton in for a hug. His body fits so perfectly in my arms.

"Goodnight."

His smile was enough to lull me to sleep each and every night. He took his father's hand as they disappeared down the hall. A quick look around the table assured me everyone had filled their bellies and it was safe to clear.

I trashed the scraps left on the plates. Before piling them into the sink, I started warm dish water and tossed a rag inside. When the temperature was perfect, I drained the towel of most of its water and headed for the table to wipe it down. Sweeping up Princeton's corn and cleaning the dishes were last on the list of things to do before I shut the kitchen down for the night.

I feel so comfortable with you. The tune was on loop in my head.

Priest's body surrounded me as I dried the few dishes we'd used. His hands rounded my waist. His chest was against my back. His head was tucked between my neck and shoulder. From side to side, he rocked us both.

"I missed you all fucking day."

"I promise not to sleep tomorrow away."

"I won't let you. I have plans for us."

"Plans?"

"Um hmm."

"What kind of plans?"

I turned around in his arms, still holding him closely.

"I want you to meet the horses."

"I'd love to."

"And jet ski on the lake."

"What about Princeton?"

"He's happiest on the water. That's why we're here so often. The jet skis are his favorite–next to the paddle boats."

"I look forward to it."

"Stay until Monday evening."

His request caught me by surprise.

"I–"

"You haven't left but all I keep thinking about is the moment you do."

"It has me holding my breath," I sighed, holding Priest's gaze.

"Stay a while longer, then."

"I'd like that. I'd like that a lot."

Feverishly, he kissed my lips. His hand cupped my butt and lifted me into the air. He placed me on the counter and immediately began fondling with the waistband of his pants. His dick sprang to life, exciting me at once. With a straightened spine, I pulled him into my hands. Up and down, I stroked his rigidness.

"Take these off," he instructed, tapping the leg of my pants.

I didn't hesitate to lift my butt so he could slide them down. The coolness of the counter raised my skin with fine bumps. Priest pulled me to the very edge and lowered his body until he was hovering over my centerpiece.

He parted my lips with two fingers, exposing my clitoris. Like a vacuum, he sucked it into his mouth and flicked his tongue backward and forward at a rapid pace. He wasn't playing fair. Not even a little.

"Uh– uhhhh. Yesss."

My body bounced from the counter, threatening to explode with each flicker of his tongue. How he was able to summon my orgasm in a matter of seconds was beyond me. He was just too damn good and I was just too damn sensitive to his touch. *To his tongue*.

"Yesssss. Uh!"

My limbs went numb. The stars appeared behind my lids, and my entire center began tingling to the point of gratifying discomfort. It was so damn good it ached.

"Ummmm. Ummmmmm. Wai– Oh God."

Priest transferred his prize from my pussy to my top set of lips. He parted them with his tongue, and coated my jaws in remembrance of me. In remembrance of what he'd just done and the yoke he was able to extract with hardly any effort.

"Uhhhhh."

He entered me from below. It felt like I'd been split in half. My walls were so tender, yet they embraced every inch of him. My contractions pulled him deeper, exposing the degree of my hunger.

"Shit, baby," he groaned against my lips.

His hands cover both ass cheeks. Slightly, he lifted me from the counter and began plowing into me. His strokes were empowering. Though slow, they were commanding. Their potency was quickly consuming me.

"Priest," I breathed into his mouth.

"Shit too good, Rose," he grunted. "Too fucking good."

The quickening of his pace led me to believe his climax was near. I was soaking wet. It was pathetic down there. The mess I'd made couldn't be cleaned with a wash rag. We'd need a shower. I was leaking profusely.

"This dick bout to cum. Fuck. This dick bout to cum."

Abruptly, Priest ejected himself. He stepped away slowly with a shake of the head.

"Off the counter. Bend over."

I couldn't keep my balance if I tried. The slippery wet counter that was covered with evidence of my explosion assisted with the impossible task he'd given. And, as soon as I'd positioned myself, he was inside of me again.

"Fuuuuuuuck." The moan had come from the depths of my soul where his dick had reached.

His hand wrapped around the back of my neck. And, the madness began.

Smack.

Smack.

Smack.

Smack.

Our bodies collided, sounding around us.

"Yes. Yes. Yesss."

Smack.

Smack.

"Goddamn," Priest fussed, "Goddamn."

Smack.

Smack.

The way he was fucking me, the way he was feeding me dick, it should've been deemed illegal. I closed my eyes, chasing the high he was promising with menacing strokes and the sound of his voice. Together, they were leading me closer to euphoria.

"That's it, dear. That's it. Arch that back and get yours."

Priest paid such close attention to detail. I was mounting and he understood it clearly. He knew how it sounded. How it felt. And, what that looked like for me. And, it wasn't until my body caved and everything around me blackened that he succumbed to his own ending.

THE GREY LIST

Saturday came and though I'd promised Priest a full day of activities, there was nothing I wanted to do more than hug the sheets with my body pressed against his. The horses he'd told me about on several occasions were as dreamy as he'd described. We spent most of the day taking them out for walks, one after the other.

Dinner was served at seven sharp. This time, it wasn't Princeton who chose our meal. And, it wasn't Priest who did the bulk of the work. I forced him out of the kitchen and into the living room for rest and relaxation while Princeton and I deepened our connection over medium-well steak, garlic potatoes, and broccoli. The meal was simple, but hearty. We all went to bed with full bellies.

In the wee hours of the night, Priest filled my belly, again. This time with dick. And, until we both drifted, he filled my ear with the sweetest nothings. I fell asleep wrapped in his arms.

Sunday was spent on the lake. Almost every water activity available, we indulged. The only activities we avoided were those that weren't safe or sensible for a five-year-old. It wasn't until six o'clock in the evening when we returned.

With exhaustion plaguing us all, Priest made the decision to order pizza instead of cooking. We piled in the family room and powered up the projector. Together, we watched Toy Story 2. By the second act, everyone was out cold.

Monday was spent in bed savoring every minute up until my departure. And, when that time came, my soul wept. My eyes stung from the tears that threatened to fall as I pulled out of the lengthy driveway and onto the street. With each mile that I traveled, I wanted to turn around and hug Priest once more. Kiss him once more.

TWELVE

Priest

Darkness surrounded us as I lowered Princeton into his carseat. My mother stood behind me, against my wishes, saying her goodbyes. From Princeton's lack of interest, I knew sleep was near. We were approaching his bedtime and I'd be surprised if he made it past the third stop sign on my mother's street before falling asleep.

"Go inside," I instructed for the second time as I closed Princeton's door.

Her stillness was baffling. Instead of heading in the opposite direction, she stood firm and crossed her arms on her chest. I didn't bother opening my door. I figured she wouldn't let me leave until she was ready, so I gave her my undivided attention.

"We're vulnerable, Dear Lady. Out here– In the open. If there was something on your mind, I really wished you'd said something before we came outside."

"I know. I– I just didn't want to be intrusive, but–"

"You can't help yourself?" I chuckled.

"I can't."

"What is it, Mother?"

She paused, taking a look around us. She stuffed her hands in the pockets of her pants and strained her pretty features. Whatever was on her mind had been bothering her for some time. I could tell by the disturbance of her prioritized peace. But, eventually, the words flowed and what came from her mouth I wasn't expecting at all.

"Who is she?"

"Mo–"

"Don't bullshit me, Priest. I know you well, son. And, I know how important companionship is to you. Lately, you've been–" she paused, struggling to express herself, "She's written all over you.

"She's made her mark. And, I'd be damned if I'm not curious as to who she is. I've seen the damage and I can't take seeing that again. I just hope she's everything you need, Priest, and not just someone you're infatuated with for the moment."

"You deserve someone who can handle your heart, son. It's one of the rarest, finest ones out there."

"She is," I confirmed.

"She is?"

"Yes, Mother. She's everything I need."

But, can't have. Not for the lifetime I need her for, anyhow.

"Good, then. I have nothing to worry about."

"You don't."

There was a pregnant pause. She was in deep thought, but I was ready to be done with the conversation. The weeks were turning over too swiftly, leaving me with less time to bask in Rather's aura. Enjoy her essence. Obsess over her presence.

"Is there anything else?"

I swung my car door open, ready to head out.

"Yes. In fact, there is."

I waited. There was no need to speak. My mother wasn't quite finished.

"Do you love her?"

Her question felt like a boulder on top of my heart. My chest tightened. The aching caused me to lift a hand and attempt to rub out the pain. The aches grew with each passing second I stared back at my mother. And when it became unbearable, the words surfaced.

"I do.

For the first time, I didn't minimize the potency of my feelings for Rather. I took full ownership of them, confessing my love to the woman who was impossible to fool. If I'd lied, she would've known instantly. But, I couldn't deny the love brewing within me for Rather. It was too precious. She was too precious. And, even in her absence, I would represent her well.

"Very much."

"Well–" she replied with a smile, "Goodnight, then, son."

"Goodnight."

2:44.

I rolled over to find the digital numbers on the clock had changed at least sixty times since I'd last had a glimpse.

Violation.

It was on rotation in my head. I'd been the head of our family since I turned thirty and there hadn't been a single instance that resulted in my disloyalty to the commandments. To the founding families are The Triad of Ara. To my family.

I didn't break code. I led by example. And, up until Rather, I'd led well.

Do you love her?

My mother didn't need to ask. She already knew. It was me that she wanted to understand it. To acknowledge it. To admit it. I had. And, now I couldn't close my eyes long enough to let sleep find me.

3:52.

Time was slipping away and I was no closer resting than I was when I laid down at eleven. Frustrated, I grabbed my phone from the nightstand. There was only one person who could put my mind at ease. She was miles away, sleeping peacefully in the room that was designed for royalty.

The phone began to ring as I began to reconsider the decision to call. Rather needed her rest, but I'd be damned if I didn't need her. After the second ring, the angelic soul that had my heart in a headlock graced the line.

"Priest," she called out to me.

Her voice was scratchy. She was in a deep sleep. I quickly regretted disturbing her but the damage had been done.

"Is everything okay?"

Now it is.

"I can't sleep."

I sat up in bed and leaned my back against the headboard.

"What's the matter?"

I'd much rather have you in my arms than be in this bed alone.

Intrusive thoughts fought for space in the moment.

"Meet me on the bridge."

From the ruffling of her covers, I knew she was getting out of bed. Her willingness and readiness to show up for me time and time again was treasured far more than she would ever know.

"Clarke?"

"Yes."

"It'll take me twenty-minutes to ma–"

I'll wait forever if that's how long it takes. It wouldn't be my first time waiting for her. I wouldn't be upset if it wasn't my last either, as long as she was coming.

"I'll see you when you get there, Rather. Drive safely."

"Okay. I love you," she rushed out, preparing to end the call.

The declaration was presented so naturally that it almost felt routine. Normal. Part of my reality and not my imagination. Though she'd rushed to get off the phone, she still hadn't hung up. Instead, labored breathing coated the line.

Her nerves were shattered. She couldn't believe she'd voice her truest feelings. She couldn't believe she'd admitted what we both already knew.

"Priest—" she breathed slowly, unsteadily.

"I love you, too."

Recanting wasn't an option, not for her and not for me. Standing in our truth was our obligation, no matter how wrong we'd deemed it. No matter how much turmoil it would cause. No matter who it would affect. No matter how forbidden it was.

Neither of us said anything more. For so long, we held the phone, silent and unmoving. I wasn't sure if we were savoring the moment or letting our transgressions marinate. Whatever the case, I sat with my head in my hands, wondering what I'd done and if there was any chance either of us could live normal lives with her closeness and my obligation to my family.

"Twenty minutes."

I nodded. "Twenty minutes."

The call ended, but I wasn't far removed from the things said during the call. Not everything, but those three words that fell from Rather's mouth so effortlessly. She'd made space for me in her heart. And, while I'd accomplished so many great things in my thirty-six years of life, conquering her heart was the greatest.

I sat at the edge of the bed with my shoulders hiked and

my palms pressing against the mattress. Not even for a second did I want to keep Rather waiting, but I needed more time with my thoughts. They'd tossed around in my head all night as I tossed in bed, but hearing her solidify everything I felt had me on a fucking rollercoaster.

When I finally got out of bed, I was in my car and on my way to the bridge in less than ten minutes. A black pullover, black sweats, and a black beanie shielded me from the November cold. I journeyed in silence. No music. No words. Nothing. My thoughts were too loud. The drumming of my heart was too intense.

Discovering I'd made it to the bridge before Rather settled my spirit. I'd gone twenty-five over the speed limit to beat her. My illegal activities had paid off. I took a seat on one of the benches and listened to the dark waters as they clashed against the shore.

So many things.

So many thoughts.

So many violations.

So many chances I had to let it go.

So many chances I had to let her go.

I didn't take any. I was already too invested. Two years of my sanity had been altered after she disrupted my world. It didn't matter that my family had arranged an even trade *—her hand in marriage for her brother's freedom.* I was invested.

"Is this seat taken?"

My eyes were still trained on the waters as I shook my head. Her fragrance was softer this time. Subtle. Sweet.

Her hand caressed the back of my neck. I closed my eyes, taking her all in without even a glance in her direction.

I didn't want to talk. I didn't want to listen. I simply wanted her in my space. If she didn't say a word, I wouldn't be opposed. The silence was enough. The craziness in my head was already too much.

"Talk to me, Priest."

With her other hand, she pulled my face in her direction. Even in her night attire, she was flawless.

"My thoughts are at war," I confessed, "You're the only person with the ability to stop it. You're my peace. I don't want anything, Rather. I don't have anything to say. I just need you near."

Her kiss was unraveling. It uprooted so many unwanted thoughts running rampant. It put me at ease and slowed my heart. The intensity of each beat remained, but they weren't as rapid. They weren't as alarming.

She pulled away too soon. I wanted her back in my space. Her lips against mine, again. Her body pressed against mine. I grabbed the bottom of her face and brought it to mine. As if she was a mind-reader, she climbed into my lap to deepen our connection and fully consume me.

Back and forward, Rather rubbed her center against me. The slip she wore underneath the ankle-length coat scrunched with every movement she made. The November chill was no match for the furnace between her legs. I could feel the fire through my pants.

Her hands roamed, searching for an escape route for my tool. I assisted by reaching into my briefs and freeing it. The satisfying sigh that came from her mouth hardened me to the point of pain.

I pulled at her gown until the end was up above her

belly button. She was pantiless. I nearly lost my shit seeing her bald pussy against my sweats.

"You like fucking with my head, Rose."

She nodded, admitting to her crime of passion. "I do."

Two fingers inside of her had her neck bending and her spine curving forward.

"Uhhhhh."

She was ready. Her temperature was just right. And, she was moist to the touch. The oven between her legs had pre-heated on the way over and was ready to bake my dish until it oozed.

Rather placed her feet on the bench, preparing to end me long before we even got started. I had the right mind to bend her ass over and fuck the filling out of her, but it would we'd be too obvious and her level of comfort would be of great concern.

I braced myself for destruction as she lowered her pussy onto my pole. She parted for me, accepting every inch. Our mouths reconnected as she began to ride me.

So poised.

So perfect.

So precious.

Rather was deeper than the waters beneath us. Her pussy felt never ending although I'd hit rock bottom and continued each time she came down on me.

"Mmmmm."

She tightened her grip around my neck.

Up.

Down.

Up.

Down.

"Ummmmm."

Up.

Down.

Up.

Down.

Her pussy was ridiculous. There wasn't a fucking thing on earth that should've felt so damn good. So inviting. So warm. So plentiful.

Her nectar narrated her movements, telling the origin story of her sopping pussy. It was the most beautiful tale. I listened closely, careful not to miss a single detail.

Her lips fell from mine. The side of her face brushed up against the stubble of my shaved beard.

Passionately, she drove her pussy into me continuously. I was unmanning right before her eyes. Each stroke of her sweetness stripped me of another layer.

Her orgasm announced itself before she could. And, when it's arrival was declared, I gripped her waist and began driving upward, digging a new path in her well for her juices to flow heavily.

"Yes. Yes. Priest. Oh God. Yes."

"Umm hmm." I encouraged her dismantling. "Cum on this motherfucker."

Her body began trembling. She could no longer support her weight. I nailed her with my hammer from below, keeping her up on her legs as my nut rose from my balls. The bulge progressed with every stroke.

"Ahhhhh! Fuck."

Like the very good girl she was, Rather came for me. I was right behind her. My ass bounced off the bench as I filled her with cum.

"I love you," breathlessly, she moaned against my cheek. "Don't ever stop."

She rested the weight of her body on mine.

"Come home with me."

"Rather, I–"

"I won't take no for an answer."

"No was never the answer."

"Turn around. Look."

Slowly, she lifted from my lap. My dick slid out of her and fell onto my sweats. She'd made a mess. Her creaminess trailed down toward the thighs of my pants. They could use a good cycle in the wash, but tossing them was the plan.

Rather settled beside me, but refused to separate completely. She laid her head on my shoulder as we both watched the sun rise slowly. It wasn't until it had taken its place in the sky that we emptied the bench.

I followed her home and parked my car in the garage alongside hers. After a shower, we climbed in bed and both drifted to sleep.

THE GREY LIST

I woke up tangled in unfamiliar sheets. However, the body beside me, bare and wrapped in the same covers, quickly dismissed my discomfort. I tapped the screen on my phone to discover it was near noon.

Princeton.

It wasn't often that I woke up in a different dwelling from my son. Each time, there was a pang of guilt that stuck with me until I saw his face again. Rather stirred in her sleep, immediately easing the internal battle I began fighting.

She was a sight I could wake up to ninety thousand times and still wouldn't grow tired. The ivory sheets against her dark skin was pure art. Images of her belonged in a gallery, one for the public to fall for just as I had.

"Sleeping beauty," I whispered in Rather's ear.

There were hardly any days off in my line of work. If I wanted to get anything done, I had to force myself out of bed and from between Rather's legs. It would be difficult, but it wasn't impossible. I was already rocking up by observing her as she slept.

"Rose."

Her features rushed to the center of her face and then relaxed again.

"Hmm?"

"Don't let the day get away from you, my dear. You should get up or you'll destroy your sleep pattern."

"Do I really have to?"

No. The word was at the tip of my tongue.

"Yes. To see me out at least. I have an appointment at three."

"Where?"

She didn't give a fuck where or why. She was prolonging the moment. I wasn't opposed, but neither did I want to tell her where I was supposed to be at three.

"My tuxedo fitting."

Her eyes popped open at once. Her upper body sprung from the bed. Frazzled and fucked well, she searched the room with her eyes.

"What time is it?"

"Almost twelve."

"God. I'm going to be late!"

"Late?"

"For my dress fitting. I'm supposed to be there at twelve-thirty. It's thirty minutes away."

"Unless you can be out of the house in five minutes, then you're already late, Rather. There's no need to rush. How about you call and see if it's possible to push your appointment back thirty minutes or so."

"She squeezed me in. She doesn't have much time to make sure the dress is perfect. I'll have at least another fitting or two to finalize things before the wedding. This is the first one. It's important."

"So is your life and your safety and the safety of everyone in your way as you try to make it on time. Call her."

"Prie–"

"Call her!" I demanded, grabbing her cell and handing it to her.

She quieted and unlocked her phone. After dialing the number, she passed it to me. There was an answer on the fourth ring.

"Cami's Bridal. How can I help you?"

"There's an appointment for Valentine at twelve thirty this afternoon."

There was a brief pause.

"Ah. Yes. In about thirty minutes."

"That appointment needs to be pushed back slightly."

"Oh no. I have a one thi–"

"Cancel it."

"I'm sorry, who is this I'm speaking with?"

"The man that is on his way down to your place of business to make a hefty contribution to your operations. Will five figures get that appointment canceled and this one pushed back?"

"Most certainly."

The response was almost instant. There was nothing else to talk about. I ended the call and handed the phone back to Rather.

"You have an hour to get dressed and to your fitting. Your life is too precious. Don't risk it for the sake of tardiness. Whatever is waiting... *whoever* is waiting can keep waiting."

Kofi had almost lost his life speeding that night. I couldn't fathom visiting a hospital room and finding Rather patched up with machines keeping her amongst the living. The lesson I'd just given was one I needed myself, but I was always careful. Always.

I doubted Rather could be under the circumstances and with the guilt of our night at the forefront of her mind. She was bound to make a mistake or become a casualty to someone else's.

"Thank you."

"You're welcome. Would you like me to take you? I'm headed that way anyway, I guess."

"No. Kleigh is meeting me there. I have to text her and tell her it's been pushed back."

I made a mental note to warn the person I'd spoken with to keep our arrangement underwraps. I didn't need Kleigh hearing about what had transpired during their appointment.

"Alright. Come on. We have to get going."

I pulled her into my arms and carried her into the bathroom where I started the shower. We'd both bathed, but after I finished with her this morning, we'd need a good scrubbing. Because we were crunched for time, sliding into her as we showered was my only option.

THIRTEEN

Priest

It had been *seventy-nine* days since Rather appeared again.

For *sixty days*, I'd been deep inside her, in every position and every chance I got.

In *eleven* days, she'd be walking down the aisle and I wasn't the man she was marrying.

Considering the code of the Triad and Kofi's pending marriage is written in stone, there's absolutely nothing left for me to do but accept my permanent position in hell. The life of leisure and liberation I once lived would be no more.

Images of her in the white dress brought a smile to my face. Kleigh had snapped the photos the day she met her at the fitting and sent them to the family's group she created without Kofi. Rather was stunning.

Her hair was swept out of her face and her smile was beaming. She looked happy. That's exactly what I wanted for her, happiness so grand she couldn't contain it. Seeing her walk down the aisle would crush my spirit but it would feed my soul.

There was someone I loved dearly benefiting from the nuptials that were sure to knot my stomach a hundred times over. But, if I had to choose between love and my brother's life, I'd choose him a hundred times over. It was easy math.

Maybe one day I'd find someone as magical as Rather. Maybe I wouldn't. What I did know was I'd only get one Kofi and it was time that nigga sat his ass down. A kid and a wife was exactly what The Triad of Ara prescribed. He was a liability to us all.

The Chemist had managed to shake himself loose of the unwanted attention, but Kofi was barking up an entirely new case with the government. Unlike Chem, he wasn't fucking a Fed. He was fucking basic, busted women who had nothing to lose but sleep at night with his dick all up their back.

His honeymoon was set to last six months. They wouldn't return to Clarke until he was tanned the color of tar. That would give us time to clean up the messes he was leaving all over the city and set him on the straight and narrow. Hopefully by then, Rather's womb would be expanding and preparing to bless the family with a child.

That was our ultimate goal. The way he cared for Princeton and would stop everything to come running if he needed his uncle was evidence he was responsible enough to father a child. More than likely, it would be just what he needed to sit down, consider his choices, and make better ones.

"Look alive, nigga!"

Kofi tossed a Red Bull in my direction.

"You're going to need that with your old ass. Princeton can't save you tonight, nigga. You're out with the boys and shit is about to get ignorant."

He wasn't telling me anything I didn't know. Chuckling, I held the can in the air and popped it. Appeasing Kofi was my sole intent tonight. Otherwise, I'd be home preparing for bed. I couldn't let him down on his night. He was preparing to commit himself and that was a huge deal to us all. It was imperative I celebrated with him.

I killed half of the can while his eyes were still trained on me.

"That's what the fuck I'm talking about. We're up all night, spending this bread and celebrating life."

He was accurate. He was turning a new leaf. Money was plentiful and it would be spent.

A flock of women boarded the private aircraft. I didn't have prior knowledge of their involvement, but I wasn't in attendance to complain. I was simply supervising to make sure my brother returned in one piece. Who he fucked wasn't my business.

As they all got seated, he slid toward me and took the seat next to me. I shut my phone down so the picture on my screen wasn't visible.

"Listen, there are five of these fine motherfuckers. I done hit 'em all but sharing is caring, right? I'm taking two for myself tonight. The thickest one and that one, Hailey. She's my favorite. You can have one for yourself. Killian already trying to stunt like his little brother and knock down two, but we're going to see if that nigga really bout the shit he claim."

"I have no interest in either of your guests. You and Killian and have them all to yourself. You and Silk. Ice. Whoever. I'm here for the fun, my bro. You can keep the pussy."

"Nigga, you sure you ain't getting poked out here?"

"Don't make me shoot you in your fucking mouth, Kofi."

"So serious," he sniggered. "But, real shit, you sure you don't want none of this pussy? It's free."

"Nothing in life is free, Kofi. And, make sure you're strapping up. Your wife is expecting an STD-free husband without a child on the way."

"And that's exactly what she'll get, police ass nigga."

"Get the fuck out of my face. I'm here for a good time. Don't ruin that for me."

"I'm not. I'm just happy your old ass out. Wheels up in five. Come alive, nigga."

It didn't matter how much of an asshole he was, Kofi owned such a huge piece of my heart. I'd clear the whole globe for him.

Berkeley City. It was my brother's destination of choice. Though it was an easy drive down to the city, the thirty-minute flight guaranteed our safety and swift return. There wouldn't be a fully sober individual leaving the strip club

Kofi had chosen and reserved the largest section they had to offer.

I sat back and watched from afar as everyone indulged in pointless debates and constant laughter. It was a blessing seeing the men I shared the same blood with make it to the age of twenty-one. Where we came from, niggas were blessed to see twelve. Our father had gotten us out of the trenches and into mansions around the city.

Though my mother was left with hundreds of thousands when her mate passed, she was afraid of draining her accounts by moving out of the hood. She hadn't worked a day in her life and didn't plan to start. The money she was in possession of would have to last a while, or at least until she found something worth investing in.

Before she could, I was born and her world changed. My father became her sole provider. Till this day, he provided for her. The money she was holding onto gained interest each year. She was sitting on a bag with the deed to her home, a new car every three years, and whatever her heart desired. Between my father and I, she didn't have to worry about anything.

By the time we were comfortable in-flight, the wheels were on the ground.

"Ready to have the night of your life?" Kofi asked, patting my shoulder.

With a shrug, I answered his question.

"This nigga uptight and shit. Needs his dick sucked. Which one of you ladies would be kind enough to loosen the tension in my big brother's spine? Nigga puts in so much fucking work he probably hasn't seen his own dick other than when he's washing niggas blo—"

"Enough."

His words were beginning to slur. His balance was questionable. Killian and I locked eyes, instantly. What was understood between us didn't need an explanation. A simple head nod assured me he was on the same page as me and letting Kofi out of our sight was not happening at any point of our night.

"I'm up for the challenge. He looks like a big boy."

The petite, caramel skinned beauty with dimples deep enough to fill with semen spoke up.

"I'd split you in half, love. Stay in your lane."

The rest of the crew erupted in laughter. Kofi pounded the seat next to him, finding my response comical. Until he had the chance to experience Rather in ways I had, he wouldn't understand my lack of interest in any other woman.

She had some shit you couldn't shake back from. Paired with her personality, aura, and essence... She was a triple threat. It wasn't easy agreeing to give yourself to anyone else when you knew you had access to something as celestial as Rather's pussy.

"As long as you piece me back together, I don't mind."

"I don't have that type of time."

Dismissing her a second time, I hoped she received the message. If not, the next words to come from my mouth wouldn't be as tolerable. They'd likely fuck up her whole night.

"Everybody out. Everybody out," Killian interjected, saving Kofi's guests from embarrassment.

One by one, we filed off the plane with Killian and I staying behind the rest of the crew.

"Four hours, maximum."

"I'm on the same time you're on," Killian agreed.

"He's already plastered. Your clip loaded?"

"And ready to eat through some flesh."

"Because someone is going to jail or to the morgue tonight if we don't keep this nigga in line."

"It won't be one of us."

"Can't be," I assured him.

"You good, though? Can't believe we got your ass out of the house."

"All hands on deck tonight. Besides, I couldn't miss his big night. This nigga won't be living the bachelor's life too much longer."

"This nigga really about to tie the knot before the both of us. Shit wild but the shit is necessary. I'm happy Pops stood ten toes down behind his decision. The last thing I want to do is lose that nigga, no matter how foolish he is."

"He is a fucking headache, but he's our headache."

"For life."

"For life."

"You ready to spend that fucking money on them hoes, nigga."

"And you talking about you're surprised I'm outside. Nigga, all he had to do was whisper strip club and I was in. Ain't shit like ass in your face, money in your pocket, and the entire world at your palms."

"Fuck celebrating that motherfucker. We're celebrating life!"

"That too." I nodded. "That too."

. . .

Kofi took the first SUV. Silk and Ice piled into the second one. Killian and I, along with two of the women from the plane, followed behind them in the third.

Left.

Right.

Light.

Right.

Three miles.

Light.

Left.

A mile.

Right.

"You have arrived at your destination."

It was a twelve-minute drive to Lust. I remembered every turn, stop light, and lengthy stretch. In the event our escape depended on our recognizance, it was important I knew how to get us back to where the fuck we'd come from.

Hastily, everyone filed out of the SUVs at the very back of the establishment. The private entrance lowered the chances of unwanted encounters. With Kofi leading the pack, it was best we stayed far away from the crowd and moved along in silence.

The bass of the speakers grew louder as the entry to the main floor opened. The hostess led us through the dimly lit space and to a section near the main stage.

"This won't work," I said to no one in particular as I pushed forward to get the attention of the hostess who'd shown us to the section.

"Hey," I called out, "Excuse me."

With her chest inflated and her braces on full display,

she turned around to face me. "How can I help you, Cutie?"

Cutie? I couldn't help the distortion of my facial features.

"You're talking to a grown ass man, love. Ain't shit cute about me."

"I–"

"Now that we've got that out of the way, this section won't work."

"That's the section you paid for." With a roll of her neck she reminded me of what I already knew and tried storming off. Before she could get far, Killian stepped in front of her and nodded in my direction.

"Ma'am, my brother was still speaking to you."

"Like I told your brother, this is the section you paid for."

"Then, I can pay for another one. We need something against the wall. Something like that."

"It's not close to the stage. Whoever reserved the section was adamant about it being close to the stage."

"And, I'm adamant about it being against the wall. We brought in enough cash to bring the motherfucking stage to us. We're not worried about that."

I took a look around, trying to find a better spot and a solution to our problem before chaos unfolded.

"That one. Give us that one."

"This one is twice that size."

"Then give us two of them motherfuckers. Baby, do you care about your job? Because it doesn't seem like you do. You're not very helpful right now. I've expressed this section doesn't work for us. Fix it or find me somebody who will. In fact, bring me the boss. I prefer conversing with peers on the same level as me. They are fluent in problem-solving. That doesn't seem to be your strength."

"One second. Let me go see what I can do."

"That's your best option."

She stormed off toward the door we'd just come through. Waiting for her to return wasn't in the plans. If she wasn't willing to make a way, I would make my own or we wouldn't be enjoying their entertainment for the night.

The duffle in Ice's hand wasn't for decoration. We weren't purse-toting, fashion-forward niggas. By definition, we were gangsters. That bag was full of bands, not air. It was bound to be a movie when the zipper was toggled, but the previews wouldn't resume until we were comfortable with our seating arrangement.

"Gather them all. We're moving."

I was still in clear view of everyone I'd come with as I stopped in front of the reserved sections that had piqued my interest. I laid the signs confirming the reservations made for them on the tables down gently and backed up in the booth until the back of my legs were pressed against the leather. A quick sweep across the club put my worries to rest. The view was flawless.

Back against the wall. My father's lesson hadn't failed us yet. Tonight wouldn't be the night we went astray.

"Perfect."

Killian gathered everyone who'd taken an interest in the section we'd been given. Kofi had yet to plant his feet, which let me know he wasn't too plastered to consider the danger of our location. Without hesitation, he followed Killian over to the sections I'd claimed for us.

"I was not feeling that shit," Kofi admitted as he slid into the booth beside me.

"Don't worry. I've got you. It's your night young nigga."

"Yes the fuck it is and it's about to get stupid."

"Have your fun. I'm your eyes and ears for the night."

Ice and Silk took the booth next to us. Killian, Kofi, and I stayed in the one at the very end.

"This section is reserved for the night. I was clear when I told you that," she sassed.

The hostess had returned with management. We'd already settled and weren't moving.

I leaned in, unbothered by her tone of voice, "And, I was clear when I told you I wanted it."

"You can't decide whe–"

"And you–" I interrupted her, "No longer have permission to speak to me. I asked for the boss. Where that nigga at, because these motherfuckers ain't it."

"Boss man sent us."

"Why isn't he here himself?"

"He's not here tonight. He's home."

"I'm sure he has a number."

I removed my cell from my pocket, ready to find out everything there was to know about the owner of Lust, down to which toothbrush he used to brush his teeth in the morning.

"There's no need to call him. We'll work it out. Move some shit around. Enjoy your night and let us know if there's anything else you need."

"Your best five."

"Come again?"

"Your best five. If they aren't here tonight, get them here by the time that bag opens. We're feeling a bit generous tonight."

Wealth was dancing in the diamonds of our watches, chains, and teeth. Killian's entire mouth was iced out. Kofi had on more jewelry than a chart-topping rapper. Me, on the other hand, preferred a more simple approach.

The new Richard Mille on my wrist made it difficult to conceal my account status, but that's exactly how it was supposed to be. My father had taught me a long time ago that a man's timepiece should announce his presence in a room before he ever had the chance to.

Just like it told the time, it would tell another man how to speak to you, how to address you, how you operated, how much work you'd put in, and how full your belly was each night you went to bed.

"Don't worry. We've got you."

The two niggas she'd brought over to assist us gave us a thumbs up and got back to business.

THE GREYLIST

I'd requested the best five in the building or in their bed and that's exactly what we'd been given. They rotated each time one of them hit the stage. It was crucial we kept our lineup fresh.

"This motherfucker gots to come home with me," Killian leaned over and said to me.

I sipped from the same cup I'd had for the last thirty minutes. He was on his sixth. I'd counted each one. Kofi had gone from sipping cups to sipping straight from the bottle. I couldn't keep up.

Though I was on my level, I was far from intoxicated. I had to be everyone's eyes. Someone had to get us back to Clarke safely and there was no doubt in my mind it would be me.

"You said that about the last three. There won't be enough room on the plane if you stay another twenty minutes, nigga. Where will we sit?"

"Plane? I'm taking her to the hotel."

His claim was news to me.

"Hotel?"

"Penthouse suites. Kofi reserved four of them in the event we decided to stay."

"Kofi has an appointment with the jeweler at noon. Has he forgotten."

"I don't think the nigga gives a fuck. He's having the time of his life."

With a shake of my head, I scoffed, "He's going to be on that plane by eleven. I don't care if I have to drag him to that motherfucker myself."

"I'll take his legs. You got his arms?" Killian looked at me.

There was a second of silence before we both sniggered.

"You're drunk."

"Then a motherfucker. But, real shit. This one, I'm taking home."

He smacked the stripper that had been working over-time in front of him on the ass. I couldn't blame him. She was gorgeous with a body that made you consider taking her fine ass out of the strip club and securing her member-ship at the country club.

"You wouldn't be wrong. Not at all."

Jeezy pounded the speakers around us, forcing everyone to yell at the top of their lungs with their chests penetrating the air. Kofi's arm went around Killian's neck as Killian turned toward me and began tapping my chest.

"Still playing with them Ms, thinking like a felon!" Killian recited the words we all knew by heart.

A few lines passed before Kofi joined him. "That work don't even come like that."

"Fuck is you selling?" I added.

"Gave you niggas a whole lane, whole lane," Killian jumped in.

"That's better than me frontin' a nigga the whole thang," I chimed in, using my free hand for emphasis.

The bass rattled every piece of glass in the establish-ment. The dancer on the stage clapped her ass to the beat, making tidal waves in the process. Everybody was up on their feet, spitting lyrics as if they applied to them.

As for us, they weren't fiction. Everything we were spit-ting were facts. Nevertheless, the unison of the entire building had the fine hairs under my Louis Vuitton jacket standing at attention.

"Love this money making like Mitch, can't leave the gammmmme," Kofi sang.

"Only thing get us excited is money and caine," Killian finished his sentence.

The Dj let the record spin, doing everybody a favor. The song could loop three times and we wouldn't be tired. The track almost felt like a personal anthem.

"I can work four pots at a time." I patted Killian's chest, reminding him of the times. "Bitch Imma robot."

"The only thing keeps crossing my mind–"

We said in unison, "I hope the doe locked."

I skipped the next line to finish my piece with, "Twenty seasons straight no stain. Let's call it fate."

I let them take the rest and settled for watching them rally around the life we'd built for ourselves with the foundation our father laid for us as children.

My brothers. They were a beautiful sight. I'd lay my life on the line for them. Any day. Any time. Any place.

The night continued without flaw. Long before the DJ was scheduled to stop spinning hits, we pushed our way through the back door. Kofi was unable to stand. One of his arms was draped over Killian and the other dangled over my shoulder.

"I love y'all. I swear," he slurred.

"Yeah," Killian replied, knowing he wouldn't shut up if no one did.

"Nah. Nah. For real. I know a nigga be fucking up. I know. But, Ima get my shit together. Y'all set me up with one of the baddest motherfuckers in all of Clarke. I've been a bitch about it, but I get it. I understand. I do. I promise."

He was rambling, but I was listening. It was this very moment I'd been waiting for all along.

"I'm ready, though. Ima buy us a fat ass crib. Have a few

kids. Sit my ass down. I can't keep up with all the women I'm fucking, their birthdays, Valentine's Day, Christmas... It's a shit show, man. Every fucking year. I'm trying to remember one birthday from this point on. Celebrate Valentine's Day with one woman. Celebrate Christmas with one woman. Stick my dick in one woman. Well, after I stick my dick in the two I have lined up for tonight."

We all joined in laughter.

"I'm taking the week to sober up and get my head in the game. Pops won't ever talk to my black ass if I fuck this up. Moms won't forgive me if I destroy *her* dream wedding. Kleigh– I can kiss my favorite person in the world goodbye if I don't come through. I can't disappoint them."

Kofi's sober thoughts were the new source of entertainment.

"Plus, that fucking maniac of a brother she has will likely kill me if I play his sister."

"It'll be war."

"Have you not heard of The Huntress nigga? We won't stand a chance. She'll take us all out before we can blink. And, if she can't get the job done, it's seven other motherfuckers that can. I guarantee you the little baby that Fed pushed out is in training right now. I'll bet my last she knows how to shoot a pistol right now."

"She's a baby," I reminded him.

"I don't give a fuck. Bet me," he challenged.

"I'm not betting you, Kofi. You're right."

I wasn't in the mood to dispute his claims.

"I don't trust the women you're contemplating taking to the penthouse that I knew nothing about."

"It's cool. They're cool. I promise. Hailey gone make sure I'm straight."

"I'm going to take the second bedroom in the suite, Boss," Silk hollered over his shoulder.

"Appreciate it."

"You know I've got his front and his back. He's alright. I can bet you that."

Silk wasn't lying. He had saved Kofi from destruction so many times I'd lost count. Tonight was more of the same. With him in the same suite as Kofi, he'd be looked after and cared for as if one of us was near.

We climbed back into the SUVs we'd come in with the same drivers at the wheels. This time, there was a woman sandwiched between Killian and I. Though he was the more responsible of the sibling pair, he wasn't above my concern.

"Killian."

"What's up?"

"I need you to tell me you can handle yourself tonight."

"You don't have to worry about me, Priest. I'm good. I can promise you that. My head is in the right place. This water will be my saving grace."

He held up the bottle in his hand.

"I had liquid IV in my cup all day. I'll be straight. I'm hydrated and will continue to hydrate."

"Good."

We arrived at *Bergamont*, our hotel of choice whenever visiting the city. It was in a secluded part of Berkeley and there were few people able to secure reservations in the prestigious dwelling. Your money had to be long and your connections had to be plentiful. Thankfully, neither was a problem for us.

It wasn't until everyone had filed out that Killian noticed I wasn't in tow. He turned back and opened the door of the SUV almost immediately.

"What you doing?" He inquired, face knotted with confusion.

"Staying overnight was never in my plans. I've made sure you and Kofi are safe. My job here is done. I'll be back in the morning to drag that nigga out of the pussy and onto the plane. Be ready."

"I got his legs," he laughed.

"You've got the legs." I confirmed.

"Bet. Be safe, nigga. See you in the morning."

"First thing."

He slammed the door and caught up to the woman waiting for him. I watched them all as they made it inside and through the lobby. When they turned the corner to get on the elevator, I tapped the seat of the driver.

"Let's go."

Twenty-three minutes later we were on the tarmac. I climbed the stairs of the plane alone. Clarke was on my radar. Soon, Berkeley would be in my rearview. There was nothing for me here. Everything I wanted, *everything I needed*, was miles and miles away.

I'm on my way.

Somberness weakened my resolve. The thirty-minute flight was the perfect reward after a night of socialization. Now that the party was over, I needed peace. *I needed her.*

It was four-thirty in the morning and I was sitting outside of Rather's home with the engine of my car running and the phone pressed against my ear.

"Hello?"

Sleeping beauty, I thought as the scratchiness of her throat coated the line.

"Rather."

"Yes?" She groaned.

"Open the garage."

"You're here?"

"I am."

"Mm kay. Is everything alright?"

"It is now."

"Okay. I'm coming down."

I ended the call and waited for the garage door to lift. It wasn't long before she appeared behind it, waiting near the garage door for me to enter. I killed the engine and stepped out, finally succumbing to the exhaustion of the full day I'd had.

I stopped a few feet short of Rather. She was in her best even when she slept. Beige slippers covered her feet. The same color pants and shirt covered the rest of her body. Pushed up over her forehead was a matching mask for her eyes. Her hair was wrapped around a big contraption that started at the center of her head and ended near her neck.

She's truly a figment of my wild imagination. If I didn't know any better, I'd swear she was made up.

The two drinks I'd consumed at *Lust* coupled with the one I had on the plane combined to give me a pleasurable buzz. I could feel the silly smile on my face, but couldn't wipe it away if I tried. But, I had no reason to. Not with Rather standing before me.

"Hey."

"Hey," I responded, taking strides to reach her.

She held out her hand, convincing me to grab hold. I followed her toward the door. She shut off the garage light just as we entered her home.

Quietly, she led me into the kitchen. We stopped near the fridge where she retrieved a bottle of water. I leaned against the counter and expanded my limbs. Her body fit perfectly between my legs.

She untwisted the cap and placed the tip of the bottle against my lips. I opened up, allowing her to pour water into my mouth. After a few seconds, she lowered it, waiting for me to consume what she'd already given.

When she felt like I was ready again, she continued. Twice more, she repeated the same steps. The empty bottle crumbled as she tossed it in the recycling bin.

"Better?"

I nodded, pulling her closer. I couldn't help but wrap her up in my arms.

"Mmmm." My body released a satisfying moan when I felt her in my palms again.

"I'm tired, baby."

"I know," I responded.

"Come on."

She stepped back and took my hand, again. Like a lovesick puppy, I followed behind her until we reached the bedroom where she got rid of my jacket. My shirt was next. Neatly, she folded it and laid it on the ottoman beside us.

She unfastened my belt and jeans before pushing them both down my legs. I stepped out of them as she eased them out of my way.

Rather was the first in bed. She pulled me down onto the mattress with her. And, instead of wrapping her in my arms. It was her arms I was wrapped in. I wouldn't protest. It was, undoubtedly, the best feeling in the world. There was no place I'd rather be.

Pressed against her chest with her legs and arms holding me as close to her as was physically possible, I found the peace I was in pursuit of.

THE GREY LIST

Sunlight greeted me with kisses on the face. The brightness reminded me why Rather slept with a mask covering her eyes. No longer was I wrapped in those long arms of hers, permanently documenting her scent in my brain.

Instinctively, I slid my hand across the bed, expecting to find a cool, empty space. To my surprise, it was Rather's frame I encountered. I pulled my eyelids apart, eager to greet her. Blurriness blinded me momentarily. When I finally regained my vision and got a glimpse of her, Rather was staring back at me.

"Good morning," cheerfully, she chortled.

"Good morning."

I didn't recognize my voice. I'd raised it so many times last night so that I was heard over the music, I'd stressed my vocal cords.

"What time is it?"

She slid down while pushing the covers back. In one swift motion, she released my dick from my briefs. It was hard as a missile anticipating take-off.

"Even if there's someplace you have to be right now, you won't make it. At least not for the next few minutes."

She'd made it clear I was stuck with her for as long as she wanted me and I couldn't protest.

Spuh!

She hawked a load of spit on the tip of my dick. My chest caved. That pretty face of hers split to accommodate me, solidifying her claims. I wasn't going any fucking where.

I placed a hand behind her head and guided myself into her mouth. Just like I'd done her insides time and time again, I fucked her warmth. The deeper I dived, the more her eyes glossed over.

"You've got it," I told her, tapping the back of her throat with each stroke.

Her body curled as her gag reflex was activated.

Fuck.

Saliva was plentiful. Her tongue swirled around the head every time I retracted.

Shit.

My ass cheeks hurt from the clenching. She was lethal in her pursuit of my semen.

"Urgh." The groan was the warning before destruction.

She was on the verge of puking. While it disgusted me to consider her meal on her good sheets, it made my dick harder and my stroke more intense.

"Don't spit up or we're starting over," I warned.

Her eyebrows furrowed on her face. She strained to keep the contents of her stomach down. The bulge of my dick started from the very beginning of my shaft and began traveling upward. I wasn't ready to bust, but I couldn't let go of Rather's head. Neither could I pull out.

"Get up," I demanded, hoping she could manage to put me out of my misery. "Get up."

She succeeded. With her knees tucked under her, she stared back at me with curious eyes.

"Take that shit off, Rather. Come sit on 'em."

Quietly, she rounded her shoulders and closed her eyes. Her demeanor changed in a split second.

"Talk to me."

Her posture was different. Her words were softer. Her apprehension was apparent.

"My period is here."

"So am I. You can get rid of them clothes or I can do it for you."

The worry lines that creased her face dissolved at once. Swollen breasts and chocolate, pebbled nipples replaced the top Rather wore to bed. She handed it over, and nodded at the fresh sheets beneath me. I lifted up from the bed and laid the shirt down.

I maneuvered Rather's body, positioning her right on top of it. She'd yet to get rid of the pants she'd worn through the night, which now made perfect sense. I slid them down her legs, expecting to find evidence of the monthly massacre.

Instead, I was met by a barely streaked sanitary pad in the center of her panties. I tossed it all into a pile beside the bed. With her body beneath mine, I placed my dick at her center.

"How are you feeling?"

"Desperate."

She swallowed hard. Rapid blinks confirmed her split nerve endings.

"I'm right here, Rose."

"Put him in."

I smiled, ready to put her out of her misery. I'd heard a handful of times that a woman's sex drive increased tremendously during her menstrual cycle. Her hormones were raging and more than likely, she was craving penetration during the very time the world had deemed it forbidden. I didn't give a fuck what rules the world had created for women's periods, but they didn't apply to me. Today, they didn't apply to Rather either.

"It's the third day," she revealed.

"I wouldn't care if it was the first, my dear."

I sealed her lips with a kiss and slid right into homebase. Her fingers tightened around my elbows.

"Uhhhh–"

Goddamn.

Upon entry, I understood my demise was near. I quickly learned it was likely the men the rules were made to protect. Because her walls were snugger. Her temperature was higher. Her depth was deeper. Her flesh was softer.

"Fuck," I whispered in her mouth. "Damn."

Passion possessed me. Pussy dominated me. I was losing the battle without even a slight chance of coming out the same man I'd gone in as.

"Umm."

The pressure was far too intense, forcing me from the bed where I hovered over Rather's body.

"My God. Mmmm."

One look at her beautiful face and I was a fucking wreck. I reached below and swirled my thumb around her clit while applying pressure. I was near my ending and I needed her to join me on the other side.

"Yessssss."

She arched her back, lifting it from the shirt underneath her. Her nipples spiked the air, inviting me in for a taste. I rounded my spine to meet her right breast.

"Priesssssst."

She was the sweetest melody on a stormy night. She was the crackling of a warm fireplace. She was the purplish hue from the sun's glow in the early morning hours when most of the world was sleeping. She was pleasure. She was pain.

Letting her go would be the hardest thing I'd ever have to do. It would cut me deeply, leaving me restless and wounded.

"Priesss— Uhhhh!."

Her contractions pulled me deeper.

"Uhhhh."

"Urgh."

I participated in the blood ritual that was sacred and rightfully so. With each stroke of my dick, the knot our souls had established tightened. The final one sealed our fates and bid us farewell, breaking my heart in half.

I collapsed onto the bed next to Rather. We both lie

speechless. The caving of our chests was the only movement made. Our sporadic breaths were the only sounds present.

The weight of our world came crashing down on me. Emotions swelled my chest. Hearing Kofi profess his intentions for their union felt more like confirmation for me than a confession of his. And, this moment felt more like closure than progress for Rather and I.

The deep, unsteady breath she pulled in sent a pang through my chest. I didn't have to look over. I didn't need to look over. I knew those big, curious eyes were no longer dry. For the life of myself, I couldn't bring myself to see tears fall down her cheeks. I couldn't see her cry. It would only make my departure much harder than it already was.

"I won't see you again, will I?"

I sifted through the words in my head, trying to find any that would heal the brokenness we'd created. There were none.

"I never said that, Rather."

She cleared her throat, trying to avoid the cracking that was inevitable. As soon as more words sprouted, so did more tears.

"You didn't have to," she paused to gather herself, "My heart said so."

"Your heart is right, Rose. I have to go and I won't return."

From my peripheral, I watched her nod. I'd confirmed her suspicions. I'd broken her heart. And, I'd ended what would go down in my history book as the greatest seventy-nine days of my life.

I didn't have the strength to look at her when I gathered my belongings. I didn't have the strength to look at her when I strolled into the bathroom. I didn't have the strength to look at her once I'd taken care of my hygiene and returned to her bedroom. And, I didn't have the strength to look at her when I exited.

As she wept, so did I. Though the tears never touched my skin, they tatted my heart. Forever, I'd be reminded of her. Of us. Of what could've been but would never be.

FOURTEEN

Rather

The blades of the ceiling fan circled, hypnotizing me and pulling me deeper into the trance I couldn't pull myself out of. The week leading up to a woman's wedding was said to be the most stressful time of a bride's life. No one mentioned the heartache. The sadness. The mourning of the life you were leaving behind to join another.

Five days.

It had been five whole days since Priest had left me in bed and I'd been unable to pull myself out of it for anything other than feeding my aching belly and emptying my bladder. I hadn't showered. I hadn't picked up a comb. I hadn't taken out the trash. I hadn't seen clearly in five whole days.

"Sssss," I winced.

My eyelids were swollen to the point of pain and tender to the touch. With each blink, it felt like shards of glass were scrapping the underside of my skin. I'd used seventy Kleenex.

Get up, Rather. Teddy's voice chastised me. I could hear the disappointment in his voice, but I was in no shape to comply.

"I can't," I choked out. "I've tried."

On queue, my phone vibrated beside me. Wishful thinking led me to the screen where I slightly prayed that Priest's contact would appear.

Kleigh. I lowered the phone onto the bed, reluctant to answer for anyone other than my sisters, mother, Teddy, or *him*.

It vibrated again. Kleigh was persistent. She wouldn't stop calling until I answered. This was *her* week. This was *her mother's* week. And, she wouldn't let me ruin it even if I tried.

"Hello?"

"Rise and shine, my girl. We have a big day. The final fitting is at four. You'll go straight to the Edgar's Hall after where hair and makeup will be waiting to get you together for the dinner tonight. But, before the dinner, we have a quick rehearsal. And then there's tomorrow!"

She was jubilant. Her joy was contagious. The way she packaged the dream she was selling and offered it to me brought a smile to my face.

"The wedding."

"Yes. The wedding!" She squealed. "Why do I sound more excited than you?"

Because you are.

"Maybe because every member of your family is present."

"Awwww, baby. I'm so sorry. My father and Chemistry said they were working to get that squared away. I'm sure between the two of them, everything will work out. They wouldn't miss your day. I know they wouldn't."

She was right. Chemistry would move waters, literally, to make it to me.

"We have dresses for all the girls according to the measurements they sent. Even little Miss Jru has a dress."

"Thank you."

"I told you I've got you and not to stress. Have you taken this week to relax like I told you?"

I've cried every day this week, Kleigh. My heart is broken. I don't know peace right now. I can't relax.

"Yes."

"Well, good, because we have a busy day ahead of us. Then, the wedding. And, after that you can spend the next six months recuperating from the eventful weekend."

"Noted."

"Alright, now get up and start getting ready. It's already one o'clock."

"Okay, okay. I'm getting up."

Two hours.

I had two hours to minimize the swelling of my eyes and reflect the same energy as my future sister-in-law. Though it wasn't looking promising, I had a group of women ready to rally behind me and help me get my shit together so my day could truly begin.

But, first, a call to my mother was essential. I needed her light and I needed her wisdom.

FaceTime was too insulting, so I opted for a phone call, instead. As the line turned over and began to ring, I rested my back against the upholstered headboard.

I could still smell Priest on my sheets. I could still hear him sleeping soundly beside me. I could still feel him inside of me.

"Rather."

Like a gentle hug after heartbreak, every girl needed from their mother, my mother's voice wrapped around me.

"Mom," I breathed out, heavily. Tears fell from my cheeks. I swiped them as quickly as they came.

"Baby, what's the matter?"

Unable to hold it in any longer, I rushed out, "I fell in love, Mom."

"Oh, baby, what's with the tears?"

"It's not with him," I cried, "It's not him."

"Rather–" she sighed, "I'm sorry."

"It's his brother I've fallen for. It's Priest."

"Baby, I have met Priest. And, as a happily married woman when I did, I must say I don't fault you. That young man is– He's–"

She stumbled over her words.

"Exactly what my heart needs."

"But can't have."

I shook my head. "It can't."

"So, hold your head high, Rather. Once the crying is over, stand tall and take your position in the family as you rightfully should. You're not the first woman to settle for what she could have instead of what she truly wanted. You won't be the last."

"It breaks my heart to know this is your reality, but it's reality nonetheless. Give yourself grace. Sulk if you want to. Cry as much as you need to. But, tomorrow, I want you standing at the altar, ten toes down, fulfilling your obligation."

"And, when it's all over, I want you to remain true to yourself, but true to the vows you've made. Waging war between brothers is not the solution. Priest was yours to have for a little while. Kofi is yours to have forever. It's not the end of your world, Rather. It's just the beginning of a new one."

I digested her words, taking them for exactly what they were. She hadn't steered me wrong in life. Today wasn't the day she'd start.

"You hear me?"

"Yes."

"Good."

I paused, preparing for the ultimate heartbreak to roll off her tongue.

"Will you make it?"

"Make what?"

"The wedding?"

"I wo–"

Ding. Dong.

The doorbell interrupted her train of thought.

"Is that your door?"

"Uh– Yes. I'm not expecting anyone. Hold on, Mom."

I lowered the phone and exited the call screen without hanging up. The camera app opened with a single tap. Darkness covered the camera in front of my home, yet the rest were crystal clear.

"Hello?" I put the phone back up to my ear.

"Yes. I'm here."

"I'm going to call you back later, okay?"

"No you're not," she fussed, "Stay on the phone with me until you find out who is behind that door."

"Okay."

I hopped off the bed and into my closet where I grabbed a pair of sweats. I wasn't one to wear them often, but for quick runs to the end of the driveway to sit the dumpster out or to the garage to retrieve something from my car they served their purpose.

I stuffed my gun in the waistline and headed downstairs. I could smell the day's debris on my body as the wind from my speed picked up. Inside the kitchen, I twisted the knobs on the stove.

Click.

Click.

Click.

Click.

Click.

Click.

I grabbed the Tiger-striped firearm and concealed my collection by turning the knobs again.

Click.

Click.

Click.

Click.

Click.

Click.

Full speed ahead, I walked toward the front door. When I was close enough, I shouted the first order.

"State your name or I'm shooting through the glass. Fair warning, I do not miss!"

I waited for a response. The silence was frustrating.

"Who the fuck are you and what the fuck do you want?"

When the silence continued, I began to pressure the trigger.

"Fine."

"It's me!"

Rome's voice stilled every muscle in my body. It gutted me of everything and then refilled me with love. Her love. Their love. Because, I knew if she was here, she hadn't come alone.

I unlocked the door and yanked it open.

"Shut up!" I cried, wrapping my arms around Rome.

Rugger was next. Then Roaman. Then Roulette. Then Range. Then Royce. My girls were here. My loves. My lifeline. My support system. *My everything*.

"Why didn't you guys tell me you were coming?" I could feel the snot dripping from my knows, but it didn't matter. Nothing mattered at the moment. Nothing but them."

"We should've so you could've bathed," Rugger grunted, pressing her way through the door.

"You funky! Like, the shit is offensive. Get back!" Roulette stepped back as she dug into her purse.

She pulled out a bottle of Dior perfume and began spritzing in my direction.

"Ugh. Smell like a box of old fruit. The hell you got going on in here?"

She stepped past me and into the house.

"She's so dramatic," Rome whispered, "But seriously, you do stink."

"Where's Mom?"

"She's flying in, in the morning with Teddy, Jru, and Egypt. He didn't want us all on the same flight."

"Always careful." I smiled, acknowledging the head of our family and his procedures.

"That's Teddy," Rome added.

"God, I've missed you all. I have so much to tell you."

"You have forty-eight hours to tell us. That's how long we're here," Rugger yelled over her shoulder as she walked past.

"Which means Mom and Chemistry only have twenty-four," Rome informed me.

The heavy breath she released told me she hated to be the bearer of bad news, but it had to be revealed.

"Shit. Mom is still on the line."

I removed my phone from my pocket to find she'd already ended the call.

"Good. She hung up already."

"She could smell the funk from that back pocket. She passed the fuck out. Now, I've got to have Chem go check on her," Roulette teased, calling our mother on her phone and walking off.

Neither of them had been to my home, but they all seemed to know every nook and cranny. Collectively, they began cleaning the mess I'd accumulated over the last five days. When Roulette reappeared, she wasn't empty-handed. She'd dug in her bag and retrieved all the goods.

"Come on. We're going upstairs to get you all the way together. I'm about to scrub your ass myself. Make sure it's nice and clean."

She led me up the stairs and into my bathroom where she stripped me bare. After starting the shower, she gave me a good once-over.

"Okay, now talk to Momma."

Roulette was the only person in the family who referred to herself as Momma, but we never revoked her right. Though she was indeed the wildest, she had the tendency to treat, talk to you, and nurture you like a mother. Just like most of us, she had no desire to birth children of her own, but she owned more than one establishment full of young, ambitious girls that she mothered better than some of the women who birthed them.

"Thing between us ended."

"You knew this was how it would play out."

I nodded. "I did. I just didn't expect it to feel like someone stole my heart out of my chest."

"They didn't. It'll hurt for a while, but you'll get through it. I promise."

"I know."

"So, are you done crying about it, babe? Because whether you want it to or not, life goes on."

"I am."

"Good. If you decide you're not, that's okay, too. I have a shoulder right here for you to cry on. I just need you to bathe first or we'll both be crying together."

"Shut up!" I chortled.

Though a chunk of me left with Priest out of my door, having my sisters around made me feel whole again. The last three months without them had been torture. I never wanted to experience life without them. They made everything alright, *even when it wasn't*.

"Come on. Get in. I have my work cut out for me."

"You're insufferable. Has anyone told you that lately?"

"Chem and he's starting to sound like a broken record."

The steam from the shower clouded the mirrors and glass all around us. When I stepped into the shower, the temperature was perfect. I reached for my loofah and was immediately scolded.

"Uh Mm. Don't touch nothing in there. I got everything you need right here."

She patted the toiletry bag she'd brought in. Roulette removed a pair of exfoliating gloves and swiped them under the water. She then lathered them until a thick foam was in both her palms. Soon after, her hands were on me, scrubbing away the pain and strife the week had caused.

By the time she grabbed the shower hose to rinse it all off, Rome had joined us. She was carrying a fluffy robe and towel. Roaman was right behind her, trying to balance four glasses of wine in her hands. Royce carried another three. Range came through the door with her intrusive thoughts brimming.

"So, is anyone going to ask her why she's been crying herself a river? I just cleaned at least a hundred snotty cloths from the floor."

"Has to be some dick," Rugger blurted entering the

bathroom with a glass of something brown and surely strong in her glass.

Roulette began her second round of cleansing.

"Spread them cheeks, Rather."

I leaned forward and placed my hands on the shower wall, assuming the position. When I was stable, I removed my hands and parted the cheeks of my ass.

"Shhhhh! Maybe it's the weight of her commitment," Rome reasoned.

"No," Roulette told them, "Rugger is right. Sis done slipped and fell on some dick. The wrong dick, might I add. The dick of the man who shares the same blood as the man she's marrying."

Gasps were echoed in the large bathroom.

"But, in her defense, she was slipping and sliding down that one first. Long before a fucking Kofi existed."

"Awwww, baby," Royce sighed.

"Damn." Range tittered.

I was rinsed for a second time. Rome stepped up, handing me the towel. I turned the water off and dried my body while still in the shower. When I emerged, I was given a glass of wine and the robe from her hands.

"And, I've fallen in love with him."

"Him who?" They asked in unison, everyone but Roulette. She was already privy to the information.

"Priest," I revealed.

A pin could drop and it would be heard a mile away. Everyone stilled. There wasn't a sound made. Not until I pushed out the breath I'd been holding, praying my sisters didn't chew into me for the choices I'd made. I should've known better than to ever believe that. Those girls were my rocks.

"Well, I could make Kofi disappear so you can have your happily ever after. He's a risk factor. His disappearance wouldn't be unlikely. After all, that's why they're eager to marry him off."

"Rugger."

She picked the dirt from beneath her nails, completely unbothered by the stale faces staring back at her.

"Anything to see my sister smile." She shrugged. "If you change your mind, don't hesitate to call. I'll be on the first thing smoking. I'm itching for an assignment."

"It won't be Kofi," I promised her. "He's a decent guy. A little wild, but he's not awful. And, we've become friends, sort of. I think it's the foundation to a happy marriage. Well, one as happy as it could be given the circumstances."

"You're a stronger sister than me because I'd try my best to sit the fellas down and have them both agree to share me. Together and separately," Roulette explained, "I have two holes. They're both fillable."

"Three," Royce corrected her.

"See, I knew I liked you better for some reason. The brother Killian wouldn't be a bad idea. Rugger showed me a picture."

"Please." She was too much at times, but I knew she was being completely honest.

Monogamy wasn't her way of life. She was a girl who liked to dibble and dabble and keep her hands in a few baskets.

"I have to be at my last fitting at four and then it's straight to the dinner for hair and makeup."

"Well, that gives us two hours of girl time. To the kitchen, shall we?"

We filed out of the bathroom. Every woman had a glass in her hand that would need to be refilled soon.

Rather

The ballroom was filled to the brim with unfamiliar faces. The guest list totaled ninety-eight people and I hadn't chosen a single one of them. Ashland was in charge of the invitations and who received one. As long as my family was in attendance, no one else mattered.

"Kleigh, this is Rugger, Range, Royce, Roulette, Rome, and Roaman," I introduced the girls.

"It's so nice to meet you all. I've heard so much about you. I'll admit I'm a bit jealous you had such beautiful women surrounding you your entire life. You girls are lucky. All I had was the guys."

She lifted her chin, angling it toward Kofi and Killian who were only a few feet away.

"Two more Chem's wouldn't be such a bad thing," Royce countered.

I heard every word shared, but my eyes were elsewhere. So was my mind and my heart. I could feel his presence, but I couldn't see him. The anchor on my chest made it evident he was near. Still, I hadn't laid eyes on him.

Curiosity guided my orbs across the room. There wasn't a sign of Priest other than my intuition and the forbidden bond we'd created over the last few months. But, he was near. I knew it and so did my heart.

He's here. I warned, preparing to encounter the man who had stolen my breath away from the very first moment I saw him two years ago.

Backward and forward, across the room, my eyes scurried in search of him until finally, the doors of the ballroom opened. I steadied my gaze and waited anxiously for confirmation of my suspicion. I wasn't prepared for what was revealed to me. I wasn't prepared for what was presented.

Dapper in a three-piece suit that was black in every aspect of the world was Priest. Just inches away, but close enough to reach out and touch, was a beautiful, caramel-skinned woman who I was sure had seen hundreds of runways in her days.

Find someone you can learn to love and don't wait until your heart gives you permission. Do it sooner than later to put us both out of our misery. I'll live my life, Priest. I want you to live yours. What's going to happen to us is inevitable. Your lonesomeness doesn't have to be. For Princeton's sake, find somebody to love.

My words replayed in my head. I'd given him specific instructions one month ago. He was simply following them. Yet, I couldn't wrap my head around the idea of him with anyone else. Neither did I want to.

Drawn to one another like moths to a flame, Priest's eyes found mine from across the room. I blinked the wetness away, encouraging the prickling of my eyes to subside. This was no place to display my pain. I'd shed enough tears. I didn't have any more to cry.

A slight head nod was all I could muster. The hand on my shoulder and the voice in my ear quickly became my saving grace.

"She's pretty," Roulette whispered.

"I hope she's worthy," I confessed, "He deserves the absolute best."

Priest's heart was pure and his intentions were good. Any woman he invested his time and energy in, even if only for a while, he meant well. He hadn't experienced many, but I had a feeling that would all change now that I was no longer occupying his bed.

I had no doubt in my mind he'd try to fuck the pain away. And, I wouldn't blame him because I feared there wasn't any other way to do so. Not even therapy would suffice.

"Everyone is taking their seats."

"Okay. I'm going to take a second to gather my bearings. My heart feels like it's breaking all over again."

"The restroom?"

I nodded.

"Do you need me to come with you?"

"I need to be alone, Roulette." Gently, I declined the offer. "Thank you."

"Don't thank me. I'll be waiting right here when you return."

I gathered a piece of my dress in my hand so I wouldn't trip over it and make a mockery of myself at my wedding dinner. Roulette kept the girls at bay. I could hear their voices fade in the background as I made my way out of the ballroom and into the hallway.

Finally alone, I breathed out the air I'd been holding hostage. I brought my trembling hand to my forehead as I traveled toward the restroom closest to the bridal suite and furthest away from the rest of the guests. My movements were unsteady. My thoughts were jumbled. And, my vision blurred.

No more tears, Rather.

I lifted my chin, trying my hardest to keep from falling apart. Just as I pushed the door to the suite, a familiar baritone soothed every inch of my being. It cupped my soul between its chords and held it closely, promising nothing but goodness.

"Rose."

I whipped my neck in the direction it had come from. There he stood with both hands in his pockets and his eyes trained on me. In silence, I watched as he struggled with his words. His feelings. His truth.

"I'm so– I'm sorry."

Sincerity and gloom were infused in each word. But it wasn't his sympathy I needed. It was his life. His love. His laughs. His legacy.

"For what, Priest?" I shook my head, confused by his words.

"The hurt, it's written all over your face. You told me that's what you wanted. Had I known, I would've come alone."

"Her?" I scoffed, taking a few steps in his direction. "You think it's her that has my heart in the bottom of my shoes?"

The question was rhetorical. He didn't answer because he knew I wasn't waiting for a response.

"It's you. And until I find the strength to forget the magic we created, it'll always be you. Please don't apologize to me for being a man, Priest. If you're going to apologize for something, let it be the fact that you can't be *my* man."

I left him standing in the hallway. There was nothing left to say. All had been said over three months.

We'd laughed and we'd loved. It was time to say our goodbyes and continue our lives as if it never happened. It didn't matter how difficult the task was. Life for us had to go on.

This wasn't a breakup. We were never supposed to happen. This was a silly game we'd played and broken hearts were the silly prizes we'd won.

Alone in the bridal suite, I patted my eyes dry for the last time. I began counting down from twenty in an effort to steady my shaky hands and jagged breathing. Slowly, my lids closed as my body began to regulate.

You're okay. Everything is okay. My father's voice played in the back of my mind. *You'll never be able to see your future if you're busy with the past.*

His advice resonated with me. It was most fitting for

the moment. If I didn't let Priest go, then I'd never learn to love Kofi. It was time to put the past three months behind me so I could begin building the foundation for a prosperous, fruitful future with my husband.

I pulled myself together and headed back into the ballroom. It was then I had a change of heart. I made a personal promise to embrace the moments leading up to the rest of my life. Ashland and Kleigh had put so much work into Kofi and I's big day. It was time to enjoy the fruit of their labor.

"There you are," Kleigh called out to me. "Kofi's been looking all over for you. Is everything okay?"

"It will be."

Kofi was waiting by our seats to take my hand. I joined him at the table that was reserved for our family and the wedding party. My nerves had settled and so had my raging heart.

Everything will be everything. I coaxed, taking Kofi's hand. He leaned in closer. His cologne was becoming more intoxicating with each passing second.

"I thought I had a runaway bride before the wedding could even begin."

"I've done many things in my life, but ran from my responsibilities has never been one."

"Good. That means I'll see you at that altar tomorrow?"

"In my white dress."

"That's what a nigga wanted to hear."

He joined his hands and clapped silently. I grabbed them and pushed them down until they fell by his sides.

"Don't start, Kofi," I warned with a smile, knowing that he hardly had any reservations.

There hadn't been a time I'd spent with him that didn't end in uncontrollable laughter. Things were always good with Kofi, which led me to believe we'd be fine. Only time would heal my brokenness and help me learn to love him. I was looking forward to the day I did.

Grace, Rather. You deserve grace.

The decor was beautiful. My dinner gown was flawless. My sisters were by my side. And, my husband-to-be was right next to me with a smile that nearly reached his ears.

Because of my status, a legal, court-appointed marriage in the United States wasn't plausible. But, we'd managed to arrange the legalization of our union in St. Catana for the following week. There, we'd participate in a smaller, more intimate ceremony for my family.

In the two hours the girls and I had alone, we'd come up with the plan and I was anxious to see it through. Our honeymoon would last over a six-month span. We'd travel the world, visiting three countries that our families deemed as safe zones.

It was crucial I kept a low profile, and steered clear of government officials. We weren't in the clear yet, but I was certain it wouldn't be long before we were.

Everyone settled around us, taking their assigned seats and preparing for the dinner to officially begin.

"Um Mm," Ashland cleared her throat as she tapped the side of the wine glass in her hand.

From the swaying of her body and her loose limbs, I could tell it wasn't the first glass of wine she'd finished.

"I'd like to start by thanking everyone for joining us

tonight. Not all of you will have the chance to witness Kofi and Rather's ceremony tomorrow, so tonight is very special. I've dreamt of this day since I found out I was pregnant with Killian."

"Standing in front of guests, saying all the great things a mother can think of about the child she birthed while everyone struggles to keep their tears at bay. Well, this isn't one of those times. Admittedly, Kofi has been a pain in our asses since he came two weeks later than his due date."

Laughter erupted.

"Even with all his foolishness, there's one thing I can't take from him. He's a good man. Marrying the woman standing next to him will be his greatest accomplishment. I can feel it. So, I'll save the tearful speech for the renewing of vows when I actually have something good to say about my son. Until then, congratulations, Kofi and Rather. May God be the center of your unity. May it last forever more."

Cheering followed Ashland's words. Kofi raised his glass and the rest of the guests joined him. I, too, raised the glass in front of me.

"To Kofi and Rather," Killian yelled.

"To Kofi and Rather," everyone chanted.

To Priest and Rather. Inescapable thoughts ruined the beauty of the moment for me.

My intuition confidently revealed I wasn't alone in my brief battle with delusion. So was he. I didn't need the carefully curated seating chart to locate him. I felt his eyes on me. His gaze was sharp and relentless.

There was a smile on every face in the building except his. He was deep in thought. Deep in regret. Deep in feelings.

I sipped the champagne from the glass, desperate to quench my thirst. Priest was all-consuming. And, though I tried to tear my eyes from him, the task proved nearly impossible.

"We're about to be served," Kleigh informed me, rescuing me from the web Priest was spinning.

"Thank you."

Mere seconds after Kleigh's forewarning the first course was served, somewhat quieting everyone around us. We'd settled for a three-course meal because I wasn't interested in the soup option and we had a long day ahead of us.

By the time the entree was in front of us, the maneuvering of Priest's muscular frame drew my attention in his direction. He placed one foot in front of the other, peeling back another layer of my sanity with each step. His beauty was breathtaking.

Until he stood in front of us, my eyes didn't leave him. They never departed from his. There was a fire brewing between my thighs. With any luck it would subside before I made it to the altar in less than twenty-four hours.

My breath hiked in my chest as his aroma swarmed my nostrils. Involuntarily, my jaw locked, fusing my mouth shut. I slid my open hands down my dress to discard the sweat. Tremors shook my body as if the temperature had lowered forty degrees in an instant. To some far away place, I wanted to disappear.

Please.

He lowered his frame to meet Kofi's ear. Just inches away, he commanded me. All of me. And, naturally, I gave him all that he requested. My eyes. My energy. My sanity. My oxygen. It wasn't until he straightened his spine and took off in the other direction that I could breathe again. See again. Think again. Smile again.

Momentarily, he halted near his assigned seat. Seconds later he was hand-in-hand with his date and the two were headed out of the ballroom. My heart fell from my chest onto the gold-trimmed plate of gourmet food.

T H E G R E Y L I S T

"Bad Boys," Rome protested.

"Boring," Rugger teased. "*Colombiana.*"

"Aren't you tired of watching that?"

"Tired of watching a master of the craft? I'm not."

"It's not your night, so you don't get to choose, anyway," Roulette stated as a matter of fact. "Tonight is all about Rather. What is it that you want to watch?"

My mind was somewhere else. My mind was with someone else. What the girls were watching at the impromptu sleepover somehow didn't matter to me. Without a doubt, no one would be watching television. It would be watching us. There was too much catching up to do and too much to talk about. No one would care who was on the screen.

Where have you gone?

Priest's whereabouts shouldn't have been my concern, but the anguish in those dark eyes concerned me.

"Rather–" Range called out. "She's talking to you, babe."

We cut the final corner in the Mercedes Sprinter. I

could hardly wait to remove my dress and trade it for the matching pajama set Rome had bought for us all.

"Sorry," I breathed, "My mind is somewhere else. I don't care what we put on. I'll watch whatever you choose."

"Does it have anything to do with that fine black brother of Kofi's?" Roulette inquired.

Nodding, I admitted the obvious.

"He left early. I can't help but wonder where he's gone."

"You don't have to wonder too long, because if I'm not mistaken, he's standing right outside of that sick ass Phantom."

Royce's words jolted me, throwing me from my seat and toward the window next to the seat in front of me. I was at the very back of the Sprinter with my legs stretched out further than my thoughts.

In all his handsome glory, Priest stood against his car with his arms folded in front of him and his chin tucked.

My God.

His presence was as daunting as it was liberating.

"Stop. Stop. Right here is fine," I yelled to the driver.

We'd made it to the edge of my driveway. Any further would force Priest to move his car. I didn't want him to move. I didn't even want him to blink until I was there. In front of him, ready and willing to listen to whatever it was he'd come to say.

"No ma'am," Roulette protested. "I'm going to beat your ass like Richie and Rhea should've if you run your tall ass out there like you have no couth. You know better, Rather."

"We don't behave in that manner. It doesn't matter that

the heart is involved. Compose yourself before you step off this bus or we can sit here all night."

"I–"

"She's right," Roaman added.

"You're too worked up, babe," Rome claimed.

"Desperate." Rugger slid in.

"Rugger!"

"Sorry. In my defense, I offered to kill the husband."

"Fix yourself, baby. Remember who you are. At whatever hour you decide to step down from this Sprinter, he'll be there. Waiting. As he should."

I lowered into the seat and tried to catch my breath. At the sight of Priest, it had escaped me. Roulette was on me in an instant, polishing my lips with a fresh coat of gloss. Rome pushed my hair out of my face and brushed it down my back with her hand. She smoothed the top down and stood back admiring her contributions shortly after.

"Feeling better?" Royce questioned.

"Much better. I'm sure I've told you all this enough times to last long after we're in the ground, but I love you."

"In this lifetime and the next, babe," Roaman declared.

"You first?" Range tilted her head toward the door.

I shook my head, unwilling to lead the way.

"You all go ahead."

One by one, they descended the steps. I was the last of the seven of us to exit. Poised and graceful, the girls led the way toward my home.

The weight of my reality made me slower. Heavier. Quieter. Though I stood tall with an erect spine, I had diminished –*internally*.

My confidence had taken a blow to the core. Optimism

had taken the back seat. My belief system was out of commission. Confusion nearly blinded me. Apprehension tugged at my heartstrings.

I rounded his car to meet him. He watched me from afar. My limbs drew closer to my body as I obliterated the distance between us. Side by side, I planted my feet in front of him.

"Rather."

He was short. He was curt. He was unmoving. The energy occupying the space between us was different. It was cold. And, it was brutal.

As quickly as my name left his throat, I regained my strength. My power was reactivated. And, the girl that had come off the bus with a bruised ego and broken heart had disappeared. Born again was the woman he'd met two years ago. The woman he invited to PS102. The woman my father had raised. The woman my brother praised.

"Priest."

"I am here as a courtesy visit from the Valentine family. During the arrangement of marriage, we were informed of the bride price your sacrifice required. Ten million in total over ten years, per your family's wishes. You'll find an initial deposit of two million dollars for the agreed amount in your account at midnight."

Those weren't the eyes I remembered. These were colder. Darker. And, soulless.

"Every two years, another two million will be wired to the account of your choosing until the sum has been met. In the event that you are to car– car– carry our namesake, an additional two million dollars per child will be delivered to you in cash on the date of birth as requested by your superiors."

He fumbled over his words. The cracking of his voice was gutting. The tremors of his chin were paralyzing. He reached behind him and slid a folder from the roof of his car. With flared nostrils, he continued.

"In addition, there is a five million dollar life insurance policy for Kofi Valentine with you serving as the sole beneficiary. If or when children are born, you will no longer be the sole beneficiary. The policy will be split even amongst you and any child who shares his DNA."

He shifted his weight from one foot to the other. He was no longer firmly planted with both feet harboring equal weight. Priest was withering.

"Hm Mm."

He cleared the trail of emotions his words were leaving behind. His spine straightened and his neck grew slightly longer after a good shake of his head.

He was decomposing before me. The Priest I knew, at least, and it was killing me softly with each movement he managed.

"Should there ever be a delay in the delivery of your funds, I am the person you are to see. If there is ever a matter that should arise during the course of your marriage that is beyond your control, I am the person you are to see. Do you understand the things I've just shared with you?"

Underneath my lids caught fire. The salty tears and mascara mix was poisoning my eyes. The damp, lengthy lashes left residue on my cheeks and my cornea with each blink.

"Rather." He demanded a response.

"Yes," I choked out.

"M– My business here has concluded."

His chin dipped near his chest. I lost those eyes in the rounding of his shoulders. The file in his hand was pushed in my direction. Reluctantly, I accepted my life's plan.

In my hands was proof that Chemistry was always twelve steps ahead of the rest of the world. My father had given my hand in marriage, but Chem had secured my future and the future of any children who were made from the union that had been arranged. They weren't in my personal plans, but should they ever come, they were covered.

Compensation, baby. If a nigga chooses to do you dirty or waste even a second of your time, make sure you're well-compensated. They say time isn't something money can buy, but that's because they've never met a woman who has punished their pockets. Be that woman. Never let them play you if they can't pay you.

Rules were rules. I didn't make them. I followed the ones put in place before me. That's how we'd gotten ourselves into the mess we were in now.

I peered at the brown folder, prolonging my departure. The dark round spot in the center shot a dagger through my heart. I lifted my head, fearful of what was waiting for me.

Priest's flared nostrils were the result of his emotional despair. So was the lone tear that had fallen.

"I—"

My chin was between his hand, suddenly. And, instead of pulling back and running in the other direction like I should've, I moved forward. Our bodies crashed into one another. Our lips collided.

Hungrily, he consumed me. His tongue roamed every inch of my mouth as if it was foreign territory. It wasn't. I wasn't. We weren't. He knew me. He knew my body. He knew my heart. He knew my mind. He knew my soul.

Painfully, Priest tore his lips from mine. Both of us stood unmoving with our chests rising and falling. My tears stained his cheeks. No words were exchanged. Not for a full minute. Just as he gathered himself and turned to leave, something in me died.

"I'm scared," I shouted, stopping him in his tracks.

With his back turned toward me, he waited for me to continue.

"I've never been afraid of anything in my life, but I am deathly afraid of losing you."

His head shook from one side to the other.

"Say something–"

He faced me. The smirk on his face was contradicting his feelings. His thoughts. His sentiments.

"Tomorrow will be the best day of your life. There's no need to be afraid. You're in good hands."

"That's untrue."

He shook his head, again.

"The day I met you was the best day of my life," I confessed, "And though good things come in threes, I find it hard to believe I'll get to meet you twice."

He lowered his chin to his chest and smiled. He was stunning. He was a dream. He was my dream.

"Goodbye, Rather."

In the middle of my driveway, with a face full of tears,

Priest left me. I retrieved my heart from the concrete. It was barely recognizable. He'd stumped all over it. He didn't understand it was his to have. He didn't know that it belonged with him.

I entered my home and quickly locked the door behind me. I pushed my back against it and pressed the file against my chest. I was sore all over.

"That's a dangerous game you're playing, baby."

I lifted my head. A single blink cleared my blurred vision. My brows cinched near the center of my forehead. The emotions I'd kept at bay erupted at once.

My legs stretched across the floor at full speed. Papers fell from my hand and littered the space around us. I didn't stop. I couldn't stop. Not until I was in his arms, my feet were off the floor, and his voice was against my cheek.

He soothed my soul. He eased the pain in my heart. He healed my wounds.

"Teddy!" I gasped, unable to form a full sentence.

Without words, he held me closely and swayed my body from one side to the other. In his arms, I wasn't the woman he'd helped me become. I was the little sister who needed the comfort of his presence and the shelter his limbs provided.

Just like that, we stood until I was able to stand on my own two feet, again. He lowered me to the floor and stood back to observe me.

"I've missed you."

"You have no idea," he tittered. "I'm no good at being away from you."

"I thought you were coming tomorrow."

"As much as I'd like to talk about the shit that's on your mind, there's a more pressing matter at hand, baby."

I shook my head and sealed my lids. The disappointment in his voice was preparing to cause irreparable damage that not even the heartbreak I was experiencing could compare to. Chemistry's questionable gaze shrunk me three sizes.

"I have it under control. Just– just please don't look at me that way."

"Rathe–"

"I'm marrying Kofi. I will fall in love with him and we will live happy lives, Chemistry."

"I'll give up everything if it means your ha–"

"Please," I begged, "That's not how this wo– how this works," I wept, "You can't save me this time, Teddy. It's time somebody saved you and if it has to be me then so be it. I'm getting down that aisle and I'm marrying that man. Because, if I don't, the order will be no more."

"We'll lose our claim to Clarke. That family's foundation will crumble. And, Priest, he'll no longer be head of the Valentines. I've been around them long enough to say with confidence that there's no better person in their family who is qualified for the job."

"I'm not leading with my feelings, Teddy. I'm leading with my head. The two are not aligned yet, but I promise they will be. I promise."

He finalized that portion of our conversation with a nod.

"Now, where's my mother, and where the hell is my niece?"

I pushed my feelings into a deep, dark place where they

were to remain. My father trusted me. He believed in me. And, I'd promised to save my sister and our brother by sacrificing myself. Nothing would change. I'd be fine. *Eventually.*

"Upstairs waiting to see Tee Rather."

I kissed Chem's cheek and headed toward the stairs. Just as I placed a foot on the first step, my cell rang. Kofi's name crossed my screen. A lump formed in my throat as I contemplated answering.

"Answer his call, Rather," Chem instructed.

"How do you know?"

The insult was written all over his handsome face. "I always know."

I slid the bar across the screen to connect the call.

"Hello?"

"It's your husband," joyfully, he replied.

My cheeks flushed. His sense of humor was medicinal.

"Your name– your name is saved in my phone, Kofi."

"Aight. Just making sure you know what time it is."

"I do."

"It's," I paused to pull the phone away from my ear and check the time. "Ten twelve."

"Which means I have an hour and forty-eight minutes to have you back home. They say it's bad luck for the groom to see the bride the day of the wedding."

"That's what I've heard."

"Then, come ride with your nigga before the clock strikes twelve, Cinderella."

"Kofi, I'm still in my dress."

"The occasion causes for something of that caliber."

"What is it?"

"If I tell you then it won't be a surprise, right?"

I nodded as if he could see me.

"Come outside, Rather. I'm pulling up."

The call ended before I could protest. There was a tingling in my gut that pushed the side of my mouth upward. Anticipation pushed my feet toward the door where I was anxious to witness Kofi's arrival.

Despite the love that I'd developed for Priest and the pain of letting him go, time with Kofi wasn't affected in the slightest. He'd been exactly who he told me he would be from the very beginning. My respect for him ran as deep as it did for the man he shared a father with.

"Rather?" Chem called out to me.

"He's here," I informed him. "I'll be back by midnight."

"I'll be waiting."

The December cold was brutal. I hurried out of the door and down to the driveway where headlights lit my path. Loud music rattled the speakers of Kofi's car. He was out in a flash, opening the passenger door.

"Your chariot awaits."

"Why, thank you, Sir."

I slid onto the soft leather. Kofi carefully stuffed the tail of my dress inside of the car and made his way back to the driver's seat. My body stiffened as he changed gears, preparing for takeoff. Slowly, he eased out of my driveway, but the snail's pace didn't last very long.

My head slammed against the headrest as his foot smashed the gas. The slightly cracked windows allowed the fresh, crisp night air in the car. It swept across my face, freeing me of my inhibitions. My heart galloped, pounding against my chest and letting me know I was alive.

"Whew," I whispered, releasing my hold on the side of the seat and relaxing.

Kofi's hand migrated to my side of the car. He intertwined our fingers and brought my left hand to his mouth as we got higher and higher in the hills of Mount Clarke. Nine minutes after we exited my driveway, we pulled into another.

After the car came to a complete stop, Kofi peered over in my direction. His baritone deepened and his vulnerability peaked. The man staring back at me felt unfamiliar. The life of the party had quickly become someone else. *Something else.*

"Welcome home, Rather."

"Home?"

He didn't answer me. Instead, he opened his door and exited the car. Within a few seconds, he was helping me out of the passenger seat. I took a step toward the front door and was immediately chastised.

"Nah. That's not how they do in them chick flicks y'all be watching."

He leaned down and scooped me right into his arms.

"Oh my God!" I blurted, finding comfort in his ability to make me laugh so easily. His charm was endearing.

Bridal-style, he carried me toward the door.

"I'm a mess right now, Rather, but I promised to clean up my act by the time we walked down that aisle. That's what I've been doing. This home is just the beginning. I have so much in store for us. Like you said back at that coffee shop, this doesn't have to be awful. It can be as beautiful as we make it."

"And, I want it to be grand. I know where you come from. I know what you're accustomed to. I know you're not a stranger to love. Though that's not where we are right now, someday we will have one of those stories we're happy to tell the youngins who ask what's the secret to a successful marriage and how we lasted so long. I'm with all of that. I want all of that."

I was at a loss for words. What I was hearing from Kofi eighty-eight days later was what I'd wanted to hear from him on day two when he stumbled into *Genre* late with a hangover.

He pushed the door open and entered our new home. It wasn't until we were over the threshold that he lowered me onto my feet. Nervously, he shoved his hands in both pockets.

"Can you see your future between these walls?"

Admittedly, I could. The warmth of the home won me over the second we stepped through the door.

"Yes."

Visibly relieved, Kofi surrounded me, wrapping his arms around my body and spinning me around. When the room stopped and my feet hit the floor, again, his body was still pressed against me. His hands pinned my face between them. His breath tickled my skin.

"Me too."

Kofi's lips crashed into mine at once, rendering me breathless.

Priest

"Priest!" The concern etched in my mother's voice was valid. "Where are you? Everyone is waiting."

The wheels of my Rolls came to a complete stop. Absentmindedly, I'd traveled thirty-five minutes. I didn't recall a single stop light, stop sign, pedestrian, crosswalk, or yield sign. Yet, I'd made it to my destination. Two hours late and without the same joy the people who'd arrived at the venue before me experienced.

Turmoil.

Darkness.

Dissatisfaction.

Hunger.
Desolation.
Fear.
Pain.
Trouble.
Unrest.
Hell.

Today, I didn't know peace because my peace was clothed in white preparing to marry the man who wasn't made for her. The man who wasn't right for her. The man I'd chosen for her.

"Priest. I asked you a question son. Where are you?"

"It's her."

I grabbed the small box from the passenger seat and exited my car. My steps were swift. I covered more ground in ten seconds than I would in two minutes on a normal day.

But this was not a normal day. This was the day *my Rose* would be walking down the aisle. This was the day she was to begin her new life. The life destined for her. The life that didn't include much of me.

"I don't understand, Priest."

I pushed through the door of the chapel.

"You asked me who she was. The woman I've fallen in love with. It's her."

"It's who, son?"

"Rather. It's Rather."

Her silence was revealing. So was my presence. There was no way in hell I would stand beside Kofi as he vowed to learn to love the woman who'd been created, especially, for me. I didn't have to learn to love Rather. I already loved her.

"Oh God, Priest. Where are you?"

All eyes were on me as I pressed through the space reserved for those responsible for making this day possible.

"I'm here, Mother."

"Here? Here where? I'm coming to find you."

The ruffling in her background muffled her words, but I still heard her clearly. She was headed for me. I was headed elsewhere. There was only one person I was interested in conversing with and he was behind the door I was standing in front of.

"There's no need."

"Priest— What are you going to do, son?"

"Something I should've done a long time ago." I killed the line and shoved the cell in my pocket.

I stepped into the groom's suite with my eyes trained on the man of the hour.

"Where the fuck you been, nigga?" Killian shouted at me. "We've been calling and tex—"

"Lower your voice," I instructed.

All chatter ceased. Silence replaced the corny jokes and obnoxious laughter of men.

"Nigga, what is the matter with you?" Confusion plagued Killian, but there was no time to explain. Kofi and I needed a minute.

"Give us the room," I demanded.

No one moved. Everyone stilled, unsure of what was happening or where to go.

"The room!" The bass increased, leaving them without room to wonder anymore.

The heels of their shoes clacked against the floor as everyone filed out. Killian stopped in front of me.

"What is happening right now?" His voice was low, not carrying very far.

"I need the room," I reminded him.

With a nod he continued out of the door. Finally, Kofi and I were alone. Sweat poured from his face. He was a nervous wreck.

A kid. I concluded.

He wasn't ready for the role he was stepping into. He still had milk on his tongue.

"You coming to tell me this is all a joke, right? That I don't actually have to go through with this shit, right?" He chuckled, pacing the floor. "What if she wakes up one day and hates me? Am I stuck in this for the rest of my life for real? Fuck. Did you niggas really think this through?"

"Kofi."

"I'm going to fuck this up. I can feel it. I don't trust myself. I'm going to fuck this up and she's going to hang my balls out to dry."

"Kofi."

"And, Hailey," he scoffed, "She's cool people. I was actually starting to like her."

"Kofi."

"Fuck, bro. This nervous shit normal?"

"KOFI!"

He stopped in his tracks and faced me.

"Why the fuck you not dressed? Where's your—"

"Kofi. There are things we need to discuss. Things that won't be easy to say or easy to hear. Things that will alter the course of our relationship. Things that will alter everything. But, I need you to exercise the utmost level of maturity, remain respectful, and think before you speak."

The pacing started again. He scratched the top of his head, unsure of what was to come, but mentally preparing himself anyway.

"What's up?"

Because there was no easy way to say what needed to be said, I didn't hesitate to do so.

"I can't let you marry her."

"If it's me you're worried about, I'm good, Priest. There's no backing out of this shit. Trust me, I've gone to Pops twelve times in the last ninety days. The answer was the same every time. This is my fate. I'm fine with that. I've spent time with her. She's a good girl, bro. A damn good girl. Everything will be kosher."

"Kofi, I don't think you understand what I'm saying."

"I do."

"You can't."

"Then what are you saying?"

He tensed, halting all movement.

"*I* can't let you marry Rather. This has absolutely nothing to do with your arrangement and everything to do with me."

"I don't follow."

"The woman you're marrying today, I'm in love with her. And, I'm not talking the kind that fades over time. I'm talking utterly obsessed. I'm talking willing to give up my seat at the head of the table and possibly tarnish the relationship I have with every member in my family."

"The kind that keeps you up at night. The kind that makes you want her every hour of every day. The kind that is in your soul. The kind that lives deep in your bones. The kind that spreads like cancer. The kind that won't allow you to stand beside your brother as he vows to love her forever because you already do."

Kofi said nothing. He simply stared at me in disbelief. And, after a few seconds, a sinful laugh erupted.

"Let me get this straight. The woman you and Pops forcing me to marry, you're fucking?"

I knew Kofi well enough to know where this conversation was headed, but preparation was key. I'd gone over countless scenarios in my head all day. Nothing he said or did at this moment would stun me.

"Remain respectful."

His anger was justified, but this wasn't the case. Kofi wasn't angry. Kofi's pride was bruised. So was mine. But, there were no egos here. It was just him and I.

"Remain respectful?"

"You understood what I said, Kofi. There's no need to question it."

I joined my hands behind my back, waiting for whatever was about to come from his mouth next.

"But, yet and still, you're fucking her?"

"Is that the only thing you took from my declaration? I love her. I am *in* love with her. That's me. From her head to her toes. She belongs to me."

"What you mean, *brother*?" Kofi chuckled, "I was just in that shit last night. Surely you don't want that no more."

His words twisted my insides. The blood drained from my veins and I flatlined. The thought of Rather giving herself to anyone other than me was repulsive. Yet and still, it made me love her no less.

She was stepping into her role. She was doing exactly

what she was supposed to. She had every right and so did Kofi. Their actions were completely justified.

"If you were inside of Rather last night then my presence should be no surprise. You know exactly why I'm here."

His news gutted me like a fucking fish, but it should've been the shedding of light on the situation at hand for Kofi. If he knew how she felt, how she smelled, how she tasted, and how she oozed, then my presence shouldn't have surprised him.

The potency of her pussy was no longer a secret. He'd taken a dive and understood the depths I was willing to go for it. *For her.*

"And, your temporary residency doesn't make me want her any less. You see, I'm a man, Kofi. Though your intention was to insult me, telling me you fucked the woman you assumed you'd be marrying doesn't. I expected you to."

I stepped closer so there was no confusion. The jab he'd thrown had rolled right off my shoulder.

"Thing is, that'll be the first and last time you slide up in my shit. That'll also be the last time you mention it. Because, it's not my feelings that you're hurting. It's your pride."

"Pride, nigga you wouldn't know shit about that," he barked.

His chest grew a full inch in height. He moved closer, completely obliterating the space between us. Because I understood where his head was and how far he was willing to take this, I braced myself for impact. The little switch in his head had been flipped. He no longer viewed me as his brother.

Right now, I was his enemy and that was alright with me as long as he understood I would treat him as such if he got out of line. I'd spared him for two years. His time was coming and if that time happened to be today, then so be it.

"Remain respectful."

I put some distance between us. His frustration was valid. His feelings were valid. I'd never discredit them.

"You been pressed for pussy your whole fucking life."

Violation.

His fist crashed into his palm. With each passing second, he was growing angrier. The insults were his defense tactic, but as long as they remained respectful, all was well. I'd let him get his shit off his chest.

"Step back," I warned, putting more space between us.

"Fuck you, my nigga."

Violation.

He stepped closer.

"Remain respectful."

"I never took you for a fraud ass nigga that'll fuck a bitch behind my back, but I guess it's like mother like son, huh."

Violation.

Unlike the others, this one wouldn't slide.

Remain respectful.

Remain respectful.

Remain respectful.

Simple instructions he couldn't follow.

"Apple don't fall far from the tree. Pops was fucking ya moms before his homie got settled under the dirt."

This time when I stepped back, it wasn't to gain distance. It was to send a blow straight into Kofi's shit.

WHAM!

Immediately, my hand curled under his mouth and nose as I bent him forward.

"Don't bleed on this motherfucking tux, nigga. I'm going to need this up off of you."

"You ready to go blow for blow with me about a bitch?"

Hearing that word come from his mouth in reference to Rather had my blood boiling, but it wasn't about her.

I leaned down near his ear, still holding my hand under his bleeding nose. "That's where you're wrong, little brother. For one, we're not going blow for blow. I'm going to beat your ass like I should've been doing every time you violated the code over the last six months."

"And, this isn't about Rather. I'd never get busy with you about a woman that is mine, been mine, and will always be mine. This is about you. You're a disrespectful motherfucker and it's time you learned your fucking lesson. So, take this shit off and let's get to it, nigga."

"Get the fuck off me."

I relieved myself of my duties and grabbed the nearest hand towel.

"Take that shit off."

I wiped my hand clean of his blood as I watched him unbutton his shirt and toss it on the back of the chair in front of the vanity. I tossed him the towel and allowed him to clean his face.

"I'm not interested in beefing with you, Kofi. But, you will respect me. You'll respect Rather. And, you damn sure will respect my mother."

"Fuck Rather. I have no interest in her anyway. I see her

as nothing more than an obstacle the family has sat in front of me. I was fine living my life as I chose."

"You were killing yourself," I reminded him.

The doors of the groom's suite burst open. In walked my father, Killian, and Chemistry. At the sight of Kofi, they all looked at me for an explanation.

"What the fuck is going on in here?" My father fumed. "What the hell happened to your face?"

"He violated," I shared.

My father's eyes tightened as he looked to Kofi and shook his head.

"Clean yourself up. You're heading down the aisle in thirty minutes or less. Goddamn, boy."

"I'm not walking down that aisle, Pops," Kofi informed him, holding the towel up to his face.

"What the hell you mean you're not walking down that aisle. Nigga, do you know how much money I spent on this fucking wedding. If I have to drag you down that aisle, you're getting down it."

"He won't be getting married today, Pops," I co-signed.

"The hell is going on? Priest, explain!"

"Rather is for me."

"Fo– for you? Nigga, have you lost your goddamn mind?"

"I have, in fact. But, I'm not willing to lose my heart, too. Consider this my resignation. I can't lead the family by example if I can't set a good one. I've broken a few commandments myself. And, as qualified as I am to run the family's empire and as much as I love it, I love Rather more. The business doesn't bring me the peace she brings. The business doesn't give Princeton what he needs. She does. I can live with my choice to step down. What I can't live with is the decision to let my brother marry the woman who has had my heart for two whole years."

"Tw– two years?" Pops drew his head back.

"Two years?" Kofi questioned.

"Another conversation for another day. Today, there's a chapel full of guests who are expecting a wedding to begin in thirty minutes."

I faced Chemistry. The look in his eyes told me this was not news to him. He'd known already. That shouldn't have been news to me, but it still caught me by surprise.

"Chemistry, if I could have your sister's hand in marriage, I'd like to give the people exactly what they came to see. A wedding between two people who love one another."

"I don't give a damn who gets married, son. It had better be some damn body. Too much money has gon–"

"Chemistry–" I urged him.

"Rather's heart is no playground, Priest," he began, "I expect you to fulfill the obligations of the arrangement and pay her accordingly. But more than the money she'll receive, the love she receives better be greater than any love the world has ever known or I will turn over every bead of soil in the world to find you. There won't be a rock you can hide under and I can't get to you."

"You're not talking to a pussy. My guns shoot like yours." I reminded him.

With a smile, he nodded, "But your aim isn't as accurate. You have my blessing."

I wasted little time stepping to the man I'd wronged and wrapping my arms around his frame. "I'm sorry, but I can't let this one get away, Kofi. She's too precious to me."

He remained silent, but the pat on my back let me know that all would be well, *eventually*.

"Pops—"

"Go ahead. We'll deal with this shit later. You niggas done ran my blood pressure through the roof. Where is my wife? Kofi, you didn't give a damn about the girl, anyway. You haven't stopped running the city since she got here. Fix your damn face and give your brother that tuxedo. Priest, you and I have unfinished business. You hear?"

"Yes."

I pushed through the door with my heart on my sleeves. There was only one person I wanted to see. My feet didn't stop moving until I reached her suite. Despite protests from those near, I entered after a warning knock.

The doors swung open and every mouth in the room hung with surprise. Rather was breathtaking. The picture I had on my lockscreen in the same dress didn't do her justice.

Her eyes grew in size at the sight of me. Nevertheless, I kept pressing until I was mere inches from her. She froze, unsure of what to say or what to do.

"Sorry to intrude, but I have a very, very important question to ask."

"Priest, what are you doing here?"

"Claiming what's mine."

"I don't understand," Rather claimed as she shook her head.

"There's no time to explain. I have less than thirty

minutes to match your fly, though I find that impossible. You're far too mesmerizing."

Nervously, she observed the room. Something told me everyone in the room were aware of our connection but the person I shared the same blood with.

"Priest?" Kleigh shrieked.

"I'm sorry, baby girl."

She rushed toward us, confusion crinkling her pretty face. A single arm halted her stride. The fierceness in the eyes of the woman who'd stopped her was taxing enough for us both.

"Sit down," she demanded, "Before I sit you down."

With a tilted head, she patted her thigh. Because I knew where Rather kept her piece, I was sure at least one of Rugger's was hiding there.

"Rugger!" Rather yelled out.

With a shrug, she folded her arms, "She hasn't shut up since we met her. My ears are on the brink of bleeding."

"You–" Rather started, again.

"Rose," I addressed her, cupping her chin.

"Yes?" She softened.

"This isn't ideal and I'm fully aware you deserve the grandest gesture, but this is where we are and my presence is all I have to display my love for you today. That and my willingness to give up everything I'm in possession of except your love. You've been exactly what I've needed over the past three months. Your blessing didn't end with me."

"It has become part of Princeton's weekly routine. Just like me, he looks forward to time with you. What you've given me, I'll spend my life trying to repay you for. In this lifetime and the others I often hear you refer to, I promise to love you, cherish you, protect you, and meet you where you are time and time again."

"My life was shitty without you. You've managed to bring me purpose, peace, and a newfound sense of priority. I'm ready to wake up to you every morning. I'm ready to wrap you in the covers every night. I'm ready to dig into the corny ass Romance novels you love so much. I'm ready for coffee in the morning. I'm ready for countless dates."

"I'm ready for extra shampoo bottles in the shower. I'm ready for around the clock therapy from the best therapist in the fucking world. I'm ready to run your bath after a long day. I'm ready to build. And, more than anything, I'm ready to give my son the mother he deserves. But, first, I need to know if you're willing to take a chance on us and meet me at the altar."

Silently, Rather nodded, trying her hardest to keep her tears from ruining her makeup. She failed miserably.

"Yes."

I released the breath I'd been holding as she wept, "I was ready the day I met you."

I practiced self-control and maintained the bit of distance between us. With every fiber in my being, I wanted to comfort her. To kiss her. To take her by the hand and leave everything and everyone behind.

But, instead, I turned and left Rather with the women who cared for her most. My absence would only last for a little while. She'd agreed to meet me at the altar. I'd be damned if I kept her waiting.

THE GREY LIST

Six women stood to the right of me. The seventh of the bridal party was on the piano, polishing the keys with her fingers. The cadence of her rendition of Etta James', *At Last*, was flawless.

Rome was gifted beyond words. They all were. Each and every one of the Childers sisters. And, I was blessed to have the chance to join their tribe.

The doors of the chapel opened and there Rather stood. A veil concealed the face I wanted to wake up to a million times or more. Since she descended the steps at *The Mansion*, I'd secretly waited for this day.

Beside her was the man who'd made it all possible. The Chemist held Rather close as they took the first step simultaneously. My heart expanded. Another step and it widened a bit more.

"Uh Mm." I cleared my throat, trying my hardest to keep my composure.

At last, my love had come along and she'd made my world a place I no longer wanted to escape. She brought light. She brought love. She brought passion. She brought purpose.

"If this motherfucker put this camera in my face again knowing my shit busted up, I'm shooting everybody in this bitch," Kofi whispered, causing Killian and I to break character.

I placed a fist over my mouth to conceal the laughter. Killian had already snorted, drawing attention to himself.

"My bad about that, man,"

"You really didn't have to do him that dirty," Killian sniggered.

"I'm suing that motherfucker. Watch."

"You gone sue me?"

"Yeah. And look at this nigga. Ugly ass. Keep getting in my fucking face."

"Kofi– stop, man." Killian's warning made me hate I couldn't see what was happening behind me.

"Chill. Just be cool, Kofi. I'll make sure he edits the pictures."

"I can't wait until this is over. I'm hitting that nigga in the back of his head."

"I said be cool."

With my eyes still trained on Rather, I watched everything around us fade to white. There was a stillness in the midst of movement. This was the calm after the storm. Everything in my world would be fine as long as she next to me.

My peace.

Just short of me, she ceased movement. Slowly, Chem lifted her veil and pulled it over her head.

My Rose.

I'd never understand God's plan when he created such a flawless creature. As if one wasn't enough, there were six others just like her. They were as beautiful as they were lethal.

My heart.

Using his thumb, Chem swiped away the fallen tears.

The way he loved and cared for her was influential. Before meeting either one of them, I knew exactly how to treat them by the way he cherished them. He'd set the tone for our union and the ones to follow.

She peered at him with so much love and admiration in her eyes. The reciprocation didn't go unnoticed. He was as fascinated with her as she was with him. Whispers were exchanged. The panged expression on Rather's face tugged at my heartstrings until finally her smile powered through.

My dear.

I took her by the hand and guided her up the two steps. At the altar, where she'd promised to meet me, we stood.

I love you. She used her hands to express.

I love you, I responded.

All over. Everywhere. So much it hurts.

That kind of pain, the best kind of pain, is the only pain you'll ever feel, I signed.

This was the woman I'd love for the rest of my life. This was the woman I'd cherish. Grow with. Grow from. Learn from. And hold onto until the end of time. I'd spent two years waiting on this woman, but the wait was finally over. She was here and she was *mine.*

SEVENTEEN

Rather

"Sleeping beauty."

The sound of his voice would never expire in my head.

"Say it," he whispered.

"Sleeping beau-ry."

Tiny chuckles followed Princeton's new attempt at a word. His vocabulary was improving and so were his social skills. My presence was the balance he needed. And, his hugs were the solution I needed. They made the world around us feel so small.

Without opening my eyes, I trailed the sound of the sniggers. Into my outstretched arms, I pulled Princeton onto the bed and underneath the covers with me. I squeezed his body close to mine.

"Beau–ty. The word is beauty."

"Beau–ty!"

"Yes."

I searched the open air with my free hand. He was near. I could smell his skin's fragrance. I could feel his presence dominating my existence. I could hear his steady breathing. And, though I couldn't see them, I could feel the ridges in the corner of his mouth that formed due to his smile.

"Good morning," Priest uttered.

He ended my misery. Against my palm, he rested his cheek. Contentment filled me to the brim. From his cheek, my hand lowered to his lips.

One.

Two.

Three.

Four.

Gently, he kissed my knuckles.

"Good morning," I yawned.

Sunlight assaulted my eyes, but with each blink I adjusted to its brutality. And, there he was, staring down at me with my hand in his. It didn't matter how many mornings I woke up to him, I still couldn't believe this was my reality. *He* was my reality.

Fourteen days.

Thirteen nights.

Waking up in Priest's bed was surreal. The sheets I'd dreamt of for many months covered my body every night. I was still waiting to be pinched. I was still waiting to wake up because there was simply no way I wasn't still dreaming.

Because we needed a plan in place for Princeton, our honeymoon would have to wait. However, our marriage was official and our license had been printed in St. Catana. We journeyed to the island for that reason alone and was back within forty-eight hours so Princeton didn't miss his father too much.

It had been two weeks since the ceremony. The thought of everything that transpired knotted my stomach and brought me joy, simultaneously. Though our worlds had been twisted upside down, our love remained intact.

"Breakfast is ready."

"Just a few more minutes with the best cuddle buddy a girl could ever ask for."

Princeton's arms snaked around my neck.

"Nah. I think that's enough. I'm not sure what this little nigga think this is."

Priest pulled on Princeton's shoulders. He paid his father no mind. His penetrating gaze nearly put me in stitches. I was trying my hardest not to laugh, but Priest was making it difficult. Watching him blossom in real time was the best part of this entire ordeal.

"Leave him alone."

I locked both arms around Princeton. He was feeding right into my antics. It was more of the same with us every day. Having me around kept a smile on Princeton's face.

He was quickly becoming my partner in crime, and making me reconsider my dreams of never bringing a child into the chaotic world we lived in. In due time, maybe I would. But, for now, he was more than enough for his father and I.

"You see the way he's looking at you. Has no one told him, I fight niggas bout you?"

"Five year olds, too?" I cackled.

"Five month olds if they look like they're trying to make a move."

"You're ridiculous."

"I'm in love, dear. That shit is ridiculous in itself."

I nodded, unable to protest his claims.

"Up, up. Breakfast is ready."

"Okay. Okay."

I buried my head between Princeton's neck and the pillow beneath us. Staying here all day was ideal, but there were a few tasks that weren't up for negotiation. I had to get out of bed and get my day started, no matter how much I wanted to stay in.

I dragged my body from the bed into the upright position. My little shadow rose from the bed as well. I stretched my arms in the air and he did the same. Before his arms came down, I scrambled my fingers across his belly.

He fell over in laughter. Giggles were so good for the soul. I'd learned that over the last two weeks. Each time I heard Princeton's, a part of me that I didn't know was broken began to heal.

Dad. I signed. *Is a hater*.

His smile widened as he looked over his shoulder at Priest. His eyes returned to me shortly after.

Mom. He placed his hand in the air with his thumb against his chin. *Is pretty*.

My heart attempted to climb through my chest. Intensely, unrhythmically, it beat against the silk clinging to my skin. My head drew backward at an alarming speed, nearing snapping my spine and paralyzing me for life. Though it was still intact, I was immobilized by both my thoughts and Princeton's words. Tears welled in my eyes as each breath I released shortened.

"Princeton."

My voice was brimming with emotions, so many that it felt pointless. So, instead of using it, I used my hands. One went against my forehead in the salute stance and then came down onto the other that was just underneath my breast bone.

Son is so smart, I declared.

Because I couldn't take the distance any longer, I grabbed hold of him and pulled him into me. Priest was mere feet away, eyes beaming with pride.

I love you, he mouthed.

In every lifetime. I responded.

T H E G R E Y L I S T

I strolled through the door of *Genre* with a new book in-hand. This time, it wasn't one from their shelves. It was the final draft of my very own publication. A local printer was able to get it printed and bound for a small fee. There were ten copies in total, nine of them were reserved for the women in my life that meant the most to me.

Mom
Range.
Rugger.
Roulette.

Roaman.
Royce.
Rome.
Egypt.
And, Kleigh.

I was pleasantly surprised by the dark figure near the edge of the patio dressed in black from head to toe. A thick coat shielded his body from the cold. Leather gloves and a black skull cap kept his hands and ears warm.

In his hands was a book from the shelves of *Genre* and a mug that resembled a tea cup. He was so consumed by the words on the pages that he wasn't aware of my presence. His stillness was entertaining. I couldn't recall a time when he was as quiet and as reserved.

"Ten o'clock on a Monday morning," I announced.

"Only you."

Kofi closed the book in his hand and took a sip from his coffee. Steam escaped the warm liquid as he placed it on the table and stood. He wrapped his arms around me.

"Good morning."

He returned to his seat, but not before sliding mine back.

"Good morning. You're early."

"And, finally realizing why your head is always in a book. Soon as I opened that one, she was busting that shit open. I'm taking that motherfucker home with me. I like her!"

"But, this time we'll pay."

"Who?"

"If we keep stealing from this beautiful business, we

won't have a place to meet for coffee a few Mondays out of the year at ten."

"You know what, you're right. You can pay for this one and the last one I stole. You owe me that, at least."

"As well as an apology. And an explanation."

"You don't owe me an explanation, Rather. You're a grown ass woman who was tossed into some shit head first– just like me. You coped with Priest. I coped by sticking my dick in every pussy I could get my hands on."

With a shrug, he took another sip from his coffee.

"Ima be shitting. I can already feel it. You smell that?"

"Smell what?"

"That fart?"

"Kofi, please don't make me puke. Why woul– Ugh."

"You chose this place. I told you coffee makes my stomach bubble."

With a roll of my eyes, I got to the point of our coffee date.

"You have to talk to your brother."

Adamantly, Kofi shook his head.

"Priest and I met before everything with Chem happened. Before I got on the plane thinking I was going for a normal girls trip and would return in a few short days, I had already claimed him as mine. Physically, I'd given myself to him. Mentally, I'd shared myself with him. Emotionally, I had no ties but I had a deep desire for them. *For him.*

"For two years, I wished I'd had another night. Maybe two. Maybe four. No amount felt like it would've been enough. I was drawn to him. He was hard to forget. I had every intention of doing that, though, no matter how hard it was.

"When I came back and you laid out a set of rules, it deflated the dream I'd had of the beginning of our partnership. Immediately, I wanted to run back to him. Still, I didn't know who he was. Not until he revealed himself to me at dinner the second time I had the pleasure of dining with the family. From that moment on, I couldn't stay away. No matter how hard I tried. And, I tried. But, some things we have no control over."

"My attraction and connection to Priest are some of those things. I'm sorry it all played out the way it did. But, the way things are right now, I can't let them stay this way. He's not himself lately. And, I doubt he will be until you pick up the phone for him or acknowledge his communication efforts when you're in the same room."

He sipped from his coffee, staring back at me.

"Say something."

Shrugging, he sat it down.

"Priest is the man for the job, Rather. I can't deny it and that's why I'm not mad anymore. I was leading with my head and not my heart when I said the things I said to my brother and was willing to brawl with him about such nonsense.

"We're bigger than that. We're better than that. It is fucked up. Yes, in every fucking way. But, when it's quiet and I really think about it... I wasn't ready for you. I doubt I would've ever been ready for you because I never chose you. There would always be some borderline resentment because I didn't have the privilege of choosing the woman I was to spend the rest of my life with. You chose Priest and that nigga chose you.

"He was willing to choose you over his position and his family. If that doesn't tell a motherfucker y'all meant to be together then I don't know what the fuck will. Because, I can look at you straight in the face and tell you right now—I'd never love you enough to choose you over my people."

"So, what's with the hostility?"

"He fucked up my pictures," Kofi admitted with a straight face. "Now, I look like mush face in all the family wedding photos. I'll never forgive that nigga for that shit. Him or that photographer. He won't be taking nobody else's pictures though."

"Kofi— What have you done?"

"That's for me to know and for you to find out, sis."

He stood on his feet and stretched his limbs. He was preparing to leave, but I wasn't quite ready for him to go. The weeks had been long and sometimes melancholy. I yearned for laughter and he could provide plenty of it.

"You're leaving already?"

"Yeah. I've got shit to do. People waiting on me."

"This is the most sane I've seen you since we met," I admitted. "It's almost bittersweet."

"Your presence served its purpose, Rather. It was my wakeup call. It gave me a chance to sit my ass down for an entire week and begin planning for something I never saw myself part of."

"What's that?"

"The future. So, in a sense, everyone got what they wanted."

Hearing Kofi confess what his family had known all along was disheartening. He was living life on the edge because he didn't imagine making it into the future they were planning for him. He wasn't rebellious. Kofi was afraid.

"Yeah." I nodded. "I suppose so."

"Thanks for the book and the coffee. I look forward to seeing you more Mondays at ten o'clock."

He tipped his head in my direction.

"Be careful, Kofi. The roads are slippery."

"I'd never fuck up a pussy appointment by wrecking the whip," he sniggered. "That's not player."

I yelled toward him, just as he took off in the other direction. "How is Hailey?"

"Hailey is good. Go see her at the bar. She's waiting to gift you a martini."

I'm waiting, too. See her soon.

With a smile, I sat back in my chair. A pleasant sigh escaped my lips as I dug into my purse to retrieve a pen. There was one more person I needed to see, but until she was ready, my written words had to suffice. On the small sheet of paper, I began the note to Kleigh that I would be stuffing inside her book and sending through the postal service.

Dear Kleigh,

I'm writing this note because I don't want to bore you with too many of my words on paper. I'd much rather see your face, hug your body, and tell you that I am sorry for what I've done to push you away. I understand your frustration and the fact you might never want to talk to me again, but the truth of the matter is I won't leave you a choice.

I value sisterhood. It's made me who I am. The last thing

I want to do is completely tarnish the relationship we were beginning to build. Despite everything that has happened, the fact of the matter is I love Priest and he loves you. My spirit won't rest until you're in my world, again. I miss you.

This is a fair warning. You have seven days to call me, send a date night invitation to my calendar, or show up at my house in new PJs. Otherwise, you'll leave me no choice but to come find you, sit you down in my chair, and treat you like a client you don't want to be until you promise all is forgiven.

I love you.
Rather Childers-Valentine.

I stared at the note on the table hoping it conveyed my truest emotions and feelings toward Kleigh's absence. Just in case I needed to ball it up and trash it, I pulled out my cell and snapped a picture.

Too much or not enough? I sent the picture to my family's group message. My mother was the first to respond.

No. It's perfect.

Girl, not you begging. Roulette was second in line.

I think that's sweet, but do you really need any more sisters? You have us.

Rome's selfishness was the cutest thing. She wanted to be the last sister and only baby. Adding Kleigh to the bunch meant there would be another sibling amongst the younger crew that included her and I.

Seven days? Rugger questioned.

She'll come around. I explained.

The rest of the girls approved the message, giving me the courage to drop it in the envelope I slid out of my purse, unfolded, and stuffed the book and note inside. I made my way to the counter and handed the cashier a fifty dollar bill.

Though she was clueless as to why I was giving it to her, she accepted it with a smile on her pretty face.

"For the two books my brother-in-law took without paying, as well as his coffee."

"Oh," she gasped, "Thank you."

"No problem. Keep the change. This place deserves it."

I exited *Genre* and headed to my car. The December cold was brutal, but the holiday cheer was plentiful.

"Whew."

I rubbed my hands together to try and increase the heat between them. The postal box on the corner made my life so much easier. I slid the large envelope from underneath my elbow and into the slot before continuing down the street.

Inside my car, I was comforted by the warmth. Princeton was heavy on my mind. Caramel popcorn, home-made juice, carrot sticks, and *Home Alone* in the theater room under heated blankets was the ideal evening for us. I couldn't wait to make it happen.

Priest was away for the day, so the car in the driveway was alarming. I drew closer to his home to see that it was Kleigh stepping out of her vehicle. The new set of wheels fit her well.

I cut into the driveway, eager to meet her at the door. She halted at the sight of me, realizing I wasn't inside and was just pulling up, too. It was too cold outside to keep her waiting, so I increased my speed and exited my car with a little more urgency than usual.

Kleigh was shivering. Something deep within told me it wasn't from the low temperature.

"I– I just sent your book off in the mail. What are you doing here?"

She angled the phone in my direction. Rugger's face on the screen wasn't surprising to me.

"Seriously, Rugger? I told you she'd come around. I could've waited seven days."

"You gave her seven days. I gave her seven minutes. It doesn't take that long to get around the bend and to her brother's home."

"Rug–"

"Kleigh now understands she's not allowed to disregard your existence. We're not there, so she is responsible for your sanity in our absence. She wanted a sister. She has seven now. Make this a lesson. We don't run from one another. We sit tight and stick it out, whatever it might be. When the rollercoaster is over, we'll all laugh about it. Isn't that right, Kleigh?"

Kleigh nodded.

"Words. Use your words," Rugger demanded.

"Yes."

"Good."

"Hang up on her," I insisted, feeling a bit awful.

Rugger wasn't for the weak. She always meant well but she always meant business. My torture tactics were almost equivalent to playdates in comparison to Rugger's. She didn't have a heart. I did.

"I can't," Kleigh whispered. "She said she'd, *you know*, kill me."

She will. I avoided the outburst and ignored my intrusive thoughts.

"Yes you can and stop whispering. She's a world away from us."

She shook her head, adamant about her stance. "She feels near."

"Trust me, she's not. Hang up. You have my permis–"

Rugger ended the call so Kleigh wouldn't have to. A sigh fell from her lips as her spine rounded and her mouth slacked.

"God, I thought today was my last day on earth."

I pulled her in for a hug. She was theatrical. Her body was trembling and her heart was racing. I could feel it against my skin.

"Dear God, honey, calm down. We'll have to give you a crash course on sisterhood before Rugger makes good on those promises."

"Thank you. I'd really appreciate it."

"I'm not serious," I chuckled, "She wouldn't. Most people don't even know the damn girl can talk. The fact she's talking to you says alot. Chaos– Quiet chaos is her language. Trust me. She's just passionate about the people she loves. If she didn't care for you, she wouldn't be on your phone. She'd be at your door."

Priest

"Meeting adjourned."

Chemistry's words sounded throughout the room. I got up from my seat and headed for the exit. Honor was right behind me. But, as we neared the exit, he started in the other direction. The Triad of Ara meeting had concluded and it was likely I wouldn't see either of the men I'd spent the last two hours with for another six months.

Because of The Chemist's legal hardships, we'd lowered the frequency. The change proved to be beneficial. There hadn't been any hiccups in our operations. All was well.

Six months ago, my position as the head of and

spokesman for the Valentine family had been compromised. Per my father's order, I was to step down and allow the second in command to take my position. Killian wasn't willing. He rejected the promotion and doubled down on his admission to keep me as head of the syndicate.

Kofi co-signed, leaving my father without a choice but to reinstate me. Six months later and the boardroom had never felt so welcoming. I was exactly where I belonged. Kofi knew it. Killian knew it. My father knew it. And, the two men I'd been in fellowship with for years knew it, too.

9:38.

When I slid into my whip, it was nearing the ten o'clock hour. I had twenty minutes to get from one end of Mount Clarke to the other. I fastened my seatbelt and hiked the volume on my stereo. Like clockwork, my wife's anthem began.

"I need a gangsta... to love me better... than all the others do," Kehlani sang, sending chills up my spine.

9:56.

I pulled into the garage and hopped out of my car. With a push of a button, it lowered behind me as I scanned the wall for my mask of choice. I slid the red one over my face and started for the door. Just as I twisted the knob, a familiar voice came over the speaker.

"Welcome back, Mr. Valentine. It's been a while." Ursula's voice was as intoxicating as I remembered. But, I was too drunk off the woman of my dreams to care.

"It has been. I've been a bit busy."

"I hear congratulations are in order."

"They are. Turns out, I didn't need you to find her for me. She was within my grasp all along."

"It's crazy how things just work themselves out, huh?"

"It's not crazy, Ursula. It's fate."

"Well, goodbyes are usually easy, but this one feels like a breakup. I will miss the two of you."

"This isn't goodbye. This is *hello*. Absolutely nothing has changed but the last name on the lease of her suite."

"That's what I like to hear, Mr. Valentine. Goodnight."

"Goodnight."

9:58.

I stepped into the suite and headed up the stairs. Hennessy and a glass sat on the counter. I rinsed it and dried it with a cloth then proceeded to open the new bottle. The brown liquor filled the glass one-fourth the way before I sat the bottle on the counter again.

Mmmm. The first sip was nostalgic.

10:00.

The time had come. My eyes were set on the door.

Knock.

Knock.

I closed my eyes, savoring the sound of knuckles against the surface.

Oh how I've missed you.

One foot in front of the other, I made my way to the door. When I stretched it open, the fiercest, sexiest being to grace the planet stood before me in a black trench coat. She pushed both sides apart by placing her hands on her hips, exposing her bare body underneath.

My dick stood at attention. The hairs on my arms and neck rose to the occasion. My heart pounded against my chest. I reminded myself to breathe, but she'd taken the oxygen out of me with her selfishness, *with her sexiness.*

She didn't move. She didn't blink. She didn't say a single word.

Good girl. I commended her.

Her obedience deserved the dick I was preparing to give her tonight. Tomorrow night. And for the rest of our lives.

Her arousal was prominent. I widened my nostrils to consume all it had to give. And, it was not until I'd had a decent helping that I decided it was time to put her out of her misery.

"Good evening, *Rose.*"

For the bonus scene of Rather that leads into book three of The Grey List, follow the link or tap here. (https://huffing tonnews.ck.page/355fc3b620)

If you're suffering from a Huffington hangover and need another shot of Rather, then read Priest's story.

Please Note: *Rather + Priest's stories are available in all formats. Both audiobooks (along with Chemistry + Egypt audiobooks) can be found on ghuffington.com. In addition, find the autographed paperbacks on ghuffington.com as well.*

HUFFINGTON NEWS

Join over 8,000 honorary Huffington residents for monthly broadcasts delivered right to their preferred devices.

Broadcasts include but aren't limited to:

- A beautiful monthly newsletter detailing everything happening in Huffington
- Extensive snippets of upcoming projects (sneak peeks)
- Release day reminders that include links (to remove the guest work from searching for books on Amazon/Ghuffington.com)
- First to hear about surprise releases
- Exclusive discounts + offers for Huffington residents
- A monthly wrap-up detailing everything that has happened in Huffington since the release of the Huffington Newsletter

Ready to become a resident?
Click here.
[https://huffingtonnews.ck.page/4693a79283]

MORE FROM GREY HUFFINGTON

Find the entire collection of Grey Huffington titles below. Titles in the catalog are available in eBook (amazon.com, + ghuffington.com), paperback (ghuffington.com), or audiobook (audible + ghuffington.com) formats.

Syx + the City
Syx + the City 2
Syx Thirty Seven
Syxth Giving
Syx Whole Weeks

Wile + Reckless
Wilde + Relentless
Wilde + Restless

Mr. Intentional
Unearth Me

The Sweetest Revenge

The Sweetest Redemption

Half + Half
The Emancipation of Emoree

Sleigh
Sleigh Squared

The Gifted
Memo
Give her Love. Give her Flowers.

Unbreak Me
Uncover Me

As we Learn
As we Love

Just Wanna Mean the Most to You
Sensitivity
10,000 Hours
Darke Hearts
muse.

Softly
Peace + Quiet
Press Rewind
Jagged Edges
My Person
The Realm of Riot Thimble
Whose Love Story is it Anyway?

Unhand Me

Home*
Blues*
31st*
Now That We're Here.*

Then Let's Fuck About It*
Giving Thanks

A Month of Sundays Ep 1
A Month of Sundays Ep 2
A Month of Sundays Ep 3
Dinner at Ever + Luca's
Saylah
The Mayor's Ball
Elm

THE EISENBERG EFFECT
Luca
Lyric
Ever*
Laike
Baisleigh*
Liam

THE DOMINO EFFECT
Ledge
Halo*
Lawe
Kleuless*

BERKELEY BRED

Malachi

Anna*

Milo

Makai

Glacier*

Mercer

Vallei*

THE GREY LIST

Chemistry "The Chemist"

Egypt

Rather "The Therapist"

—

* signifies the publication is available EXCLUSIVELY on ghuffington.com.

—

Prefer Audiobooks?

Did you know **there's a library FULL of audiobooks on ghuffington.com** for the lovers who listen?

We're building so you can continue to listen to the books you've been hearing good things about. There are currently over 17 audiobooks waiting for you to indulge.

In addition to our audiobook library, we have an audiobook

club for those who care to save 40-50% off their audiobooks. **Heard is not mandatory to shop audiobooks but we do recommend taking a look at the perks.**

Audiobooks Available (**exclusively on GHuffington.com**)

Chemistry
Egypt
Ever
Baisleigh
Halo
Kleuless
Anna
Glacier
Vallei (coming soon)
Muse.
Elm.
Sensitivity
The Realm of Riot Thimble
Whose Love Story is it Anyway?
Unhand Me

THE HUNTRESS

If you're here, it means you've finished Rather. Thanks for supporting my new release. **Please do me a favor and leave your review on Amazon and Goodreads**. Simply copy and paste that review on ghuffington.com for the Rather product listing here.

Six months later...

Though the sun was shining brightly and the clouds yesterday's storm brought along had cleared, there was a stillness, a darkness that hovered over me. I swiped the lone tear from my eye, wondering if the pain ever went away or if it just rested for days or weeks at a time until you felt a little too happy, a little too alive, and a little too free before reminding you to sit the fuck down and remember.

Remember the aches.

Remember the tears.

Remember the restlessness.

Remember the new reality death forced you into.

"I'd be foolish to wish you were here," I tittered, "Because, all that wishing will get me nowhere. My heart will still be broken and you'll still be right here where we left you with all these decorations Jru keeps littering your memorial with."

My niece was the way to my heart. Two whole days with her and I still hadn't had my fix of the growing toddler. A pressing matter was the cause of Priest's impromptu visit to St. Catana.

Simultaneously, my heart and head were aching from missing my family. Instead of coming alone and only for the few hours he intended to be here, Priest brought me along and extended his trip for my appeasement.

Seeing my family did wonders for the heart. Egypt was glowing. Roaman was sharpening her mind and skills by servicing the St. Catana locals.

Roulette had friended a local bar owner and turned her business into a cash cow. Rome was entertaining the children by offering free ballet lessons in a small studio Teddy created for her with around-the-clock security. Range had her head in her books, studying cases because the crime rate in St. Catana didn't exist. It was pure paradise.

Royce was still hands-on with our family's operation though everything was virtual. Our mother was mourning and living out her wildest dreams of being a grandparent. CJ had her wrapped around her little fingers.

Rugger.

It was Rugger who worried me. She'd yet to plant both feet on the ground and adjust to the ways of St. Catana. She was hungry. She was unfulfilled. She was thirsty for blood. I could see the longing in her eyes each time I saw that pretty face of hers.

"She knows her grandpa. She knows you well. We make sure of it. Ri-thee. That's what she calls you," I chuckled, resting my butt on the grass in front of his headstone.

I was careful not to damage any of the gadgets Jru had left. I wouldn't hear the end of her little rant if I did. Pinwheels pierced the dirt. There were at least ten of them. Toy guns were lined neatly against the headstone. A picture of Jru in a bathing suit with gargles laid flat against the ground.

Daily, she and my mother took a walk to the gravesite. She was familiar with the patch of land. She was comfortable here. She'd made this place her own.

"I miss you," I choked, trying my hardest not to break.

Naturally, I fought to remain poised and collected in front of my father, but I was losing the battle with my emotions.

"I miss you deeply. Every day. It's so hard to– to– I just never imagined my life without you. Not now and not ever. I feel so lost sometimes. I just want to hear your voice. Hear your sound advice. Your wisdom was my guidance. Now that you're gone– I– I find it hard to continue life with a smile... *with joy... with happiness*. It feels like a lie."

I wiped the tears from my cheeks and tried settling my raging heart.

"But it's not. It's not a lie. I met a man, Richie. You know him so I don't have to tell you I made a good decision," I wept, unable to control my emotions any longer.

This time, I didn't want to try because I knew it was useless. That's how much my husband meant to me. At the sound of his name, my heart grew three times its size. At the thought of him, I was overcome with so many good things it hurt.

His existence brought me so much pain. The kind that wasn't rooted in agony, but in contentment, satisfaction, gratitude, and an abundance of love. He was my completion. My comfort. My everything.

"But, I did. I made a good decision. I made the right decision, even though it wasn't the decision you'd made for me. Priest was the one for me all along, Richie. He's kind. He's reassuring. He's attentive. He's welcoming. He's confident. He's vulnerable. He's open. He's mature. He's light. He's love."

I wiped my nose with the back of my hand.

"And, he's my husband."

A full minute passed. Silence lulled my heart. I swallowed the lump in my throat and regained control of myself.

"What hurts me the most about all of this–" pausing, I stretched my lips into a smile. "Is you never got to see me in my dress. I'm the first of all your girls to wed and you didn't have the chance to walk me down the aisle. You waited so long. I'm so sorry we couldn't make that dream of yours come true sooner."

"Rather–" Priest's voice rattled me to the core.

My body clung to both syllables for support.

"Yes?" I asked without looking in his direction.

"We must leave now."

I lifted a hand in the air. Priest grabbed hold and lifted me from the ground.

"Are you finished here?"

"Yes, until next time. Don't keep me away from him too long. He'll begin to think I don't miss him."

"He knows you do," Priest assured me as we started toward the tarmac.

The sound of toy guns rattling against one another and pinwheels spinning stopped me in my tracks. I turned to find Jru's decor creating the sweetest, softest melody.

"He knows," I said to Priest before continuing down the road with him by my side.

The subtle sign was enough to put my worries to rest. *He knows.*

I'd bid everyone a farewell. Visiting Richie was the very last thing on my list of to-dos. The heaviness his absence plagued me with was not a feeling I was fond of. I'd prolong its presence as often as I could.

"After you Mrs. Valentine," Priest sniggered.

Though he was displaying the manners his family had stored within him from a child, he wanted to watch me climb the steps almost purely for personal gain. He'd been feeding me well and the few pounds I'd packed on had gone to all the right places.

I had a hard time deciphering if it was Priest's weight or the grown woman's weight everyone warned you about as a young adult. Maybe it was a mixture of both. Nevertheless, he was drawn to it. *Drawn to me.*

"Childers-Valentine," I reminded him from the first step.

He was still at the bottom, waiting to climb up. I shook my head, knowing he wouldn't follow until I was out of sight. When I rounded the corner and greeted the first crew member, I could finally hear his footsteps nearing.

"Good evening, ma'am."

"Good evening."

"Good evening." Priest nodded at the flight attendant as he wrapped his arms around me and pushed me forward.

There was a stirring of my juices that I was certain would ruin my panties.

Am I even wearing pan–

"I can smell you from all the way up here, but your eagerness will have to practice patience."

"Why," I whispered as if others could hear us.

I had plans for Priest and they couldn't wait until we landed. They needed progress now.

Just as the word left my mouth, the door of the restroom at the back of the main cabin opened. With a drying cloth in her hand, Rugger stepped out. My brows drew near the center of my forehead as confusion etched my features.

"Hello, Rather."

I waited for an explanation that I realized wouldn't come. Rugger made herself comfortable in the first seat on the aircraft, just inches away from where Priest and I stood.

"What are you doing here? We're preparing for takeoff."

"So am I."

"Rugger–"

"I've been in a state of unrest since we landed in Catana. This isn't home for us. We have a home and it's about time I did what I do best so we can return unscathed."

My heart pumped wildly.

"This is home for Chem," I reminded her.

"Which is why I'm not returning, baby. But, the rest of you must."

I followed the voice behind us and was met with the same dark eyes I shared with all my siblings. Chem stood with his hands gathered in front of him and a gaze void of emotion. The logical, sensible version of him had vanished.

The Chemist staring back at me was one I knew all too well. I whipped my head in Rugger's direction, realizing the best parts of her had vanished into thin air as well. And, unknowingly, I was reintroduced to the coldest, darkest version of the woman I loved dearly. *The Huntress* had returned and her mission was in motion.

"Well, then." My smile wasn't to be mistaken. Their admission was music to me. "I'd love a new client list."

"One is waiting," Rugger claimed, crossing one leg over the other.

Rugger.
The Huntress
Fall 2024.
Available for pre-order on Amazon.

For Priest's story, visit ghuffington.com.